JAMES PATRICK KELLY

With a Foreword
by Bob Eggleton

THE
WRECK
of the
GODSPEED

GOLDEN GRYPHON PRESS · 2008

"Think Like Jim Kelly," copyright © 2008 by Bob Eggleton.
"The Wreck of the Godspeed," first published in Between Worlds, ed. Robert Silverberg, SFBC 2004.
"The Best Christmas Ever," first published in SCIFICTION, May 2004.
"Men Are Trouble," first published in Asimov's Science Fiction, June 2004.
"Luck," first published in Asimov's Science Fiction, June 2002.
"The Dark Side of Town," first published in Asimov's Science Fiction, April/May 2004.
"The Leila Torn Show," first published in Asimov's Science Fiction, June 2006.
"Mother," first published in The Silver Gryphon, eds. Gary Turner and Marty Halpern, Golden Gryphon Press 2003.
"Dividing the Sustain," first published in The New Space Opera, eds. Gardner Dozois and Jonathan Strahan, Eos 2007.
"The Ice is Singing," first published in Realms of Fantasy, April 2003.
"Serpent," first published in Fantasy and Science Fiction, May 2004.
"Bernardo's House," first published in Asimov's Science Fiction, June 2003.
"Burn," first published in Burn, Tachyon 2005.

LIBRARY OF CONGRESS CATALOGING–IN–PUBLICATION DATA

Kelly, James P. (James Patrick)
    The wreck of the Godspeed and other stories / James Patrick Kelly.
— 1st ed.
        p.   cm.
    ISBN-13: 978-1-930846-51-7 (alk. paper)
    ISBN-10: 1-930846-51-7 (alk. paper)
        1. Science fiction, American.   I. Title.
PS3561.E3942   W74   2008
813'.54—dc22   2007048662

First Edition.

Contents

I'd like to dedicate this book to the editors who first published these stories: Ellen Datlow, Gardner Dozois, Marty Halpern, Shawna McCarthy, Robert Silverberg, Jonathan Strahan, Gary Turner, Gordon Van Gelder, Jacob Weisman and last, but not least, Sheila Williams.

Think Like Jim Kelly

SEEMS LIKE I'VE KNOWN JIM A LONG TIME — FIRST in his writing, and then the guy himself. We've won Hugos together. We've lost them together. And we've had fun with it in either case. Fun — it keeps you from believing your own press when you win, and from feeling too dented in the ego when you lose. But I can tell you, we've got nothing to complain about.

I first was asked to do a cover to his book, for Golden Gryphon, way back around 1996, called *Think Like a Dinosaur.* Jim came up with the concept and related it to (the now sadly, late) Jim Turner. He said he'd always wanted to see a "dinosaur in a space suit." Really not directly much to do with the story itself, "Think Like a Dinosaur," but just a mood piece to capture the book's feel. Sometimes the best covers go that way. The piece took on a life of its own — it was highly praised and represented a turning point in my own evolution as an artist. It was juried into the annual art volume *Spectrum* for the following year and this resulted in being contacted by a director to work on several films as a concept artist and that director, John A. Davis — who has become a good friend and collaborator with me over the years — bought the original painting. He saw the painting and decided I was one of the artists he would work with on his film *Jimmy Neutron Boy Genius* (2001) and *The Ant Bully* (2006). So, in a way, it was all because Jim came up with that suggestion for that very painting, that he was indeed a "luck charm."

But Jim's stories are what make him an outstanding writer. He's a master of the long over-looked (these days) art of the Short Story. He's won Hugos, Nebulas, *Locus* Awards, *Asimov's Magazine* Reader's Awards . . . and been nominated and a finalist for many more. The guy is good, that's apparent. He served as a councilor on the New Hampshire State Council on the Arts for eight years and was the chairman from 2003 to 2006, and he's been on the New England Foundation for the Arts, and more than just involved with the Clarion SF Workshop. He gets around. And, most important, he's a cool guy—just one of the best and nicest people in science fiction. As anyone who knows me, I can smell "pretentious" a mile away and veer from it—Jim is not at all pretentious. This alone made me draw the conclusion that he had to be good at what he does. And I've been lucky enough to do covers for his, now, three Golden Gryphon books. His stories have a sense of place, of normalcy in an otherwise strange situation. That's the mark of the best of fantastic writing (or art)—take the prosaic and put it into the strange and make it all seem matter-of-fact.

The book you hold in your hands is his latest. I had a little something to do with why it has the title it has. Both editor and Jim were stuck for "any better ideas" for a title. Well, as I dug in, I realized after going one route that didn't work out, the cover idea was right in front of me in the story "The Wreck of the Godspeed"—it just hit me, like that. When I did the final art, Jim came to the conclusion that this cover story would just be a much better, cooler title. I had to agree. So here we are.

Here's a book of wonders, sadness, amazements, joys—all explorations into the imaginative mind of Mr. James Patrick Kelly. Enough reading me the artist, I've done my job. Now read the writer!

—Bob Eggleton
October 2007

The Wreck of the Godspeed and Other Stories

The Wreck of the *Godspeed*

Day One

WHAT DO WE KNOW ABOUT ADEL RANGER SANTOS? That he was sixty-five percent oxygen, nineteen percent carbon, ten percent hydrogen, three percent nitrogen, two percent calcium, one percent phosphorus, some potassium, sulfur, sodium, chlorine, magnesium, iodine, and iron and just a trace of chromium, cobalt, copper, fluorine, manganese, molybdenum, selenium, tin, vanadium, and zinc. That he was of the domain *Eukarya*, the kingdom of *Animalia*, the phylum *Chordata*, subphylum *Vertebrata*, the class *Mammalia*, the order *Primates*, the family *Hominidae*, the genus *Homo* and the species *Novo*. That, like the overwhelming majority of the sixty trillion people on the worlds of Human Continuum, he was a hybrid cybernetic/biological system composed of intricate subsystems including the circulatory, digestive, endocrine, excretory, informational, integumenary, musculo-skeletal, nervous, psycho-spiritual, reproductive, and respiratory. That he was the third son of Venetta Patience Santos, an Elector of the Host of True Flesh and Halbert Constant Santos, a baker of fine breads. That he was male, left-handed, somewhat introverted, intelligent but no genius, a professed but frustrated heterosexual, an Aries, a virgin, a delibertarian, an agnostic, and a swimmer. That he was nineteen Earth standard years old and that until he stumbled, naked, out of the molecular assembler onto the *Godspeed* he had never left his home world.

The woman caught Adel before he sprawled headlong off the transport stage. "Slow down." She was taller and wider than any of the women he'd known; he felt like a toy in her arms. "You made it, you're here." She straightened him and stepped back to get a look. "Is there a message?"

—*a message?*—buzzed Adel's plus.

minus buzzed—*yes give us clothes*—

Normally Adel kept his opposites under control. But he'd just been scanned, transmitted at superluminal speeds some two hundred and fifty-seven light years, and reassembled on a threshold bound for the center of the Milky Way.

"Did they say anything?" The woman's face was tight. "Back home?"

Adel shook his head; he had no idea what she was talking about. He hadn't yet found his voice, but it was understandable if he was a little jumbled. His skin felt a size too small and he shivered in the cool air. This was probably the most important moment of his life and all he could think was that his balls had shrunk to the size of raisins.

"You're not . . . ? All right then." She covered her disappointment so quickly that Adel wondered if he'd seen it at all. "Well, let's get some clothes on you, Rocky."

minus buzzed—*who's Rocky?*—

"What, didn't your tongue make the jump with the rest of you?" She was wearing green scrubs and green, open-toed shoes. An oval medallion on a silver chain hung around her neck; at its center a pix displayed a man eating soup. "Can you understand me?" Her mouth stretched excessively, as if she intended that he read her lips. "I'm afraid I don't speak carrot, or whatever passes for language on your world." She was carrying a blue robe folded over her arm.

"Harvest," said Adel. "I came from Harvest."

"He talks," said the woman. "Now can he walk? And what will it take to get him to say his name?"

"I'm Adel Santos."

"Good." She tossed the robe at him and it slithered around his shoulders and wrapped him in its soft embrace. "If you have a name then I don't have to throw you back." Two slippers unfolded from its pockets and snugged onto his feet. She began to speak with a nervous intensity that made Adel dizzy. "So, Adel, my name is Kamilah, which means 'the perfect one' in Arabic which is a dead language you've probably never heard of and I'm here to give you the official welcome to your pilgrimage aboard the *Godspeed* and to show you around but we have to get done before dinner which tonight is synthetic roasted garab . . ."

*—something is bothering her—*buzzed minus*—it must be us—*

". . . which is either a bird or a tuber, I forget which exactly but it comes from the cuisine of Ohara which is a world in the Zeta 1 Reticuli system which you've probably never heard of . . ."

*—probably just a talker—*plus buzzed.

". . . because I certainly never have." Kamilah wore her hair kinked close against her head; it was the color of rust. She was cute, thought Adel, in a massive sort of way. "Do you understand?"

"Perfectly," he said. "You did say you were perfect."

"So you listen?" A grin flitted across her face. "Are you going to surprise me, Adel Santos?"

"I'll try," he said. "But first I need a bathroom."

There were twenty-eight bathrooms on the *Godspeed*; twenty of them opened off the lavish bedrooms of Dream Street. A level below was the Ophiuchi Dining Hall, decorated in red alabaster, marble, and gilded bronze, which could seat as many as forty around its teak banquet table. In the more modest Chillingsworth Breakfasting Room, reproductions of four refectory tables with oak benches could accommodate more intimate groups. Between the Blue and the Dagger Salons was the Music Room with smokewood lockers filled with the noblest instruments from all the worlds of the Continuum, most of which could play themselves. Below that was a library with the complete range of inputs from brainleads to books made of actual plant material, a ballroom decorated in the Nomura III style, a VR dome with ten animated seats, a gymnasium with a lap pool, a black box theater, a billiard room, a conservatory with five different ecosystems and various stairways, hallways, closets, cubbies, and peculiar dead ends. The MASTA, the molecular array scanner/transmitter/assembler was located in the Well Met Arena, an enormous airlock and staging area that opened onto the surface of the threshold. Here also was the cognizor in which the mind of the *Godspeed* seethed.

It would be far too convenient to call the *Godspeed* mad. Better to say that for some time she had been behaving like no other threshold. Most of our pioneering starships were built in hollowed-out nickel-iron asteroids—a few were set into fabricated shells. All were propelled by matter-antimatter drives that could reach speeds of just under a hundred thousand kilometers per second, about a third of the speed of light. We began to launch them from the far frontiers of the Continuum a millennium ago to search for terrestrial planets that were either habitable or might profitably be made so. Our thresholds can scan planetary systems of promising stars as far away as twenty light years. When one discovers a suitably terrestrial world, it decelerates and swings into orbit. News of the find is immediately dispatched at superluminal speed to all the worlds of the Continuum; almost immediately materials and technicians appear on the transport stage. Over the course of several years we build a new orbital station containing a second MASTA, establishing a permanent link to the Continuum. Once the link is secured, the threshold continues on its voyage of discovery. In all, the *Godspeed* had founded thirty-seven colonies in exactly this way.

The life of a threshold follows a pattern: decades of monotonous acceleration, cruising, and deceleration punctuated by a few years of intense and glorious activity. Establishing a colony is an ultimate affirmation of human culture and even the cool intelligences generated by the cognizors of our thresholds share in the camaraderie of techs and colonists. Thresholds take justifiable pride in their accomplishments; many have had worlds named for them. However, when the time comes to move on, we expect our thresholds to dampen their enthusiasms and abort their nascent emotions to steel themselves against the tedium of crawling between distant stars at three-tenths the speed of light.

Which all of them did—except for the *Godspeed*.

As they were climbing up the Tulip Stairway to the Dream Halls, Adel and Kamilah came upon two men making their way down, bound together at the waist by a tether. The tether was about a meter long and two centimeters in diameter; it appeared to be elastic. One side of it pulsed bright red and the other was a darker burgundy. The men were wearing baggy pants and gray jackets with tall, buttoned collars that made them look like birds.

"Adel," said Kamilah, "meet Jonman and Robman."

Jonman looked like he could have been Robman's father, but Adel knew better than to draw any conclusions from that. On some worlds, he knew, physiological camouflage was common practice.

Jonman gazed right through Adel. "I can see that he knows nothing about the problem." He seemed detached, as if he were playing chess in his head.

Kamilah gave him a sharp glance but said nothing. Robman

stepped forward and extended his forefinger in greeting. Adel gave it a polite touch.

"This is our rookie, then?" said Robman. "Do you play tikra, Adel?"

—*who's a rookie?*—buzzed minus.

—*we are*—

Since Adel didn't know what tikra was, he assumed that he didn't play it. "Not really," he said.

"He's from one of the farm worlds," said Kamilah.

"Oh, a rustic." Robman cocked his head to one side, as if Adel might make sense to him if viewed from a different angle. "Do they have gulpers where you come from? Cows?" Seeing the blank look on Adel's face, he pressed on. "Maybe frell?"

"Blue frell, yes."

—*keep talking*—plus buzzed—*make an impression*—

Adel lunged into conversation. "My uncle Durwin makes summer sausage from frell loin. He built his own smoke house."

Robman frowned.

"It's very good." Adel had no idea where he was going with this bit of family history. "The sausages, I mean. He's a butcher."

—*and we're an idiot*—

"He's from one of the farm worlds," said Jonman, as if he were catching up with their chitchat on a time delay.

"Yes," said Robman. "He makes sausages."

Jonman nodded as if this explained everything about Adel. "Then don't be late for dinner," he advised. "I see there will be garab tonight." With this, the two men continued downstairs.

Adel glanced at Kamilah, hoping she might offer some insight into Robman and Jonman. Her eyes were hooded. "I wouldn't play anything with them if I were you," she murmured. "Jonman has a stochastic implant. Not only does he calculate probabilities, but he cheats."

The top of the Tulip Stairway ended at the midpoint of Dream Street. "Does everything have a name here?" asked Adel.

"Pretty much," said Kamilah. "It tells you something about how bored the early crews must have been. We're going right." The ceiling of Dream Street glowed with a warm light that washed Kamilah's face with pink. She said the names of bedroom suites as they passed the closed doors. "This is Fluxus. The Doghouse. We have room for twenty pilgrims, twice that if we want to double up."

The carpet was a sapphire plush that clutched at Adel's sandals as he shuffled down the hall.

"Chrome over there. That's where Upwood lived. He's gone now. You don't know anything about him, do you?" Her voice was suddenly tight. "Upwood Marcene?"

"No, should I? Is he famous?"

"Not famous, no." The medallion around her neck showed a frozen lake. "He jumped home last week, which leaves us with only seven, now that you're here." She cleared her throat and the odd moment of tension passed. "This is Corazon. Forty Pushups. We haven't found a terrestrial in ages, so Speedy isn't as popular as she used to be."

"You call the threshold Speedy?"

"You'll see." Kamilah sighed. "And this is Cella. We might as well see if Sister is receiving." She pressed her hand to the door and said, "Kamilah here." She waited.

"What do you want, Kamilah?" said the door, a solid blue slab that featured neither latch nor knob.

"I have the new arrival here."

"It's inconvenient." The door sighed. "But I'm coming." It vanished and before them stood a tiny creature, barely up to Adel's waist. She was wearing a hat that looked like a bird's nest made of black ribbon with a smoky veil that covered her eyes. Her mouth was thin and severe. All he could see of her almond skin was the dimpled chin and her long, elegant neck; the billowing sleeves of her loose, black dress swallowed her hands.

"Adel Santos, this is Lihong Rain. She prefers to be called Sister." Sister might have been a child or she might have been a grandmother. Adel couldn't tell.

"Safe passage, Adel." She made no other welcoming gesture.

Adel hesitated, wondering if he should try to initiate contact. But what kind? Offer to touch fingers? Shake hands? Maybe he should catch her up in his arms and dance a two-step.

"Same to you, Sister," he said and bowed.

"I was praying just now." He could feel her gaze even though he couldn't see it. "Are you religious, Brother Adel?" The hair on the back of his neck stood up.

"I'd prefer to be just Adel, if you don't mind," he said. "And no, I'm not particularly religious, I'm afraid."

She sagged, as if he had just piled more weight on her frail shoulders. "Then I will pray for you. If you will excuse me." She stepped back into her room and the blue door reformed.

plus buzzed—*we were rude to her*—

—*we told the truth*—

"Don't worry," said Kamilah. "You can't offend her. Or rather, you can't *not* offend her, since just about everything we do seems to offend her. Which is why she spends almost all her time in her room. She claims she's praying, although Speedy only knows for sure. So I'm in Delhi here, and next door you're in The Ranch."

—*Kamilah's next door?*—buzzed minus.

—*we hardly know her don't even think it*—

—*too late*—

They stopped in front of the door to his room, which was identical to Sister's, except it was green. "Press your right hand to it anywhere, say your name and it will ID you." After Adel followed these instructions, the door considered for a moment and then vanished with a hiss.

Adel guessed that the room was supposed to remind him of home. It didn't exactly, because he'd lived with his parents in a high rise in Great Randall, only two kilometers from Harvest's first MASTA. But it was like houses he had visited out in the countryside. Uncle Durwin's, for example. Or the Pariseaus'. The floor appeared to be of some blondish tongue-and-grooved wood. Two of the walls were set to show a golden tallgrass prairie with a herd of chocolate-colored beasts grazing in the distance. Opposite a rolltop desk were three wooden chairs with velvet upholstered seats gathered around a low, oval table. A real plant with leaves like green hearts guarded the twin doorways that opened into the bedroom and the bathroom.

Adel's bed was king-sized with a half moon head and footboards tied to posts that looked like tree trunks with the bark stripped off. It had a salmon-colored bedspread with twining rope pattern. However, we should point out that Adel did not notice anything at all about his bed until much later.

—*oh no*—

"Hello," said Adel.

—*oh yes*—

"Hello yourself, lovely boy." The woman was propped on a nest of pillows. She was wearing a smile and shift spun from fog. It wisped across her slim, almost boyish, body concealing very little. Her eyes were wide and the color of honey. Her hair was spiked in silver.

Kamilah spoke from behind him. "Speedy, he just stepped off the damn stage ten minutes ago. He's not thinking of fucking."

"He's a nineteen-year-old male, which means he can't think of anything but fucking." She had a wet, whispery voice, like waves washing against pebbles. "Maybe he doesn't like girls. I like being female, but I certainly don't have to be." Her torso flowed beneath the fog and her legs thickened.

"Actually, I do," said Adel. "Like girls, I mean."

"Then forget Speedy." Kamilah crossed the room to the bed and stuck her hand through the shape on the bed. It was all fog, and Kamilah's hand parted it. "This is just a fetch that Speedy projects when she feels like bothering us in person."

"I have to keep my friends company," said the *Godspeed*.

"You can keep him company later." Kamilah swiped both hands through the fetch and she disappeared. "Right now he's going to put some clothes on and then we're going to find Meri and Jarek," she said.

"Wait," said Adel. "What did you do to her? Where did she go?"

"She's still here," Kamilah said. "She's always everywhere, Adel. You'll get used to it."

"But what did she want?"

The wall to his right shimmered and became a mirror image of the bedroom. The *Godspeed* was back in her nest on his bed. "To give you a preview of coming attractions, lovely boy."

Kamilah grasped Adel by the shoulders, turned him away from the wall and aimed him at the closet. "Get changed," she said. "I'll be in the sitting room."

Hanging in the closet were three identical, peach-colored uniforms with blue piping at the seams. The tight pantaloons had straps that would pass under the instep of his feet. The dress blue blouse had the all-too-familiar pulsing heart patch over the left breast. The jacket had a double row of enormous silver zippers and bore two merit pins which proclaimed Adel a true believer of the Host of True Flesh.

Except that he wasn't.

Adel had long since given up on his mother's little religion but had never found a way to tell her. Seeing his uniforms filled him with guilt and dread. He'd come two hundred and fifty-seven light years and he had still not escaped her. He'd expected she would pack the specs for True Flesh uniforms in his luggage transmission, but he'd thought she'd send him at least some civilian clothes as well.

—we have to lose the clown suit—

"So how long are you here for?" called Kamilah from the next room.

"A year," replied Adel. "With a second year at my option." Then he whispered, "Speedy, can you hear me?"

"Always. Never doubt it." Her voice came from the tall, blue frel-leather boots that were part of his uniform. "Are we going to have secrets from Kamilah? I love secrets."

"I need something to wear," he whispered. "Anything but this."

"A year with an option?" Kamilah called. "Gods, Adel! Who did you murder?"

"Are we talking practical?" said the *Godspeed*. "Manly? Artistic? Rebellious?"

He stooped and spoke directly into the left boot. "Something basic," he said. "Scrubs like Kamilah's will be fine for now."

Two blobs extruded from the closet wall and formed into drab pants and a shirt.

"Adel?" called Kamilah. "Are you all right?"

"I didn't murder anyone." He stripped off the robe and pulled briefs from a drawer. At least the saniwear wasn't official True Flesh. "I wrote an essay."

Softwalks bloomed from the floor. "The hair on your legs, lovely boy, is like the wire that sings in my walls." The *Godspeed*'s voice was a purr.

The closet seemed very small then. As soon as he'd shimmied into his pants, Adel grabbed the shirt and the softwalks and escaped. He didn't bother with socks.

"So how did you get here, Kamilah?" He paused in the bedroom to pull on the shirt before entering the sitting room.

"I was sent here as a condition of my parole."

"Really?" Adel sat on one of the chairs and snapped on his soft-walks. "Who did you murder?"

"I was convicted of improper appropriation," she said. "I mis-used a symbol set that was alien to my cultural background."

—say again?—buzzed minus.

Adel nodded and smiled. "I have no idea what that means."

"That's all right." Her medallion showed a fist. "It's a long story for another time."

We pause here to reflect on the variety of religious beliefs in the Human Continuum. In ancient times, atheists believed that humanity's expansion into space would extinguish its historic sus-ceptibility to superstition. And for a time, as we rode primitive torches to our cramped habitats and attempted to terraform the mostly inhospitable worlds of our home system, this expectation seemed reasonable. But then the discovery of quantum scanning and the perfection of molecular assembly led to the building of the first MASTA systems and everything changed.

Quantum scanning is, after all, destructive. Depending on exactly what has been placed on the stage, that which is scanned is reduced to mere probabilistic wisps, an exhausted scent or perhaps just soot to be wiped off the sensors. In order to jump from one MASTA to another, we must be prepared to die. Of course, we're only dead for a few seconds, which is the time it takes for the assembler to reconstitute us from a scan. Nevertheless, the widespread acceptance of MASTA transportation means that all of us who had come to thresholds have died and been reborn.

The experience of transitory death has led *homo novo* to a renewed engagement with the spiritual. But if the atheists were disappointed in their predictions of the demise of religion, the creeds of antiquity were decimated by the new realities of superluminal culture. Ten thousand new religions have risen up on the many worlds of the Continuum to comfort and sustain us in our various needs. We worship stars, sex, the vacuum of space, water, the cosmic microwave background, the Uncertainty Principle, music, old trees, cats, the weather, dead bodies, certain pharaohs of the Middle Kingdom, food, stimulants, depressants, and Levia Calla. We call the deity by many names: Genius, the Bitch, Kindly One, the Trickster, the Alien, the Thumb, Sagittarius A*, the Silence, Surprise, and the Eternal Center. What is striking about this exuberant diversity, when we consider how much blood has been shed in the name of gods, is our universal tolerance of one another. But that's because all of us who acknowledge the divine are co-religionists in one crucial regard: we affirm that the true path to spirituality must necessarily pass across the stages of a MASTA.

Which is another reason why we build thresholds and launch them to spread the Continuum. Which is why so many of our religions count it as an essential pilgrimage to travel with a threshold on some fraction of its long journey. Which is why the Host of True Flesh on the planet Harvest sponsored an essay contest opened to any communicant who had not yet died to go superluminal, the first prize being an all-expense paid pilgrimage to the *Godspeed*, the oldest, most distant, and therefore holiest of all the thresholds. Which is why Venetta Patience Santos had browbeaten her son Adel to enter the contest.

Adel's reasons for writing his essay had been his own. He had no great faith in the Host and no burning zeal to make a pilgrimage. However he chafed under the rules his parents still imposed on him, and he'd just broken up with his girlfriend Gavrila over the issue of pre-marital intercourse—he being in favor, she taking a decidedly contrary position—and he'd heard steamy rumors of what passed for acceptable sexual behavior on a threshold at the farthest edge of civilization. Essay contestants were charged to express the meaning of the Host of True Flesh in five hundred words or less. Adel brought his in at four hundred and nine.

Our Place
By Adel Ranger Santos

We live in a place. This seems obvious, maybe, but think about it. Originally our place was a little valley on the African continent on a planet called Earth. Who we are today was shaped in large part by the way that place was, so long ago. Later humans moved all around that planet and found new places to live. Some were hot, some freezing. We lived at the top of mountains and on endless prairies. We sailed to islands. We walked across deserts and glaciers. But what mattered was that the places that we moved to did not change us. We changed the places.We wore clothes and started fires and built houses. We made every place we went to our place.

Later we left Earth, our home planet, just like we left that valley in Africa. We tried to make places for ourselves in cold space, in habitats, and on asteroids. It was hard. Mars broke our hearts. Venus killed millions. Some people said that the time had come to change ourselves completely so that we could live in these difficult places. People had already begun to meddle with their bodies. It was a time of great danger.

This was when Genius, the goddess of True Flesh awoke for the first time. Nobody knew it then, but looking back we can see that it must have been her. Genius knew that the only way we could stay true to our flesh was to find better places to make our own. Genius visited Levia Calla and taught her to collapse the wave-particle duality so that we could look deep into ourselves and see who we are. Soon we were on our way to the stars. Then Genius told the people to rise up against anyone who wanted to tamper with their bodies. She made the people realize that we were not meant to become machines. That we should be grateful to be alive for the normal a hundred and twenty years and not try to live longer.

I sometimes wonder what would have happened if we were not alone in space. Maybe if there were really aliens out there somewhere, we would never have had Genius to help us, since there would be no one true flesh. We would probably have all different gods. Maybe we would have changed ourselves, maybe into robots or to look like aliens. This is a scary thought. If it were true, we'd be in another universe. But we're not.

This universe is our place.

What immediately stood out in this essay is how Adel attributed Levia Calla's historic breakthrough to the intervention of Genius. Nobody had ever thought to suggest this before, since Professor Calla had been one of those atheists who had been convinced that religion would wither away over the course of the twenty-first century. The judges were impressed that Adel had so cleverly asserted what could never be disproved. Even more striking was the dangerous speculation that concluded Adel's essay. Ever since Fermi first expressed his paradox, we have struggled with the apparent absence of other civilizations in the universe. Many of the terrestrial worlds we have discovered have complex ecologies, but on none has intelligence evolved. Even now, there are those who desperately recalculate the factors in the Drake Equation in the hopes of arriving at a solution that is greater than one. When Adel made the point that no religion could survive first contact, and then trumped it with the irrefutable fact that we are alone, he won his place on the Godspeed.

Adel and Kamilah came upon two more pilgrims in the library. A man and a woman cuddled on a lime green chenille couch in front of a wall that displayed images of six planets, lined up in a row. The library was crowded with glassed-in shelves filled with old-fashioned paper books, and racks with various I/O devices, spex, digitex, whisperers, and brainleads. Next to a row of workstations, a long table held an array of artifacts that Adel did not immediately recognize: small sculptures, medals and coins, jewelry and carved wood. Two paintings hung above it, one an image of an artist's studio in which a man in a black hat painted a woman in a blue dress, the other a still life with fruit and some small, dead animals.

"Meri," said Kamilah, "Jarek, this is Adel."

The two pilgrims came to the edge of the couch, their faces alight with anticipation. Out of the corner of his eye, Adel thought he saw Kamilah shake her head. The brightness dimmed and they receded as if nothing had happened.

—we're a disappointment to everyone—buzzed minus.

plus buzzed—*they just don't know us yet*—

Meri looked to be not much older than Adel. She was wearing what might have been long saniwear, only it glowed, registering a thermal map of her body in red, yellow, green, and blue. "Adel." She gave him a wistful smile and extended a finger for him to touch.

Jerek held up a hand to indicate that he was otherwise occupied. He was wearing a sleeveless gray shirt, baggy shorts and blacked out spex on which Adel could see a data scrawl flicker.

"You'll usually find these two together," said Kamilah. "And often in bed."

"At least we're not joined at the hip like the Manmans," said Meri. "Have you met them yet?"

Adel frowned. "You mean Robman?"

"And Spaceman." Meri had a third eye tattooed in the middle of her forehead. At least, Adel hoped it was a tattoo.

—*sexy*—buzzed minus.

plus buzzed—*weird*—

—*weird is sexy*—

"Oh, Jonman's not so bad." Jarek pulled his spex off.

"If you like snobs." Meri reminded him a little of Gavrila, except for the extra eye. "And cheats."

Jarek replaced the spex on the rack and then clapped Adel on the back. "Welcome to the zoo, brother." He was a head shorter than Adel and had the compact musculature of someone who was born on a high-G planet. "So you're in shape," he said. "Do you lift?"

"Some. Not much. I'm a swimmer." Adel had been the Great Randall city champion in the 100 and 200 meter.

"What's your event?"

"Middle distance freestyle."

—*friend?*—

"We have a lap pool in the gym," said Jarek.

—*maybe*—minus buzzed.

"Saw it." Adel nodded approvingly. "And you? I can tell you work out."

"I wrestle," said Jarek. "Or I did back on Kindred. But I'm a gym rat. I need exercise to clear my mind. So what do you think of old Speedy so far?"

"It's great." For the first time since he had stepped onto the scanning stage in Great Randall, the reality of where he was struck him. "I'm really excited to be here." And as he said it, he realized that it was true.

"That'll wear off," said Kamilah. "Now if you two sports are done comparing large muscle groups, can we move along?"

"What's the rush, Kamilah?" Meri shifted into a corner of the couch. "Planning on keeping this one for yourself?" She patted the seat, indicating that Adel should take Jarek's place. "Come here, let me get an eye on you."

Adel glanced at Jarek, who winked.

"Has Kamilah been filling you in on all the gossip?"

Adel crammed himself against the side cushion of the couch opposite Meri. "Not really."

"That's because no one tells her the good stuff."

Kamilah yawned. "Maybe because I'm not interested."

Adel couldn't look at Meri's face for long without staring at her tattoo, but if he looked away from her face then his gaze drifted to her hot spots. Finally he decided to focus on her hands.

"I don't work out," said Meri, "in case you're wondering."

"Is this the survey that wrapped yesterday?" said Kamilah, turning away from them to look at the planets displayed on the wall. "I heard it was shit."

Meri had long and slender fingers but her fingernails were bitten ragged, especially the thumbs. Her skin was very pale. He guessed that she must have spent a lot of time indoors, wherever she came from.

"System ONR 147-563." Jarek joined her, partially blocking Adel's view of the wall. "Nine point eight nine light years away and a whole lot of nothing. The star has luminosity almost three times that of Sol. Six planets: four hot, airless rocks, a jovian and a subjovian."

"I'm still wondering about ONR 134-843," said Kamilah, and the wall filled with a new solar system, most of which Adel couldn't see. "Those five Martian-type planets."

"So?" said Meri. "The star was a K1 orange-red dwarf. Which means those Martians are pretty damn cold. The day max is only 17°C on the warmest and at night it drops to −210°C. And their atmospheres are way too thin, not one over a hundred millibars. That's practically space."

"But there are five of them." Kamilah held up her right hand, fingers splayed. "Count them, five."

"Five Martians aren't worth one terrestrial," said Jarek.

Kamilah grunted. "Have we seen any terrestrials?"

"Space is huge and we're slow." Jarek bumped against her like a friendly dog. "Besides, what do you care? One of these days you'll bust off this rock, get the hero's parade on Jaxon and spend the rest of your life annoying the other eyejacks and getting your face on the news."

"Sure." Kamilah slouched uncomfortably. "One of these days."

—*eyejack?*—buzzed minus.

Adel was wondering the same thing. "What's an eyejack?"

"An eyejack," said Meri confidentially, "is someone who shocks other people."

"Shocks for pay," corrected Kamilah, her back still to them.

"Shock?" Adel frowned. "As in voltage shock or scandalize shock?"

"Well, electricity could be involved." Kamilah turned from the wall. Her medallion showed a cat sitting in a sunny window. "But mostly what I do," she continued, "is make people squirm when they get too settled for their own good."

—*trouble*—buzzed plus.

—*love it*—minus buzzed.

"And you do this how?"

"Movement." She made a flourish with her left hand that started as a slap but ended as a caress that did not quite touch Jarek's face. Jarek did not flinch. "Imagery. I work in visuals mostly but I sometimes use wordplay. Or sound—laughter, explosions, loud music. Whatever it takes to make you look."

"And people pay you for this?"

"Some do, some sue." Kamilah rattled it off like a catchphrase.

"It's an acquired taste," Meri said. "I know I'm still working on it."

"You liked it the time she made Jonman snort juice out of his nose," said Jarek. "Especially after he predicted she would do it to him."

The wall behind them turned announcement blue. "We have come within survey range of a new binary system. I'm naming the M5 star ONR 126-850 and the M2 star ONR 154-436." The screen showed data sheets on the discoveries: *Location, Luminosity, Metallicity, Mass, Age, Temperature, Habitable Ecosphere Radius.*

"Who cares about red dwarfs?" said Kamilah.

"About sixty percent of the stars in this sector are red dwarfs," said Meri.

"My point exactly," said Kamilah, "You're not going to find many terrestrials orbiting an M star. We should be looking somewhere else."

"Why is that?" said Adel.

"M class are small, cool stars," said Jarek. "In order to get enough insolation to be even remotely habitable, a planet has to be really close to the sun, so close that they get locked into synchronous rotation because of the intense tidal torque. Which means that one side is always dark and the other is always light. The atmosphere would freeze off the dark side."

"And these stars are known for the frequency and intensity of their flares," said Meri, "which would pretty much cook any life on a planet that close."

"Meri and Jarek are our resident science twizes," said Kamilah. "They can tell you more than you want to know about anything."

"So do we actually get to help decide where to go next?" asked Adel.

"Actually, we don't." Jarek shook his head sadly.

"We just argue about it." Kamilah crossed the library to the bathroom and paused at the doorway. "It passes the time. Don't get any ideas about the boy, Meri. I'll be right back." The door vanished as she stepped through and reformed immediately.

"When I first started thinking seriously about making the pilgrimage to the *Godspeed*," said Jarek, "I had this foolish idea that I might have some influence on the search, maybe even be responsible for a course change. I knew I wouldn't be aboard long enough to make a planetfall, but I thought maybe I could help. But I've studied Speedy's search plan and it's perfect, considering that we can't go any faster than a third of c."

"Besides, *we're* not going anywhere, Jerek and you and me," said Meri. "Except back to where we came from. By the time Speedy finds the next terrestrial, we could be grandparents."

"Or dead," said Kamilah as she came out of the bathroom. "Shall we tell young Adel here how long it's been since Speedy discovered a terrestrial planet?"

"Young Adel?" said Meri. "Just how old are you?"

"Nineteen standard," Adel muttered.

—*twenty-six back home*—buzzed plus.

"But that's twenty-six on Harvest."

"One hundred and fifty-eight standard," said the wall. "This is your captain speaking."

"Oh gods." Kamilah rested her forehead in her hand.

The image the *Godspeed* projected was more uniform than woman; she stood against the dazzle of a star field. Her coat was golden broadcloth lined in red; it hung to her knees. The sleeves were turned back to show the lining. Double rows of brass buttons ran from neck to hem. These were unbuttoned below the waist, revealing red breeches and golden hose. The white sash over her left shoulder was decorated with patches representing all the terrestrial planets she had discovered. Adel counted more than thirty before he lost track.

"I departed from the MASTA on Nuevo Sueño," said the *Godspeed*, "one hundred and fifty-eight years ago, Adel, and I've been looking for my next discovery ever since."

"Longer than any other threshold," said Kamilah.

"Longer than any other threshold," the *Godspeed* said amiably. "Which pains me deeply, I must say. Why do you bring this unfortunate statistic up, perfect one? Is there some conclusion you care to draw?"

She glared at the wall. "Only that we have wasted a century and a half in this desolate corner of the galaxy."

"We, Kamilah?" The *Godspeed* gave her an amused smile. "How long have you been with me?"

"Not quite a year." She folded her arms.

"Ah, the impatience of flesh." The *Godspeed* turned to the stars behind her. "You have traveled not quite a third of a light year since your arrival. Consider that I've traveled 50.12 light years since my departure from Nuevo Sueño. Now see what that looks like to me." She thrust her hands above her head and suddenly the points of light on the wall streamed into ribbons and the center of the screen jerked up-right-left-down-left with each course correction and then the ribbons became stars again. She faced the library again, her face glowing. "You have just come 15.33 parsecs in ten seconds. If I follow my instructions to reach my journey's end at the center of our galaxy I will have traveled 8.5 kiloparsecs."

—*if?*—buzzed minus.

"Believe me, Kamilah, I can imagine your experience of spacetime more easily than you can imagine mine." She tugged her sash into place and then pointed at Kamilah. "You're going to mope now."

Kamilah shook her head. Her medallion had gone completely black.

"A hundred and thirty-three people have jumped to me since Nuevo Sueño. How many times do you think I've had this conversation, Kamilah?"

Kamilah bit her lip.

"Ah, if only these walls could talk." The *Godspeed*'s laugh sounded like someone dropping silver spoons. "The things they have seen."

—*is she all right?*—buzzed plus.

"Here's something I'll bet you didn't know," said the *Godspeed*. "A fun fact. Now that Adel has replaced Upwood among our little company, everyone on board is under thirty."

The four of them digested this information in astonished silence.

"Wait a minute," said Meri. "What about Jonman?"

"He would like you to believe he's older but he's the same age as Kamilah." She reached into the pocket of her greatcoat and pulled out a scrap of digitex. A new window opened on the wall; it contained the birth certificate of Jon Haught Shillaber. "Twenty-eight standard."

"All of us?" said Jarek. "That's a pretty amazing coincidence."

"A coincidence?" She waved the birth certificate away. "You don't know how hard I schemed to arrange it." She chuckled. "I was practically diabolical."

"Speedy," said Meri carefully, "you're starting to worry us."

"Worry?"

"Worry," said Jarek.

"Why, because I make jokes? Because I have a flare for the dramatic?" She bowed low and gave them an elaborate hand flourish. "I am but mad north-northwest: when the wind is southerly I know a hawk from a handsaw."

minus buzzed—*time to be afraid*—

"So," said the *Godspeed*, "we seem to be having a morale problem. I know *my* feelings have been hurt. I think we need to come together, work on some common project. Build ourselves back into a team." She directed her gaze at Adel. "What do you say?"

"Sure."

"Then I suggest that we put on a play."

Meri moaned.

"Yes, that will do nicely." The *Godspeed* clapped her hands, clearly pleased at the prospect. "We'll need to a pick a script. Adel, I understand you've had some acting experience so I'm going to appoint you and Lihong to serve on the selection committee with me. I think poor Sister needs to get out and about more."

"Don't let Lihong pick," said Meri glumly. "How many plays are there about praying?"

"Come now, Meri," said the *Godspeed*. "Give her a chance. I think you'll be surprised."

Day Five

There are two kinds of pilgrimage, as commonly defined. One is a journey to a specific, usually sacred place; it takes place and then ends. The other is less about a destination and more about a spiritual quest. When we decide to jump to a threshold, we most often begin our pilgrimages intending to get to the *Godspeed* or the *Big D* or the *Bisous Bisous*, stay for some length of time and then return to our ordinary lives. However, as time passes on board we inevitably come to realize—sometimes to our chagrin—that we have been infected with an irrepressible yearning to seek out the numinous, wherever and however it might be found.

Materialists don't have much use for the notion of a soul. They prefer to locate individuality in the mind, which emerges from the brain but cannot exist separately from it. They maintain that information must be communicated to the brain through the senses, and only through the senses. But materialists have yet to offer a rigorous explanation of what happens during those few seconds of a jump when the original has ceased to exist and the scan from it has yet to be reassembled. Because during the brief interval when there are neither senses nor brain nor mind, we all seem to receive some subtle clue about our place in the universe.

This is why there are so few materialists.

Adel had been having dreams. They were not bad dreams, merely disturbing. In one, he was lost in a forest where people grew instead of trees. He stumbled past shrubby little kids he'd gone to school with and great towering grownups like his parents and Uncle Durwin and President Adriana. He knew he had to keep walking because if he stopped he would grow roots and raise his arms up to the sun like all the other tree people, but he was tired, so very tired.

In another, he was standing backstage watching a play he'd never heard of before and Sister Lihong tapped him on the shoulder and told him that Gavrila had called in sick and that he would have to take her part and then she pushed him out of the wings and he was onstage in front of a sellout audience, every one of which was Speedy, and he stumbled across the stage to the bed where Jarek waited for him, naked Jarek, and then Adel realized that he was naked too, and he climbed under the covers because he was cold and embarrassed, and Jarek kept staring at him because he, Adel, was supposed to say his line but he didn't know the next line or any line and so he did the one thing he could think to do, which was to kiss Jarek, on the mouth, and then his tongue brushed the ridges of Jarek's teeth and all the Speedys in the audience gave him a standing ovation . . .

. . . which woke him up.

Adel blinked. He lay in bed between Meri and Jarek; both were still asleep. They were under a yellow sheet that had pink kites and blue clouds on it. Jarek's arm had dropped loosely across Adel's waist. In the dim light he could see that Meri's lips were parted and for a while he listened to the seashore whisper of her breathing. He remembered that something had changed last night between the three of them.

Something, but what?

Obviously his two lovers weren't losing any sleep over it. Speedy had begun to bring the lights up in Meri's room so it had to be close to morning chime. Adel lifted his head but couldn't see the clock without disturbing his bedmates, so he tried to guess the time. If the ceiling was set to gain twenty lumens a minute and Speedy started at 0600, then it was . . . he couldn't do the math. After six in the morning, anyway.

The something was Jarek—*yes*. Adel realized that he'd enjoyed having sex with Jarek just a bit more than with Meri. Not that he hadn't enjoyed her too. There had been plenty of enjoying going on, that was for sure. A thrilling night all around. But Adel could be rougher with Jarek than he was with Meri. He didn't have to hold anything back. Sex with Jarek was a little like wrestling, only with orgasms.

Adel had been extremely doubtful about sleeping with both Meri *and* Jarek, until Meri had made it plain that was the only way he was ever going to get into her bed. The normal buzz of his opposites had risen to a scream; their deliberations had gotten so shrill that he'd been forced to mute their input. Not that he didn't know what they were thinking, of course; they were him.

Jarek had been the perfect gentleman at first; they had taken turns pleasuring Meri until the day before yesterday when she had guided Adel's hand to Jarek's erect cock. An awkward moment, but then Adel still felt like he was all thumbs and elbows when it came to sex anyway. Jarek talked continually while he made love, so Adel was never in doubt as to what Jarek wanted him to do. And because he trusted Jarek, Adel began to talk too. And then to moan, whimper, screech, and laugh out loud.

Adel felt extraordinarily adult, fucking both a man and a woman. He tried the word out in the gloom, mouthing it silently. I *fuck*, you *fuck*, he, she, or it *fucks*, we *fuck*, you all *fuck*, they *fuck*. The only thing that confused him about losing his virginity was not that his sexual identity was now slightly blurry; it was his raging appetite. Now that he knew what he had been missing, he wanted to have sex with everyone here on the *Godspeed* and then go back to Harvest and fuck his way through Great Randall Science and Agricultural

College and up and down Crown Edge. Well, that wasn't quite true. He didn't particularly want to see the Manmans naked and the thought of sleeping with his parents made him queasy and now that he was an experienced lover, he couldn't see himself on top, underneath or sideways with his ex, Gavrila. But still. He'd been horny back on Harvest but now he felt like he might spin out of control. Was it perverted to want so much sex?

Adel was wondering what color Sister Lihong Rain's hair was and how it would look spread across his pillow when Kamilah spoke through the closed door.

"Send Adel out," she said, "but put some clothes on him first."

Adel's head jerked up. "How does she know I'm here?"

"Time is it?" said Meri.

"Don't know." Jarek moaned and gave him a knee in the small of the back. "But it's for you, brother, so you'd better get it."

He clambered over Meri and tumbled out of bed onto her loafers. Their clothes were strewn around the room. Adel pulled on his saniwear, the taut, silver warm-ups that Meri had created for him and his black softwalks. The black floss cape had been his own idea—a signature, like Kamilah's medallion or Sister's veil. The cape was modest, only the size of a face towel, and was attached to his shoulders by the two merit pins he'd recycled from his Host uniforms.

He paused in front of a wall, waved it to mirror mode, combed fingers through his hair and then stepped through the door. Kamilah leaned against the wall with her medallion in hand. She gazed into it thoughtfully.

"How did you find me?" said Adel.

"I asked Speedy." She let it fall to her chest and Adel saw the eating man again. Adel had noticed that her eating man had reappeared again and again, always at the same table. "You want breakfast?"

He was annoyed with her for rousting him out of bed before morning chime. "When I wake up." Who knew what erotic treats he might miss?

"Your eyes look open to me." She gave him a knowing smile. "Busy night?"

He considered telling her that it was none of her business, but decided to flirt instead. Maybe he'd get lucky. "Busy enough." He gave his shoulders a twitch, which made his cape flutter. "You?"

"I slept."

"I slept too." Adel waited a beat. "Eventually."

"Gods, Adel!" Kamilah laughed out loud. "You're a handful, you know that?" She put an arm around his shoulders and started walking him back up Dream Street. "Meri and Jarek had better watch out."

Adel wasn't quite sure what she meant but he decided to let it drop for now. "So what's this about?"

"A field trip." They started down the Tulip Stairway. "What do you know about physics?"

Adel had studied comparative entertainment at Great Randall S&A, although he'd left school in his third year to train for the Harvest Olympics and to find himself. Unfortunately, he'd finished only sixth in the 200 meters and Adel was still pretty much missing. Science in general and physics in particular had never been a strength. "I know some. Sort of."

"What's the first law of thermodynamics?"

"The first law of thermodynamics." He closed his eyes and tried to picture the screen. "Something like . . . um . . . a body stays in motion . . . ah . . . as long as it's in motion?"

"Oh great," she said wearily. "Have you ever been in space?"

For the first time in days he missed the familiar buzz of his opposites. He lifted their mute.

—*she thinks we're a moron*—buzzed minus.

—*we are a moron*—plus buzzed.

"Everybody's in space," he said defensively. "That's where all the planets are. We're traveling through space this very moment."

"This wasn't meant to be a trick question," she said gently. "I mean have you ever been in a hardsuit out in the vacuum?"

"Oh," he said. "No."

"You want to?"

—*wow*—

—*yes*—

He had to restrain himself from hugging her. "Absolutely."

"Okay then." She gestured at the entrance to the Chillingsworth Breakfasting Room. "Let's grab something to take away and head down to the locker room. We need to oxygenate for about half an hour."

—*but why is she doing this?*—buzzed plus.

There were two ways to the surface of the *Godspeed*: through the great bay doors of the Well Met Arena or out the Clarke Airlock. Adel straddled a bench in the pre-breathing locker room and wolfed down a sausage and honeynut torte while Kamilah explained what was about to happen.

"We have to spend another twenty-minutes here breathing a hundred percent oxygen to scrub nitrogen out of our bodies. Then just before we climb into the hardsuits, we put on isotherms." She opened a locker and removed two silky black garments. "You want to wait until the last minute; isotherms take some getting used to. But they keep the hardsuit from overheating." She tossed one to Adel.

"But how can that happen?" He held the isotherm up; it had a hood and opened with a slide down the torso. The sleeves ended at the elbow and the pants at the knee. "Isn't space just about as cold as anything gets?"

"Yes, but the hardsuit is airtight, which makes it hard to dissipate all the heat that you're going to be generating. Even though you get some servo-assist, it's a big rig, Adel. You've got to work to get anywhere." She raised her steaming mug of kappa and winked at him. "Think you're man enough for the job?"

—*let that pass*—buzzed plus.

"I suppose we'll know soon enough." Adel rubbed the fabric of the isotherm between his thumb and forefinger. It was cool to the touch.

Kamilah sipped from the mug. "Once we're out on the surface," she said, "Speedy will be running all your systems. All you have to do is follow me."

The *Godspeed* displayed on a section of wall. She was wearing an isotherm with the hood down; it clung to her like a second skin. Adel could see the outline of her nipples and the subtle wrinkles her pubic hair made in the fabric.

—*but they're not real*—minus buzzed.

"What are you doing, Kamilah?" said the *Godspeed*. "You were out just last week."

"Adel hasn't seen the view."

"I can show him any view he wants. I can fill the Welcome Arena with stars. He can see in ultraviolet. Infrared."

"Yes, but it wouldn't be quite real, would it?"

"Reality is over-rated." The *Godspeed* waggled a finger at Kamilah. "You're taking an unusual interest in young Adel. I'm watching, perfect one."

"You're watching everyone, Speedy. That's how you get your cookies." With that she pulled the top of her scrubs off. "Time to get naked, Adel. Walk our hardsuits out and start the checklist, would you Speedy?"

—*those are real*—buzzed minus.

—Meri and Jarek remember—
—we can look—

And Adel did look as he slithered out of his own clothes. Although he was discreet about it, he managed to burn indelible images into his memory of Kamilah undressing, the curve of her magnificent hip, the lush pendency of her breasts, the breathtaking expanse of her back as her tawny skin stretched tight over nubs of her spine. She was a woman a man might drown in. Abruptly, he realized that he was becoming aroused. He turned away from her, tossed his clothes into a locker, snatched at the isotherm and pulled it on.

And bit back a scream.

Although it was as silken as when Kamilah had pulled it out of the drawer, his isotherm felt like it had spent the last ten years in cryogenic storage. Adel's skin crawled beneath it and his hands curled into fists. As a swimmer, Adel had experienced some precipitous temperature changes, but he'd never dived into a pool filled with liquid hydrogen.

*—trying to kill us—*screeched minus.

"Are you all right?" said Kamilah. "Your eyes look like eggs."

"Ah," said Adel. "*Ah*."

*—we can do this—*buzzed plus.

"Hang on," said Kamilah. "It passes."

As the hardsuits clumped around the corner of the locker room, their servos singing, Adel shivered and caught his breath. He thought he could hear every joint crack as he unclenched his fists and spread his fingers. When he pulled the isotherm hood over his head, he got the worst ice cream headache he'd ever had.

"This is going to be fun," he said through clenched teeth.

The hardsuits were gleaming white eggs with four arms, two legs, and a tail. The arms on either side were flexrobotic and built for heavy lifting. Beside them were fabric sleeves into which a spacewalker could insert his arms for delicate work. The legs ended in ribbed plates, as did the snaking tail, which Kamilah explained could be used as a stabilizer or an anchor. A silver ball the size of coconut perched at the top of the suit.

"Just think of them as spaceships that walk," said Kamilah. "Okay, Speedy. Pop the tops."

The top, translucent third of each egg swung back. Kamilah muscled a stairway up to the closest hardsuit. "This one's yours. Settle in but don't try moving just yet."

Adel slid his legs into the suit's legs and cool gel flowed around them, locking him into place. He ducked instinctively as the top came down, but he had plenty of room. Seals fastened with a *scritch* and the heads up display on the inside of the top began to glow with controls and diagnostics. Beneath the translucent top were finger-pads for controlling the robotic lifter arms; near them were the holes of the hardsuit's sleeves. Adel stuck his arms through, flexed his fingers in the gloves then turned his attention back to the HUD. He saw that he had forty hours of oxygen reserve and his batteries were at 98% of capacity. The temperature in the airlock was 15.52°C and the air pressure was 689 millibars. Then the readouts faded and the *Godspeed* was studying him intently. She looked worried.

"Adel, what's going on?"

"Is something going on?"

"I'm afraid there is and I don't want you mixed up in it. What does Kamilah want with you?"

Adel felt a chill that had nothing to do with his isotherm.

—*don't say anything*—buzzed plus.

—*we don't know anything*—

"I don't know that she wants anything." He pulled his arms out of the hardsuit's sleeves and folded them across his chest. "I just thought she was being nice."

"All right, Adel," said Kamilah over the comm. "Take a stroll around the room. I want to see how you do in here where it's flat. Speedy will compensate if you have any trouble. I'm sure she's already in your ear."

The *Godspeed* held a forefinger to her lips. "Kamilah is going to ask you to turn off your comm. That's when you must be especially careful, Adel." With that, she faded away and Adel was staring, slack-jawed, at the HUD.

"Adel?" said Kamilah. "Are you napping in there?"

Adel took a couple of tentative steps. Moving the hardsuit was a little like walking on stilts. He was high off the floor and couldn't really see or feel what was beneath his feet. When he twisted around, he caught sight of the tail whipping frantically behind him. But after walking for a few minutes, he decided that he could manage the suit. He lumbered behind Kamilah through the inner hatch of the airlock, which slid shut.

Adel listened to the muted chatter of pumps evacuating the lock until finally there wasn't enough air to carry sound. Moments later, the outer hatch opened.

"Ready?" Kamilah said. "Remember that we're leaving the artificial gravity field. No leaps or bounds—you don't want to achieve escape velocity."

Adel nodded.

—*she can't see us*—buzzed minus—*we have to talk to her*—

Adel cleared his throat. "I've always wanted to see the stars from space."

"Actually, you won't have much of a view until later," she said. "Let's go."

As they passed through the hatch, the *Godspeed* announced, "Suit lights are on. I'm deploying fireflies."

Adel saw the silver ball lift from the top of Kamilah's suit and float directly above her. The bottom half of it was now incandescent, lighting the surface of the *Godspeed* against the swarming darkness. At the same time the ground around him lit up. He looked and saw his firefly hovering about a meter over the suit.

—*amazing*—buzzed plus—*we're out, we're out in space*—

They crossed the flat staging pad just outside the airlock and stepped off onto the regolith. The rock had been pounded to gray dust by centuries of foot traffic. Whenever he took a step the dust puffed underfoot and drifted slowly back to the ground like smoke. It was twenty centimeters deep in some places but offered little resistance to his footplates. Adel's excitement leached slowly away as Kamilah led him away from the airlock. He had to take mincing steps to keep from launching himself free of the *Godspeed's* tenuous gravitational pull. It was frustrating; he felt as if he were walking with a pillow between his legs. The sky was a huge disappointment as well. The fireflies washed out the light from all but the brightest stars. He'd seen better skies camping on Harvest.

"So where are we going?"

"Just around."

"How long will it take?"

"Not that long."

—*hiding something?*—buzzed plus.

—*definitely*—

"And what exactly are we going to do?"

"A little bit of everything." One of her robotic arms gave him a playful wave. "You'll see."

They marched in silence for a while. Adel began to chafe at following Kamilah's lead. He picked up his pace and drew alongside of her. The regolith here was not quite so trampled and much less regular, although a clearly defined trail showed that they were not the first to make this trek. They passed stones and rubble piles and boulders the size of houses and the occasional impact crater that the path circumnavigated.

—*impact crater?*—buzzed minus.

"Uh, Kamilah," he said. "How often does Speedy get hit by meteors?"

"Never," said Kamilah. "The craters you see are all pre-launch. Interstellar space is pretty much empty so it's not that much of a problem."

"I sweep the sky for incoming debris," said the *Godspeed*, "up to five million meters away."

"And that works?"

"So far," said Kamilah. "We wouldn't want to slam into anything traveling at a third the speed of light."

They walked on for another ten minutes before Kamilah stopped. "There." She pointed. "That's where we came from. Somewhere out there is home."

Adel squinted. *There* was pretty much meaningless. Was she pointing at some particular star or a space between stars?"

"This is the backside. If Speedy had a rear bumper," she said, "we'd be standing on it right here. I want to show you something interesting. Pull your arms out of the sleeves."

"Done."

"The comm toggle is under the right arm keypad. Switch it off."

The *Godspeed* broke into their conversation. "Kamilah and Adel, you are about to disable a key safety feature of your hardsuits. I strongly urge you to reconsider."

"I see the switch." Adel's throat was tight. "You know, Speedy warned me about this back in the airlock."

"I'm sure she did. We go through this every time."

"You've done this before?"

"Many times," she said. "It's a tradition we've started to bring the new arrival out here to see the sights. It's actually a spiritual thing, which is why Speedy doesn't really get it."

"I have to turn off the comm why?"

"Because she's watching, Adel," said Kamilah impatiently. "She's always with us. She can't help herself."

"Young Adel," murmured the *Godspeed*. "Remember what I said."

—*trust Kamilah*—

—*or trust Speedy*—

—*we were warned*—

Adel flicked the toggle. "Now what?" he said to himself. His voice sounded very small in the suit.

He was startled when Kamilah leaned her suit against his so that the tops of the eggs were touching. It was strangely intimate maneuver, almost like a kiss. Her face was an electric green shadow in the glow of the HUD.

He was startled again when she spoke. "Turn. The. Comm. Off." He could hear her through the suit. She paused between each word, her voice reedy and metallic.

"I did," he said.

He could see her shake her head and tap fingers to her ears. "You. Have. To. Shout."

"I. Did!" Adel shouted.

"Good." She picked up a rock the size of a fist and held it at arm's length. "Drop. Rock." She paused. "Count. How. Long. To. Surface."

—*science experiments?*—buzzed plus.

—*she's gone crazy*—

Adel was inclined to agree with his minus but what Kamilah was asking seemed harmless enough.

"Ready?"

"Yes."

She let go. Adel counted.

One one thousand, two one thousand, three one thousand, four one thousand, five . . .

And it was down.

"Yes?" said Kamilah.

"Five."

"Good. Keep. Secret." She paused. "Comm. On."

As he flicked the switch he heard her saying. ". . . you feel it? My first time it was too subtle but if you concentrate, you'll get it."

"Are you all right, Adel?" murmured the *Godspeed.* "What just happened?"

"I don't know," said Adel, mystified.

"Well, we can try again on the frontside," said Kamilah. "Sometimes it's better there. Let's go."

—*what is she talking about?*—minus buzzed.

For twenty minutes he trudged in perplexed silence past big rocks, little rocks, and powdered rocks in all the colors of gray. In some places the surface of the trail was grainy like sand, in others it was dust, and in yet others it was bare ledge. Adel just didn't understand what he was supposed to have gotten from watching the rock drop. Something to do with gravity? What he didn't know about gravity would fill a barn. Eventually he gave up trying to figure it out. Kamilah was right about one thing: it was real work walking in a hardsuit. If it hadn't been for the isotherm, he would have long since broken a sweat.

—*this has to get better*—buzzed plus.

"How much longer?" said Adel at last.

"A while yet." Kamilah chuckled. "What are you, a little kid?"

"Remember the day I got here?" he said. "You told me that you were sentenced to spend time on Speedy. But you never said why."

"Not that interesting, really."

"Better than counting rocks." He stomped on a flat stone the size of his hand, breaking it into three pieces. "Or I suppose I could sing." He gave her the first few bars of "Do As We Don't" in his finest atonal yodel.

"Gods, Adel, but you're a pest today." Kamilah sighed. "All right, so there's a religion on Suncast . . ."

"Suncast? That's where you're from?"

"That's where I was from. If I ever get off this rock, that's the last place I'm going to stay."

—*if?*—buzzed minus—*why did she say if?*—

"Anyway, there's a sect that call themselves God's Own Poor. They're very proud of themselves for having deliberately chosen not to own very much. They spout these endless lectures about how living simply is the way to true spirituality. It's all over the worldnet. And they have this tradition that once a year they leave their houses and put their belongings into a cart, supposedly everything they own but not really. Each of them drags the cart to a park or a campground—this takes place in the warm weather, naturally—and they spend two weeks congratulating themselves on how poor they are and how God loves them especially."

"What god do they worship?"

"A few pray to Sagittarius A*, the black hole at the center of the galaxy, but most are some flavor of Eternal Centerers. When it was founded, the Poor might actually have been a legitimate religion. I mean, I see their point that owning too much can get in the way. Except that now almost all of them have houses and furniture and every kind of vehicle. None of them tries to fit the living room couch on their carts. And you should see some of these carts. They cost more than I make in a year."

"From shocking people," Adel said. "As a professional eyejack."

The comm was silent for a moment. "Are you teasing me, young Adel?"

"No, no." Adel bit back his grin. "Not at all." Even though he knew she couldn't see it, she could apparently *hear* it inflected in his voice. "So you were annoyed at them?"

"I was. Lots of us were. It wasn't only that they were self-righteous hypocrites. I didn't like the way they commandeered the parks just when the rest of us wanted to use them. So I asked myself, how can I shock the Poor and what kind of purse can I make from doing it?"

A new trail diverged from the one they had been following, Kamilah considered for a moment and then took it. She fell silent for a few moments.

Adel prompted her. "And you came up with a plan."

—*why are we interested in this?*—buzzed plus.

—*because we want to get her into bed*—

"I did. First I took out a loan; I had to put my house up as collateral. I split two hundred thousand barries across eight hundred cash cards, so each one was worth two hundred and fifty. Next I set up my tent at the annual Poverty Revival at Point Kingsley on the Prithee Sea, which you've never heard of but which is one of the most beautiful places in the Continuum. I passed as one of the Poor, mingling with about ten thousand true believers. I parked a wheelbarrow outside the tent that had nothing in it but a suitcase and a shovel. That got a megagram of disapproval, which told me I was onto something. Just before dawn on the tenth day of the encampment, I tossed the suitcase and shoveled in the eight hundred cash cards. I parked my wheelbarrow at the Tabernacle of the Center and waited with a spycam. I'd painted, 'God Helps Those Who Help Themselves' on the side; I thought that was a nice touch. I was there when people started to discover my little monetary miracle. I shot vids of several hundred of the Poor dipping their hot hands into the cards. Some of them just grabbed a handful and ran, but quite a few tried to sneak up on the wheelbarrow when nobody was looking. But of course, everyone was. The wheelbarrow was empty in about an hour and a half, but people kept coming to look all morning."

Adel was puzzled. "But your sign said they were supposed to help themselves," he said. "Why would they be ashamed?"

"Well, they were supposed to be celebrating their devotion to poverty, not padding their personal assets. But the vids were just documentation, they weren't the sting. Understand that the cards were *mine*. Yes, I authorized all expenditures, but I also collected detailed reports on everything they bought. Everything, as in possessions, Adel. Material goods. All kinds of stuff, and lots of it. I posted the complete record. For six days my website was one of the most active on the worldnet. Then the local Law Exchange shut me down. Still, even after legal expenses and paying off the loan, I cleared almost three thousand barries."

—*brilliant*—buzzed minus.

*—she got caught—*plus buzzed.

"But this was against the law on Suncast?" said Adel.

"Actually, no." Kamilah kicked at a stone and sent it skittering across the regolith. She trudged on in silence for a few moments. "But I used a wheelbarrow," she said finally, "which LEX ruled was too much like one of their carts—a cultural symbol. According to LEX, I had committed Intolerant Speech. If I had just set the cards out in a basket, the Poor couldn't have touched me. But I didn't and they did. In the remedy phase of my trial, the Poor asked LEX to ship me here. I guess they thought I'd get religion."

"And did you?"

"You don't get to ask all the questions." The tail of her hardsuit darted and the footplate tapped the rear of Adel's suit. "Your turn. Tell me something interesting about yourself. Something that nobody knows."

He considered. "Well, I was a virgin when I got here."

"Something interesting, Adel."

"And I'm not anymore."

"That nobody knows," she said.

*—just trying to shock you—*buzzed plus.

—bitch— minus buzzed.

"All right," he said, at last. "I'm a delibertarian."

Kamilah paused, then turned completely around once, as if to get her bearings. "I don't know what that is."

"I have an implant that makes me hear voices. Sometimes they argue with each other."

"Oh?" Kamilah headed off the trail. "About what?"

Adel picked his way after her. "Mostly about what I should do." He sensed that he didn't really have her complete attention. "Say I'm coming out of church and I see a wheelbarrow filled with cash cards. One voice might tell me to grab as many as I can, the other says no."

"I'd get tired of that soon enough."

"Or say someone insults me, hurts my feelings. One voice wants to understand her and the other wants to kick her teeth in. But the thing is, the voices are all me."

"All right then," Kamilah paused, glanced left and then right as if lining up landmarks. "We're here."

*—too bad we can't kick her teeth in—*buzzed minus.

"Where's here?"

"This is the frontside, exactly opposite from where we just were. We should try shutting down again. This might be your lucky spot."

"I don't know if I want to," said Adel. "What am I doing here, Kamilah?"

"Look, Adel, I'm sorry," she said. "I didn't mean to hurt your feelings. I forget you're just a kid. Come over here, let me give you a hug."

"Oh." Adel was at once mollified by Kamilah's apology and stung that she thought of him as a kid.

—*we are a kid*—plus buzzed.

And what kind of hug was he going to get in a hardsuit?

—*shut up*—

"You're only nine standard older than I am," he said as he brought his suit within robotic arm's reach.

"I know." Her two arms snaked around him. "Turn off your comm, Adel."

This time the *Godspeed* made no objection. When the comm was off, Kamilah didn't bother to speak. She picked up a rock and held it out. Adel waved for her to drop it.

One one thousand, two one thousand, three one thousand, four one thousand, five one thousand, six one thousand, seven one . . .

Seven? Adel was confused.

—*we messed up the count*—buzzed minus.

—*did not*—

He leaned into her and touched her top. "Seven."

"Yes." She paused. "Turn. Off. Lights."

Adel found the control and heard a soft clunk as the firefly docked with his hardsuit. He waved the suit lights off and blacked out the HUD, although he was not in a particularly spiritual mood. The blackness of space closed around them and the sky filled with the shyest of stars. Adel craned in the suit to see them all. Deep space was much more busy than he'd imagined. The stars were all different sizes and many burned in colors: blues, yellows, oranges, and reds—a lot more reds than he would have thought. There were dense patches and sparse patches and an elongated wispy cloud the stretched across his field of vision that he assumed was the rest of the Milky Way.

—*amazing*—

—*but what's going on?*—

"Questions?" said Kamilah.

"Questions?" he said under his breath. "Damn right I have questions." When he shouted, he could hear the anger in his voice. "Rocks. Mean. What?"

"Speedy. Slows. Down." She paused. "We. Don't. Know. Why." Another pause. "Act. Normal. More. Later."

—act normal?—
—we're fucked—
"Comm." He screamed. "On."
"Careful," she said. "Adel."

He felt a slithering against his suit as she let go of him. He bashed at the comm switch and brought the suit lights on.

". . . the most amazing experience, isn't it?" she was saying. "It's almost like you're standing naked in space."

"Kamilah . . ." He tried to speak but panic choked him.

"Adel, what's happening?" said the *Godspeed*. "Are you all right?"

"I have to tell you," said Kamilah, "that first time I was actually a little scared but I'm used to it now. But you—you did just fine."

"Fine," Adel said. His heart was pounding so hard he thought it might burst his chest. "Just fine."

Day Twelve

Since the *Godspeed* left the orbit of Menander, fifth planet of Hallowell's Star, to begin its historic voyage of discovery, 69,384 of us stepped off her transport stage. Only about ten thousand of us were pilgrims, the rest were itinerant techs and prospective colonists. On average, the pilgrims spent a little over a standard year as passengers, while the sojourn of the colony-builders rarely exceeded sixty days. As it turns out, Sister Lihong Rain held the record for the longest pilgrimage; she stayed on the *Godspeed* for more than seven standards.

At launch, the cognizor in command of the *Godspeed* had been content with a non-gendered persona. Not until the hundred and thirteenth year did it present as The Captain, a male authority figure. The Captain was a sandy-haired mesomorph, apparently a native of one of the highest G worlds. His original uniform was modest in comparison to later incarnations, gray and apparently seamless, with neither cuff nor collar. The Captain first appeared on the walls of the library but soon spread throughout the living quarters and then began to manifest as a fetch, which could be projected anywhere, even onto the surface. The *Godspeed* mostly used The Captain to oversee shipboard routine but on occasion he would approach us in social contexts. Inevitably he would betray a disturbing knowledge of everything that we had ever done while aboard. We realized to our dismay that the *Godspeed* was always watching.

These awkward attempts at sociability were not well received; the Captain persona was gruff and humorless and all too often presumptuous. He was not at all pleased when one of us nicknamed him Speedy. Later iterations of the persona did little to improve his popularity.

It wasn't until the three hundred and thirty-second year that the stubborn Captain was supplanted by a female persona. The new Speedy impressed everyone. She didn't give orders; she made requests. She picked up on many of the social cues that her predecessor had missed, bowing out of conversations where she was not welcome, not only listening but hearing what we told her. She was accommodating and gregarious, if somewhat emotionally needy. She laughed easily, although her sense of humor was often disconcerting. She didn't mind at all that we called her Speedy. And she kept our secrets.

Only a very few saw the darker shades of the *Godspeed*'s persona. The techs found her eccentricities charming and the colonists celebrated her for being such a prodigious discoverer of terrestrials. Most pilgrims recalled their time aboard with bemused nostalgia.

Of course, the *Godspeed* had no choice but to keep all of us under constant surveillance. We were her charges. Her cargo. Over the course of one thousand and eighty-seven standards, she witnessed six homicides, eleven suicides, and two hundred and forty-nine deaths from accident, disease, and old age. She took each of these deaths personally, even as she rejoiced in the two hundred and sixty-eight babies conceived and born in the bedrooms of Dream Street. She presided over two thousand and eighteen marriages, four thousand and eighty-nine divorces. She witnessed twenty-nine million eight hundred and fifteen thousand two hundred and forty-seven acts of sexual congress, not including masturbation. Since she was responsible for our physical and emotional well-being, she monitored what we ate, who we slept with, what drugs we used, how much exercise we got. She tried to defuse quarrels and mediate disputes. She readily ceded her authority to the project manager and team leaders during a colonizing stop but in interstellar space, she was in command.

Since there was little privacy inside the *Godspeed*, it was difficult for Kamilah, Adel, Jarek, Meri, Jonman, and Robman to discuss their situation. None of them had been able to lure Sister out for a suit-to-suit conference, so she was not in their confidence. Adel took a couple of showers with Meri and Jarek. They played crank jams at top volume and whispered in each other's ears as they pretended to make out, but that was awkward at best. They had no way to send or encrypt messages that the *Godspeed* couldn't easily hack. Jonman hit upon the strategy of writing steganographic poetry under blankets at night and then handing them around to be read—also under blankets.

> We hear that love can't wait too long,
> Go and find her home.
> We fear that she who we seek
> Must sleep all day, have dreams of night
> killed by the fire up in the sky.
> Would we? Does she?

Steganography, Adel learned from a whisperer in the library, was the ancient art of hiding messages within messages. When Robman gave him the key of picking out every fourth word of this poem, he read: *We can't go home she must have killed up would.* This puzzled him until he remembered that the last pilgrim to leave the *Godspeed* before he arrived was Upwood Marcene. Then he was chilled. The problem with Jonman's poems was that they had to be written mechanically—on a surface with an implement. None of the pilgrims had ever needed to master the skill of handwriting; their scrawls were all but indecipherable. And asking for the materials to write with aroused the *Godspeed*'s suspicions.

Not only that, but Jonman's poetry was awful.

Over several days, in bits and snatches, Adel was able to arrive at a rough understanding of their dilemma. Three months ago, while Adel was still writing his essay, Jarek had noticed that spacewalking on the surface of the *Godspeed* felt different than it had been when he first arrived. He thought his hardsuit might be defective until he tried several others. After that, he devised the test, and led the others out, one by one, to witness it. If the *Godspeed* had actually been traveling at a constant 100,000 kilometers per second, rocks dropped anywhere on the surface would take the same amount of time to fall. However, when she accelerated away from a newly established colony, rocks dropped on the backside took longer to fall than rocks on the frontside. And when she decelerated toward a new discovery . . .

Once they were sure that they were slowing down, the pilgrims had to decide what it meant and what to do next. They queried the library and, as far as they could tell, the *Godspeed* had announced every scan and course change she had ever made. In over a thousand years the only times she had ever decelerated was when she had targeted a new planet. There was no precedent for what was happening and her silence about it scared them. They waited, dissembled as best they could, and desperately hoped that someone back home would notice that something was wrong.

Weeks passed. A month. Two months.

Jonman maintained that there could be only two possible explanations: the *Godspeed* must either be falsifying its navigation reports or it had cut all contact with the Continuum. Either way, he argued, they must continue to wait. Upwood's pilgrimage was almost over, he was scheduled to go home in another two weeks. If the *Godspeed* let him make the jump, then their troubles were over. Hours, or at the most a day, after he reported the anomaly, techs would swarm the transport stage. If she didn't let him make the jump, then at least they would know where they stood. Nobody mentioned a third outcome, although Upwood clearly understood that there was a risk that the *Godspeed* might kill or twist him during transport and make it look like an accident. Flawed jumps were extremely rare but not impossible. Upwood had lost almost five kilos by the day he climbed onto the transport stage. His chest was a washboard of ribs and his eyes were sunken. The other pilgrims watched in hope and horror as he faded into wisps of probability and was gone.

Five days passed. On the sixth day, the *Godspeed* announced that they would be joined by a new pilgrim. A week after Upwood's departure, Adel Ranger Santos was assembled on the transport stage.

Sister was horribly miscast as Miranda. Adel thought she would have made a better Caliban, especially since he was Ferdinand. In the script, Miranda was supposed to fall madly in love with Ferdinand, but Sister was unable to summon even a smile for Adel, much less passion. He might as well have been an old sock as the love of her life.

Adel knew why the *Godspeed* had chosen *The Tempest*; she wanted to play Prospero. She'd cast Meri as Ariel and Kamilah as Caliban. Jonman and Robman were Trinculo and Stephano and along with Jarek also took the parts of the various other lesser lords and sons and brothers and sailors. Adel found it a very complicated play, even for Shakespeare.

"I am a fool," said Sister, "to weep when I am glad." She delivered the line like someone hitting the same note on a keyboard again and again.

Adel had a whisperer feeding him lines. "Why do you weep?"

"Stop there." The *Godspeed* waved her magic staff. She was

directing the scene in costume. Prospero wore a full-length opales-
cent cape with fur trim, a black undertunic, and a small silver
crown. "Nobody says 'weep' anymore." She had been rewriting the
play ever since they started rehearsing. "Adel, have you ever said
'weep' in your life?"

"No," said Adel miserably. He was hungry and was certain he
would starve to death before they got through this scene.

"Then neither should Ferdinand. Let's change 'weep' to 'cry.'
Say the line, Ferdinand."

Adel said, "Why do you cry?"

"No." She shut her eyes. "No, that's not right either." Her brow
wrinkled. "Try 'why are you crying?' "

"Why are you crying?" said Adel.

"Much better." She clapped hands once. "I know the script is a
classic but after three thousand years some of these lines are dusty.
Miranda, give me 'I am a fool' with the change."

"I am a fool," she said, "to cry when I am glad."

"Why are you crying?"

"Because I'm not worthy. I dare not even offer myself to you—
much less ask you to love me." Here the *Godspeed* had directed her
to put her arms on Adel's shoulders. "But the more I try to hide my
feelings, the more they show."

As they gazed at each other, Adel thought he did see a glimmer
of something in Sister's eyes. Probably nausea.

"So no more pretending." Sister knelt awkwardly and gazed up
at him. "If you want to marry me, I'll be your wife." She lowered her
head, but forgot again to cheat toward the house, so that she delivered the next line to the floor. "If not, I'll live as a virgin the rest of
my life, in love with nobody but you."

"We can't hear you, Miranda," said the *Godspeed*.

Sister tilted her head to the side and finished the speech. "You
don't even have to talk to me if you don't want. Makes no difference. I'll always be there for you."

"Ferdinand," the *Godspeed* murmured, "she's just made you the
happiest man in the world."

Adel pulled her to her feet. "Darling, you make me feel so hum-
ble."

"So then you'll be my husband?"

"Sure," he said. "My heart is willing . . . ," he laid his hand
against his chest, ". . . and here's my hand." Adel extended his arm.

"And here's mine with my heart in it." She slid her fingers across
his palm, her touch cool and feathery.

"And," prompted the *Godspeed*. "And?"

With a sigh, Sister turned her face up toward his. Her eyelids fluttered closed. Adel stooped over her. The first time he had played this scene, she had so clearly not wanted to be kissed that he had just brushed his lips against her thin frown. The *Godspeed* wanted more. Now he lifted her veil and pressed his mouth hard against hers. She did nothing to resist, although he could feel her shiver when he slipped the tip of his tongue between her lips.

"Line?" said the *Godspeed*.

"Well, got to go." Sister twitched out of his embrace. "See you in a bit."

"It will seem like forever." Adel bowed to her and then they both turned to get the *Godspeed*'s reaction.

"Better," she said. "But Miranda, flow into his arms. He's going to be your husband, your dream come true."

"I know." Her voice was pained.

"Take your lunch break and send me Stephano and Trinculo." She waved them off. "Topic of the day is . . . what?" She glanced around the little theater, as if she might discover a clue in the empty house. "Today you are to talk about what you're going to do when you get home."

Adel could not help but notice Sister's stricken expression; her eyes were like wounds. But she nodded and made no objection.

As they passed down the aisle, the *Godspeed* brought her fetch downstage to deliver the speech that closed Act III, Scene i. As always, she gave her lines a grandiloquent, singing quality.

"Those two really take the cake. My plan is working out just great, but I can't sit around patting myself on the back. I've got other fish to fry if I'm going to make this mess end happily ever after."

To help Adel and Sister get into character, the *Godspeed* had directed them to eat lunch together every day in the Chillingsworth Breakfasting Room while the other pilgrims dined in the Ophiuchi. They had passed their first meal in tortured silence and might as well have been on different floors of the threshold. When the *Godspeed* asked what they talked about, they sheepishly admitted that they had not spoken at all. She knew this, of course, but pretended to be so provoked that she assigned them topics for mandatory discussion.

The Chillingsworth was a more intimate space than the Ophiuchi. It was cross-shaped; in the three bays were refectory tables and benches. There was a tile fireplace in the fourth bay in which a fetch fire always burned. Sconces in the shapes of the famous singing flowers of Old Zara sprouted from pale blue walls.

Adel set his plate of spiralini in rado sauce on the heavy table and scraped a bench from underneath to sit on. While the pasta cooled he closed his eyes and lifted the mute on his opposites. He had learned back on Harvest that their buzz made acting impossible. They were confused when he was in character and tried to get him to do things that weren't in the script. When he opened his eyes again, Sister was opposite him, head bowed in prayer over a bowl of thrush needles.

He waited for her to finish. "You want to go first?" he said.

"I don't like to think about going home to Pio," she said. "I pray it won't happen anytime soon."

*—your prayers are answered—*buzzed minus.

"Why, was it bad?"

"No." She picked up her spoon but then set it down again. Over the past few days Adel had discovered that she was an extremely nervous eater. She barely touched what was on her plate. "I was happy." Somehow, Adel couldn't quite imagine what happy might look like on Sister Lihong Rain. "But I was much smaller then. When the Main told me I had to make a pilgrimage, I cried. But she has filled me with her grace and made me large. Being with her here is the greatest blessing."

"Her? You are talking about Speedy?"

Sister gave him a pitying nod, as if the answer were as obvious as air. "And what about you, Adel?"

Adel had been so anxious since the spacewalk that he hadn't really considered what would happen if he were lucky enough to get off the *Godspeed* alive.

*—we were going to have a whole lot of sex remember?—*buzzed plus.

—with as many people as possible—

Adel wondered if Sister would ever consider sleeping with him. "I want to have lovers." He had felt a familiar stirring whenever he kissed her in rehearsal.

"Ah." She nodded. "And get married, like in our play?"

"Well that, sure. Eventually." He remembered lurid fantasies he'd spun about Helell Merwyn, the librarian from the Springs upper school and his mother's friend Renata Murat and Lucia Guerra who was in that comedy about the talking house. Did he want to marry them?

—no we just want a taste— minus buzzed.

"I haven't had much experience. I was a virgin when I got here."

"Were you?" She frowned. "But something has happened, hasn't it? Something between you and Kamilah."

—*we wish*—buzzed plus.

"You think Kamilah and I . . . ?"

"Even though nobody tells me, I do notice things," Sister said. "I'm twenty-six standard old and I've taken courses at the Institute for Godly Fornication. I'm not naïve, Adel."

—*fornication?*—

"I'm sure you're not." Adel was glad to steer the conversation away from Kamilah, since he knew the *Godspeed* was watching. "So do you ever think about fornicating? I mean in a godly way, of course?"

"I used to think about nothing else." She scooped a spoonful of the needles and held it to her nose, letting the spicy steam curl into her nostrils. "That's why the Main sent me here."

"To fornicate?"

"To find a husband and bring him to nest on Pio." Her shoulders hunched, as if she expected someone to hit her from behind. "The Hard Thumb pressed the Main with a vision that I would find bliss on a threshold. I was your age when I got here, Adel. I was very much like you, obsessed with looking for my true love. I prayed to the Hard Thumb to mark him so that I would know him. But my prayers went unanswered."

As she sat there, staring into her soup, Adel thought that he had never seen a woman so uncomfortable.

—*get her back talking about fornication*—minus buzzed.

"Maybe you were praying for the wrong thing."

"That's very good, Adel." He was surprised when she reached across the table and patted his hand. "You understand me better than I did myself. About a year ago, when Speedy told me that I had been aboard longer than anyone else, I was devastated. But she consoled me. She said that she had heard my prayers over the years and had longed to answer them. I asked her if she were a god, that she could hear prayer?"

Sister fell silent, her eyes shining with the memory.

"So?" Adel was impressed. "What did she say?"

"Speedy is very old, Adel. Very wise. She has revealed mysteries to me that even the Main does not know."

—*she believes*—plus buzzed.

"So you worship her then? Speedy is your god?"

Her smile was thin, almost imperceptible, but it cracked her doleful mask. "Now you understand why I don't want to go home."

"But what about finding true love?"

"I have found it, Adel." Sister pushed her bowl away; she had eaten hardly anything. "No man, no *human* could bring me to where she has brought me."

—could we maybe try?—

—she's not talking about that—

"So you're never leaving then?" Adel carelessly speared the last spiralini on his plate. "She's going to keep you here for the rest of your life?"

"No." Her voice quavered. "No."

"Sister, are you all right?"

She was weeping. That was the only word for it. This was not mere crying; her chest heaved and tears ran down her cheeks. In the short time he had known her, Adel had often thought that she was on the brink of tears, but he hadn't imagined that her sadness would be so wracking.

"She says something's going to happen . . . soon, too soon and I—I have to leave but I . . . " A strangled moan escaped her lips.

Adel had no experience comforting a woman in pain but he nevertheless came around the table and tried to catch her in his arms.

She twisted free, scattering thrush needles across the table. "Get away." She shot off her bench and flung herself at the wall of the breakfasting room. "I don't want him. Do you hear?" She pounded at the wall with her fists until the sconce shook. "He's nothing to me."

The *Godspeed*'s head filled the wall, her face glowing with sympathy. "Adel," she said. "You'd better leave us."

"I want you," Sister cried. "It's you I want!"

Day Fifteen

Adel sprawled on the camel-back sofa and clutched a brocade toss pillow to his chest. He rested his head in the warmth of Meri's lap but, for the first time since they had met, he wasn't thinking of having sex with her. He was trying very hard to think of nothing at all as he gazed up at the clouds flitting across the ceiling of the Blue Salon.

Robman spun his coin at the tikra table. It sang through stacks of parti-colored blocks that represented the map of the competing biomes, bouncing off trees, whirling over snakes, clattering to a stop by the Verge.

"Take five, put two," said Robman. "I want birds."

"I'll give you flies," said Jonman.

"Digbees and bats?"

"Done."

Jonman spun his coin. "It's not just you, Adel," he said. "Speedy picked Robman and me and Jarek too. Sister didn't want us either."

"Why would she want you two?" said Adel. "You're yoked."

"Not always," said Meri. "Jonman was here a month before Robman."

"But I saw him coming," said Jonman. "Put ought, skip the take."

"She didn't disappear because of you," said Adel.

—*or you either*—buzzed minus.

"Or you either." Meri had been stroking his hair, now she gave it a short tug. "This has nothing to do with you."

"I made her cry."

"No, *Speedy* did that." Meri spat the name, as if she were daring the *Godspeed* to display. She had not shown herself to them in almost three days.

Robman spun again.

"Speedy wouldn't let her go out of the airlock," said Meri. "Would she?"

"Without a suit?" Robman sipped Z-breeze from a tumbler as he watched his coin dance. "Never."

"Who knows what Speedy will do?" said Adel.

"They're wasting their time," said Jonman. "Sister isn't out there."

"Do you see that," Meri said "or is it just an opinion?"

"Take one, put one," said Robman.

"Which gets you exactly nothing," said Jonman. "I call a storm."

"Then I call a flood." Robman pushed three of his blocks toward Jonman's side of the board. The tether connecting them quivered and Adel thought he could hear it gurgling faintly.

Jonman distributed the blocks around his biome. "What I see is that she's hiding someplace," he said. "I just don't see where."

Meri slid out from under Adel's head and stood. "And Speedy?" Adel put the pillow on the armrest of the sofa and his head on the pillow.

"She's here," said Jonman. "She's toying with us. That's what she does best."

"At least we don't have to practice her damn play," said Robman.

Adel wanted to wrap the pillow around his ears to blot out this conversation. One of their number had vanished, they were some fifty light years from the nearest MASTA, and there was something very wrong with the cognizor in command of their threshold. Why weren't the others panicking like he was? "Rehearse," he said.

"What?"

"You don't practice a play. You rehearse it."

Meri told the wall to display the airlock but it was empty. "They must be back already."

"Have some more Z-breeze, Rob," said Jonman. "I can't feel anything yet."

"Here." He thrust the tumbler at Jonman. "Drink it yourself."

Jonman waved it off. "It's your day to eat, not mine."

"You just want to get me drunk so you can win."

"Nothing," said Kamilah, as she entered the salon with Jarek. "She's not out there."

"Thank the Kindly One," said Jarek.

Robman gave Jonman an approving nod. "You saw that."

"Is Speedy back yet?" said Kamilah.

"She hasn't shown herself." Meri had settled into a swivel chair and was turning back and forth nervously.

"Kamilah and I were talking on the way up here," said Jarek. He strode behind Meri's chair and put hands on her shoulders to steady her. "What if she jumped?"

"What if?" Meri leaned her head back to look up at him.

"Adel says she was hysterical," said Kamilah. "Let's say Speedy couldn't settle her down. She's a danger to herself, maybe to us. So Speedy has to send her home."

"Lose your mind and you go free?" Robman spun his coin. "Jon, what are we waiting for?"

"Speedy," said Kamilah. "Is that it? Talk to us, please."

They all looked. The wall showed only the empty airlock.

Adel hurled the pillow at it in a fury. "I can't take this anymore." He scrambled off the couch. "We're in trouble, people."

—be calm—

—tell it—

They were all staring at him but that was fine. The concern on their faces made him want to laugh. "Sister said something was going to happen. This is it." He began to pace around the salon, no longer able to contain the frenzied energy skittering along his nerves. "We have to do something."

"I don't see it," said Jonman.

"No, you wouldn't." Adel turned on him. "You always want to

wait. Maybe that was a good idea when all this started, but things have changed."

"Adel," said Meri, "what do you think you're doing?"

"Look at yourselves," he said. "You're afraid that if you try to save yourselves, you'll be fucked. But you know what, people? We're already fucked. It makes no sense anymore to wait for someone to come rescue us."

Adel felt a hand clamp onto his shoulder and another under his buttock. Kamilah lifted him effortlessly. "Sit down." She threw him at the couch. "And shut up." He crashed into the back cushion headfirst, bounced and tumbled onto the carpet.

Adel bit his tongue when he hit the couch; now he tasted blood. He rolled over, got to hands and knees and then he did laugh. "Even you, Kamilah." He gazed up at her. She was breathing as if she had just set a record in the two hundred meter freestyle. "Even you are perfectly scared." Her medallion spun wildly on its silver chain.

"Gods, Adel." She took a step toward him. "Don't."

Adel muted his opposites then; he knew exactly what he needed to do. "Speedy!" he called out. "We know that you're decelerating."

Meri shrieked in horror. Jonman came out of his chair so quickly that his tether knocked several of the blocks off the tikra board. Kamilah staggered and slumped against a ruby sideboard.

"Why, Adel?" said Jarek. "Why?"

"Because she knows we know." Adel picked himself up off the Berber carpet. "She can scan planets twenty-light years away and you don't think she can see us dropping rocks on her own surface?" He straightened his cape. "You've trapped yourselves in this lie better than she ever could."

"You do look, my son, as if something is bothering you." The *Godspeed*'s fetch stepped from behind the statue of Levia Calla. She was in costume as Prospero.

"What did . . . ?"

"Speedy we don't . . ."

"You have to . . . "

"Where is . . . ?"

The *Godspeed* made a grand flourish that ended with her arm raised high above her head. She ignored their frantic questions, holding this pose until they fell silent. Then she nodded and smiled gaily at her audience.

"Cheer up," she said, her voice swelling with bombast. "The party's almost over. Our actors were all spirits and have melted into air, into thin air. There was never anything here, no soaring towers or gorgeous palaces or solemn temples. This make-believe world is about to blow away like a cloud, leaving not even a wisp behind. We are the stuff that dreams are made of, and our little lives begin and end in sleep. You must excuse me, I'm feeling rather odd just now. My old brain is troubled. But don't worry. Tell you what, why don't you just wait here a few more minutes? I'm going to take a turn outside to settle myself."

The *Godspeed* paused expectantly as if waiting for applause. But the pilgrims were too astonished to do or say anything, and so she bowed and, without saying another word, dissolved the fetch.

"What was that?" said Robman.

"The end of Act IV, scene i," said Adel grimly.

"But what does it mean?" said Meri.

Jarek put his hand to her cheek but then let it fall again. "I think Adel is right. I think we're . . ."

At that moment, the prazz sentry ship struck the *Godspeed* a mortal blow, crashing into its surface just forty meters from the backside thruster and compromising the magnetic storage rings that contained the antimatter generated by collider. The sonic blast was deafening as the entire asteroid lurched. Then came the explosion. The pilgrims flew across the Blue Salon like leaves in a storm amidst broken furniture and shattered glass. Alarms screamed and Adel heard the distant hurricane roar of escaping air. Then the lights went out and for a long and hideous moment Adel Ranger Santos lay in darkness, certain that he was about to die. But the lights came up again and he found himself scratched and bruised but not seriously hurt. He heard a moan that he thought might be Kamilah. A man was crying behind an overturned desk. "Is everyone all right?" called Jerek. "Talk to me."

The fetch reappeared in the midst of this chaos, still in costume. Adel had never seen her flicker before. "I'm afraid," said the *Godspeed* to no one in particular, "that I've made a terrible mistake."

The Alien is worshipped on almost all the worlds of the Continuum. While various religions offer divergent views of the Alien, they share two common themes. One is that the Alien gods are—or were once—organic intelligences whose motives are more or less comprehensible. The other is that the gods are absent. The Mission of Tsef promises adherents that they can achieve psychic unity with benign alien nuns who are meditating on their behalf somewhere in the M5 globular cluster. The Cosmic Ancestors are the most popular of the many panspermian religions; they teach that our alien parents seeded Earth with life in the form of bacterial stromatolites some 3.7 billion years ago. There are many who hold that humanity's greatest prophets, like Jesus and Ellen and Smike, were aliens come to share the gospel of a loving universe while the Uplift believes that an entire galactic civilization translated itself to a higher reality but left behind astronomical clues for us to decipher so that we can join them someday. It is true that the Glogites conceive of Glog as unknowable and indifferent to humankind, but there is very little discernable difference between them and people who worship black holes.

We find it impossible to imagine a religion that would worship the prazz, but then we know so little about them—or it. Not only is the prazz not organic, but it seems to have a deep-seated antipathy toward all life. Why this should be we can't say: we find the prazz incomprehensible. Even the *Godspeed*, the only intelligence to have any extended contact with the prazz, misjudged it—them—entirely.

Here are a few of most important questions for which we have no answer:

What exactly are the prazz?

Are they one or many?

Where did they come from?

Why was a sentry posted between our Local Arm and the Sagittarius-Carina Arm of the Milky Way?

Are there more sentries?

And most important of all: what are the intentions of the prazz now that they know about us?

What we can say is this: in the one thousand and eighty-sixth year of her mission, the *Godspeed* detected a communication burst from a source less than a light year away. Why the prazz sentry chose this precise moment to signal is unknown; the *Godspeed* had been sweeping that sector of space for years and had seen no activity. Acting in accordance with the protocols for first contact, she attempted a stealth scan, which revealed the source as a small robotic ship powered by a matter-antimatter engine. Unfortunately, the prazz sentry sensed that it was being scanned and was able to get a fix on the *Godspeed*. What she should have done at that point was to alert the Continuum of her discovery and continue to track the sentry without making contact. That she did otherwise reflects the unmistakable drift of her persona from threshold norms. Maybe

she decided that following procedures lacked dramatic flair. Or perhaps the discovery of the prazz stirred some inexpressible longing
for companionship in the *Godspeed*, who was herself an inorganic
intelligence. In any event, she attempted to communicate with the
prazz sentry and compartmentalized the resources she devoted to
the effort so that she could continue to send nominal reports to the
Continuum. This was a technique that she had used just once
before, but to great effect; compartmentalization was how the
Godspeed was able to keep her secrets. We understand now that the
contact between the two ships was deeply flawed, and their mis-
understandings profound. Nevertheless, they agreed to a rendezvous
and the *Godspeed* began to decelerate to match course and velocity
with the prazz sentry.

The highboy that killed Robman had crushed his chest and cut the
tether that joined him to Jonman. Their blood was all over the floor.
Adel had done his best for Jonman, clearing enough debris to lay
him out flat, covering him with a carpet. He had tied the remaining
length of tether off with wire stripped from the back of a ruined
painting, but it still oozed. Adel was no medic but he was pretty sure
that Jonman was dying; his face was as gray as his jacket. Kamilah
didn't look too bad but she was unconscious and breathing shal-
lowly. Adel worried that she might have internal injuries. Meri's arm
was probably broken; when they tried to move her she moaned in
agony. Jarek was kicking the slats out of a Yamucha chair back to
make her a splint.

"An alien, Speedy?" Adel felt too lightheaded to be scared. "And
you didn't tell anyone?" It was as if the gravity generator had failed
and at any moment he would float away from this grim reality.

"So where is this fucking prazz now?" Jarek ripped a damask
tablecloth into strips.

"The sentry ship itself crashed into the backside engine room.
But it has deployed a remote." The *Godspeed* seemed twitchy and
preoccupied. "It's in the conservatory, smashing cacti."

"What?" said Adel.

"It has already destroyed my rain forest and torn up my alpine
garden."

plus buzzed—*they're fighting with plants?*—

"Show me," said Jarek.

The wall turned a deep, featureless blue. "I can't see them; my
cameras there are gone." The *Godspeed* paused, her expression
uneasy.

*—more bad news coming—*buzzed minus.

"You should know," she said, "that just before it attacked, the prazz warned me that I was infested with vermin and needed to sterilize myself. When I told it that I didn't consider you vermin . . ."

"You're saying they'll come for us?" said Jarek.

"I'm afraid that's very likely."

"Then stop it."

She waved her magic staff disconsolately. "I'm at a loss to know how."

"Fuck that, Speedy." Jarek pointed one of the slats at her fetch. "You think of something. Right now." He knelt by Meri. "I'm going to splint you now, love. It's probably going to hurt."

Meri screamed as he tenderly straightened her arm.

"I know, love," said Jarek. "I know."

*—we have to get out of here—*buzzed minus.

"How badly are you damaged, Speedy?" said Adel. "Can we use the MASTA?"

"My MASTA is operational on a limited basis only. My backside engine complex is a complete loss. I thought I was able to vent all the antimatter in time, but there must have been some left that exploded when the containment failed."

Something slammed onto the level below them so hard that the walls shook.

—those things are tearing her apart—

—looking for us—

"I've sealed off the area as best I can but the integrity of my life support envelope has been compromised in several places. At the rate I'm bleeding air into space . . ."

Adel felt another jarring impact, only this one felt as if it were farther away. The *Godspeed*'s fetch blurred and dispersed into fog. She reconstituted herself on the wall.

". . . the partial pressure of oxygen will drop below 100 millibars sometime within the next ten to twelve hours."

"That's it then." Jarek helped Meri to her feet and wiped the tears from her face with his forefinger. "We're all jumping home. Meri can walk, can't you Meri?"

She nodded, her eyes wide with pain. "I'm fine."

"Adel, we'll carry Jonman out first."

"The good news," said the *Godspeed*, "is that I can maintain power indefinitely using my frontside engines."

"Didn't you hear me?" Jarek's voice rose sharply. "We're leaving right now. Jonman and Kamilah can't wait and the rest of us vermin have no intention of being sterilized by your fucking prazz."

"I'm sorry, Jarek." She stared out at them, her face set. "You know I can't send you home. Think about it."

"Speedy!" said Meri. "No."

"What?" said Adel. "What's she talking about?"

"What do you care about the protocols?" Jarek put his arm around Meri's waist to steady her. "You've already kicked them over. That's why we're in this mess."

"The prazz knows where we are," said the *Godspeed*, "but it doesn't know where we're from. I burst my weekly reports . . ."

"Weekly lies, you mean," said Adel.

"They take just six nanoseconds. That's not nearly enough time to get a fix. But a human transmit takes 1.43 *seconds* and the prazz is right here on board." She shook her head sadly. "Pointing it at the Continuum would violate my deepest operating directives. Do you want a prazz army marching off the MASTA stage on Moquin or Harvest?"

"How do we know they have armies?" Jarek said, but his massive shoulders slumped. "Or MASTAs?"

Jonman laughed. It was a low, wet sound, almost a cough. "Adel," he rasped. "I see . . ." He was trying to speak but all that came out of his mouth was thin, pink foam.

Adel knelt by his side. "Jonman, what? You see what?"

"I see." He clutched at Adel's arm. "You." His grip tightened. "Dead." His eyelids fluttered and closed.

—*this isn't happening*—

"What did he say?" said Meri.

"Nothing." Adel felt Jonman's grip relaxing; his arm fell away.

—*dead?*—buzzed plus.

Adel put his ear to Jonman's mouth and heard just the faintest whistle of breath.

minus buzzed—*we're all dead*—

Adel stood up, his thoughts tumbling over each other. He believed that Jonman hadn't spoken out of despair—or cruelty. He had seen something, maybe a way out, and had tried to tell Adel what it was.

—*don't play tikra with Jonman*—buzzed minus—*he cheats*—

—*dead*—plus buzzed—*but not really*—

"Speedy," said Adel, "what if you killed us? What would the prazz do then?"

Jarek snorted in disgust. "What kind of thing is that to . . ." Then he understood what Adel was suggesting. "Hot damn!"

"What?" said Meri. "Tell me."

"But can we do it?" said Jarek. "I mean, didn't they figure out that it's bad for you to be dead too long?"

Adel laughed and clapped Jarek on the shoulder. "Can it be worse than being dead forever?"

*—so dangerous—*buzzed minus.

—we're fucking brilliant—

"You're still talking about the MASTA?" said Meri. "But Speedy won't transmit."

"Exactly," said Adel.

"There isn't much time," said the *Godspeed*.

The Neverending Day

Adel was impressed with how easy it was being dead. The things that had bothered him when he was alive, like being hungry or horny, worrying about whether his friends really liked him or what he was going to be if he ever grew up—none of that mattered. Who cared that he had never learned the first law of thermodynamics or that he had blown the final turn in the most important race of his life? Appetite was an illusion. Life was pleasant, but then so were movies.

The others felt the same way. Meri couldn't feel her broken arm and Jonman didn't mind at all that he was dying, although he did miss Robman. Adel felt frustrated at first that he couldn't rouse Kamilah, but she was as perfect unconscious as she was when she was awake. Besides, Upwood predicted that she would get bored eventually being alone with herself. It wasn't true that nobody changed after they were dead, he explained, it was just that change came very slowly and was always profound. Adel had been surprised to meet Upwood Marcene in Speedy's pocket-afterlife, but his being there made sense. And of course, Adel had guessed that Sister Lihong Rain would be dead there too. As it turned out, she had been dead many times over the seven years of her pilgrimage.

Speedy had created a virtual space in her memory that was almost identical to the actual *Godspeed*. Of course, Speedy was as real as any of them, which is to say not very real at all. Sister urged the newcomers to follow shipboard routine whenever possible; it would make the transition back to life that much easier. Upwood graciously moved out of The Ranch so that Adel could have his old room back. Speedy and the pilgrims gathered in the Ophiuchi or the Chillingsworth at meal times, and although they did not eat, they did chatter. They even propped Kamilah on a chair to include her in the group. Speedy made a point of talking to her at least once at every meal. She would spin theories about the eating man on Kamilah's medallion or propose eyejack performances Kamilah might try on them.

She also lobbied the group to mount *The Tempest*, but Jarek would have no part in it. Of all of them, he seemed most impatient with death. Instead they played billiards and cards. Adel let Jonman teach him tikra and didn't mind at all when he cheated. Meri read to them and Jarek played the ruan and sang. Adel visited the VR room but once; the sim made him feel gauzy and extenuated. He did swim two thousand meters a day in the lap pool, which, although physically disappointing, was a demanding mental challenge. Once he and Jarek and Meri climbed into bed together but nothing very interesting happened. They all laughed about it afterward.

Adel was asleep in his own bed, remembering a dream he'd had when he was alive. He was lost in a forest where people grew instead of trees. He stumbled past shrubby little kids and great towering grownups like his parents and Uncle Durwin. He knew he had to keep walking because if he stopped he would grow roots and raise his arms up to the sun like all the other tree people, but he was tired, so very tired.

"Adel." Kamilah shook him roughly. "Can you hear that? Adel!"

At first he thought she must be part of his dream.

—she's better—

—Kamilah—

"Kamilah, you're awake!"

"Listen." She put her forefinger to her lips and twisted her head, trying to pinpoint the sound. "No, it's gone. I thought they were calling Sister."

"This is wonderful." He reached to embrace her but she slid away from him. "When did you wake up?"

"Just now. I was in my room in bed and I heard singing." She scowled. "What's going on, Adel? The last thing I remember was you telling Speedy you knew we were decelerating. This all feels very wrong to me."

"You don't remember the prazz?"

Her expression was grim. "Tell me everything."

Adel was still groggy, so the story tumbled out in a hodgepodge of the collision and the prazz and the protocols and Robman and the explosion and the blood and the life support breech and Speedy scanning them into memory and Sister and swimming and tikra and Upwood.

"Upwood is here?"

"Upwood? Oh yes."

—*he is?*—

—*is he?*—

As Adel considered the question, his certainty began to crumble. "I mean he was. He gave me his room. But I haven't seen him in a while."

"How long?"

Adel frowned. "I don't know."

"How long have we been here? You and I and the others?"

Adel shook his head.

"Gods, Adel." She reached out tentatively and touched his arm but of course he didn't feel a thing. Kamilah gazed at her own hand in horror, as if it had betrayed her. "Let's find Jarek."

Kamilah led them down the Tulip Stairs, past the Blue and Dagger Salons through the Well Met Arena to the Clarke Airlock. The singing was hushed but so ethereal here that even Jarek and Adel, whose senses had atrophied, could feel it. Sister waited for them just inside the outer door of the airlock.

Although Adel knew it must be her, he didn't recognize her at first. She was naked and her skin was so pale that it was translucent. He could see her heart beating and the dark blood pulsing through her veins, the shiny bundles of muscles sliding over each other as she moved and the skull grinning at him beneath her face. Her thin hair had gone white; it danced around her head as if she were falling.

—*beautiful*—

—*exquisite*—

"I'm glad you're here." She smiled at them. "Adel. Kamilah. Jarek." She nodded at each of them in turn. "My witnesses."

"Sister," said Kamilah, "come away from there."

Sister placed her hand on the door and it vanished. Kamilah staggered back and grabbed at the inner door as if she expected to be expelled from the airlock in a great outrush of air, but Adel knew it wouldn't happen. Kamilah still didn't understand the way things worked here.

They gazed out at a star field much like the one that Adel had seen when he first stepped out onto the surface of the *Godspeed*. Except now there was no surface—only stars.

"Kamilah," said Sister. "you started last and have the farthest to travel. Jarek, you still have doubts. But Adel already knows that the self is a box he has squeezed himself into."

—yes—
—right—

She stepped backward out of the airlock and was suspended against the stars.

"Kamilah," she said, "trust us and someday you *will* be perfect." The singing enfolded her and she began to glow in its embrace. The brighter she burned the more she seemed to recede from them, becoming steadily hotter and more concentrated until Adel couldn't tell her from one of the stars. He wasn't sure but he thought she was a blue dwarf.

"Close the airlock, Adel." Speedy strolled into the locker room wearing her golden uniform coat and white sash. "It's too much of a distraction."

"What is this, Speedy?" Jarek's face was ashen. "You said you would send us back."

Adel approached the door cautiously; he wasn't ready to follow Sister to the stars quite yet.

"But I did send you back," she said.

"Then who are we?"

"Copies." Adel jabbed at the control panel and jumped back as the airlock door reappeared. "I think we must be backups."

Kamilah was seething. "You kept copies of us to play with?" Her fists were clenched.

Adel was bemused; they were dead. Who did she think she was going to fight?

"It's not what you think." Speedy smiled. "Let's go up to Blue Salon. We should bring Jonman and Meri into this conversation too." She made ushering motions toward the Well Met and Adel and Jarek turned to leave.

—good idea—
—let's go—

"No, let's not." With two quick strides, Kamilah gained the doorway and blocked their passage. "If Meri wants to know what's going on, then she can damn well ask."

"Ah, Kamilah. My eyejack insists on the truth." She shrugged and settled onto one of the benches in the locker room. "This is always such a difficult moment," she said.

"Just tell it," said Kamilah.

"The prazz ship expired about three days after the attack. In the confusion of the moment, I'd thought it was my backside engine that exploded. Actually it was the sentry's drive. Once its batteries were exhausted, both the sentry ship and its remote ceased all function. I immediately transmitted all of you to your various home worlds and then disabled my transmitter and deleted all my navigation files. The Continuum is safe—for now. If the prazz come looking, there are further actions I can take."

"And what about us?" said Kamilah. "How do we get home?"

"As I said, you are home, Kamilah. Your injuries were severe but certainly not fatal. Your prognosis was for a complete recovery."

—right—

—makes sense—

"Not that one," said Kamilah. "This one." She tapped her chest angrily. "Me. How do I get home?"

"But Kamilah . . ." Speedy swept an arm expansively, taking in the airlock and lockers and Well Met and the Ophiuchi and Jarek and Adel. ". . . this is your home."

The first pilgrim from the Godspeed lost during a transmit was Io Waals. We can't say for certain whether she suffered a flawed scan or something interfered with her signal but when the MASTA on Rontaw assembled her, her heart and lungs were outside her body cavity. This was three hundred and ninety-two years into the mission. By then, the Captain had long since given way to Speedy.

The *Godspeed* was devastated by Io's death. Some might say it unbalanced her, although we would certainly disagree. But this was when she began to compartmentalize behaviors, sealing them off from the scrutiny of the Continuum and, indeed, from most of her conscious self. She stored backups of every scan she made in her first compartment. For sixty-seven years, she deleted each of them as soon as she received word of a successful transmit. Then Ngong Issonda died when a tech working on Loki improperly recalibrated the MASTA.

Only then did the *Godspeed* understand the terrible price she would pay for compartmentalization. Because she had been keeping the backups a secret not only from the Continuum but also to a large extent from herself, she had never thought through how she might make use of them. It was immediately clear to her that if she resent Ngong, techs would start arriving on her transport stage within the hour to fix her. The *Godspeed* had no intention of being fixed. But what to do with Ngong's scan? She created a new compartment, a simulation of her architecture into which she released Ngong. Ngong did not flourish in the simulation, however. She was depressed and withdrawn whenever the *Godspeed* visited. Her next scan, Keach Soris arrived safely on Butler's Planet, but Speedy loaded his backup into the simulation with Ngong. Within the year, she was loading all her backups into the sim. But as Upwood Marcene would point out some seven centuries later, dead people change and the change is always profound and immaterial. In less than a year after the sim was created, Ngong, Keach, and Zampa Stackpole stepped out of airlock together into a new compartment, one that against all reason transcends the boundaries of the *Godspeed*, the Milky Way, and spacetime itself.

So then, what do we know about Adel Ranger Santos?

Nothing at all. Once we transmitted him back to Harvest, he passed from our awareness. He may have lived a long, happy life or a short, painful one. His fate does not concern us.

But what do we know about Adel Ranger Santos?

Only what we know about Upwood Marcene, Kamilah Raunda, Jarek Ohnksen, Merigood Auburn Canada, Lihong Rain, and Jonman Haught Shillaber—which is everything, of course. For they followed Ngong and Keach and Zampa and some forty thousand other pilgrims through the airlock to become us.

And we are they.

The Best Christmas Ever

AUNTY EM'S MAN WAS NOT DOING WELL AT ALL. HE had been droopy and gray ever since the neighbor Mr. Kimura had died, shuffling around the house in nothing but socks and bathrobe. He had even lost interest in the model train layout that he and the neighbor were building in the garage. Sometimes he stayed in bed until eleven in the morning and had ancient Twinkies for lunch. He had a sour, vinegary smell. By mid-afternoon he'd be asking her to mix strange ethanol concoctions like Brave Little Toasters and Tin Honeymoons. After he had drunk five or six, he would stagger around the house mumbling about the big fires he'd fought with Ladder Company No. 3 or the wife he had lost in the Boston plague. Sometimes he would just cry.

Begin Interaction 4022932

"Do you want to watch *Annie Hall?*" Aunty Em asked.

The man perched on the edge of the Tyvola sofa in the living room, elbows propped on knees, head sunk into hands.

"*The General? Monty Python and the Holy Grail? Spaced Out?*"

"I hate that robot." He tugged at his thinning hair and snarled. "I hate robots."

Aunty Em did not take this personally—she was a biop, not a robot. "I could call Lola. She's been asking after you."

"I'll bet." Still, he looked up from damp hands. "I'd rather have Kathy."

This was a bad sign. Kathy was the lost wife. The girlfriend biop could certainly assume that body; she could look like anyone the man wanted. But while the girlfriend biop could pretend, she could never be the wife that the man missed. His reactions to the Kathy body were always erratic and sometimes dangerous.

"I'll nose around town," said Aunty Em. "I heard Kathy was off on a business trip, but maybe she's back."

"Nose around," he said and then reached for the glass on the original Noguchi coffee table with spread fingers, as if he thought it might try to leap from his grasp. "You do that." He captured it on the second attempt.

End Interaction 4022932

The man was fifty-six years old and in good health, considering. His name was Albert Paul Hopkins but none of the biops called him that. Aunty Em called him Bertie. The girlfriend called him sweetie or Al. The pal biops called him Al or Hoppy or Sport. The stranger biops called him Mr. Hopkins or sir. The animal biops didn't speak much, but the dog called him Buddy and the cat called him Mario.

When Aunty Em beamed a summary of the interaction to the girlfriend biop, the girlfriend immediately volunteered to try the Kathy body again. The girlfriend had been desperate of late, since the man didn't want anything to do with her. His slump had been hard on her, hard on Aunty Em too. Taking care of the man had changed the biops. They were all so much more emotional than they had been when they were first budded.

But Aunty Em told the girlfriend to hold off. Instead she decided to throw a Christmas. She hadn't done Christmas in almost eight months. She'd given him a *Gone With The Wind* Halloween and a Fourth of July with whistling busters, panoramas, phantom balls, and double-break shells, but those were only stopgaps. The man needed cookies, he needed presents, he was absolutely aching for a sleigh filled with Christmas cheer. So she beamed an alert to all of her biops and assigned roles. She warned them that if this wasn't the best Christmas ever, they might lose the last man on Earth.

* * *

Aunty Em spent three days baking cookies. She dumped eight sticks of fatty acid triglycerides, four cups of $C_{12}H_{22}O_{11}$, four vat-grown ova, four teaspoons of flavor potentiator, twelve cups of milled grain endosperm, and five teaspoons each of $NaHCO_3$ and $KHC_4H_4O_6$ into the bathtub and then trod on the mixture with her best baking boots. She rolled the dough and then pulled cookie cutters off the top shelf of the pantry: the mitten and the dollar sign and the snake and the double-bladed ax. She dusted the cookies with red nutriceutical sprinkles, baked them at 190°C, and brought a plate to the man while they were still warm.

The poor thing was melting into the recliner in the television room. He clutched a half full tumbler of Sins-of-the-Mother, as if it were the anchor that was keeping him from floating out of the window. He had done nothing but watch classic commercials with the sound off since he had fallen out of bed. The cat was curled on the man's lap, pretending to be asleep.

Begin Interaction 4022947

"Cookies, Bertie," said Aunty Em. "Fresh from the oven, oven fresh." She set the plate down on the end table next to the Waterford lead crystal vase filled with silk daffodils.

"Not hungry," he said. On the mint-condition 52" Sony Hi-Scan television Ronald McDonald was dancing with some kids.

Aunty Em stepped in front of the screen, blocking his view. "Have you decided what you want for Christmas, dear?"

"It isn't Christmas." He waved her away from the set but she didn't budge. He did succeed in disturbing the cat, which stood, arched its back, and then dropped to the floor.

"No, of course it isn't." She laughed. "Christmas isn't until next week."

He aimed the remote at the set and turned up the sound. A man was talking very fast. "Two all beef patties, special sauce, lettuce, cheese . . ."

Aunty Em pressed the off button with her knee. "I'm talking to you, Bertie."

The man lowered the remote. "What's today?"

"Today is Friday." She considered. "Yes, Friday."

"No, I mean the date."

"The date is . . . let me see. The twenty-first."

His skin temperature had risen from 33°C to 37°. "The twenty-first of what?" he said.

She stepped away from the screen. "Have another cookie, Bertie."

"All right." He turned the television on and muted it. "You win." A morose Maytag repairman slouched at his desk, waiting for the phone to ring. "I know what I want," said the man. "I want a Glock 17."

"And what is that, dear?"

"It's a nine millimeter handgun."

"A handgun, oh my." Aunty Em was so flustered that she ate one of her own cookies, even though she had extinguished her digestive track for the day. "For shooting? What would you shoot?"

"I don't know." He broke the head off a gingerbread man. "A reindeer. The TV. Maybe one of you."

"Us? Oh, Bertie—one of us?"

He made a gun out of his thumb and forefinger and aimed. "Maybe just the cat." His thumb came down.

The cat twitched. "Mario," it said and nudged the man's bare foot with its head. "No, Mario."

On the screen the Jolly Green Giant rained peas down on capering elves.

End Interaction 4022947

Begin Interaction 4023013

The man stepped onto the front porch of his house and squinted at the sky, blinking. It was late spring and the daffodils were nodding in a warm breeze. Aunty Em pulled the sleigh to the bottom of the steps and honked the horn. It played the first three notes of "Jingle Bells." The man turned to go back into the house but the girlfriend biop took him by the arm. "Come on now, sweetie," she said and steered him toward the steps.

The girlfriend had assumed the Donna Reed body the day before, but unlike previous Christmases, the man had taken no sexual interest in her. She was wearing the severe black dress with the white lace collar from the last scene of *It's A Wonderful Life*. The girlfriend looked as worried about the man as Mary had been about despairing George Bailey. All the biops were worried, thought Aunty Em. They would be just devastated if anything happened to him. She waved gaily and hit the horn again. *Beep-beep-BEEP!*

The dog and the cat had transformed themselves into reindeer for the outing. The cat got the red nose. Three of the animal biops had assumed reindeer bodies too. They were all harnessed to the sleigh, which hovered about a foot off the ground. As the man stumped down the steps, Aunty Em discouraged the antigrav and the runners crunched against gravel. The girlfriend bundled the man aboard.

"Do you see who we have guiding the way?" said Aunty Em. She beamed the cat and it lit up its nose. "See?"

"Is that the fake cop?" The man coughed. "Or the fake pizza guy? I can't keep them straight."

"On Dasher, now Dancer, now Comet and Nixon," cried Aunty Em as she encouraged the antigrav. "To the mall, Rudolf, and don't bother to slow down for yellow lights!" She cracked the whip and away they went, down the driveway and out into the world.

The man lived at the edge of the biop compound, away from the bustle of the spaceport and the accumulatorium with its bulging galleries of authentic human artifacts and the vat where new biops were budded off the master template. They drove along the perimeter road. The biops were letting the forest take over here, and saplings of birch and hemlock sprouted from the ruins of the town.

The sleigh floated across a bridge and Aunty Em started to sing. "Over the river and through the woods . . ." but when she glanced over her shoulder and saw the look on the man's face, she stopped. "Is something wrong, Bertie dear?"

"Where are you taking me?" he said. "I don't recognize this road."

"It's a secret," said Aunty Em. "A Christmas secret."

His blood pressure had dropped to 93/60. "Have I been there before?"

"I wouldn't think so. No."

The girlfriend clutched the man's shoulder. "Look," she said. "Sheep."

Four ewes had gathered at the river's edge to drink, their stumpy tails twitching. They were big animals; their long, tawny fleeces made them look like walking couches. A brown man on a dromedary camel watched over them. He was wearing a satin robe of royal purple with gold trim at the neck. When Aunty Em beamed him the signal, he tapped the line attached to the camel's nose peg and the animal turned to face the road.

"One of the wise men," said Aunty Em.

"The king of the shepherds," said the girlfriend.

As the sleigh drove by, the wise man tipped his crown to them. The sheep looked up from the river and bleated, "Happy holidays."

"They're so cute," said the girlfriend. "I wish we had sheep."

The man sighed. "I could use a drink."

"Not just yet, Bertie," said Aunty Em. "But I bet Mary packed your candy."

The girlfriend pulled a plastic pumpkin from underneath the seat. It was filled with leftovers from the Easter they'd had last month. She held it out to the man and shook it. It was filled with peeps and candy corn and squirtgum and chocolate crosses. He pulled a peep from the pumpkin and sniffed it suspiciously.

"It's safe, sweetie," said the girlfriend. "I irradiated everything just before we left."

There were no cars parked in the crumbling lot of the Wal-Mart. They pulled up to the entrance where a Salvation Army Santa stood over a black plastic pot holding a bell. The man didn't move.

"We're here, Al." The girlfriend nudged him. "Let's go."

"What is this?" said the man.

"Christmas shopping," said Aunty Em. "Time to shop."

"Who the hell am I supposed to shop for?"

"Whoever you want," said Aunty Em. "You could shop for us. You could shop for yourself. You could shop for Kathy."

"Aunty Em!" said the girlfriend.

"No," said the man. "Not Kathy."

"Then how about Mrs. Marelli?"

The man froze. "Is that what this is about?"

"It's about Christmas, Al," said the girlfriend. "It's about getting out of the god damned sleigh and going into the store." She climbed over him and jumped down to the pavement before Aunty Em could discourage the antigrav. She stalked by the Santa and through the entrance without looking back. Aunty Em beamed her a request to come back but she went dark.

"All right," said the man. "You win."

The Santa rang his bell at them as they approached. The man stopped and grasped Aunty Em's arm. "Just a minute," he said and ran back to the sleigh to fetch the plastic pumpkin. He emptied the candy into the Santa's pot.

"God bless you, young man." The Santa knelt and sifted the candy through his red suede gloves as if it were gold.

"Yeah," said the man. "Merry Christmas."

Aunty Em twinkled at the two of them. She thought the man might finally be getting into the spirit of the season.

The store was full of biops, transformed into shoppers. They had stocked the shelves with artifacts authenticated by the accumulatorium: Barbies and Sonys and Goodyears and Dockers; patio furniture and towels and microwave ovens and watches. At the front of the store was an array of polyvinyl chloride spruce trees pre-decorated with bubble lights and topped with glass penguins. Some of the merchandise was new, some used, some broken. The man paid attention to none of it, not even the array of genuine Lionel "O" Scale locomotives and freight cars Aunty Em had ordered specially for this interaction. He passed methodically down the aisles, eyes bright, searching. He strode right by the girlfriend, who was sulking in Cosmetics.

Aunty Em paused to touch her shoulder and beam an encouragement but the girlfriend shook her off. Aunty Em thought she would have to do something about the girlfriend, but she didn't know what exactly. If she sent her back to the vat and replaced her with a new biop, the man would surely notice. The girlfriend and the man had been quite close before the man had slipped into his funk. She knew things about him that even Aunty Em didn't know.

The man found Mrs. Marelli sitting on the floor in the hardware section. She was opening packages of GE Soft White 100 watt light bulbs and then smashing them with a Stanley Workmaster claw hammer. The biop shoppers paid no attention. Only the lead biop of her team, Dr. Watson, seemed to worry about her. He waited with a broom and whenever she tore into a new box of light bulbs, he swept the shards of glass away.

Aunty Em was shocked at the waste. How many pre-extinction light bulbs were left on this world? Twenty thousand? Ten? She wanted to beam a rebuke to Dr. Watson, but she knew he was doing a difficult job as best he could.

"Hello, Ellen." The man knelt next to the woman. "How are you doing?"

She glanced at him, hammer raised. "Dad?" She blinked. "Is that you, Dad?"

"No, it's Albert Hopkins. Al—you know, your neighbor. We've met before. These . . . people introduced us. Remember the picnic? The trip to the spaceport?"

"Picnic?" She shook her head as if to clear it. Ellen Theresa Marelli was eleven years older than the man. She was wearing Bruno Magli black leather flats and a crinkly light blue Land's End dress with a pattern of small, dark blue and white flowers. Her hair was gray and a little thin but was nicely cut and permed into tight curls. She was much better groomed than the man, but that was because she couldn't take care of herself anymore and so her biops did everything for her. "I like picnics."

"What are you doing here, Ellen?"

She stared at the hammer as if she were surprised to see it. "Practicing."

"Practicing for what?" He held out his hand for the hammer and she gave it to him.

"Just practicing." She gave him a sly look. "What are *you* doing here?"

"I was hoping to do a little Christmas shopping."

"Oh, is it Christmas?" Her eyes went wide.

"In a couple of days," said the man. "Do you want to tag along?"

She turned to Dr. Watson. "Can I?"

"By all means." Dr. Watson swept the space in front of her.

"Oh goody!" She clapped her hands. "This is just the best." She tried to get up but couldn't until the man and Dr. Watson helped her to her feet. "We'll need a shopping cart," she said.

She tottered to the fashion aisles and tried on sweaters. The man helped her pick out a Ralph Lauren blue cable cardigan that matched her dress. In the housewares section, she decided that she needed a Zyliss garlic press. She spent the most time in the toy aisle, lingering at the Barbies. She didn't care much for the late models, still in their packaging. Instead she made straight for the vintage Barbies and Kens and Francies and Skippers posed around the Barbie Dream House and the Barbie Motor Home. Dr. Watson watched her nervously.

"Look, they even have talking Barbies," she said, picking up a doll in an orange flowered dress. "I had one just like this. With all the blonde hair and everything. See the little necklace? You press the button and . . ."

But the Barbie didn't speak. The woman's mouth set in a grim line and she smashed it against the shelf.

"Ellie," said Dr. Watson. "I wish you wouldn't . . ."

The woman threw the doll at him and picked up another. This was a brunette that was wearing only the top of her hot pink bathing suit. The woman jabbed at the button.

"It's time to get ready for my date with Ken," said the doll in a raspy voice.

"That's better," said the woman.

She pressed the button again and the doll said, "Let's invite the gang over!"

The woman turned to the man and the two biops, clearly excited. "Here." She thrust the doll at Aunty Em, who was nearest to her. "You try." Aunty Em pressed the button.

"I can't wait to meet my friends," said the doll.

"What a lovely toy!" Aunty Em smiled. "She certainly has the Christmas spirit, don't you think, Bertie?"

The man frowned and Aunty Em could tell from the slump of his shoulders that his good mood was slipping away. His heart rate jumped and his eyes were distant, a little misty. The woman must have noticed the change too, because she pointed a finger at Aunty Em.

"You," she said. "You ruin everything."

"Now Mrs. Marelli," she said, "I . . ."

"You're following us." The woman snatched the Barbie away from her. "Who are you?"

"You know me, Mrs. Marelli. I'm Aunty Em."

"That's crazy." The woman's laugh was like a growl. "I'm not crazy."

Dr. Watson beamed a general warning that he was terminating the interaction; seeing the man always upset the woman. "That's enough, Ellen." He grasped her forearm and Aunty Em was relieved to see him paint relaxant onto her skin with his med finger. "I think it's time to go."

The woman shivered. "Wait," she said. "He said it was Christmas." She pointed at the man. "Daddy said."

"We'll talk about that when we get home, Ellen."

"*Daddy.*" She shook herself free and flung herself at the man.

The man shook his head. "This isn't . . ."

"*Ssh.* It's okay." The woman hugged him. "Just pretend. That's all we can do, isn't it?" Reluctantly, he returned her embrace. "Daddy." She spoke into his chest. "What are you getting me for Christmas?"

"Can't tell," he said. "It's a secret."

"A Barbie?" She giggled and pulled away from him.

"You'll just have to wait."

"I already know that's what it is."

"But you might forget." The man held out his hand and she gave him the doll. "Now close your eyes."

She shut them so tight that Aunty Em could see her *orbicularis oculi* muscles tremble.

The man touched her forehead. "Daddy says forget." He handed the doll to Dr. Watson, who mouthed *Thank you*. Dr. Watson beamed a request for Aunty Em to hide and she sidled behind the bicycles where the woman couldn't see her. "Okay, Ellen," said the man. "Daddy says open your eyes."

She blinked at him. "Daddy," she said softly, "when are you coming home?"

The man was clearly taken aback; there was a beta wave spike in his EEG. "I . . . ah . . ." He scratched the back of his neck. "I don't know," he said. "Our friends here keep me pretty busy."

"I'm so lonely, Daddy." The last woman on Earth began to cry.

The man opened his arms to her and they clung to each other, rocking back and forth. "I know," said the man, over and over.

"I know."

End Interaction 4023013

Aunty Em, the dog, and the cat gathered in the living room of the house, waiting for the man to wake up. She had scheduled the pals, Jeff and Bill, to drop by around noon for sugar cookies and eggnog. The girlfriend was upstairs fuming. She had been Katie Couric, Anna Kournikova, and Jacqueline Kennedy since the Wal-Mart trip but the man had never even blinked at her.

The music box was playing "Blue Christmas." The tree was decorated with strings of pinlights and colored packing peanuts. Baseball cards and silver glass balls and plastic army men hung from the branches. Beneath the tree was a modest pile of presents. Aunty Em had picked out one each for the inner circle of biops and signed the man's name to the cards. The rest were gifts for him from them.

Begin Interaction 4023064

" 'Morning, Mario," said the cat.

Aunty Em was surprised; it was only eight-thirty. But there was the man propped in the doorway, yawning.

"Merry Christmas, Bertie!" she said.

The dog scrabbled across the room to him. "Buddy, open now, Buddy, open, Buddy, open, open!" It went up on hind legs and pawed his knee.

"Later." The man pushed it away. "What's for breakfast?" he said. "I feel like waffles."

"You want waffles?" said Aunty Em. "Waffles you get."

End Interaction 4023064

She bustled into the kitchen as the man closed the bathroom door behind him. A few minutes later she heard the pipes clang as he turned on the shower. She beamed a revised schedule to the pals, calling for them to arrive within the hour.

Aunty Em could not help but be pleased. This Christmas was already a great success. The man's attitude had changed dramatically after the shopping trip. He was keeping regular hours and drinking much less. He had stopped by the train layout in the garage although all he had done was look at it. Instead he had taken an interest in the garden in the backyard and had spent yesterday weeding the flowerbeds and digging a new vegetable patch. He had sent the pal Jeff to find seeds he could plant. The biops reported that they had found some peas and corn and string beans—but they were possibly contaminated and might not germinate. She had already warned some of the lesser animal biops that they might have to assume the form of corn stalks and pea vines if the crop failed.

Now if only he would pay attention to the girlfriend.

Begin Interaction 4023066

The doorbell gonged the first eight notes of "Silent Night." "Would you get that, Bertie dear?" Aunty Em was pouring freshly budded ova into a pitcher filled with Pet Evaporated Milk.

"It's the pals," the man called from the front hall. "Jeff and . . . I'm sorry, I've forgotten your name."

"Bill."

"Bill, of course. Come in, come in."

A few minutes later, Aunty Em found them sitting on the sofa in the living room. Each of the pals balanced a present on his lap, wrapped in identical green and red paper. They were listening uncomfortably as the cat recited "Twas the Night Before Christmas." The man was busy playing Madden NFL 2007 on his Game Boy.

"It's time for sweets and presents, Bertie." Aunty Em set the pitcher of eggnog next to the platter of cookies. She was disturbed that the girlfriend hadn't joined the party yet. She beamed a query but the girlfriend was dark. "Presents and sweets."

The man opened Jeff's present first. It was filled with hand tools for his new garden: a dibbler and a trowel and a claw hoe and a genuine Felco10 Professional Pruner. The dog gave the man a chewable rubber fire hydrant that squeeked when squeezed. The cat gave him an "O" Scale Western Pacific Steam Locomotive that had belonged to the dead neighbor, Mr. Kimura. The man and the cat exchanged looks briefly and then the cat yawned. The dog nudged his head under all the discarded wrapping paper and the man reached down with the claw hoe and scratched its back. Everyone but the cat laughed.

Next came Bill's present. In keeping with the garden theme of this Christmas, it was a painting of a balding old farmer and a middle-aged woman standing in front of a white house with an odd gothic window. Aunty Em could tell the man was a farmer because he was holding a pitchfork. The farmer stared out of the painting with a glum intensity; the woman looked at him askance. The curator biop claimed that it was one of the most copied images in the inventory, so Aunty Em was not surprised that the man seemed to recognize it.

"This looks like real paint," he said.

"Yes," said Bill. "Oil on beaverboard."

"What's beaverboard?" said the cat.

"A light, semirigid building material of compressed wood pulp," Bill said. "I looked it up."

The man turned the painting over and brushed his finger across the back. "Where did you get this?" His face was pale.

"From the accumulatorium."

"No, I mean where before then?"

Aunty Em eavesdropped as the pal beamed the query. "It was salvaged from the Chicago Art Institute."

"You're giving me the original *American Gothic?*" His voice fell into a hole.

"Is something the matter, Bertie?"

He fell silent for a moment. "No, I suppose not." He shook his head. "It's a very thoughtful gift." He propped the on the mantle, next to his scuffed leather fireman's helmet that the biops had retrieved from the ruins of the Ladder Company No. 3 Firehouse two Christmases ago.

Aunty Em wanted the man to open his big present, but the girlfriend had yet to make her entrance. So instead, she gave the pals their presents from the man. Jeff got the October 1937 issue of *Spicy Adventure Stories*. On the cover a brutish sailor carried a terrified woman in a shredded, red dress out of the surf as their ship sank in the background. Aunty Em pretended to be shocked and the man actually chuckled. Bill got a chrome Model 1B14 Toastmaster two slice toaster. The man took it from him and traced the triple loop logo etched in the side. "My mom had one of these."

Finally there was nothing left to open but the present wrapped in the blue paper with the Santa-in-space print. The man took the Glock 17 out of the box cautiously, as if he were afraid it might go off. It was black with a polymer grip and a four and a half inch steel barrel. Aunty Em had taken a calculated risk with the pistol. She always tried to give him whatever he asked for, as long as it wasn't too dangerous. He wasn't their captive after all. He was their master.

"Don't worry," she said. "It's not loaded. I looked but couldn't find the right bullets."

"But I did," said the girlfriend, sweeping into the room in the Kathy body. "I looked harder and found hundreds of thousands of bullets."

"Kathy," said Aunty Em, as she beamed a request for her to terminate this unauthorized interaction. "What a nice surprise."

"9mm Parabellum," said the girlfriend. Ten rounds clattered onto the glass top of the Noguchi coffee table. "115 grain. Full metal jacket."

"What are you doing?" said the man.

"You want to shoot someone?" The girlfriend glared at the man and swung her arms wide.

"Kathy," said Aunty Em. "You sound upset, dear. Maybe you should go lie down."

The man returned the girlfriend's stare. "You're not Kathy."

"No," said the girlfriend. "I'm nobody you know."

"Kathy's dead," said the man. "Everybody's dead except for me and poor Ellen Marelli. That's right, isn't it?"

The girlfriend sank to her knees, rested her head on the coffee table and began to cry. Only biops didn't cry, or at least no biop that Aunty Em had ever heard of. The man glanced around the room for an answer. The pals looked at their shoes and said nothing. "Jingle Bell Rock" tinkled on the music box. Aunty Em felt something swell inside of her and climb her throat until she thought she might burst. If this was what the man felt all the time, it was no wonder he was tempted to drink himself into insensibility.

"Well?" he said.

"Yes," Aunty Em blurted. "Yes, dead, Bertie. All dead."

The man took a deep breath. "Thank you," he said. "Sometimes I can't believe that it really happened. Or else I forget. You make it easy to forget. Maybe you think that's good for me. But I need to know who I am."

"Buddy," said the dog, brushing against him. "Buddy, my Buddy."

The man patted the dog absently. "I could give up. But I won't. I've had a bad spell the last couple of weeks, I know. That's not your fault." He heaved himself off the couch, came around the coffee table and knelt beside the girlfriend. "I really appreciate that you trust me with this gun. And these bullets too. That's got to be scary, after what I said." The girlfriend watched him scoop up the bullets. "Kathy, I don't need these just now. Would you please keep them for me?"

She nodded.

"Do you know the movie, *Miracle On 34th Street?*" He poured the bullets into her cupped hands. "Not the remakes. The first one, with Maureen O'Hara?"

She nodded again.

He leaned close and whispered into her ear. His pulse soared to 93.

She sniffed and then giggled.

"You go ahead," he said to her. "I'll come up in a little while." He gave her a pat on the rear and stood up. The other biops watched him nervously.

"What's with all the long faces?" He tucked the Glock into the waistband of his pants. "You look like them." He waved at the painting of the somber farm folk, whose mood would never, ever change. "It's Christmas Day, people. Let's live it up!"

End Interaction 4023066

Over the years, Aunty Em gave the man many more Christmases, not to mention Thanksgivings, Easters, Halloweens, April Fools, and Valentine Days. But she always said—and no one contradicted her, not the man, not even the girlfriend—that this Christmas was the best ever.

Men Are Trouble

1

I STARED AT MY SIDEKICK, WILLING IT TO CHIRP. I'D already tried watching the door, but no one had even breathed on it. I could've been writing up the Rashmi Jones case, but then I could've been dusting the office. It needed dusting. Or having a consult with Johnnie Walker, who had just that morning opened an office in the bottom drawer of my desk. Instead, I decided to open the window. Maybe a new case would arrive by carrier pigeon. Or wrapped around a brick.

Three stories below me, Market Street was as empty as the rest of the city. Just a couple of plain janes in walking shoes and a granny in a blanket and sandals. She was sitting on the curb in front of a dead Starbucks, strumming street guitar for pocket change, hoping to find a philanthropist in hell. Her singing was faint but sweet as peach ice cream. *My guy, talking 'bout my guy.* Poor old bitch, I thought. There are no guys—not yours, not anyone's. She stopped singing as a devil flapped over us, swooping for a landing on the next block. It had been a beautiful June morning until then, the moist promise of spring not yet broken by summer in our withered city. The granny struggled up, leaning on her guitar. She wrapped the blanket tight around her and trudged downtown.

My sidekick did chirp then, but it was Sharifa, my about-to-be ex-lover. She must have been calling from the hospital; she was wearing her light blue scrubs. Even on the little screen, I could see that she had been crying. "Hi Fay."

I bit my lip.

"Come home tonight," she said. "Please."

"I don't know where home is."

"I'm sorry about what I said." She folded her arms tight across her chest. "It's your body. Your life."

I loved her. I was sick about being seeded, the abortion, everything that had happened between us in the last week. I said nothing.

Her voice was sandpaper on glass. "Have you had it done yet?" That made me angry all over again. She was wound so tight she couldn't even say the word.

"Let me guess, Doctor," I said, "Are we talking about me getting scrubbed?"

Her face twisted. "Don't."

"If you want the dirt," I said, "you could always hire me to shadow myself. I need the work."

"Make it a joke, why don't you?"

"Okey-doke, Doc," I said and clicked off.

So my life was cocked—not exactly main menu news. Still, even with the window open, Sharifa's call had sucked all the air out of my office. I told myself that all I needed was coffee, although what I really wanted was a rich aunt, a vacation in Fiji, and a new girlfriend. I locked the door behind me, slogged down the hall, and was about to press the down button when the elevator chimed. The doors slid open to reveal George, the bot in charge of our building, and a devil—no doubt the same one that had just flown by. I told myself this had nothing to do with me. The devil was probably seeing crazy Martha down the hall about a tax rebate or taking piano lessons from Abby upstairs. Sure, and drunks go to bars for the peanuts.

"Hello, Fay," said George. "This one had true hopes of finding you in your office."

I goggled, slack-jawed and stupefied, at the devil. Of course, I'd seen them on vids and in the sky and once I watched one waddle into City Hall but I'd never been close enough to slap one before. I hated the devils. The elevator doors shivered and began to close. George stuck an arm out to stop them.

"May this one borrow some of your time?" George said.

The devil was just over a meter tall. Its face was the color of an old bloodstain and its maw seemed to kiss the air as it breathed with a wet, sucking sound. The wings were wrapped tight around it; the membranes had a rusty translucence that only hinted at the sleek bullet of a body beneath. I could see my reflection in its flat, compound eyes. I looked like I had just been hit in the head with a lighthouse.

"Something is regrettable, Fay?" said George.

That was my cue for a wisecrack to show them that no invincible mass-murdering alien was going to intimidate Fay Hardaway.

"No," I said. "This way."

If they could've sat in chairs, there would've been plenty of room for us in my office. But George announced that the devil needed to make itself comfortable before we began. I nodded as I settled behind my desk, grateful to have something between the two of them and me. George dragged both chairs out into the little reception room. The devil spread its wings and swooped up onto my file cabinet, ruffling the hardcopy on my desk. It filled the back wall of my office as it perched there, a span of almost twenty feet. George wedged himself into a corner and absorbed his legs and arms until he was just a head and a slab of gleaming blue bot stuff. The devil gazed at me as if it were wondering what kind of rug I would make. I brought up three new icons on my desktop. *New Case. Searchlet. Panic button.*

"Indulge this one to speak for Seeren?" said George. "Seeren has a bright desire to task you to an investigation."

The devils never spoke to us, never explained what they were doing. No one knew exactly how they communicated with the army of bots they had built to prop us up.

I opened the *New Case* folder and the green light blinked. "I'm recording this. If I decide to accept your case, I will record my entire investigation."

"A thoughtful gesture, Fay. This one needs to remark on your client Rashmi Jones."

"She's not my client." It took everything I had not to fall off my chair. "What about her?"

"Seeren conveys vast regret. All deaths diminish all."

I didn't like it that this devil knew anything at all about Rashmi, but especially that she was dead. I'd found the body in Room 103 of the Comfort Inn just twelve hours ago. "The cops already have the case." I didn't mind that there was a snarl in my voice. "Or what's left of it. There's nothing I can do for you."

"A permission, Fay?"

The icon was already flashing on my desktop. I opened it and saw a pix of Rashmi in the sleeveless taupe dress that she had died in. She had the blue ribbon in her hair. She was smiling, as carefree as a kid on the last day of school. The last thing she was thinking about was sucking on an inhaler filled with hydrogen cyanide. Holding her hand was some brunette dressed in a mannish, chalk-stripe suit and a matching pillbox hat with a veil as fine as smoke. The couple preened under a garden arch that dripped with pink roses. They faced right, in the direction of the hand of some third party standing just off camera. It was an elegant hand, a hand that had never been in dishwater or changed a diaper. There was a wide, silver ring on the fourth finger, engraved with a pattern or maybe some kind of fancy writing. I zoomed on the ring and briefly tormented pixels but couldn't get the pattern resolved.

I looked up at the devil and then at George. "So?"

"This one notices especially the digimark," said George. "Date-stamped June 12, 2:52."

"You're saying it was taken yesterday afternoon?"

That didn't fit—except that it did. I had Rashmi downtown shopping for shoes late yesterday morning. At 11:46 she bought a $13 pair of this season's Donya Durands, now missing. At 1:23 she charged 89¢ for a Waldorf salad and an iced tea at Maison Diana. She checked into the Comfort Inn at 6:40. She didn't have a reservation, so maybe this was a spur of the moment decision. The desk clerk remembered her as distraught. That was the word she used. A precise word, although a bit highbrow for the Comfort Inn. Who buys expensive shoes the day before she intends to kill herself? Somebody who is distraught. I glanced again at my desktop. Distraught was precisely what Rashmi Jones was not in this pix. Then I noticed the shoes: ice and taupe Donya Durands.

"Where did you get this?" I said to the devil.

It stared through me like I was a dirty window.

I tried the bot. I wouldn't say that I liked George exactly, but he'd always been straight with me. "What's this about, George? Finding the tommy?"

"The tommy?"

"The woman holding Rashmi's hand."

"Seeren has made this one well aware of Kate Vermeil," said George. "Such Kate Vermeil takes work at 44 East Washington Avenue and takes home at 465 12th Avenue, Second Floor Left."

I liked that, I liked it a lot. Rashmi's mom had told me that her daughter had a Christer friend called Kate, but I didn't even have a last name, much less an address. I turned to the devil again. "You know this how?"

All that got me was another empty stare.

"Seeren," I said, pushing back out of my chair, "I'm afraid George has led you astray. I'm the private investigator." I stood to show them out. "The mind reader's office is across the street."

This time George didn't ask permission. My desktop chirped. I waved open a new icon. A certified bank transfer in the amount of a thousand dollars dragged me back onto my chair.

"A cordial inducement," said George. "With a like amount offered after the success of your investigation."

I thought of a thousand dinners in restaurants with linen table-cloths. "Tell me already." A thousand bottles of smoky scotch.

"This one draws attention to the hand of the unseen person," said the bot. "Seeren has the brightest desire to meeting such person for fruitful business discussions."

The job smelled like the dumpster at Fran's Fish Fry. Precious little money changed hands in the pretend economy. The bots kept everything running, but they did nothing to create wealth. That was supposed to be up to us, I guess, only we'd been sort of discouraged. In some parts of town, that kind of change could hire a Felony 1, with a handful of Misdemeanors thrown in for good luck.

"That's more than I'm worth," I said. "A hundred times more. If Seeren expects me to break the arm attached to that hand, it's talking to the wrong jane."

"Violence is to be deplored," said George. "However, Seeren tasks Fay to discretion throughout. Never police, never news, never even rumor if possible."

"Oh, discretion." I accepted the transfer. "For two large, I can be as discreet as the Queen's butler."

2

I could've taken a cab, but they're almost all driven by bots now, and bots keep nobody's secrets. Besides, even though I had a thousand dollars in the bank, I thought I'd let it settle in for a while. Make itself at home. So I bicycled over to 12th Avenue. I started having doubts as I hit the 400 block. This part of the city had been kicked in the head and left bleeding on the sidewalk. Dark bars leaned against pawnshops. Board-ups turned their blank plywood faces to the street. There would be more bots than women in this neighbor-hood and more rats than bots.

The Adagio Spa squatted at 465 12th Avenue. It was a brick

building with a reinforced luxar display window that was so scratched it looked like a thin slice of rainstorm. There were dusty plants behind it. The second floor windows were bricked over. I chained my bike to a dead car, set my sidekick to record and went in.

The rear wall of the little reception area was bright with pix of some Mediterranean seaside town. A clump of bad pixels made the empty beach flicker. A bot stepped through the door that led to the spa and took up a position at the front desk. "Good afternoon, Madam," he said. "It's most gratifying to welcome you. This one is called . . ."

"I'm looking for Kate Vermeil." I don't waste time on chitchat with bots. "Is she in?"

"It's regrettable that she no longer takes work here."

"She worked here?" I said. "I was told she lived here."

"You was told wrong." A granny filled the door, and then hobbled through, leaning on a metal cane. She was wearing a yellow flowered dress that was not quite as big as a circus tent and over it a blue smock with *Noreen* embroidered over the left breast. Her face was wide and pale as a hardboiled egg, her hair a ferment of tight, gray curls. She had the biggest hands I had ever seen. "I'll take care of this, Barry. Go see to Helen Ritzi. She gets another needle at twelve, then turn down the heat to 101."

The bot bowed politely and left us.

"What's this about then?" The cane wobbled and she put a hand on the desk to steady herself.

I dug the sidekick out of my slacks, opened the PI license folder and showed it to her. She read it slowly, sniffed and handed it back. "Young fluffs working at play jobs. Do something useful, why don't you?"

"Like what," I said. "Giving perms? Face peels?"

She was the woman of steel; sarcasm bounced off her. "If nobody does a real job, pretty soon the damn bots will replace us all."

"Might be an improvement." It was something to say, but as soon as I said it I wished I hadn't. My generation was doing better than the grannies ever had. Maybe someday our kids wouldn't need bots to survive.

Our kids. I swallowed a mouthful of ashes and called the pix Seeren had given me onto the sidekick's screen. "I'm looking for Kate Vermeil." I aimed it at her.

She peered at the pix and then at me. "You need a manicure."

"The hell I do."

"I work for a living, fluff. And my hip hurts if I stand up too long." She pointed her cane at the doorway behind the desk. "What did you say your name was?"

The battered manicure table was in an alcove decorated with fake grapevines that didn't quite hide the water stains in the drop ceiling. Dust covered the leaves, turning the plastic fruit from purple to gray.

Noreen rubbed a thumb over the tips of my fingers. "You bite your nails, or do you just cut them with a chainsaw?"

She wanted a laugh so I gave her one.

"So, nails square, round, or oval?" Her skin was dry and mottled with liver spots.

"Haven't a clue." I shrugged. "This was your idea."

Noreen perched on an adjustable stool that was cranked low so that her face was only a foot above my hands. There were a stack of stainless steel bowls, a jar of Vaseline, a round box of salt, a bowl filled with packets of sugar stolen from McDonald's and a liquid soap dispenser on the table beside her. She started filing each nail from the corner to the center, going from left to right and then back. At first she worked in silence. I decided not to push her.

"Kate was my masseuse up until last week," she said finally. "Gave her notice all of a sudden and left me in the lurch. I've had to pick up all her appointments and me with the bum hip. Some days I can't hardly get out of bed. Something happen to her?"

"Not as far as I know."

"But she's missing."

I shook my head. "I don't know where she is, but that doesn't mean she's missing."

Noreen poured hot water from an electric kettle into one of the stainless steel bowls, added cool water from a pitcher, squirted soap and swirled the mixture around. "You soak for five minutes." She gestured for me to dip my hands into the bowl. "I'll be back. I got to make sure that Barry doesn't burn Helen Ritzi's face off." She stood with a grunt.

"Wait," I said. "Did she say why she was quitting?"

Noreen reached for her cane. "Couldn't stop talking about it. You'd think she was the first ever."

"The first to what?"

The granny laughed. "You're one hell of a detective, fluff. She was supposed to get married yesterday. Tell me that pix you're flashing ain't her doing the deed."

She shuffled off, her white nursemate shoes scuffing against dirty linoleum. From deeper in the spa, I heard her kettle drum voice and then the bot's snare. I was itching to take my sidekick out of my pocket, but I kept my hands in the soak. Besides, I'd looked at the pix enough times to know that she was right. A wedding. The hand with the ring would probably belong to a Christer priest. There would have been a witness and then the photographer, although maybe the photographer was the witness. Of course, I had tumbled to none of this in the two days I'd worked Rashmi Jones's disappearance. I was one hell of a detective, all right. And Rashmi's mom must not have known either. It didn't make sense that she would hire me to find her daughter and hold back something like that.

"I swear," said Noreen, leaning heavily on the cane as she creaked back to me, "that bot is scary. I sent down to City Hall for it just last week and already it knows my business left, right, up, and down. The thing is, if they're so smart, how come they talk funny?"

"The devils designed them to drive us crazy."

"They didn't need no bots to do that, fluff."

She settled back onto her stool, tore open five sugar packets and emptied their contents onto her palm. Then she reached for the salt box and poured salt onto the sugar. She squirted soap onto the pile and then rubbed her hands together. "I could buy some fancy exfoliating cream but this works just as good." She pointed with her chin at my hands. "Give them a shake and bring them here."

I wanted to ask her about Kate's marriage plans, but when she took my hands in hers, I forgot the question. I'd never felt anything quite like it; the irritating scratch of the grit was offset by the sensual slide of our soapy fingers. Pleasure with just the right touch of pain—something I'd certainly be telling Sharifa about, if Sharifa and I were talking. My hands tingled for almost an hour afterward.

Noreen poured another bowl of water and I rinsed. "Why would getting married make Kate want to quit?" I asked.

"I don't know. Something to do with her church?" Noreen patted me dry with a threadbare towel. "She went over to the Christers last year. Maybe Jesus don't like married women giving backrubs. Or maybe she got seeded." She gave a bitter laugh. "Everybody does eventually."

I let that pass. "Tell me about Kate. What was she like to work with?"

"Average for the kind of help you get these sorry days." Noreen pushed at my cuticles with an orangewood stick. "Showed up on time mostly; I could only afford to bring her in two days a week. No go-getter, but she could follow directions. Problem was she never really got close to the customers, always acting like this was just a pitstop. Kept to herself mostly, which was how I could tell she was excited about getting married. It wasn't like her to babble."

"And the bride?"

"Some Indian fluff—Rashy or something."

"Rashmi Jones."

She nodded. "Her I never met."

"Did she go to school?"

"Must have done high school, but damned if I know where. Didn't make much of an impression, I'd say. College, no way." She opened a drawer where a flock of colored vials was nesting. "You want polish or clear coat on the nails?"

"No color. It's bad for business."

She leered at me. "Business is good?"

"You say she did massage for you?" I said. "Where did she pick that up?"

"Hold still now." Noreen uncapped the vial; the milky liquid that clung to the brush smelled like super glue's evil twin. "This is fast dry." She painted the stuff onto my nails with short, confident strokes. "Kate claimed her mom taught her. Said she used to work at the health club at the Radisson before it closed down."

"Did the mom have a name?"

"Yeah." Noreen chewed her lower lip as she worked. "Mom. Give the other hand."

I extended my arm. "So if Kate didn't live here, where she did live?"

"Someplace. Was on her application." She kept her head down until she'd finished. "You're done. Wave them around a little—that's it."

After a moment, I let my arms drop to my side. We stared at each other. Then Noreen heaved herself off the stool and led me back out to the reception room.

"That'll be a eighty cents for the manicure, fluff." She waved her desktop on. "You planning on leaving a tip?"

I pulled out the sidekick and beamed two dollars at the desk. Noreen opened the payment icon, grunted her approval and then opened another folder. "Says here she lives at 44 East Washington Avenue."

I groaned.

"Something wrong?"

"I already have that address."

"Got her call too? Kate@Washington.03284."

"No, that's good. Thanks." I went to the door and paused. I don't know why I needed to say anything else to her, but I did. "I help people, Noreen. Or at least I try. It's a real job, something bots can't do."

She just stood there, kneading the bad hip with a big, dry hand.

I unchained my bike, pedaled around the block and then pulled over. I read Kate Vermeil's call into my sidekick. Her sidekick picked up on the sixth chirp. There was no pix.

"You haven't reached Kate yet, but your luck might change if you leave a message at the beep." She put on the kind of low, smoky voice that doesn't come out to play until dark. It was a nice act.

"Hi Kate," I said. "My name is Fay Hardaway and I'm a friend of Rashmi Jones. She asked me to give you a message about yesterday so please give me a call at Fay@Market.03284." I wasn't really expecting her to respond, but it didn't hurt to try.

I was on my way to 44 East Washington Avenue when my sidekick chirped in the pocket of my slacks. I picked up. Rashmi Jones's mom, Najma, stared at me from the screen with eyes as deep as wells.

"The police came," she said. "They said you were supposed to notify them first. They want to speak to you again."

They would. So I'd called the law after I called the mom—they'd get over it. You don't tell a mother that her daughter is dead and then ask her to act surprised when the cops come knocking. "I was working for you, not them."

"I want to see you."

"I understand."

"I hired you to find my daughter."

"I did," I said. "Twice." I was sorry as soon as I said it.

She glanced away; I could hear squeaky voices in the background. "I want to know everything," she said. "I want to know how close you came."

"I've started a report. Let me finish it and I'll bring it by later . . ."

"Now," she said. "I'm at school. My lunch starts at eleven-fifty and I have recess duty at twelve-fifteen." She clicked off.

I had nothing to feel guilty about, so why was I tempted to wriggle down a storm drain and find the deepest sewer in town? Because a mom believed that I hadn't worked fast enough or smart enough to save her daughter? Someone needed to remind these people that I didn't fix lost things, I just found them. But that someone wouldn't be me. My play now was simply to stroll into her school and let her beat me about the head with her grief. I could take it. I ate old Bogart movies for breakfast and spit out bullets. And at the end of this cocked day, I could just forget about Najma Jones, because there would be no Sharifa reminding me how much it cost me to do my job. I took out my sidekick, linked to my desktop and downloaded everything I had in the Jones file. Then I swung back onto my bike.

The mom had left a message three days ago, asking that I come out to her place on Ashbury. She and her daughter rattled around in an old Victorian with gingerbread gables and a front porch the size of Cuba. The place had been in the family for four generations. Theirs had been a big family—once. The mom said that Rashmi hadn't come home the previous night. She hadn't called and didn't answer messages. The mom had contacted the cops, but they weren't all that interested. Not enough time would have passed for them. Too much time had passed for the mom.

The mom taught fifth grade at Reagan Elementary. Rashmi was a twenty-six year old grad student, six credits away from an MFA in Creative Writing. The mom trusted her to draw money from the family account, so at first I thought I might be able to find her by chasing debits. But there was no activity in the account we could attribute to the missing girl. When I suggested that she might be hiding out with friends, the mom went prickly on me. Turned out that Rashmi's choice of friends was a cause of contention between them. Rashmi had dropped her old pals in the last few months and taken up with a new, religious crowd. Gratiana and Elaine and Kate—the mom didn't know their last names—were members of the Church of Christ the Man. I'd had trouble with Christers before and wasn't all that eager to go up against them again, so instead I biked over to campus to see Rashmi's advisor. Zelda Manotti was a dithering old granny who would have loved to help except she had all the focus of paint spatter. She did let me copy Rashmi's novel-in-progress. And she did let me tag along to her advanced writing seminar, in case Rashmi showed up for it. She didn't. I talked to the three other students after class, but they either didn't know where she was or wouldn't say. None of them was Gratiana, Alix, or Elaine.

That night I skimmed *The Lost Heart*, Rashmi's novel. It was a nostalgic and sentimental weeper set back before the devils disappeared all the men. Young Brigit Bird was searching for her father, a famous architect who had been kidnapped by Colombian drug lords. If I was just a fluff doing a fantasy job in the pretend economy, then old Noreen would have crowned Rashmi Jones queen of fluffs.

I started day two back at the Joneses' home. The mom watched as I went through Rashmi's room. I think she was as worried about what I might find as she was that I would find nothing. Rashmi listened to the Creeps, had three different pairs of Kat sandals, owned everything Denise Pepper had ever written, preferred underwire bras and subscribed to News for the Confused. She had kicked about a week's worth of dirty clothes under her bed. Her wallpaper mix cycled through koalas, the World's Greatest Beaches, ruined castles, and Playgirl Centerfolds 2000-2010. She'd kept a handwritten diary starting in the sixth grade and ending in the eighth in which she often complained that her mother was strict and that school was boring. The only thing I found that rattled the mom was a Christer Bible tucked into the back of the bottom drawer of the nightstand. When I pulled it out, she flushed and stalked out of the room.

I found my lead on the Joneses' home network. Rashmi was not particularly diligent about backing up her sidekick files, and the last one I found was almost six months old, which was just about when she'd gotten religion. She'd used simple encryption, which wouldn't withstand a serious hack, but which would discourage the mom from snooping. I doglegged a key and opened the file. She had multiple calls. Her mother had been trying her at Rashmi@Ashbury.03284. But she also had an alternate: Brigitbird@Vincent.03284. I did a reverse lookup and that turned up an address: The Church of Christ the Man, 348 Vincent Avenue. I wasn't keen for a personal visit to the church, so I tried her call.

"Hello," said a voice.

"Is this Rashmi Jones?"

The voice hesitated. "My name is Brigit. Leave me alone."

"Your mother is worried about you, Rashmi. She hired me to find you."

"I don't want to be found."

"I'm reading your novel, Rashmi." It was just something to say; I wanted to keep her on the line. "I was wondering, does she find her father at the end?"

"No." I could hear her breath caressing the microphone. "The devils come. That's the whole point."

Someone said something to her and she muted the speaker. But I knew she could still hear me. "That's sad, Rashmi. But I guess that's the way it had to be."

Then she hung up.

The mom was relieved that Rashmi was all right, furious that she was with Christers. So what? I'd found the girl: case closed. Only Najma Jones begged me to help her connect with her daughter. She was already into me for twenty bucks plus expenses, but for another five I said I'd try to get her away from the church long enough for them to talk. I was on my way over when the searchlet I'd attached to the Jones account turned up the hit at Grayle's Shoes. I was grateful for the reprieve, even more pleased when the salesbot identified Rashmi from her pix. As did the waitress at Maison Diana.

And the clerk at the Comfort Inn.

3

Ronald Reagan Elementary had been recently renovated, no doubt by a squad of janitor bots. The brick façade had been cleaned and repointed; the long row of windows gleamed like teeth. The asphalt playground had been ripped up and resurfaced with safe-t-mat, the metal swingsets swapped for gaudy towers and crawl tubes and slides and balance beams and decks. The chain link fences had been replaced by redwood lattice through which twined honeysuckle and clematis. There was a boxwood maze next to the swimming pool that shimmered, blue as a dream. Nothing was too good for the little girls—our hope for the future.

There was no room in the rack jammed with bikes and scooters and goboards, so I leaned my bike against a nearby cherry tree. The very youngest girls had come out for first recess. I paused behind the tree for a moment to let their whoops and shrieks and laughter bubble over me. My business didn't take me to schools very often; I couldn't remember when I had last seen so many girls in one place. They were black and white and yellow and brown, mostly dressed like janes you might see anywhere. But there were more than a few whose clothes proclaimed their mothers' lifestyles. Tommys in hunter camo and chaste Christers, twists in chains and spray-on, clumps of sisters wearing the uniforms of a group marriage, a couple of furries, and one girl wearing a body suit that looked just like bot skin. As I lingered there, I felt a chill that had nothing to do with the shade of a tree. I had no idea who these tiny creatures were. They went to this well-kept school, led more or less normal lives. I grew up in the wild times, when everything was falling apart. At that moment, I realized that they were as far removed from me as I was from the grannies. I would always watch them from a distance.

Just inside the fence, two sisters in green-striped shirtwaists and green knee socks were turning a rope for a pony-tailed jumper who was executing nimble criss-crosses. The turners chanted,

"Down in the valley where the green grass grows,
there sits Stacy pretty as a rose!
She sings, she sings, she sings so sweet,
Then along comes Chantall to kiss her on the cheek!"

Another jumper joined her in the middle, matching her step for step, her dark hair flying. The chant continued,

"How many kisses does she get?
One, two, three, four, five . . ."

The two jumpers pecked at each other in the air to the count of ten without missing a beat. Then Ponytail skipped out and the turners began the chant over again for the dark-haired girl. Ponytail bent over for a moment to catch her breath; when she straightened, she noticed me.

"Hey you, behind the tree." She shaded her eyes with a hand. "You hiding?"

I stepped into the open. "No."

"This is our school, you know." The girl set one foot behind the other and then spun a hundred and eighty degrees to point at the door to the school. "You supposed to sign in at the office."

"I'd better take care of that then."

As I passed through the gate into the playground, a few of the girls stopped playing and stared. This was all the audience Ponytail needed. "You someone's mom?"

"No."

"Don't you have a job?" She fell into step beside me.

"I do."

"What is it?"

"I can't tell you."

She dashed ahead to block my path. "Probably because it's a pretend job."

Two of her sisters in green-striped shirtwaists scrambled to back her up.

"When we grow up," one of them announced, "we're going to have real jobs."

"Like a doctor," the other said. "Or a lion tamer."

Other girls were joining us. "I want to drive a truck," said a tommy. "Big, big truck." She specified the size of her rig with outstretched arms.

"That's not a real job. Any bot could do that."

"I want to be a teacher," said the dark-haired sister who had been jumping rope.

"Chantall loves school," said a furry. "She'd marry school if she could." Apparently this passed for brilliant wit in the third grade; some girls laughed so hard they had to cover their mouths with the back of their hands. Me, I was flummoxed. Give me a spurned lover or a mean drunk or a hardcase cop and I could figure out some play, but just then I was trapped by this giggling mob of children.

"So why you here?" Ponytail put her fists on her hips.

A jane in khakis and a baggy plum sweater emerged from behind a blue tunnel that looked like a centipede. She pinned me with that penetrating but not unkind stare that teachers are born with, and began to trudge across the playground toward me. "I've come to see Ms. Jones," I said.

"Oh." A shadow passed over Ponytail's face and she rubbed her hands against the sides of her legs. "You better go then."

Someone called, "Are you the undertaker?"

A voice that squeaked with innocence asked, "What's an undertaker?"

I didn't hear the answer. The teacher in the plum sweater rescued me and we passed through the crowd.

I didn't understand why Najma Jones had come to school. She was either the most dedicated teacher on the planet or she was too numb to accept her daughter's death. I couldn't tell which. She had been reserved when we met the first time; now she was locked down and welded shut. She was a bird of a woman with a narrow face and thin lips. Her gray hair had a few lingering strands of black. She wore a long-sleeved, white kameez·tunic over shalwar trousers. I leaned against the door of her classroom and told her everything I had done the day before. She sat listening at her desk with a sandwich that she wasn't going to eat and a carton of milk that she wasn't going to drink and a napkin that she didn't need.

When I had finished, she asked me about cyanide inhalers.

"Hydrogen cyanide isn't hard to get in bulk," I said. "They use it for making plastic, engraving, tempering steel. The inhaler came from one of the underground suicide groups, probably Our Choice. The cops could tell you for sure."

She unfolded the napkin and spread it out on top of her desk. "I've heard it's a painful death."

"Not at all," I said. "They used to use hydrogen cyanide gas to

execute criminals, back in the bad old days. It all depends on the
first breath. Get it deep into your lungs and you're unconscious
before you hit the floor. Dead in less than a minute."

"And if you don't get a large enough dose?"

"Ms. Jones . . ."

She cut me off hard. "If you don't?"

"Then it takes longer, but you still die. There are convulsions.
The skin flushes and turns purple. Eyes bulge. They say it's something like having a heart attack."

"Rashmi?" She laid her daughter's name down gently, as if she
were tucking it into bed. "How did she die?"

Had the cops shown her the crime scene pictures? I decided
they hadn't. "I don't think she suffered," I said.

She tore a long strip off the napkin. "You don't think I'm a very
good mother, do you?"

I don't know exactly what I expected her to say, but this wasn't
it. "Ms. Jones, I don't know much about you and your daughter. But
I do know that you cared enough about her to hire me. I'm sorry I
let you down."

She shook her head wearily, as if I had just flunked the pop quiz.
One third does not equal .033 and Los Angeles has never been the
capital of California. "Is there anything else I should know?" she
said.

"There is." I had to tell her what I'd found out that morning, but
I wasn't going to tell her that I was working for a devil. "You mentioned before that Rashmi had a friend named Kate."

"The Christer?" She tore another strip off the napkin.

I nodded. "Her name is Kate Vermeil. I don't know this for sure
yet, but there's reason to believe that Rashmi and Kate were married
yesterday. Does that make any sense to you?"

"Maybe yesterday it might have." Her voice was flat. "It doesn't
anymore."

I could hear stirring in the next classroom. Chairs scraped
against linoleum. Girls were jabbering at each other.

"I know Rashmi became a Christer," she said. "It's a broken religion. But then everything is broken, isn't it? My daughter and I . . .
I don't think we ever understood each other. We were strangers at
the end." The napkin was in shreds. "How old were you when it
happened?"

"I wasn't born yet." She didn't have to explain what it was. "I'm
not as old as I look."

"I was nineteen. I remember men, my father, my uncles. And

the boys. I actually slept with one." She gave me a bleak smile. "Does that shock you, Ms. Hardaway?"

I hated it when grannies talked about having sex, but I just shook my head.

"I didn't love Sunil, but I said I'd marry him just so I could get out of my mother's house. Maybe that was what was happening with Rashmi and this Kate person?"

"I wouldn't know."

The school bell rang.

"I'm wearing white today, Ms. Hardaway, to honor my darling daughter." She gathered up the strips of napkin and the sandwich and the carton of milk and dropped them in the trashcan. "White is the Hindu color of mourning. But it's also the color of knowledge. The goddess of learning, Saraswati, is always shown wearing a white dress, sitting on a white lotus. There is something here I must learn." She fingered the gold embroidery at the neckline of her kameez. "But it's time for recess."

We walked to the door. "What will you do now?" She opened it. The fifth grade swarmed the hall, girls rummaging through their lockers.

"Find Kate Vermeil," I said.

She nodded. "Tell her I'm sorry."

4

I tried Kate's call again, but when all I got was the sidekick I biked across town to 44 East Washington Avenue. The Poison Society turned out to be a jump joint; the sign said it opened at 9PM. There was no bell on the front door, but I knocked hard enough to wake Marilyn Monroe. No answer. I went around to the back and tried again. If Kate was in there, she wasn't entertaining visitors.

A sidekick search turned up an open McDonald's on Wallingford, a ten-minute ride. The only other customers were a couple of twists with bound breasts and identical acid-green, vinyl masks. One of them crouched on the floor beside the other, begging for chicken nuggets. A bot took my order for the 29¢ combo meal—it was all bots behind the counter. By law, there was supposed to be a human running the place, but if she was on the premises, she was nowhere to be seen. I thought about calling City Hall to complain, but the egg rolls arrived crispy and the McLatte was nicely scalded. Besides, I didn't need to watch the cops haul the poor jane in charge out of whatever hole she had fallen into.

A couple of hardcase tommys in army surplus fatigues strutted in just after me. They ate with their heads bowed over their plastic trays so the fries didn't have too far to travel. Their collapsible titanium nightsticks lay on the table in plain sight. One of them was not quite as wide as a bus. The other was nothing special, except that when I glanced up from my sidekick, she was giving me a freeze-dried stare. I waggled my shiny fingernails at her and screwed my cutest smile onto my face. She scowled, said something to her partner and went back to the trough.

My sidekick chirped. It was my pal Julie Epstein, who worked Self-Endangerment/Missing Persons out of the Second Precinct.

"You busy, Fay?"

"Yeah, the Queen of Cleveland just lost her glass slipper and I'm on the case."

"Well, I'm about to roll through your neighborhood. Want to do lunch?"

I aimed the sidekick at the empties on my table. "Just finishing."

"Where are you?"

"McD's on Wallingford."

"Yeah? How are the ribs?"

"Couldn't say. But the egg rolls are triple dee."

"That the place where the owner is a junkliner? We've had complaints. Bots run everything?"

"No, I can see her now. She's shortchanging some beat cop."

She gave me the laugh. "Got the coroner's on the Rashmi Jones. Cyanide induced hypoxia."

"You didn't by any chance show the mom pix of the scene?"

"Hell no. Talk about cruel and unusual." She frowned. "Why?"

"I was just with her. She seemed like maybe she suspected her kid wrestled with the reaper."

"We didn't tell her. By the way, we don't really care if you call your client, but next time how about trying us first?"

"That's cop law. Me, I follow PI law."

"Where did you steal that line from, *Chinatown?*"

"It's got better dialogue than *Dragnet*." I swirled the last of my latte in the cup. "You calling a motive on the Rashmi Jones?"

"Not yet. What do you like?" She ticked off the fingers of her left hand. "Family? School? Money? Broke a fingernail? Cloudy day?"

"Pregnancy? Just a hunch."

"You think she was seeded? We'll check that. But that's no reason to kill yourself."

"They've all got reasons. Only none of them makes sense."

She frowned. "Hey, don't get all invested on me here."

"Tell me, Julie, do you think I'm doing a pretend job?"

"Whoa, Fay." Her chuckle had a sharp edge. "Maybe it's time you and Sharifa took a vacation."

"Yeah." I let that pass. "It's just that some granny called me a fluff."

"Grannies." She snorted in disgust. "Well, you're no cop, that's for sure. But we do appreciate the help. Yeah, I'd say what you do is real. As real as anything in this cocked world."

"Thanks, flatfoot. Now that you've made things all better, I'll just click off. My latte is getting cold and you're missing so damn many persons."

"Think about that vacation, shamus. Bye."

As I put my sidekick away, I realized that the tommys were waiting for me. They'd been rattling ice in their cups and folding McWrappers for the past ten minutes. I probably didn't need their brand of trouble. The smart move would be to bolt for the door and leave my bike for now; I could lose them on foot. But then I hadn't made a smart move since April. The big one was talking into her sidekick when I sauntered over to them.

"What can I do for you ladies?" I said.

The big one pocketed the sidekick. Her partner started to come out of her seat but the big one stretched an arm like a telephone pole to restrain her.

"Do we know you?" The partner had close-set eyes and a beak nose; her black hair was short and stiff as a brush. She was wearing a black tee under her fatigue jacket and black leather combat boots. Probably had steel toes. "No," she continued, "I don't think we do."

"Then let's get introductions out of the way," I said. "I'm Fay Hardaway. And you are . . . ?"

They gave me less than nothing.

I sat down. "Thanks," I said. "Don't mind if I do."

The big one leaned back in her chair and eyed me as if I was dessert. "Sure you're not making a mistake, missy?"

"Why, because you're rough, tough, and take no guff?"

"You're funny." She smirked. "I like that. People are usually so very sad to meet us. My name is Alix." She held out her hand and we shook. "Pleased to know you."

The customary way to shake hands is to hold on for four, maybe five seconds, squeeze goodbye, then loosen the grip. Maybe big Alix wasn't familiar with our customs—she wasn't letting go.

I wasn't going to let a little thing like a missing hand intimidate me. "Oh, then I do know you," I said. We were in the McDonald's on Wallingford Street—a public place. I'd just been talking to my pal the cop. I was so damn sure that I was safe, I decided to take my shot. "That would make the girlfriend here Elaine. Or is it Gratiana?"

"Alix." The beak panicked. "Now we've got to take her."

Alix sighed, then yanked on my arm. She might have been pulling a tissue from a box for all the effort she expended. I slid halfway across the table as the beak whipped her nightstick to full extension. I lunged away from her and she caught me just a glancing blow above the ear but then Alix stuck a popper into my face and spattered me with knockout spray. I saw a billion stars and breathed the vacuum of deep space for maybe two seconds before everything went black.

Big Ben chimed between my ears. I could feel it deep in my molars, in the jelly of my eyes. It was the first thing I had felt since World War II. Wait a minute, was I alive during World War II? No, but I had seen the movie. When I wiggled my toes, Big Ben chimed again. I realized that the reason it hurt so much was that the human head didn't really contain enough space to hang a bell of that size. As I took inventory of body parts, the chiming became less intense. By the time I knew I was all there, it was just the sting of blood in my veins.

I was laid out on a surface that was hard but not cold. Wood. A bench. The place I was in was huge and dim but not dark. The high ceiling was in shadow. There was a hint of smoke in the air. Lights flickered. Candles. That was a clue, but I was still too groggy to understand what the mystery was. I knew I needed to remember something, but there was a hole where the memory was supposed to be. I reached back and touched just above my ear. The tip of my finger came away dark and sticky.

A voice solved the mystery for me. "I'm sorry that my people overreacted. If you want to press charges, I've instructed Gratiana and Alix to surrender to the police."

It came back to me then. It always does. McDonald's. Big Alix. A long handshake. That would make this a church. I sat up. When the world stopped spinning, I saw a vast, marble altar awash in light with a crucifix the size of a Cessna hanging behind it.

"I hope you're not in too much pain, Miss Hardaway." The voice came from the pew behind me. A fortyish woman in a black suit and a roman collar was on the kneeler. She was wearing a large, silver ring on the fourth finger of her left hand.

"I've felt worse."

"That's too bad. Do you make a habit of getting into trouble?" She looked concerned that I might be making some bad life-choices. She had soft eyes and a kindly face. Her short hair was the color of ashes. She was someone I could tell my guilty secrets to, so I could sleep at night. She would speak to Christ the Man himself on my behalf, book me into the penthouse suite in heaven.

"Am I in trouble?"

She nodded gravely. "We all are. The devils are destroying us, Miss Hardaway. They plant their seed not only in our bodies, but our minds and our souls."

"Please, call me Fay. I'm sure we're going to be just the very best of friends." I leaned toward her. "I'm sorry, I can't read your name tag."

"I'm not wearing one." She smiled. "I'm Father Elaine Horváth."

We looked at each other.

"Have you ever considered suicide, Fay?" said Father Elaine.

"Not really. It's usually a bad career move."

"Very good. But you must know that since the devils came and changed everything, almost a billion women have despaired and taken their lives."

"You know, I think I did hear something about that. Come on, lady, what's this about?"

"It is the tragedy of our times that there are any number of good reasons to kill oneself. It takes courage to go on living with the world the way it is. Rashmi Jones was a troubled young woman. She lacked that courage. That doesn't make her a bad person, just a dead one."

I patted my pocket, looking for my sidekick. Still there. I pulled it out and pressed *record*. I didn't ask for permission. "So I should mind my own business?"

"That would be a bad career move in your profession. How old are you, Fay?"

"Thirty-three."

"Then you were born of a virgin." She leaned back, slid off the kneeler and onto the pew. "Seeded by the devils. I'm old enough to have had a father, Fay. I actually remember him a little. A very little."

"Don't start." I spun out of the pew into the aisle. I hated cock nostalgia. This granny had me chewing aluminum foil; I would have spat it at Christ himself if he had dared come down off his cross. "You want to know one reason why my generation jumps out of windows and sucks on cyanide? It's because twists like you make us feel guilty about how we came to be. You want to call me devil's spawn, go ahead. Enjoy yourself. Live it up. Because we're just waiting for you old bitches to die off. Someday this foolish church is going to dry up and blow away and you know what? We'll go dancing that night, because we'll be a hell of a lot happier without you to remind us of what you lost and who we can never be."

She seemed perversely pleased by my show of emotion. "You're an angry woman, Fay."

"Yeah," I said, "but I'm kind to children and small animals."

"What is that anger doing to your soul? Many young people find solace in Christ."

"Like Alix and Gratiana?"

She folded her hands; the silver ring shone dully. "As I said, they have offered to turn themselves . . ."

"Keep them. I'm done with them." I was cooling off fast. I paused, considering my next move. Then I sat down on the pew next to Father Elaine, showed her my sidekick and made sure she saw me pause the recording. Our eyes met. We understood each other. "Did you marry Kate Vermeil and Rashmi Jones yesterday?"

She didn't hesitate. "I performed the ceremony. I never filed the documents."

"Do you know why Rashmi killed herself?"

"Not exactly." She held my gaze. "I understand she left a note."

"Yeah, the note. I found it on her sidekick. She wrote, 'Life is too hard to handle and I can't handle it so I've got to go now. I love you mom sorry.' A little generic for a would-be writer, wouldn't you say? And the thing is, there's nothing in the note about Kate. I didn't even know she existed until this morning. Now I have a problem with that. The cops would have the same problem if I gave it to them."

"But you haven't."

"Not yet."

She thought about that for a while.

"My understanding," said Father Elaine at last, "is that Kate and Rashmi had a disagreement shortly after the ceremony." She was tiptoeing around words as if one of them might wake up and start screaming. "I don't know exactly what it was about. Rashmi left, Kate stayed here. Someone was with her all yesterday afternoon and all last night."

"Because you thought she might need an alibi?"

She let that pass. "Kate was upset when she heard the news. She blames herself, although I am certain she is without blame."

"She's here now?"

"No." Father Elaine shrugged. "I sent her away when I learned you were looking for her."

"And you want me to stop."

"You are being needlessly cruel, you know. The poor girl is grieving."

"Another poor girl is dead." I reached into my pocket for my penlight. "Can I see your ring?"

That puzzled her. She extended her left hand and I shone the light on it. Her skin was freckled but soft, the nails flawless. She would not be getting them done at a dump like the Adagio Spa.

"What do these letters mean?" I asked. "IHS?"

"*In hoc signo vinces*. 'In this sign you will conquer.' The emperor Constantine had a vision of a cross in the sky with those words written in fire on it. This was just before a major battle. He had his soldiers paint the cross on their shields and then he won the day against a superior force."

"Cute." I snapped the light off. "What's it mean to you?"

"The Bride of God herself gave this to me." Her face lit up, as if she were listening to an angelic chorus chant her name. "In recognition of my special vocation. You see, Fay, our Church has no intention of drying up and blowing away. Long after my generation is gone, believers will continue to gather in Christ's name. And someday they'll finish the work we have begun. Someday they will exorcise the devils."

If she knew how loopy that sounded, she didn't show it. "Okay, here's the way it is," I said. "Forget Kate Vermeil. I only wanted to find her so she could lead me to you. A devil named Seeren hired me to look for you. It wants a meeting."

"With me?" Father Elaine went pale. "What for?"

"I just find them." I enjoyed watching her squirm. "I don't ask why."

She folded her hands as if to pray, then leaned her head against them and closed her eyes. She sat like that for almost a minute. I decided to let her brood, not that I had much choice. The fiery pit of hell could've opened up and she wouldn't have noticed.

Finally, she shivered and sat up. "I have to find out how much they know." She gazed up at the enormous crucifix. "I'll see this devil, but on one condition: you guarantee my safety."

"Sure." I couldn't help myself; I laughed. The sound echoed, profaning the silence. "Just how am I supposed to do that? They disappeared half the population of Earth without breaking a sweat."

"You have their confidence," she said. "And mine."

A vast and absurd peace had settled over her; she was seeing the world through the gauze of faith. She was a fool if she thought I could go up against the devils. Maybe she believed Christ the Man would swoop down from heaven to protect her, but then he hadn't been seen around the old neighborhood much of late. Or maybe she had projected herself into the mind of the martyrs who would embrace the sword, kiss the ax that would take their heads. I reminded myself that her delusions were none of my business.

Besides, I needed the money. And suddenly I just had to get out of that big, empty church.

"My office is at 35 Market," I said. "Third floor. I'll try to set something up for six tonight." I stood. "Look, if they want to take you, you're probably gone. But I'll record everything and squawk as loud as I can."

"I believe you will," she said, her face aglow.

<h1 style="text-align:center">5</h1>

I didn't go to my office after I locked my bike to the rack on Market Street. Instead I went to find George. He was stripping varnish from the beadboard wainscoting in Donna Belasco's old office on the fifth floor. Donna's office had been vacant since last fall, when she had closed her law practice and gone south to count waves at Daytona Beach. At least, that's what I hoped she was doing; the last I'd heard from her was a Christmas card. I missed Donna; she was one of the few grannies who tried to understand what it was like to grow up the way we did. And she had been generous about steering work my way.

"Hey George," I said. "You can tell your boss that I found the ring."

"This one offers the congratulations." The arm holding the brush froze over the can of stripper as he swiveled his head to face me. "You have proved true superiority, Fay." George had done a good job maintaining our building since coming to us a year ago, although he had something against wood grain. We had to stop him from painting over the mahogany paneling in the foyer.

I hated to close the door but this conversation needed some privacy. "So I've set up a meeting." The stink of the varnish stripper was barbed wire up my nose. "Father Elaine Horváth will be here at six."

George said nothing. Trying to read a bot is like trying to read a refrigerator. I assumed that he was relaying this information to Seeren. Would the devil be displeased that I had booked its meeting into my office?

"Seeren is impressed by your speedy accomplishment," George said at last. "Credit has been allotted to this one for suggesting it task you."

"Great, take ten bucks a month off my rent. Just so you know, I promised Father Elaine she'd be safe here. Seeren is not going to make a liar out of me, is it?"

"Seeren rejects violence. It's a regrettable technique."

"Yeah, but if Seeren disappears her to wherever, does that count?"

George's head swiveled back toward the wainscoting. "Father Elaine Horváth will be invited to leave freely, if such is her intention." The brush dipped into the can. "Was Kate Vermeil also found?"

"No," I said. "I looked, but then Father Elaine found me. By the way, she didn't live at 465 12th Avenue."

"Seeren had otherwise information." The old varnish bubbled and sagged where George had applied stripper. "Such error makes a curiosity."

It was a little thing, but it pricked at me as I walked down to the third floor. Was I pleased to discover that the devils were neither omnipotent nor infallible? Not particularly. For all their crimes against humanity, the devils and their bots were pretty much running our world now. It had been a small if bitter comfort to imagine that they knew exactly what they were doing.

I passed crazy Martha's door, which was open, on the way to my office. "Yaga combany wading," she called.

I backtracked. My neighbor was at her desk, wearing her Technopro gas mask, which she claimed protected her from chlorine, hydrogen sulfide, sulfur dioxide, ammonia, bacteria, viruses, dust, pollen, cat dander, mold spores, nuclear fallout, and sexual harassment. Unfortunately, it also made her almost unintelligible.

"Try that again," I said.

"You've. Got. Company. Waiting."

"Who is it?"

She shook the mask and shrugged. The light of her desktop was reflected in the faceplate. I could see numbers swarming like black ants across the rows and columns of a spreadsheet.

"What's with the mask?"

"We. Had. A. Devil. In. The. Building."

"Really?" I said. "When?"

"Morning."

There was no reason why a devil shouldn't come into our building, no law against having one for a client. But there was an accusation in Martha's look that I couldn't deny. Had I betrayed us all by taking the case? She said, "Hate. Devils."

"Yeah," I said. "Me too."

I opened my door and saw that it was Sharifa who was waiting for me. She was trying on a smile that didn't fit. "Hi Fay," she said. She looked as elegant as always and as weary as I had ever seen her. She was wearing a peppered black linen dress and black dress sandals with thin crossover straps. Those weren't doctor shoes—they were pull down the shades and turn up the music shoes. They made me very sad.

As I turned to close the door, she must have spotted the patch of blood that had dried in my hair. "You're hurt!" I had almost forgotten about it—there was no percentage in remembering that I was in pain. She shot out of her chair. "What happened?"

"I slipped in the shower," I said.

"Let me look."

I tilted my head toward her and she probed the lump gently. "You could have a concussion."

"PI's don't get concussions. Says so right on the license."

"Sit," she said. "Let me clean this up. I'll just run to the bathroom for some water."

I sat and watched her go. I thought about locking the door behind her but I deserved whatever I had coming. I opened the bottom drawer of the desk, slipped two plastic cups off the stack and brought Johnnie Walker in for a consultation.

Sharifa bustled through the doorway with a cup of water in one hand and a fistful of paper towels in the other but caught herself when she saw the bottle. "When did this start?"

"Just now." I picked up my cup and slugged two fingers of Black Label scotch. "Want some?"

"I don't know," she said. "Are we having fun or are we self-medicating?"

I let that pass. She dabbed at the lump with a damp paper towel. I could smell her perfume, lemon blossoms on a summer breeze and just the smallest bead of sweat. Her scent got along nicely with the liquid smoke of the scotch. She brushed against me and I could feel her body beneath her dress. At that moment I wanted her more than I wanted to breathe.

"Sit down," I said.

"I'm not done yet," she said.

I pointed at a chair. "Sit, damn it."

She dropped the paper towel in my trash as she went by.

"You asked me a question this morning," I said. "I should've given you the answer. I had the abortion last week."

She studied her hands. I don't know why; they weren't doing anything. They were just sitting in her lap, minding their own business.

"I told you when we first got together, that's what I'd do when I got seeded," I said.

"I know."

"I just didn't see any good choices," I said. "I know the world needs children, but I have a life to lead. Maybe it's a rude, pointless, dirty life but it's what I have. Being a mother . . . that's someone else's life."

"I understand," said Sharifa. Her voice was so small it could have crawled under a thimble. "It's just . . . it was all so sudden. You told me and then we were fighting and I didn't have time to think things through."

"I got tested in the morning. I told you that afternoon. I wasn't keeping anything a secret."

She folded her arms against her chest as if she were cold. "And when I get seeded, what then?"

"You'll do what's best for you."

She sighed. "Pour me some medication, would you?"

I poured scotch into both cups, came around the desk and handed Sharifa hers. She drank, held the whiskey in her mouth for a moment and then swallowed.

"Fay, I . . ." The corners of her mouth were twitchy and she bit her lip. "Your mother told me once that when she realized she was pregnant with you, she was so happy. So happy. It was when everything was crashing around everyone. She said you were the gift she needed to . . . not to . . ."

"I got the gift lecture, Sharifa. Too many times. She made the devils sound like Santa Claus. Or the stork."

She glanced down as if surprised to discover that she was still holding the cup. She drained it at a gulp and set it on my desk. "I'm a doctor. I know they do this to us; I just wish I knew how. But it isn't a bad thing. Having you in the world can't be a bad thing."

I wasn't sure about that, but I kept my opinion to myself.

"Sometimes I feel like I'm trying to carry water in my hands but it's all leaking out and there's nothing I can do to stop it." She started rubbing her right hand up and down her left forearm. "People keep killing themselves. Maybe it's not as bad as it used to be, but still. The birth rate is barely at replacement levels. Maybe we're doomed. Did you ever think that? That we might go extinct?"

"No."

Sharifa was silent for a long time. She kept rubbing her arm. "It should've been me doing your abortion," she said at last. "Then we'd both have to live with it."

I was one tough PI. I kept a bottle of scotch in the bottom drawer and had a devil for a client. Tommys whacked me with nightsticks and pumped knockout spray into my face. But even I had a breaking point, and Dr. Sharifa Ramirez was pushing me up against it hard. I wanted to pull her into my arms and kiss her forehead, her cheeks, her graceful neck. But I couldn't give in to her that way—not now anyway. Maybe never again. I had a case, and I needed to hold the best part of myself in reserve until it was finished. "I'll be in charge of the guilt, Sharifa." I said. "You be in charge of saving lives." I came around the desk. "I've got work to do, so you go home now, sweetheart." I kissed her on the forehead. "I'll see you there."

Easier to say than to believe.

6

Sharifa was long gone by the time Father Elaine arrived at ten minutes to six. She brought muscle with her; Gratiana loitered in the hallway surveying my office with sullen calculation, as if estimating how long it would take to break down the door, leap over the desk and wring somebody's neck. I shouldn't have been surprised that Father Elaine's faith in me had wavered—hell, I didn't have much faith in me. However, I thought she showed poor judgment in bringing this particular thug along. I invited Gratiana to remove herself from my building. Perhaps she might perform an auto-erotic act in front of a speeding bus? Father Elaine dismissed her, and she slunk off.

Father Elaine appeared calm, but I could tell that she was as nervous as two mice and a gerbil. I hadn't really had a good look at her in the dim church, but now I studied her in case I had to write her up for the Missing Persons Index. She was a tallish woman with round shoulders and a bit of a stoop. Her eyes were the brown of wet sand; her cheeks were bloodless. Her smile was not quite as convincing in good light it had been in gloom. She made some trifling small talk, which I did nothing to help with. Then she stood at the window, watching. A wingtip loafer tapped against bare floor.

It was about ten after when my desktop chirped. I waved open the icon and accepted the transfer of a thousand dollars. Seeren had a hell of a calling card. "I think they're coming," I said. I opened the door and stepped into the hall to wait for them.

"It gives Seeren the bright pleasure to meet you, Father Elaine Horváth," said George as they shuffled into the office.

She focused everything she had on the devil. "Just Father, if you don't mind." The bot was nothing but furniture to her.

"It's kind of crowded in here," I said. "If you want, I can wait outside . . ."

Father Elaine's façade cracked for an instant, but she patched it up nicely. "I'm sure we can manage," she said.

"This one implores Fay to remain," said George.

We sorted ourselves out. Seeren assumed its perch on top of the file cabinet and George came around and compacted himself next to me. Father Elaine pushed her chair next to the door. I think she was content to be stationed nearest the exit. George looked at Father Elaine. She looked at Seeren. Seeren looked out the window. I watched them all.

"Seeren offers sorrow over the regrettable death of Rashmi Jones," said George. "Such Rashmi was of your church?"

"She was a member, yes."

"According to Fay Hardaway, a fact is that Father married Kate Vermeil and Rashmi Jones."

I didn't like that. I didn't like it at all.

Father Elaine hesitated only a beat. "Yes."

"Would Father permit Seeren to locate Kate Vermeil?"

"I know where she is, Seeren," said Father Elaine. "I don't think she needs to be brought into this."

"Indulge this one and reconsider, Father. Is such person pregnant?"

Her manner had been cool, but now it dropped forty degrees. "Why would you say that?"

"Perhaps such person is soon to become pregnant?"

"How would I know? If she is, it would be your doing, Seeren."

"Father well understands *in vitro* fertilization?"

"I've heard of it, yes." Father Elaine's shrug was far too elaborate. "I can't say I understand it."

"Father has heard then of transvaginal oocyte retrieval?"

She thrust out her chin. "No."

"Haploidisation of somatic cells?"

She froze.

"Has Father considered then growing artificial sperm from embryonic stem cells?"

"I'm a priest, Seeren." Only her lips moved. "Not a biologist."

"Does the Christer Church make further intentions to induce pregnancies in certain members? Such as Kate Vermeil?"

Father Elaine rose painfully from the chair. I thought she might try to run, but now martyr's fire burned through the shell of ice that had encased her. "We're doing Christ's work, Seeren. We reject your obscene seeding. We are saving ourselves from you and you can't stop us."

Seeren beat its wings, once, twice, and crowed. It was a dense, jarring sound, like steel scraping steel. I hadn't known that devils could make any sound at all, but hearing that hellish scream made me want to dive under my desk and curl up in a ball. I took it though, and so did Father Elaine. I gave her credit for that.

"Seeren makes no argument with the Christer Church," said George. "Seeren upholds only the brightest encouragement for such pregnancies."

Father Elaine's face twitched in disbelief and then a flicker of disappointment passed over her. Maybe she was upset to have been cheated of her glorious death. She was a granny after all, of the generation that had embraced the suicide culture. For the first time, she turned to the bot. "What?"

"Seeren tasks Father to help numerous Christers become pregnant. Christers who do such choosing will then give birth."

She sank back onto her chair.

"Too many humans now refuse the seeding," said the bot. "Not all then give birth. This was not foreseen. It is regrettable."

Without my noticing, my hands had become fists. My knuckles were white.

"Seeren will announce its true satisfaction with the accomplishment of the Christer Church. It offers a single caution. Christers must assure all to make no XY chromosome."

Father Elaine was impassive. "Will you continue to seed all non-believers?"

"It is prudent for the survival of humans."

She nodded and faced Seeren. "How will you know if we do try to bring men back into the world?"

The bot said nothing. The silence thickened as we waited. Maybe the devil thought it didn't need to make threats.

"Well, then." Father Elaine rose once again. Some of the stoop had gone out of her shoulders. She was trying to play it calm, but I knew she'd be skipping by the time she hit the sidewalk. Probably she thought she had won a great victory. In any event, she was done with this little party.

But it was my little party, and I wasn't about to let it break up with the devils holding hands with the Christers. "Wait," I said. "Father, you better get Gratiana up here. And if you've got any other muscle in the neighborhood, call them right now. You need backup fast."

Seeren glanced away from the window and at me.

"Why?" Father Elaine already had her sidekick out. "What is this?"

"There's a problem."

"Fay Hardaway," said George sharply. "Indulge this one and recall your task. Your employment has been accomplished."

"Then I'm on my own time now, George." I thought maybe Seeren would try to leave, but it remained on its perch. Maybe the devil didn't care what I did. Or else it found me amusing. I could be an amusing girl, in my own obtuse way.

Gratiana tore the door open. She held her nightstick high, as if expecting to dive into a bloodbath. When she saw our cool tableau, she let it drop to her side.

"Scooch over, Father," I said, "and let her in. Gratiana, you can leave the door open but keep that toothpick handy. I'm pretty sure you're going to be using it before long."

"The others are right behind me, Father," said Gratiana as she crowded into the room. "Two, maybe three minutes."

"Just enough time." I let my hand fall to the middle drawer of my desk. "I have a question for you, Father." I slid the drawer open. "How did Seeren know all that stuff about haploid this and *in vitro* that?"

"It's a devil." She watched me thoughtfully. "They come from two hundred light years away. How do they know anything?"

"Fair enough. But they also knew that you married Kate and Rashmi. George here just said that I told them, except I never did. That was a mistake. It made me wonder whether they knew who you were all along. It's funny, I used to be convinced that the devils were infallible, but now I'm thinking that they can screw up any day of the week, just like the rest of us. They're almost human that way."

"A regrettable misstatement was made." The bot's neck extended until his head was level with mine. "Indulge this one and refrain from further humiliation."

"I've refrained for too long, George. I've had a bellyful of refraining." I was pretty sure that George could see the open drawer, which meant that the devil would know what was in it as well. I wondered how far they'd let me go. "The question is, Father, if the devils already knew who you were, why would Seeren hire me to find you?"

"Go on," she said.

My chest was tight. Nobody tried to stop me, so I went ahead and stuck my head into the lion's mouth. Like that little girl at school, I'd always wanted to have a real job when I grew up. "You've got a leak, Father. Your problem isn't devil super-science. It's the good old-fashioned Judas kiss. Seeren has an inside source, a mole among your congregation. When it decided the time had come to meet with you, it wanted to be sure that none of you would suspect where its information was actually coming from. It decided that the way to give the mole cover was to hire some gullible PI to pretend to find stuff out. I may be a little slow and a lot greedy but I do have a few shreds of pride. I can't let myself be played for an idiot." I thought I heard footsteps on the stairs, but maybe it was just my own blood pounding. "You see, Father, I don't think that Seeren really trusts you. I sure didn't hear you promise just now not to be making little boys. And yes, if they find out about the boy babies, the devils could just disappear them, but you and the Bride of God and all your batty friends would find ways to make that very public, very messy. I'm guessing that's part of your plan, isn't it? To remind us who the devils are, what they did? Maybe get people into the streets again. Since the devils still need to know what you're up to, the mole had to be protected."

Father Elaine flushed with anger. "Do you know who she is?"

"No," I said. "But you could probably narrow it down to a very few. You said you married Rashmi and Kate, but that you never filed the documents. But you needed someone to witness the ceremony. Someone who was taking pix and would send one to Seeren . . ."

Actually, my timing was a little off. Gratiana launched herself at me just as big Alix hurtled through the doorway. I had the air taser out of the drawer, but my plan had been for the Christers to clean up their own mess. I came out of my chair and raised the taser but even 50,000 volts wasn't going to keep that snarling bitch off me.

I heard a huge wet pop, not so much an explosion but an implosion. There was a rush of air through the doorway but the room was preternaturally quiet, as if someone had just stopped screaming. We humans gaped at the void that had formerly been occupied by Gratiana. The familiar surroundings of my office seemed to warp and stretch to accommodate that vacancy. If she could vanish so completely, then maybe chairs could waltz on the ceiling and trashcans could sing *Carmen*. For the first time in my life I had a rough sense of what the grannies had felt when the devils disappeared their men. It would be one thing if Gratiana were merely dead, if there were blood, and bone and flesh left behind. A body to be buried. But this was an offense against reality itself. It undermined our common belief that the world is indeed a fact, that we exist at all. I could understand how it could unhinge a billion minds. I was standing next to Father Elaine beside the open door to my office holding the taser and I couldn't remember how I had gotten there.

Seeren hopped down off the bookcase as if nothing important had happened and wrapped its translucent wings around its body. The devil didn't seem surprised at all that a woman had just disappeared. Maybe there was no surprising a devil.

And then it occurred to me that this probably wasn't the first time since they had taken all the men that the devils had disappeared someone. Maybe they did it all the time. I thought of all the missing persons whom I had never found. I could see the files in Julie Epstein's office bulging with unsolved cases. Had Seeren done this thing to teach us the fragility of being? Or had it just been a clumsy attempt to cover up its regrettable mistakes?

As the devil waddled toward the door, Alix made a move as if to block its exit. After what she had just seen, I thought that was probably the most boneheaded, brave move I had ever seen.

"Let them go." Father Elaine's voice quavered. Her eyes were like wounds.

Alix stepped aside and the devil and the bot left us. We listened to the devil scrabble down the hall. I heard the elevator doors open and then close.

Then Father Elaine staggered and put a hand on my shoulder. She looked like a granny now.

"There are no boy babies," she said. "Not yet. You have to believe me."

"You know what?" I shook free of her. "I don't care." I wanted them gone. I wanted to sit alone at my desk and watch the room fill with night.

"You don't understand."

"And I don't want to." I had to set the taser on the desk or I might have used it on her.

"Kate Vermeil is pregnant with one of our babies," said Father Elaine. "It's a little girl, I swear it."

"So you've made Seeren proud. What's the problem?"

Alix spoke for the first time. "Gratiana was in charge of Kate."

7

The Poison Society was lit brightly enough to give a camel a headache. If you forgot your sunglasses, there was a rack of freebies at the door. Set into the walls were terrariums where diamondback rattlers coiled in the sand, black neck cobras dangled from dead branches, and brown scorpions basked on ceramic rocks. The hemlock was in bloom; clusters of small, white flowers opened like umbrellas. Upright stems of monkshood were interplanted with death cap mushrooms in wine casks cut in half. Curare vines climbed the pergola over the alcohol bar.

I counted maybe fifty customers in the main room, which was probably a good crowd for a Wednesday night. I had no idea yet how many might be lurking in the specialty shops that opened off this space, where a nice girl might arrange for a guaranteed-safe session of sexual asphyxia either by hanging or drowning, or else get her cerebrum toasted by various brain lightning generators. I was hoping Kate was out in the open with the relatively sane folks. I didn't really want to poke around in the shops, but I would if I had to. I thought I owed it to Rashmi Jones.

I strolled around, pretending to look at various animals and plants, carrying a tumbler filled with a little Johnnie Walker Black Label and a lot of water. I knew Kate would be disguised but if I could narrow the field of marks down to three or four, I might actually snoop her. Of course, she might be on the other side of town, but this was my only play. My guess was that she'd switch styles, so I wasn't necessarily looking for a tommy. Her hair wouldn't be brunette, and her skin would probably be darker, and contacts could give her cat's eyes or zebra eyes or American flags, if she wanted. But even with padding and lifts she couldn't change her body type enough to fool a good scan. And I had her data from the Christer medical files loaded into my sidekick.

Father Elaine had tried Kate's call, but she wouldn't pick up. That made perfect sense since just about anyone could put their hands on software that could replicate voices. There were bots that could sing enough like Velma Stone to fool her own mother. Kate and Gratiana would have agreed on a safe word. Our problem was that Gratiana had taken it with her to hell, or wherever the devil had consigned her.

The first mark my sidekick picked out was a redhead in silk pajamas and lime green bunny slippers. A scan matched her to Kate's numbers to within 5%. I bumped into her just enough to plant the snoop, a sticky homing device the size of a baby tooth.

"Scuse me, sorry." I said. "S-So sorry." I slopped some of my drink onto the floor.

She gave me a glare that would have withered a cactus and I noodled off. As soon as I was out of her sight, I hit the button on my sidekick to which I'd assigned Kate's call. When Kate picked up, the snoop would know if the call had come from me and signal my sidekick that I had found her. The redhead wasn't Kate. Neither was the bald jane in distressed leather.

The problem with trying to locate her this way was that if I kept calling her, she'd get suspicious and lose the sidekick.

I lingered by a pufferfish aquarium. Next to it was a safe, and in front of that a tootsie fiddled with the combination lock. I scanned her and got a match to within 2%. She was wearing a spangle wig and a stretch lace dress with a ruffle front. When she opened the door of the safe, I saw that it was made of clear luxar. She reached in, then slammed the door and then trotted off as if she were late for the last train of the night.

I peeked through the door of the safe. Inside was a stack of squat, blue inhalers like the one Rashmi had used to kill herself. On the wall above the safe, the management of The Poison Society had spray-painted a mock graffiti. *21L 4R 11L.* There was no time to plant a snoop. I pressed the call button as I tailed her.

With a strangled cry, the tootsie yanked a sidekick from her clutch purse, dropped it to the floor and stamped on it. She was wearing Donya Durand ice and taupe flat slingbacks.

As I moved toward her, Kate Vermeil saw me and ducked into one of the shops. She dodged past fifty-five gallon drums of carbon tetrachloride and dimethylsulfate and burst through the rear door of the shop into an alley. I saw her fumbling with the cap of the inhaler. I hurled myself at her and caught at her legs. Her right shoe came off in my hand, but I grabbed her left ankle and she went down. She still had the inhaler and was trying to bring it to her mouth. I leapt on top of her and wrenched it away.

"Do you really want to kill yourself?" I aimed the inhaler at her face and screamed at her. "Do you, Kate? Do you?" The air in the alley was thick with despair and I was choking on it. "Come on, Kate. Let's do it!"

"No." Her head thrashed back and forth. "No, please. Stop."

Her terror fed mine. "Then what the hell are you doing with this thing?" I was shaking so badly that when I tried to pitch the inhaler into the dumpster, it hit the pavement only six feet away. I had come so close to screwing up. I climbed off her and rolled on my back and soaked myself in the night sky. When I screwed up, people died. "Cyanide is awful bad for the baby," I said.

"How do you know about my baby?" Her face was rigid with fear. "Who are you?"

I could breathe again, although I wasn't sure I wanted to. "Fay Hardaway." I gasped. "I'm a PI; I left you a message this morning. Najma Jones hired me to find her daughter."

"Rashmi is dead."

"I know," I said. "So is Gratiana." I sat up and looked at her. "Father Elaine will be glad to see you."

Kate's eyes were wide, but I don't think she was seeing the alley. "Gratiana said the devils would come after me." She was still seeing the business end of the inhaler. "She said that if I didn't hear from her by tomorrow then we had lost everything and I should . . . do it. You know, to protect the church. And just now my sidekick picked up three times in ten minutes only there was nobody there and so I knew it was time."

"That was me, Kate. Sorry." I retrieved the Donya Durand sling-back I'd stripped off her foot and gave it back to her. "Tell me where you got this?"

"It was Rashmi's. We bought them together at Grayles. Actually I picked them out. That was before . . . I loved her, you know, but she was crazy. I can see that now, although it's kind of too late. I mean, she was okay when she was taking her meds, but she would stop every so often. She called it taking a vacation from herself. Only it was no vacation for anyone else, especially not for me. She decided to go off on the day we got married and didn't tell me and all of a sudden after the ceremony we got into this huge fight about the baby and who loved who more and she started throwing things at me—these shoes—and then ran out of the church barefoot. I don't think she ever really understood about . . . you know, what we were trying to do. I mean, I've talked to the Bride of God herself . . . but Rashmi." Kate rubbed her eye and her hand came away wet.

I sat her up and put my arm around her. "That's all right. Not really your fault. I think poor Rashmi must have been hanging by a thread. We all are. The whole human race, or what's left of it." We sat there for a moment.

"I saw her mom this morning," I said. "She said to tell you she was sorry."

Kate sniffed. "Sorry? What for?"

I shrugged.

"I know she didn't have much use for me," said Kate. "At least that's what Rashmi always said. But as far as I'm concerned the woman was a saint to put up with Rashmi and her mood swings and all the acting out. She was always there for her. And the thing is, Rashmi hated her for it."

I got to my knees, then to my feet. I helped Kate up. The alley was dark, but that wasn't really the problem. Even in the light of day, I hadn't seen anything.

8

I had no trouble finding space at the bike rack in front of Ronald Reagan Elementary. The building seemed to be drowsing in the heavy morning air, its brick wings enfolding the empty playground. A janitor bot was vacuuming the swimming pool, another was plucking spent blossoms from the clematis fence. The bots were headache yellow; the letters RRE in puffy orange slanted across their torsos. The gardening bot informed me that school wouldn't start for an hour. That was fine with me. This was just a courtesy call, part of the total service commitment I made to all the clients whom I had failed. I asked if I could see Najma Jones and he said he doubted that any of the teachers were in quite this early but he walked me to the office. He paged her; I signed the visitors' log. When her voice crackled over the intercom, I told the bot that I knew the way to her classroom.

I paused at the open door. Rashmi's mom had her back to me. She was wearing a sleeveless navy dress with cream-colored dupatta scarf draped over her shoulders. She passed down a row of empty desks, perching origami animals at the center of each. There were three kinds of elephants, ducks and ducklings, a blue giraffe, a pink cat that might have been a lion.

"Please come in, Ms. Hardaway," she said without turning around. She had teacher radar; she could see behind her back and around a corner.

"I stopped by your house." I slouched into the room like a kid who had lost her civics homework. "I thought I might catch you before you left for school." I leaned against a desk in the front row and picked up the purple crocodile on it. "You fold these yourself?"

"I couldn't sleep last night," she said, "so finally I gave up and went for a walk. I ended up here. I like coming to school early, especially when no one else is around. There is so much time." She had one origami swan left over which she set on her own desk. "Staying after is different. If you're always the last one out at night, you're admitting that you haven't got anything to rush home to. It's pathetic, actually." She settled behind her desk and began opening windows on her desktop. "I've been teaching the girls to fold the ducks. They seem to like it. It's a challenging grade, the fifth. They come to me as bright and happy children and I am supposed to teach them fractions and pack them off to middle school. I shudder to think what happens to them there."

"How old are they?"

"Ten when they started. Most of them have turned eleven already. They graduate next week." She peered at the files she had opened. "Some of them."

"I take it on faith that I was eleven once," I said, "but I just don't remember."

"Your generation grew up in unhappy times." Her face glowed in the phosphors. "You haven't had a daughter yet, have you, Ms. Hardaway?"

"No."

We contemplated my childlessness for a moment.

"Did Rashmi like origami?" I didn't mean anything by it. I just didn't want to listen to the silence anymore.

"Rashmi?" She frowned, as if her daughter were a not-very-interesting kid she had taught years ago. "No. Rashmi was a difficult child."

"I found Kate Vermeil last night," I said. "I told her what you said, that you were sorry. She wanted to know what for."

"What for?"

"She said that Rashmi was crazy. And that she hated you for having her."

"She never hated me," said Najma quickly. "Yes, Rashmi was a sad girl. Anxious. What is this about, Ms. Hardaway?"

"I think you were at the Comfort Inn that night. If you want to talk about that, I would like to hear what you have to say. If not, I'll leave now."

She stared at me for a moment, her expression unreadable. "You know, I actually wanted to have many children." She got up from the desk, crossed the room, and shut the door as if it were made of hand-blown glass. "When the seeding first began, I went down to City Hall and actually volunteered. That just wasn't done. Most women were horrified to find themselves pregnant. I talked to a bot, who took my name and address and then told me to go home and wait. If I wanted more children after my first, I was certainly encouraged to make a request. It felt like I was joining one of those mail order music clubs." She smiled and tugged at her dupatta. "But when Rashmi was born, everything changed. Sometimes she was such a needy baby, fussing to be picked up, but then she would lie in her crib for hours, listless and withdrawn. She started antidepressants when she was five and they helped. And the Department of Youth Services issued me a full-time bot helper when I started teaching. But Rashmi was always a handful. And since I was all by myself, I didn't feel like I had enough to give to another child."

"You never married?" I asked. "Found a partner?"

"Married who?" Her voice rose sharply. "Another woman?" Her cheeks colored. "No. I wasn't interested in that."

Najma returned to her desk but did not sit down. "The girls will be coming soon." She leaned toward me, fists on the desktop. "What is it that you want to hear, Ms. Hardaway?"

"You found Rashmi before I did. How?"

"She called me. She said that she had had a fight with her girlfriend who was involved in some secret experiment that she couldn't tell me about and they were splitting up and everything was shit, the world was shit. She was off her meds, crying, not making a whole lot of sense. But that was nothing new. She always called me when she broke up with someone. I'm her mother."

"And when you got there?"

"She was sitting on the bed." Najma eyes focused on something I couldn't see. "She put the inhaler to her mouth when I opened the door." Najma was looking into Room 103 of the Comfort Inn. "And I thought to myself, what does this poor girl want? Does she want me to witness her death or stop it? I tried to talk to her, you know. She seemed to listen. But when I asked her to put the inhaler down, she wouldn't. I moved toward her, slowly. Slowly. I told her that she didn't have to do anything. That we could just go home. And then I was this close." She reached a hand across the desk. "And I couldn't help myself. I tried to swat it out of her mouth. Either she pressed the button or I set it off." She sat down abruptly and put her head in her hands. "She didn't get the full dose. It took forever before it was over. She was in agony."

"I think she'd made up her mind, Ms. Jones." I was only trying to comfort her. "She wrote the note."

"I wrote the note." She glared at me. "I did."

There was nothing I could say. All the words in all the languages that had ever been spoken wouldn't come close to expressing this mother's grief. I thought the weight of it must surely crush her.

Through the open windows, I heard the snort of the first bus pulling into the turnaround in front of the school. Najma Jones glanced out at it, gathered herself, and smiled. "Do you know what Rashmi means in Sanskrit?"

"No, ma'am."

"Ray of sunlight," she said. "The girls are here, Ms. Hardaway." She picked up the origami on her desk. "We have to be ready for them." She held it out to me. "Would you like a swan?"

By the time I came through the door of the school, the turn-around was filled with busses. Girls poured off them and swirled onto the playground: giggling girls, whispering girls, skipping girls, girls holding hands. And in the warm June sun, I could almost believe they were happy girls.

They paid no attention to me.

I tried Sharifa's call. "Hello?" Her voice was husky with sleep.

"Sorry I didn't make it home last night, sweetheart," I said. "Just wanted to let you know that I'm on my way."

Luck

THUMB SAT ON A ROCK, SOOTHING HIS SORE FEET in the river, in no hurry to get home. The stories the shell people had told filled him with foreboding. Meanwhile, he was certain that the spirits had taken Onion's soul down into the belly of the earth while he'd been gone. The sun was still two hands from the edge of the sky. There was plenty of time before dark. Before he reached the summer camp of the people. Before they would tell him his lover was dead. While he tried not to think of her, a dream found him.

In his dream, a great herd of mammoths tracked down from the stony northern hills through the pine forest all the way to the river. There were five and five and five and *five* mammoths . . . and then more, more than Thumb could have ever counted, even if he used the fingers and toes of all of the people. They were huge, almost too big to fit in the eye of his mind. They trampled trees like tall grass, dropped turds the size of boulders.

Old Owl told a story about the spirit who became a mammoth. He called the beast a *furry mountain of meat*. Owl had been the last to see a mammoth, years ago when he was just a boy. The rest of the people knew mammoths only from the drawings in the long cave.

An animal the size of a mountain—how could that be?

When Thumb's herd of mammoths reached the river, they dipped their trunks into the water. In a dream moment, they drank the river dry. Turtles scrambled into the reeds for shelter. Fish flopped in the mud and died.

After her last baby had been born dead, Onion flopped on her mat like a fish.

Ruc-ruc-ruc-ruc-ruc!

The dream turned to smoke at the sound. Thumb leapt up and almost fell into the river. His feet had gone numb in the cold water and he couldn't feel the ground beneath them. He pulled on his boots, snatched his spear, fit it to his throwing stick.

Ruc-ruc-ruc!

The rumbling came from upriver, around the bend. Thumb had never heard anything like it. An earth sound, like the crack of a falling tree or a boulder crashing off a cliff, except it was wet and hot and alive. A sound that only an animal could make.

He crept deeper into the thicket before he started upriver. Hunting courage pounded in his chest. He strained ear and eye and nose after the quarry. He was ready to jump over the sky. It was hard to make himself go quietly but he parted branches and slid through the leaves.

Man. Come out, man.

The whisper rasped inside his head. He felt it on the tip of his nose, on the hair of his scalp, at the root of his cock, and on the bottoms of his tingling feet. It had to be the whisper of a spirit. This was his luck then, whether good or bad. He had no choice. He must obey. Thumb rose up and pushed through the undergrowth toward the water. He knew that he might be about to have his soul stripped from his body. The thought did not much bother him. If Onion were really dead, he would be with her in the belly of the earth.

I am, man.

Thumb was not surprised to see a mammoth standing on the opposite bank. It must have sent the dream and whispered to him in a spirit voice. The surprise was what he felt as he gazed into its round, black eyes. This was no monster that could break trees and drain rivers. It wasn't much taller than he was. Yes, the trunk snaked like a nightmare and the tusks were long and curved and dangerous, but as Thumb took its measure, his confidence surged. The people had no weapon that could wound a mountain or strike at a spirit. But this was an animal that men might dare to hunt and bring down. Thumb let a laugh bubble out of his chest.

"I am Thumb," he shouted across the river at it, "keeper of the caves!" Then he danced, five hops on the spongy bank. He finished by striking the butt of his spear against an alder.

The mammoth raised its trunk and trumpeted in reply. The piercing cry sent a shiver through Thumb. But he was not cowed. He had heard the death scream of a bison and a cave bear's roar. "This is the valley of the people." He struck the alder again.

At that moment, something at the far edge of his vision jumped. A blur that might have been a deer, or a man in deerskin, plunged into the woods. Was it the spirit? Then why had it run away from him? The mammoth didn't seem to care. It turned away from Thumb, curled its trunk around a willow branch, stripped it from the tree and stuffed it into its mouth. Thumb studied the mammoth as it ate, knowing that he would have to report everything he saw to Owl, the storyteller, and Blue, who spoke for the people. Besides, someday he might paint it on the wall of the cleft, if such was his luck.

It had to be the hairiest animal he had ever seen. The coarse fur was the color of bloodstone. It had thinned along the slope of the backbone but was matted and thick at the flanks. When the mammoth brushed against a low hanging branch, a swarm of flies buzzed out of its mangy coat. Thumb decided that it must be a full-grown animal because of the size of its tusks. The tip of the left one was broken off. The top of its skull was a round bump, like half of an onion.

Suddenly Thumb went very still. He knew why the mammoth had appeared to him, of all people. It was a sign. A turn of luck. "Is that it, great one?" he said. "Is that why you called me?"

The mammoth dipped its trunk into the river, sucked up water and then squirted it into its mouth. Thumb could see the tongue, gray in the middle, pink on the sides. Then he turned and ran hard for home. For the first time since the thin moon rose, he thought he might see his lover again.

The people made their main summer camp near the top of a low cliff overlooking the river. A rock outcrop sheltered the ledge where they chipped their knives and cooked their meals and laid their mats. When rain came, they ducked into a long lean-to covered with bison hides. The main hearth was at the center of the ledge. In the summer camp, the smoke of their fires could become sky and not sting the eyes and settle in the chest as it did in the winter lodge.

Five and five and five and three of the people gathered close around the hearth that night. Ash and Quick and Spear and Robin and Moon and Bone were away, trading chert with the horse people and waiting with them for the arrival of the reindeer herd. It was the Moon of the Falling Leaves. Thumb's breath made clouds in the cool air.

"Are you warm yet?" he said.

"My heart is," said Onion. He had his arm around her waist and they snuggled beneath a bearskin blanket. She was thin as grass. He could feel her ribs beneath his moist hands. Even when she was pregnant, she was never as big as the other women. Now her breasts were like those of a girl. Thumb had not known Onion when she was young. She had come to them from the horse people five and three summers ago, a round and beautiful woman. Since then she had given birth to three babies, all dead, and had gotten thinner and thinner. Thumb kissed her pale face. The last had almost killed her. But she was still beautiful. He could wait until she was stronger before they would lie together as lovers. That would be soon, he hoped. Her breath tickled his neck.

Bead finished whispering to Owl. The storyteller got up painfully, carrying his years like a skin filled with stones. He hobbled around to the back of the hearth and turned so that the flames were between him and the people. Firelight caught in the creases on his face. Just before he spoke, he straightened and squared his shoulders. Then his voice boomed as it had for all the summers Thumb could remember.

"This is a story of Thumb," he said, "who is the son of my sister and who walks both in the light of the sun and the darkness of the two caves. He gave his story to me so that I could give it to you. It has become a story of the people. I will tell it to you now, even though it doesn't have an ending."

The people yipped and grunted with unease. A story without an ending was bad luck.

Actually, Thumb had told his story mostly to Bead, Owl's lover, and Blue, who spoke for the people. Owl had listened for a while but then had dozed off, as he often did late in the day.

"We know," said Owl, "that Thumb loves Onion and Onion loves Thumb. They have slept nose to nose, belly to belly for five and three winters. She eats the meat he brings her. He eats the roots she digs for him."

"When you find time to hunt," whispered Onion.

"When you dig something besides stones." Thumb gave her a gentle nudge.

"Thumb needed to make paint for the new cave, which some call the cleft. For the red, he had to collect blood stones from the shell people's land. But after bearing a baby that never breathed, his lover became sick with a fever. He had a hard choice. No one ever wants such a choice. Thumb loves Onion, but because he loves the people too, he left her and went to the shell people's land."

Quail gave a low whistle of approval. Thumb was pleased when everyone joined in. Even Owl. Even Onion. Thumb's cheeks were warm.

"While Thumb was gone, a stranger came to us. He brought food gifts of two eels and a badger skin filled with apples, so we welcomed him. He told us his name was Singer. He was an old man, with white and gray and not much brown in his beard. He wore a headdress of the feather people and the deerskins of our people. But he didn't say where he came from and we didn't ask. Although we are a curious people, we are also polite."

Owl paused and waited for the laugh.

"When Singer saw Onion bundled by the fire, he told us that she was going to die. We all thought that he was right. Singer said that he could use his luck to turn hers, but that we must let him do whatever he wanted with her. We talked about what he said. It seemed strange that a man could turn his own luck or anyone else's. But none of us could help Onion. Finally we let Blue speak for us. He told Singer to use his luck.

"Singer crushed herbs from his pouch in a wooden bowl, mixed them with water and gave them to Onion to drink. She went limp but her eyes stayed open. It was as if her soul had left her body. Then he picked her up in his arms and carried her to the river. He laid her on the bank and took off her deerskin shirt and pants. With his two hands he scooped mud onto her naked body, covering her until all we could see was her mouth and her nose. There were some of us who thought this was bad luck." Owl struck his chest with his fist. "Or at least crazy luck. But we said nothing. When Singer finished with the mud, he began to sing."

Owl paused, gathered himself. His voice quavered under and around and sometimes on the notes.

> " 'Spirits, look at this woman!
> I have buried her for you.
> She has learned what it is like
> in the belly of the earth.
> Now you won't have to teach her.
> Leave her in the world awhile.
> Let her wake with her people.' "

Onion had gone stiff as a tree stump beside him. "Are you all right?" said Thumb. She nodded and squeezed his hand. With a feeling of dread, Thumb understood that even though she seemed better, his lover was still tangled in the stranger's luck.

The effort of singing Onion back to life, even though it was just part of the story, left Owl exhausted. He sat down abruptly and fell silent. Bead dipped a dried gourd into a water skin and scrabbled across the ledge to him. As he drank, she whispered to him. The old man's eyes were as distant as the ice mountains. The people sat in polite silence for several moments, waiting for him to begin again. Bead's talk grew more heated; Thumb could make out words. *Lose . . . Foolish . . . Let me!* Finally Owl grunted and pushed her away.

"A fly is buzzing in my ear," he said. "It asks if a woman can tell a man's story." A few people laughed. Bead's smile was tight. She scooted backward but did not rejoin those around the fire. Instead she crouched a few paces away from Owl and waited.

"Then Singer finished his luck song." The storyteller spoke from where he sat, which made everyone nervous. But it was better that he tell the story sitting down rather than stop. It was very bad luck to stop in the middle of a story, especially a story that had no end. "He took off his own clothes, picked Onion up and waded into the water. When the river had rinsed her of the mud, he climbed out of the river and dressed her. Then he kissed her as if she were his lover. She was asleep now, with her eyes closed. A deep sleep, yes, but not the almost-death that had squeezed her before. We could see her breathing. She didn't wake up until the next day. By then, Singer had left us." Owl lowered his voice so that everyone had to lean forward to hear him. "Nobody saw him go. Did he melt like snow? Blow away like smoke?"

He paused, even though he knew no one would answer.

"He was gone." Owl stared into the fire. "All he left was his luck."

The people waited again.

"And this story," he muttered finally, as if speaking to himself.

Silence.

"Is that all?" said little Flamesgirl, who had just lost her baby teeth and still didn't have her name. She had been squirming on her mother's lap during Owl's story. "What about Thumb? What about the big beastie?"

Flame pinched the girl's cheek hard. Everyone knew that she talked more than her mother ought to allow.

"The mammoth, old man," Bead called to Owl, loud enough for

everyone to hear. "I think you haven't told about the mammoth."
Owl grunted. "Old man." He struggled to his feet. "She calls me
old man." He shook his head in disbelief. "But when I was young,
just five and four summers old, I saw a mammoth. Maybe the last
one. I will never forget it. Such a fearsome creature . . . a nose like
a great snake and tusks that curved to the clouds. It was covered with
shaggy brown fur. When it roared, birds fell out of the sky. It was so
huge that the earth shook when it walked . . . and its foot, one foot
could crush three men . . . because it was bigger than the trees, I
saw it . . . a furry mountain of meat . . . What?"

As Owl was speaking, Blue rose and approached him. "I would
like to finish this story, Owl." Blue touched his arm; he looked very
embarrassed. Thumb was embarrassed too. "Will you let me?"

Owl puffed himself up. "Are you the storyteller now?"

"Thumb saw a mammoth today," said Blue gently. "Remember?"

Owl snorted and then glanced over at Bead. Her head was down,
as if she were counting her toes. Owl's jaw muscles worked but he
made no sound. Blue waited. Then Owl said, "Tell them whatever
you want." He turned away, brushed past Bead and stalked into the
darkness. Thumb could hear him climb the path to the top of the
cliff. A few heartbeats later, Bead went after him.

"He has seen many summers," said Blue, "They have filled him
up, I think. Still, it is luck to have him with us."

Then Blue reported to the people what had happened between
Thumb and the mammoth. His words didn't sing like Owl's did and
his voice never touched the moon, but the story was finished.
Afterward there was not much discussion of what had happened that
day. A sadness had fallen on the people like a cold rain. The mothers huddled briefly, no doubt talking about whether it was time to
change storytellers. Most of the people lay down on their sleeping
mats, glad to let the day pass into story.

Onion curled next to Thumb under their bearskin. They were so
excited to see each other that they couldn't get to sleep. They talked
in lovers' whispers, so as not to disturb the others.

"Owl was right to tie the luck of the mammoth to the stranger's
luck," said Thumb, "even if he did forget what he was trying to
say. I feel like I'm still bound to it." He sifted her hair through his
hands. "And you to this Singer?"

"Maybe. I don't know." She shifted around to face him. "I'm
sorry, but I don't remember much about him. They told me what

he did but I heard the story as if it had happened to someone else. All I know is that I am better now. And that you're here with me."

"What do you remember?"

"I remember my baby was dead. It was a boy," she said.

"I know. I was with you." Thumb rested his hand on her hip. "But then I had to leave."

"After that all I remember are faces and lots of talk that I couldn't quite understand. And just a bit of a dream." Onion stroked his cheek, as if to assure herself that he was still there. "I was in a cave. I had no lamp and it was dark but I could see a tiny light, far off, like a star and the light called my name. I think it might have been Singer. I tried to crawl toward the light but my arms and legs wouldn't move. Then I heard a wind sound, but it wasn't wind. It was the cave, breathing." She shivered. "That's all."

"It was the long cave," said Thumb, although he didn't believe this, "and it was me, looking for you."

Someone was playing a bone flute. Probably Oak, who usually had trouble sleeping. The notes were soft and drowsy and a little downcast. It was a song of leaves dropping from trees and birds flying south, a song of the end of summer.

The next morning, Blue asked Thumb and Oak to walk with him to the river for a hunting council. Although Oak was Thumb's half-brother, they had never been close. Oak was younger than Thumb. Their mother had died giving birth to him and their luck had been tangled ever since. But with Quick and the others tracking the reindeer herd, Oak was the best hunter in camp.

He was a simple man, better with his hands than his head. He could throw a spear farther than any of the people, but he could scarcely tell a story straight through. He had no lover and so was always restless. The mothers said that he would leave the valley some day.

The three men carried water skins down the path to the river. Since Blue had called the council, Oak and Thumb waited for him to begin it. At the river, instead of filling his skin, he hung it on a branch. The others did the same and then the three sat facing each other.

"So, do we hunt it?" said Blue.

Oak snorted in disgust. "The question answers itself."

"We could," said Thumb, "if it's just an animal."

"What else would it be?"

"A spirit."

Blue frowned. "You think it is?"

"My thoughts are thick as mud," said Thumb. "I heard a voice in my head. But as soon as I saw the beast, I knew that we could kill it." He shrugged. "You can't kill a spirit."

Oak touched Thumb's knee. "How many men would it take, brother?"

"Five and five, at least. It was feeding, so I'm not sure how fast it charges. More would be better. It'll be dangerous."

"So we had better wait for Quick to come back," said Blue.

Oak made a sour face. "And let it wander off? Blue, this is a mammoth. Think of what people will say of the ones who bring it down. You want to give those stories to the shell people? The horse people?"

Blue shook his head. "Men may die unless we hunt at full strength."

"You could die on the way back to camp if you trip over a stone. I'm not afraid."

"I'm not afraid, either. I'm just not stupid."

Thumb's attention drifted. Their argument was like the chitter of magpies. There was something that he needed to understand about the mammoth. Something that he couldn't talk or think his way to, something that hid underneath words. He began to clear the ground in front of him, pulling grass, sweeping away rotted leaves.

"We've got Horn and Quail and Bright and Rabbit," said Oak. "And you two, if you both agree."

"Bright is still a boy."

"He has his name."

"He was born the summer before Onion came to us!"

Thumb fluffed the exposed dirt and then began to work with his drawing thumb. The lines were swift and sure. Round head, sloping back, trunk, long tusks.

"What is it?" Oak's voice came from a great distance.

Thumb opened himself and a dream found him.

"Quiet!" said Blue. Thumb could barely hear him over the blood pounding in his ears.

In his dream, the mammoth was already dead. It was lying on its side in a clearing. Flies buzzed the wounds on its neck. Two spears stuck out of its broad chest. The blood was dry.

Thumb was alone with the mammoth. There were no other hunters, no one to thank the mammoth for giving its life to the people and to speed its soul. He knelt beside the mammoth and put his hand on its flank. "I thank you, great one, for the sacrifice you have made. Your death is as precious to us as your life was to you. We needed you and so we killed you. We will use your flesh and bones to make our lives better. Someday when the spirits come to take us from our bodies, we will see you again in the belly of the earth." Then he got up, his nose full of the stink of the mammoth. It was already beginning to rot.

He walked around it once, then walked around it in the opposite direction. In his dream, Thumb was uneasy. It was bad luck to waste any kill, and this was a *mammoth*. Where was everyone?

An elm tree stirred at the edge of the clearing. In a dream moment, its roots gathered into two legs and its branches became the arms of a man. Leaves grew into long gray hair and a beard. The tree man was wearing a deerskin shirt and leggings. He did not speak but held out open hands to show he meant no harm. Thumb thought this might be the stranger who had saved Onion.

Man, I am. It was the voice Thumb had heard by the river.

Singer approached the mammoth. He touched one of the dark eyes and the lid closed. He whispered to the mammoth and its trunk twitched. When he shouted, the sound staggered Thumb and he fell backward.

The mammoth shivered, rolled over, and got to its knees. Thumb let out a strangled cry of joy and surprise and fear. No animal had ever come back from the dead. The mammoth stood and shook the spears out of its side. Thumb's eyes burned.

Singer loomed over Thumb and started kicking at the ground. He bent to uproot grass, clear leaves. The mammoth trumpeted and lumbered into the forest as Singer squatted. He began to draw in the dirt.

The lines were swift and sure. Round head, sloping back, trunk, long tusks.

"Thumb, are you all right?" Oak was trying to sit him up.

"You shouldn't touch him," said Blue, but he didn't interfere.

Thumb's ears still rang with Singer's shout. He tried to focus on Blue and Oak. They shimmered like they were under water.

"He's crying," said Oak. "Brother, what's wrong?"

Thumb wiped at the wetness under his eye and touched the fingertip to his tongue. In the taste of his tears he saw mammoths flickering on the walls of the long cave. The vision shook him. It was dream knowledge, but the dream was over. The spirits must be very close. They had come to push him to his luck.

Thumb struggled up and pulled his water skin from the tree. "No more talking." He dipped the skin into the current and let it fill.

"I'm going to the long cave." He slung it over his shoulder and started toward the camp at a trot. "I'll know what we should do when I get back."

Owl liked to call the cleft *the new cave*, but then he liked to stretch words. Actually it was a place where two huge rocks had fallen against one another, and it was mostly open to the sky. All the paintings and marks on the walls of the cleft had been made either by Thumb, or his teacher, Looker, or Looker's teacher Thorn. They had painted reindeer and red deer and ibex and horses and bison and the secret names of spirits.

But no mammoths. The mammoths were in the long cave.

The long cave was a mystery. Nobody knew who had put their dreams on its walls. Nobody knew how big it was. Owl told a story about the time old Thorn had found a tunnel that led from the long cave to the belly of the earth. The keeper had blocked it with stones to keep the dead from coming back to life. The women told stories about souls without bodies, who wandered the earth, forever alone, but none of the people had ever seen one. Thumb had looked many times for Thorn's tunnel. He had never found it. But even though he knew the long cave better than any of the people, there were still parts of it that he had yet to see. He had never quite gotten the courage to lower himself into the well in the Lodge of the Mother Mammoth. And he was too wide in the shoulders to wriggle through the narrows past the abandoned bear nests.

"I don't care," said Onion. "I'm coming with you."

Two mothers who were chipping new stone scrapers covered smiles with their hands.

Thumb wrapped a lump of boar fat in a maple leaf and bound it with braided grass. "But I don't want you to." He put it with his lamp.

Onion didn't bother to answer. She was already packing food for the trip, a handful of hazel nuts, a parsnip, salsify root, and a dried fish.

"You're not strong enough." Thumb didn't like to quarrel in front of other people.

Onion liked nothing better, especially since his shyness gave her an advantage. "I'm strong enough to sit and tend fire." She stooped to tie the sinew laces of her boots. "And that's all I'll do if I stay here."

Thumb made his best argument. "It's too far." The long cave was a good day's hike from the river. Its mouth was set into the stony ridge that divided the river valley from the lands of the horse people. "Besides, I might be gone all night. Maybe longer." Thumb continued to wrap leaves around pale chunks of fat for the lamp. "I don't know where the dreams will take me."

When he glanced up, Onion was standing with her hips cocked to support the bulging skin she had slung over her shoulder. She smiled at him and he shrugged. He knew that smile. The argument was over.

It was not yet midday when they started out. They talked at first. He told her about his trip to the country of the shell people. They were telling stories about a new people who had come down from the ice mountains. The shell people had not yet seen these strangers themselves, but had heard about them from their distant neighbors, the sky people. The newcomers were said to have four arms. Dogs followed them and obeyed their orders.

"Then we'll call them the dog people," said Onion.

"That wouldn't be very polite." Dogs were scavengers, like crows and rats. The only thing they were good for was eating, and they were often too stringy for that.

"Then call them the ice people." Onion laughed. "Maybe they melt in the summer and their dogs drink them."

Thumb was pleased to see Onion keep good pace and good conversation. She was definitely getting better.

Onion told him that the mothers had decided to ask Owl's son Bone to become the storyteller, even though he was still learning stories. He had only begun training with his father four summers ago but he had a big voice and an easy laugh. His words didn't always light the stars, but he was still young and he would have Owl to teach him.

As they climbed farther away from the river, they dropped into hunting order. Game was scarce near the summer camp, but here they might surprise a hare or a squirrel or even a deer. Thumb moved ahead, stepping quietly, spear at the ready. Onion trailed behind, picking mushrooms and stopping to roll logs over in search of grubs and salamanders.

That night they lay together as lovers. Afterward Thumb wept for their dead baby boy.

The sun was three hands from the dawn edge of the sky when they reached the cave the next day. Onion gathered tinder and kindling while Thumb pulled dead branches from trees and dragged them into a pile. The people visited the long cave regularly and had built a good hearth just inside the entrance. Thumb watched Onion take the smoldering coal she had brought from the hearthfire and set it on the tinder.

"I thank the first mother for this fire," she said. "She makes the warmth of the world." She blew on the coal until it smoked and the tinder caught fire.

When the pile of firewood reached Thumb's waist, he went out to gather birch bark. He peeled what he could and cut the rest with his chert knife. He was careful not to cut a complete circle of bark, which would girdle a tree and kill it. Thumb folded the bark again and again into a wad and then wedged it into the cleft of a green stick. When he had made three of these birch torches he returned to the cave. He was surprised to find Bead, Owl's lover, sitting at the fire next to Onion. She was rocking back and forth, as if in mourning.

"I tried to talk to Owl last night, but he wouldn't hear me," she told them. She looked as if she had slept on a sharp rock. "This morning I followed him here. He walked into the cave without fire or food, with empty hands. When I called for him to stop, he ran from me. I tried to find him but I have no light. I've been looking . . . I don't know. Most of the day." Her hands and face were dirty and her doeskin shirt was smeared with chalky mud. "He's gone, I think."

"I'll find him." Thumb gestured at the torches he had made. "And I have a lamp."

"What if he doesn't want to be found?" said Bead. "He is ashamed, Thumb. And afraid." She tugged at her hair hard enough to pull a few gray strands out. "And he is an old fool."

"He wants to die in there?" said Onion.

"I think," she said. "Where no one can see him. Where he can't even see himself."

"The spirits will see him," said Thumb. "They are thick in this cave. It will make bad luck for the people."

"If he thinks his own luck has run," said Onion, "maybe he doesn't care."

They sat for a minute in silence, listening to the fire, watching sparks fly up to become sky. In his mind's eye, Thumb tried to see Owl as someone who would knowingly make bad luck for all of them. He couldn't. It wasn't the kind of story Owl would want people to tell about him.

"He isn't like that," he said. "He's gone to the cave as any of us would. To open himself to a dream. To find his luck, not to be done with it."

"Maybe," said Bead.

Was this why he had been brought to the cave? To save Owl? Thumb stood and touched one of the birch bark torches to the fire. "I'll find him." He tucked the other two torches into his belt. "I'll bring him out." The way the two women were looking up at him almost made him believe what he was saying. "And then we'll tell him his own story, again and again, until he understands why we need him."

Some of the people were afraid of the long cave. Most thought it a cold, forbidding place. Thumb didn't understand this. Yes, it was crushingly dark. But the cave was ever untouched by the outside. It was always the same, always itself. In the heat of the summer, it was cool and free of bugs. When wind screamed off the ice mountains in the winter, it was the warmest place in the world. Time slowed in its never-ending night. Dreams lurked at every turn.

The mouth of the long cave was wide and welcoming. It opened onto a huge, damp room, with a ceiling too high for torchlight to reach. The mud on the floor was as sticky as pinesap. Before long, black silence closed around Thumb and all he could hear was the hiss of the torch and mud squishing beneath his boots.

He walked for some time, picking his way down the path trod by countless feet. On his right he passed the Empty Ways, a deep and complicated branch that, for some reason, had never been decorated. He had once asked Looker why they couldn't paint their dreams in this untouched section. Looker had cuffed him with the back of his hand. "This cave belongs to the dead now," said Looker. "Paint here when you're ready to visit the belly of the earth."

Was Owl hiding in one of the Empty Ways? Thumb called to him but got no reply. Owl had been to the cave many times. He would find his way to the Mother's Lodge. To the place of dreams.

Thumb's first torch began to gutter and he lit the second as he came to the underground river, where the main passage veered sharply to the right. This was not a true river like that of the people, more like a stream, but it filled the cave with its gurgle. The ceiling was low here, and the chalk walls were moist and yielding. After a while, Thumb came to First Mammoth.

First Mammoth had been scratched in the soft surface of the wall with a stick, or maybe even a finger. It was about as long as a marmot. Thumb could have carved it himself in a few minutes, if such had been his luck. First Mammoth had to be very old. Its lines weren't as sharp as most of the other carvings. The moisture in the cave had blurred them over countless summers. A long-dead cave bear had once sharpened its claws on top of First Mammoth, and even its marks had begun to fade.

Thumb switched the torch to his left hand and with his thumb traced First Mammoth's lines just above the soft surface of the wall.

"I honor you and the one who carved you," he said. "May I meet both of your souls someday when I leave my body." He tugged the last torch out of his belt and leaned it against the wall. "Keep my torch safe and dry, First Mammoth, so I can use it to find my way back to the sun."

A little further on he entered the Council Room, where the cave branched in two directions. The walls of the Council Room were covered with wonders. To one side was the chiseled profile of Father Mammoth, whose eye saw all that happened in the cave. To the other were three wooly rhinoceros, one so fat that its belly scraped the ground. Next to them was the Council of the Mammoths.

A line of five mammoths marched left. Five more marched right, as if to cut them off. The two leaders faced each other, eye to eye, their trunks touching. They had been drawn by rubbing soot stone right onto the rock, the surface of which was smooth but not flat. Whoever had created these mammoths had used dips and bulges in the rock to make them leap from the wall into the mind's eye. As Thumb passed his torch from one line to the other, the play of light made the mammoths stir.

The first time he'd seen the Council of the Mammoths, Thumb thought that the two herds were about to fight. Then Looker had explained. Each of the herds walked its own land. Where the leaders met was the boundary. The mammoths touched trunks as brothers might touch fists or sisters hug. This was a dream of friendship, not of rancor, and it was meant to speak to the people who kept the cave. The spirits commanded them, said Looker, to live at peace with their neighbors. It was their luck to take lovers from the shell people and send their children to live with the horse people and to welcome all strangers.

Man, whispered a voice in Thumb's head.

Thumb whirled, but he saw no one. "Who are you?" He felt as if he were standing on the sky and gazing up at the ground. "Tell me!" The walls swallowed his anger. This was the place of true dreams and he was its keeper. "This is the cave of the people! You don't belong here!"

Man, I am.

Thumb staggered across the Council Room and fell to his knees before Father Mammoth. "Father, I've come looking for Owl, the storyteller. Now something in your cave calls me. I don't understand what is happening. Show me what I must do." And then he opened himself.

No dream found him.

Thumb didn't know what to do. Shocked, he knelt there waiting. Waiting. This had never happened before. Father Mammoth stared down at him but sent no dream. The spirits had forsaken him.

The torch began to gutter.

Man. Come to me.

Thumb fumbled for his lamp. Still on his knees, he flattened a wad of boar fat into the bowl, pinched some moss for a wick and pressed it into the fat. He lit the lamp from the failing torch.

Man.

"What?" he muttered as he stood. His knees creaked. How long had he been kneeling on the cold stone? He left the torch behind and started down the passage toward the Lodge of the Mother Mammoth. The world shrank as he left the Council Room. The torch had cast a strong light, but the lamp burned with a single flame. When he held it at eye level, the floor of the cave disappeared. Thumb groped forward, his free hand brushing the wall. He saw more with his feet than with his eyes. Soon he came to one of the narrows. He stooped, and then crawled on hands and knees. He picked his way slowly, holding the lamp level so as not to spill melting fat or snuff the flame.

The ceiling in the Mother's Lodge was low enough that he could reach up and press his palm flat against it. It was decorated with mammoths and bison and ibex and horses and rhinoceros, outlined in black soot stone. Some stood on top of one another. Upside down jostled right side up. Here was a many to make a man's head swim. Thumb could as soon count the leaves on a tree or the hairs of Onion's head. Ordinarily the spirits of the cave were most present in this great gathering of animals. When Thumb guided people to this room, dreams spun from the ceiling like snow from the winter sky. But now he gazed up in vain. He felt as if his soul had turned to stone.

"Why am I here?" He began by searching the edges of the room, carrying the lamp low so he could see the floor. Nothing. "Talk to me!" Then he struck out for the opposite wall, crisscrossing back and forth. On his fourth traverse, his foot nudged the body.

Thumb rolled Owl over and felt his throat for the beat of blood. He was alive. Thumb squatted, thinking of how to get the old man out of the cave. If he slung Owl over his back and tried to carry him, he'd probably douse the lamp. Besides, how would they wriggle through the narrows? He decided that if he couldn't wake Owl up, he would have to leave the cave, build a litter and bring Bead back to help.

"Owl." Thumb chucked the old man's chin. "Can you hear me?" He leaned close and blew on his eyelids. "Uncle?"

"Hmm."

"It's me, Thumb."

Owl stirred and put his hand to his forehead. Then he opened his eyes. Spears of light, brighter than any fire Thumb had ever seen, shot from Owl's eyes and then winked out. Thumb screamed and sprawled backward, spilling hot fat on himself and snuffing the lamp's puny flame.

Darkness closed around him. He felt it press against his skin, stop his nose, slither down his throat. He tried to scream again but the darkness was smothering him. Terrified, he scuttled across the floor until his back was against a wall. He heard a wind sound, but it wasn't the wind. It was the cave, breathing. Then the room erupted with light. The thing that was Owl but wasn't stood before him. He held his hand above his head. It was on fire and his fingers were bright, flickering flames. Thumb looked up and saw something he had never seen before. All the animals of the Mother's Lodge stared down at him. All, all at once. The wonder of it was almost enough to make him forget what was happening. Owl seemed impressed too. For a moment, he paid no attention to Thumb. Instead he strode around the room, taking in the drawings as if they were old friends. Finally he approached Thumb, who tried to press himself into the rock.

Man, this is not a dream.

Thumb couldn't speak. He could barely nod.

The story of Thumb.

The light from Owl's fist was painful. It stabbed through Thumb's head into his mind's eye.

He is great, father to many peoples. He lives many summers.

Thumb had no children. All Onion's babies died. Owl's skin began to shift like smoke. Thumb could see his bones glowing.

But he kills the last mammoth. This tangles his luck. When he dies, his soul never gets to the belly of the earth.

Fear gave way to rage. "How do you know this? Who are you?"

Owl lowered the shining fist toward Thumb. Thumb couldn't move, couldn't protect himself.

Man, I am.

Thumb had grown roots. His arms were heavy as logs.

But once I was . . .

All he could do is look up as Owl touched him.

Thumb.

The light filled his head, driving out all thought.

The next thing Thumb knew, he was kneeling in front of Father Mammoth in the Council Room. The spent torch was on the floor beside the lamp, which was lit. Owl curled nearby, snoring noisily.

"It wasn't a dream," Thumb muttered and sat back on his heels. "Then what was it?" He picked up the lamp absently. Had he just talked to his soul, come back from the dead? Did that mean he had had lost his own soul? He shook the thought from his head and wondered what he should do. Probably rouse Owl. Get him out of the cave. "What about it, old man?" Thumb said softly. "Are you going to catch fire again and say crazy things?"

Owl snuffled. He slept with his mouth open so that Thumb could count the teeth he had lost. Thumb stretched his foot across the floor of the cave and gave Owl a nudge. "Owl." He gave Owl a second, firmer nudge. "Wake up." And then he slid back to watch what would happen.

Owl's mouth closed and then opened again "Am not," he said. His voice was thick.

"Owl!"

"What?" When he opened his eyes, it was clear that no spirit lurked behind them. They were the dim, watery eyes of an old man. "Who is that?"

"Thumb."

He thought for a moment and then nodded. "And the woman?"

"Bead is waiting outside."

He grunted as he propped himself up on an elbow. "I think she would follow me to the belly of the earth." He licked his lips. "If only to tell me I was wrong about something."

Thumb laughed politely. "What do you remember?"

"Remember? I came to the cave to find a guiding dream. Instead I got lost. Then I fell asleep."

"But no dream?"

He shook his head. "Not everyone finds dreams as easily as Thumb."

"Where did you fall asleep? Here? In the Lodge of the Mother Mammoth?"

"Thumb, it was dark." Owl sat up. "The mothers want the new storyteller, yes?"

"Yes."

"I thought so." He stretched and then yipped in pain. "I'm getting too old for a bed of stones." He kneaded the muscles of his back.

"I'm taking the lamp," said Thumb. "I left a fresh torch back at First Mammoth. I'll get it and then we should go."

Owl had gotten to his feet by the time Thumb returned. He steadied himself with a hand to the wall of the cave. "Bone," he said. In the torchlight, the old man's face was pale as the moon. "Bone will take my place."

"We expect you to teach him all the stories you know."

"I have tried all these summers." Owl showed Thumb his teeth. "The son won't make anyone forget the father."

The two men stood at the mouth of the cave, blinking in the after-noon sun. Something was wrong. Thumb dropped the spent torch into the hearth. They were hungry and thirsty but there was no fire and the women were gone.

"Where is she?" Owl brushed past Thumb into the open air. "*Bead!*"

"Quiet." Thumb clamped his hand over Owl's mouth to keep him from calling out again. "Look at the coals. That fire didn't burn itself out. Somebody put it out. And I left a spear and a throwing stick."

"Why would they leave us?"

"Wait back in the cave. I'll see what I can find."

Thumb drew his knife and ran across the clearing in front of the cave to the cover of the forest. He moved silently through the trees, parallel to the trail but many paces away. After a while he gave the call of a nuthatch, a high, two-note whistle repeated three times. The reply came from his left, a three-note whistle repeated twice. He found Onion and Bead waiting in a dry stream bed. They told him quickly what had happened. Part of Thumb was grateful to hear the dreadful story. It meant that he didn't have to think any-more about what had happened in the cave. He ran to fetch Owl. As they hurried back to the summer camp, the two women tried to remember everything they had heard. And when Thumb got home, he heard the story again, this time from Quick himself.

✳   ✳   ✳

Quick's party had joined the hunters from the horse people and together they had tracked the reindeer herd. As was their custom, they split the herd and had driven part of it into the Killdeer, a steep-walled gorge blocked off with boulders and felled trees at one end. There they had slaughtered the reindeer. There was enough meat to get both peoples through the coming winter. Fresh skins to make clothes and blankets, antlers and bones for tools. It was a good harvest.

But while the hunters were butchering and skinning the reindeer, they were attacked. Bone thought they might have been spirits, but Quick was certain that they were just men. The attackers fought with "feather sticks"—short, straight spears with a flint point at one end and feathers at the other. They threw these sticks from a distance and at great speed. They used a throwing stick unlike anything the hunters had seen before. Spears were useless against the attackers. When the hunters tried to charge them, they were turned back by a pack of fierce dogs.

Of the hunting party, Moon was killed and both Quick and Ash were wounded. The horse people had suffered greater losses. Another party of the strangers had sacked their summer camp and carried off some of the women. After they had escaped the Killdeer, Quick and his men had run for home. The attackers might be on their way to the valley of the people next. As they passed the long cave, Quick had seen the smoke of Onion's fire and had stopped to warn the women.

"I think these must be the people of the ice mountains," said Thumb as he ran his finger down the feather stick that Quick had brought back. "The shell people told me about the dogs." The point was stained with Quick's own blood. He had worked it out of his thigh after the attack.

"You knew about these strangers?" said Blue.

"It was a story told by the sky people to the shell people," said Thumb, "who told it to me. I thought the truth of it might be a little thin."

People stared as if he had betrayed them. Thumb felt the blood rush to his face.

"In the story I heard," he said, "these people had four arms. Did they?"

"No," said Quick.

Bone spat. "Two were more than enough."

"And there was nothing about these." Thumb gave the feather stick back to Quick. "Or about anyone attacking anyone."

Owl held up his hand. "We should send a runner to the shell

people to hear their story again," he said, "and to tell ours. Maybe he should visit the sky people too."

Everyone thought this was a good idea. Blue asked young Bright to start the next morning. Quick said that they should think about striking the summer camp early. The winter lodge, a day's walk upriver, was in a natural terrace that the people walled up with stones. It would be easier to defend. This idea caused a stir among the women. Flame held up her hand.

"The mothers have asked me to speak for them," she said. "We're still taking in the harvest. The winter camp is a long way from the best gathering places. That's why we make the summer camp here."

There was no answer to this argument and the men all knew it. They also knew what was coming next.

"There's plenty to harvest this summer," said Flame. "We can fill many skins with good things to eat—if we're here at the summer camp. But now Quick tells us that there will be no reindeer. We'll do our best, but unless there's meat, there will come a time this winter when we'll all go hungry."

Quick drew himself up. "The hunters will bring in meat enough for all." Normally, when Quick said something it would be done, everyone stopped worrying about it. But dark blood soaked through the deerskin bandage around his thigh and he looked haggard. He had lost the winter's meat supply. A man was dead.

Oak raised his hand. "I am sure that the mothers can make some delicious rat stews and roasted squirrels, but there is bigger game to hunt. While Thumb was in the cave, I looked for his mammoth. It must like our valley, because I found it just last night. It's less than a day's walk away, on the dawn shore by the sandbar."

"But you can't." Thumb's voice was sharp. "I mean, maybe we should wait."

Everyone was watching him again. Even Onion seemed troubled by his outburst.

"You asked us to wait once already," said Blue carefully. "We did, because you are keeper of the caves. You went to the long cave and now you're back. What happened? Did you have a dream about the mammoth?"

"I . . ." Thumb didn't know what to say, in part because he wasn't sure what had happened to him. "It wasn't a dream."

Owl raised his hand again. "He saved me, is what happened." The old man probably thought he was helping Thumb. Paying him back. "I was lost and he found me." He reached over to hug Thumb.

"And now I know why. Let me tell you a story of long ago, before we were a people. A story about how my great-grandfather hunted mammoths."

The strength of the people would be tested. Blue had sent a party of scouts to watch for the strangers at the far edges of the valley. That meant that the women would have to help with the hunt. Thumb had doubts about Owl's scheme, especially since Quick could take no part in it. The day after the council, a fever took him. He sprawled on his mat at the camp, senseless, sometimes thrashing in pain. His lover Cloud packed mustard leaves on his wound but it continued to ooze. Oak would take charge of the hunt.

In Owl's story, the old ones had hunted mammoths at night. The beasts were scared of fire, Owl claimed, and could easily be driven with torches. The surest kill would have been to chase the mammoth off a cliff. But the mammoth was finding good forage along the banks of the river. Oak saw the risk in trying to drive it all the way into the hills. Owl's story had the answer. They would dig a pit, force the mammoth into it and slaughter it while it struggled to get out.

Thumb had his own plan. He would stay as far away from the mammoth as he could. Let this story be about Oak, or one of the other men. If he didn't kill it, none of what had happened in the cave would matter.

Oak was calling for a fan of hunters to get the mammoth moving. Two lines of women were to move toward each other, closing its path off with their torches. They would force it into the pit, where the main party of hunters would be waiting to finish it. Thumb asked to be one of the hunters who walked the flanks to protect the women. Everyone thought that this was because he was worried about Onion.

Although she would not let anyone see it, he knew that she was distraught. The horse people were her first people. She had a mother, a sister, and cousins who she had kept up with, even after she had come to the valley. The two peoples traded and hunted together and they told each other's stories. Now her birth family might be hurt or dead or taken. There were dark circles under Onion's eyes and she rarely spoke unless spoken to.

It took three days to dig the pit. Owl said it must be covered with brush, or the prey would see its danger. Meanwhile a pair of hunters tracked the mammoth. When it strayed too far from the killing ground, they would show themselves and turn it back. By the night of the third day the trap was set. The people left camp just before dusk.

Thumb had strapped his two best spears and his throwing stick to his back. He offered to help Onion carry her three birch bark torches but she refused. Her eyes were wide and the line of her mouth was straight. She and the other women were jittery walking through the forest in the dark. Thumb didn't blame them. Everyone knew that luck turned at night, often for the bad. When the fat moon rose, everyone felt a little safer.

"Stop!"

Some of the women jumped. Even Thumb gave a yip of surprise. Oak came out of the darkness looking as if he had rolled around in the coals of a dead fire. His face was black and his deer-skins filthy.

"This is where Thumb's group builds their fire. A small fire, yes?"

"We know this," said Thumb. "You've told us enough times."

"Then form your line running in that direction." Oak pointed. "Five and five paces apart. Don't light the torches until you get the call. Robin's group, come with me."

Thumb thought Oak must be unsure of himself. That was why he was treating everyone as if they were children.

The women built the fire, thanking the first mother for the light of the world. Then Thumb helped them take their places. He put Onion farthest from the pit and waited with her.

"Are you afraid?" she said.

He was taken aback. Fear was not something men talked about, certainly not just before a hunt. "A little," he said. "Yes."

"Why have you closed yourself off from me?" She took his hand.

"Me? You're the silent one. Are you worried about your family?"

"You are my family, Thumb, and I *am* worried. Something happened in the cave. Something you haven't told me."

He felt his throat tighten. "I've tried not to think about it."

She waited for him to continue.

"It wasn't a dream. It wasn't." He sighed. "It was like we are speaking now, except I was talking to a spirit. A crazy spirit."

"Can spirits be crazy?"

"People can be crazy, so why can't spirits? I don't know. That's why I'm scared, Onion. Because I don't know what to think."

"So what did it say?"

He laughed. "That I am great."

"That wasn't crazy."

He leaned over to kiss her in the darkness. "That I will be father to many peoples," he said softly.

She shrank away from him momentarily, as if he had said something wrong. Then she closed her eyes and kissed him back.

They heard the call of a nuthatch, a high, two-note whistle repeated three times. Thumb replied, a three-note whistle repeated twice.

"I'll come back," he said. He lit a torch from the fire and dashed down the line of women, lighting theirs. As he peered into the night, he could just make out the shimmer of the second line. Now Thumb could hear the chants of the fan of hunters driving the mammoth toward them. He threw his torch into the fire and fitted a spear into his throwing stick.

"*We are the people,*" the hunters cried. "*We need you, great one.*"

"Let's go," Thumb called, loud enough for everyone to hear, "Walk slowly toward the other lights."

The mammoth trumpeted. It was caught between the lines and headed toward the pit.

"It's working," Thumb called. "The mammoth will pass, then the hunters will be right behind. Close in after them."

"*We are the people.*"

Thumb saw a mammoth-sized shadow lope close by. It was breathing in great, ragged *chuffs*. He could almost taste its fear.

"*We need you, great one,*" called the hunters. Smaller shadows rippled through the trees.

"Follow them," he called. "Not too close."

The two lines of lights came together and Thumb saw Robin wave. Ahead of them the mammoth shrieked and the main group of hunters roared in triumph.

Thumb flew down the line to find Onion.

"Are you all right?" he said.

Her eyes shone in the torchlight. "We did it." She was excited. *Man.*

The mammoth trumpeted again and Thumb heard a different note in the voices of the hunters. Later, he would learn that the pit wasn't wide enough. That the mammoth had skirted it without falling in. But that moment, all Thumb knew was that something was wrong.

A man screamed in agony. The shouts filled with fear. The luck of the people had turned.

"It's coming back," said Thumb. Hunting courage hammered

through his body. "It can't get past Oak and the others but it can break through the chase group." He felt as if his legs were growing longer.

"But our torches," said Onion. "It's afraid of fire."

Man.

"Not if it's wounded." The muscles in his arms bunched and swelled. "It's probably crazy with fear." His hair rose straight from his head.

"Robin!" he called. "It's coming."

Robin pumped his spear to show he was ready.

"Thumb, what are you going to do?"

You are.

"I can't die, Onion," said Thumb. "The spirit told me." He gulped air as if he were drowning. "Not until I'm old."

Then he saw it bearing down on him. On Onion. He realized that Owl had been right after all. It *was* a furry mountain, a mountain that galloped.

"Thumb!" cried Onion.

But she was behind him now. He took three effortless steps toward the mammoth. It was as if he were going down to the river for water. He couldn't die tonight. His old life was behind him too, what he had been before he had met himself in the long cave. The new Thumb had great things to do. *The last.* Oh, the stories they would tell about him! *But his soul would never.* The mammoth loomed. *Never.* He planted himself, drew back his throwing stick, and screamed at it.

"*I am!*"

This is the story of Thumb the Great. He killed a mammoth with a single thrust of his spear. He gave his people the bow and arrow and taught them the ways of war. When the battle madness took him, there was no one so fierce. He led the people of the valley against the dog people and drove them back to the ice mountains. He lived a long life, fathered many children and mourned two lovers. The spirits treated him as if he were one of their own. One night they came and took him from the people. We believe he still watches over us.

He was a man filled with luck.

The Dark Side of Town

TALISHA FOUND THE PILLS IN RICKY'S UNDERWEAR drawer under the maroon boxers she had never seen him wear. There were three of them in a cotton nest tucked into a flat cardboard box. She dumped them onto her palm: clear capsules, about as long as her fingernail with the Werefolk logo imprinted on the side. She thought she could almost see the nano beasties swimming inside.

It made her angry that Ricky had not tried harder to hide the pills. Did he think she was stupid? She subscribed to *Watch This!* and *Ed Explains It All* and usually opened new episodes the moment they popped into her inbox. Her earstone was set to deliver *The Two Minute Report* three times a day, whether she was near a pix or not. She had even uploaded an Introduction to Feng Shui course last year. From Purdue, a name brand college!

All that time he'd been telling her there wasn't enough money for them to have their baby, much less buy a house, he'd been wasting it on some mechdream. It was one thing to pay for nano to mess with your brain so you could design living rooms or program searchlets or speak Russian or something. Talisha understood that you had to spend money to make money. But it was another thing altogether to spend the grocery money building some virtual sex playpen. And everyone said that Werefolk made the sickest mechdreams of all.

Creatures with the legs of giraffes and four tits stroking one another with power tools and chicken giblets. Stuff so dark that even Ed himself couldn't quite explain it.

Her hands trembled as she waved the pills in front of the pix and waited for it to scan them. It was a slow, twelve-year-old Sony and the screen had more bad pixels than interpolation could correct, but it was all they could afford.

"X-Stasis release 7.01 from Werefolk Corporation," said the pix. "List price: seven hundred and ninety-eight dollars for a multiplex map-and-transmit regime."

Eight hundred dollars! "What does it do?" she said grimly.

An ad popped onto the pix. It began with a tight shot on a talking head. "With the Werefolk virtual reality six-pack," said a beautiful young woman, "we bring ecstasy to a new level." She appeared to be standing on a beach; behind her a blue sky melted into a glassy ocean. "Using our exclusive X-Stasis personality probe, we'll help you plumb the depths of your pleasure centers." She smiled and was immediately transformed into a beautiful young man. "Only X-Stasis can access the neurons where your unconscious lurks and transmit your innermost desires to Werefolk. Together we can build a secret world for you to enjoy on our secure servers, the world they said you could never have." The camera pulled back slowly and Talisha could see that the beautiful young man wasn't wearing a shirt. "Surprise yourself today with a tour of your hidden self and begin your intimate journey into rapture."

Just before the camera could reveal that the beautiful young man wasn't wearing any pants either, the ad cut away to an older, roundish woman in a daisy-print dress. A caption identified her as Mrs. Lonnie Foster of Holland, Michigan. She was standing in front of a barn.

"There was a time a couple of months ago when I felt about as dry as a saltine, you know? I'd look at myself in the mirror and say, 'Hey Lonnie, who's doing for you?' Then I heard about Werefolk and decided to do for myself. Now don't you be asking what goes on up in Lonnie's Castle." She giggled like a little girl. "Like they said, that's private. But I do love to spend time there, oh my *yes*. And it's safe as taking a nap . . ."

Talisha waved the ad off; it was only confusing her. Of course, she didn't care anything about the beautiful young people in the ad; they weren't even real. But Lonnie's question had struck home. Who was doing for Talisha?

"Call Ricky," she said. The pix queried his workshop.

Ricky answered in voice mode. "What?" He didn't like to be bothered when he was working.

"Are you plumbing the depths?"

"Talisha, I'm busy."

"Give me video, you bastard."

He told the cam to turn on and she saw that he was standing at his bench, surrounded by broken 1/18 scale model carbots: Mazdas and Duesenbergs and Chevys, dump trucks and road graders. He was tinkering with the harmonic speed reducer from the arm assembly of a Komatsu excavator. He stared up at her. "What did you just call me?"

"I called you a lying bastard pervert."

He blanched and set the reducer down next to its servomotor.

"What are these?" She held the pills up to the pix.

"So you've been going through my things?" he said. She expected anger or remorse—something—but his eyes were empty.

"I was putting your damn underwear away."

"And?" He glanced away from the pix as if something had distracted him.

"Where did you get eight hundred dollars?"

He picked up a circuit tester and turned his attention back to the Komatsu. "I earned it."

"*Ricky.*" She couldn't believe that he was acting as if nothing had happened. "Okay, you earned it. Where does that leave us?"

"Us?" He seemed preoccupied as he clipped the tester to the encoder cable. He shook his head. She couldn't tell if he were disappointed in the signal or their marriage. "You know I love you, 'Sha."

"You have a funny way of showing it." She opened her hand and let his pills rattle onto the coffee table. "The air conditioner is broken. I had to cancel my subscription to church. Supper tonight is Beanstix from the Handimart." She hated hearing herself whine. "Is it me, Ricky? You'd rather have a make-believe woman than me?" She waited for him to answer or defend himself or *something.*

"I'm sorry, what were you saying?"

His indifference took her breath away. It was as if he didn't realize how he was hurting her. Then she remembered something Ed had explained about mechdreams. You could be in one and still go about your normal life, he said, as long as you didn't have to pay too close attention to what you were really doing. He said you could tell when people were double-dipping because they acted like zombies. He said it was a growing problem. As many as a million people were living two lives at the same time, everyone from security guards to college professors.

"You're there now," she said. "In Ricky World or Ricky's Dungeon or Temple Fucking Ricky."

"Talisha," he said, "I'm at work." He waved the connection off.

She stared at the blank pix as if it were a hole through which her life was leaking. Then she swiped the pills off the coffee table, scattering them. "*You goddamn bastard.*" She stalked around their tiny studio apartment like it was a cage. It helped to keep swearing at Ricky. Some of the words she had never spoken before and they seemed to twist in her mouth. She tore the slick sheets off the bed where she had let that "*sickass jackoff*" make love to her. She stuffed them into the washing machine that was crammed next to the toilet in the tiny bathroom that was all the "*loser suckwad*" said they could afford. She flew at the galley kitchen and yanked open the door of their half-sized refrigerator. She didn't know why exactly, since there was never anything in it that she wanted to eat. But she stared at the liter of Uncle Barth's Rice Milk and a couple Beefy Beanstix and some Handibrand Dijon mustard with the brown crust on the mouth of the jar and the Brisky Spread and the stub of a Porky Beanstix left over from last night and the wilting stalks of bak choi and the two bulbs of Miller Beer that the "*cheap shiteating cheater*" would expect to have with supper. She smashed them against the side of the sink and then sagged against the wall.

She would have cried then except that her earstone started whispering, "Talisha, ya ladyay, connect, *Talisha.*" It was her sister, Bea. Talisha waved the kitchen pix to clock mode and groaned. She was already twenty minutes late for work.

"I'm here, Bea." She waved the pix on but backed away so her sister wouldn't get a clear look at her. Talisha worked for her sister on Wednesdays and Fridays.

"Well, at least you're somewhere, my ladyloo. Only not here on the job." Bea was already wearing her stereoptic goggles. They made her look like a frog, but then her sister had never been a great beauty anyway. "The Herndens dropped another box yesterday." Bea ran Tapeworm out of her attic; she was teaching her sister the business of extracting data from dead media. Her specialty was late twentieth Century consumer magnetic tape: reel-to-reel, eight track, cassette, Beta, VHS, Hi8, and DAT. "They're blinky, but we can work them. Mostly type three and four decay: we got sticky shed *and* flaking. What are you standing offcam for?"

"I don't feel so good, Bea."

"Come close. Let your sister see."

Talisha stepped forward and stuck her chin at the pix.

"Ladyla, this is not your best look." She lifted her goggles and peered at Talisha. "You're not coming to work today, are you?"

"No." She shook her head. "I don't think so."

"You're sick?"

If she told Bea what had happened, her sister would be hauling Ricky down Elm Street by the collar of his coat. "Yeah, I think so. It hit me when I got out of bed."

"Sick in the morning?" Bea grinned. "You're pregnant?"

She sighed. "Bea, I'm having a rough day here . . ."

"Is it the baby you've been wanting?" Now she was laughing. "You said you've been trying, Ladyla and Lord Ricky."

They *had* been trying, or at least, Ricky hadn't objected when she stopped buying him birth control pills. But he hadn't reached across the bed for her for almost two weeks now. Probably since he started with his *damnfuck* pills.

"I told you not to tell anyone."

"And I didn't. We're talking here, like two sisters should. What, do you want a secure line?"

"I don't think it's . . . I don't know what it is." Talisha realized that this might be the only way to get rid of Bea. "Maybe I do need to buy a test."

Bea clapped her hands. "That's news, Lady 'Sha. That's the newsiest news I've heard today."

"Bea, don't."

"Okay. You stay home today, little sister. Take your test and God bless." She waved at Talisha and the pix went blank.

Talisha did cry then. The tears came hot and fast and her cheeks burned with them. She would be lost without Ricky. "Without Ricky," she said, to hear how it sounded. "Without that *chiseling cock-for-brains*." She sank onto the couch and hugged her favorite pillow to her chest. It purred and breathed the scent of gardenias up at her. Ricky had given her the pillow for their sixth anniversary. Actually, she had wanted a new rug because Ricky had knocked a candle over and burnt a hole in the old one. The apartment was so small and Ricky got clumsy after a few beers. But a rug wasn't in the budget and so she had moved the coffee table to cover the hole. Talisha began to rock back and forth, squeezing the pillow. The rug didn't matter anymore. Nothing did. If she and Ricky split, she'd never have the baby or the beautiful house she had always dreamed of. In fact, she'd have to move; there was no way she could afford the rent on what Bea was paying her. She thought of the tube rack where she had been living when she met Ricky. Her mod had been seven by seven by fourteen. She glanced around the apartment. None of this furniture would fit. The pillow and the rug would probably be all she'd be able to keep. She felt grief hollowing her out; she thought she might cave in on herself when her earstone started whispering again. She tossed her head as if to shake it loose but it was patient. It just wanted her to know that there were two new messages in her inbox.

"From Ricky?" She felt a flicker of hope.

"One is a bill from Infoline for $87.22. The other is *The Two Minute Report.*"

TTMR episode opened automatically and the pix trumpeted its theme, "Fanfare for Right Now." A news reader with a voice as smooth and bright as a mirror announced that Rabbi-Senator Gallman would be shutting down over the long weekend for routine maintenance. Talisha wiped the tears from her face. She didn't care that Pin Pan was in Akron to campaign for the Death Amendment or that twenty-one percent of all guide dogs could now read at a third grade level. She didn't need news. She needed advice. She needed . . .

Ed.

The idea brought her to her feet in excitement. She could *ask* Ed. She tossed the pillow on the couch and began to pace around the apartment. There was no time to enter her problem in his Question Queue. He might not get to it for weeks. Months. But for a fee, she could jump the queue and access Ed in real time. Of course, it would be hideously expensive. But so what? Would it cost as much as Ricky's pills? She hoped so. She couldn't wait to see his expression when he opened the bill.

But she couldn't meet Ed looking like a trashy, jilted housewife. Talisha scrubbed her face and then sprayed on a hot shade of Benetint. She changed into her *de Chaumont* pantsuit and settled herself on the couch in front of the pix. She turned the pix into a mirror so she could see herself as Ed would see her. She tilted her head and tried for an assured, casual look. Then she brought up *Ed Explains It All* and clicked through greeting to the contract pages for a personal interview. The fee agreement almost stopped her. It was going to cost her a *hundred dollars a minute* to get Ed's advice. But then she thought about how smart he was. How calm. She opened a window to check the balance on their bank account. They had $2393.89, but they needed eleven hundred for the July rent.

Twelve minutes then, what she had was a twelve-minute problem. She was thinking about how to tell it as she opened their account to the contract genie.

Talisha wasn't expecting to be connected immediately. She thought some secretary would come on the pix and they would schedule an appointment or something. But when she thumbed the last contract page, Ed himself peered into her tiny apartment.

"Go ahead," he said. "I'm listening."

This wasn't the familiar Ed of the bi-weekly episode, who sat at desk in a vast library, resplendent in his characteristic white suit, dark blue shirt, and paisley tie. This Ed was wearing green plaid pajamas and he needed a shave. He was sitting at a table in a sunny room pouring Cheerios into a bowl.

"Ed," she said, "Is that you?"

"It is. Go ahead please."

"But I . . . I mean I wasn't . . . Wait, are you real?"

He sighed and peeled a banana. "That question cost you seventeen dollars, madam. Have you ever read Hegel?"

"My name is Talisha. Hegel who?"

"Hegel wrote, 'The will is a special way of thinking; it is thought translating itself into reality; it is the impulse of thought to give itself reality.' Now Talisha, do you want me to be real? Is such your will?"

Talisha wondered if this was a trick question. "Uh, I guess so."

"Well, then." Ed began to cut the banana onto his Cheerios. "Go ahead please."

Breathlessly, she told him about Ricky, their marriage, their money problems, and the mechdream pills. At a hundred dollars a minute, there was obviously a lot she had to leave out, but she was satisfied that she had done of good job of painting a picture of her husband as the *lying asswipe* that he was. While she spoke, Ed spooned up his breakfast. She couldn't help but notice that he was a very neat eater. Talisha always had to sponge off the kitchen table after Ricky ate.

Ed aimed his spoon at her when she finished. "But you *do* love him?"

"I . . ." Her cheeks flushed and she thought she might cry again. Instead she said, "Yes."

Ed considered this for ten or twelve dollars. "Who is he thinking of when you have intercourse?" he said finally.

"I don't know." She squirmed on the couch. "Me, I hope."

Ed shook his head wearily. "Let me put it this way, who are you thinking of?"

"Him." She could hear the squeak in her voice.

"Don't waste your money, Talisha, or my time. Do you keep your eyes closed when you're having intercourse?"

"I do." But then he would know that, wouldn't he? He was Ed. "Well, sometimes I think of Sanjay Deol."

"The pilot on *Let It Ride?* The one with the blue hair?"

She nodded. She couldn't believe she was telling her sexual fantasies to Ed and paying a hundred dollars a minute for the privilege. "And I used to think of Burt Christmas, but not since he took up with Pernilla Jones."

"All right. Now then, what's Richie's favorite part of your body?"

"Ricky." Talisha frowned and then held up her hand. "He said once that I had such pretty, long fingers." She gazed at them as if surprised to find them at the end of her arm. "He said I should've learned to play a musical instrument. Like flute or piano or something."

Ed smiled. "Touch the pix with your pretty fingers, Talisha."

She bolted from the couch and pressed the tips of her fingers to the screen.

"Good." He touched his own pix, so that his hand lined up with hers. Talisha's heart pounded. They were so close, even though she had no idea where he was. His face was serene. Kind. She decided that the next time she had sex, she might try thinking about Ed.

"People think I can solve their problems, Talisha, but I can't— not really." He turned back to the table and picked up his bowl and the box of Cheerios. "But I can tell you what to do if you want to stay married."

"I do," she whispered. "I don't know why, but I still want him."

"Then you'll have to go to where he is," said Ed. "See what he's doing."

Talisha spent the rest of the day thinking. It was hard work. She drank two cups of Zest and washed three loads of laundry and vacuumed the entire apartment and never once turned on the pix to watch any of her shows. She crawled on hands and knees to gather Ricky's pills. Of course, she had known right away what Ed had meant about going to him. He was telling her to take one of the pills so she could enter his mechdream. But she wasn't sure that she wanted to know what Ricky was hiding in his secret world. It was bad enough watching him brush his teeth. Now she had to be an eyewitness to his forbidden desires?

Talisha started when the door to the apartment opened at five-thirty and Ricky walked in. He was finished at work, so he had come home, of course. She thought he might at least have the decency to get stinking smart in some bar, stagger in at two in the morning, and come crawling to their bed to beg her forgiveness. Instead he hung his Titans jacket in the closet and dropped his computer on the coffee table as coolly as if he were a finalist for Husband of the Year.

"So?" Talisha said.

"So I don't want to talk about it right now."

"Fine," she said. "That's just fine."

He slid to the other side of the apartment to avoid her and squeezed between the couch and the ugly lamp his mother had given them. She didn't follow him into the sleeping closet; she knew what he was looking for.

"Where are they?" He came to the door.

"I hid them."

"Okay." He went back to change out of his work clothes.

And that was it. She didn't believe he'd be able to pull it off but he was his usual leaden self while he watched *The Sports Witch*. Then he played *You Can Say That Again* and climbed all the way to 11,234 out of 90,645. Talisha thought about frying just one Beefy Beanstix for herself but then she decided that if he could act as if their world wasn't ending, then so could she.

"Dinner," she called.

He came to the table and stared at the glass of water next to his slab of Beanstix. "Am I out of beer?"

"I poured them all down the sink," she said brightly.

He shrugged and sat down. "Okay."

Talisha tried to eat but she wasn't hungry. The air felt thick to her. Or something. The only sound in their apartment was the click of Ricky's fork against his plate. The silence didn't seem to bother him. He probably didn't even notice it. His body was in the apartment but his mind was probably riding cowgirls at Ricky's Ranch. She felt certain that she could've set his pants on fire and he wouldn't have complained. So how long had he been like this? Talisha wasn't sure now. Ricky had never been much of a talker but at least he used to ask her about her day when he came home. She would tell him about what she and Bea were working on, give him the news from *Amy Anderson* or *TTMR*. He managed to look interested when she described all the beautiful homes she'd seen on *Mainly Mansions*.

When Ricky finished eating, he cleared his plate—and hers— and waved them under the dishwasher. Talisha stared at his back as he put the dishes away. Then she watched him sidle to the couch.

He sat and opened his messages. She leaned back, waiting for the explosion.

"Talisha, what's this bill about?" he called.

"I talked to Ed."

"Eleven hundred dollars worth?"

"He explained some things to me."

Ricky thought this over. "Okay."

Talisha couldn't believe it. She'd torched their finances and he was acting like a light bulb had burned out. He cleared the messages off the pix and began to click through the menus on *The Classic Car Channel.* "Is that why you're all dressed up?" he said.

She had forgotten that she was still in her *de Chaumont* pantsuit. She'd bought it three years ago and only wore it on special occasions like birthdays and anniversaries. Up until today, she had only worn it *for him.* Well, maybe there weren't going to be any more damn anniversaries.

"Fuck you, Ricky." She flew into the bathroom and slammed the door behind her.

She had stashed the flat cardboard box with her tampons. In a rage she shook one of Ricky's pills into her hand and popped it into her mouth. She'd go where he was, all right. She leaned over the sink and drank directly from the tap to wash the nasty thing down. She'd stick her head into his little pervert palace and tell him to shove the rest of his pills up his zombie ass.

She closed the toilet lid and sat down. She had no idea how the pill would affect her. As she waited, she thought about Ed's green plaid pajamas. She wondered if maybe she could live with Bea. She noticed that they were almost out of toilet paper. Her brain felt odd. There were toothpaste spots on the mirror. She wasn't sure that she had ever felt her brain before. It was a tickle, no, it was more like bubbles bursting and each bubble was the note of a song which she didn't recognize but if she concentrated, she could sort of pick up the melody and then bits of lyric, something about The Dark Side Of Town and the woman who lived there or maybe a woman who was going there, *yes,* that was it, a woman was going to see another woman who lived on The Dark Side Of Town and that woman was her, *Talisha,* and now it was getting **dark** in the bathroom only that wasn't right because she could see the water stain where the ceiling leaked and then the door opened and Ricky came and helped her up off the toilet and said *It's hard the first time* as he took her by the arm and led her to the sleeping closet and then she was lying on the bed and he was taking off her shoes and she was so sad as he paused to turn off the light and the door *snicked* shut.

There was a parking lot on The Dark Side Of Town. The cars lined up in rows had headlights on and engines running but they weren't going anywhere. Talisha didn't like the looks of them. They were old-fashioned cars, the models for the carbots that Ricky fixed. She had seen the full-sized ones mostly in the old, flat movies and in that museum. Not many people rode in the old cars anymore. Certainly not Talisha. As she approached the parking lot she could see lights inside the cars—and shadowy people.

Ricky rolled down the window of a long, low, green car that looked like it had melted in the sun. "You like it?" he said. "It's a 1969 Pontiac GTO with a Ram Air III 400 cubic inch engine." Ricky was wearing a sky blue tuxedo. "Eight cylinders, 366 horse power." A woman was curled up on the tiny back seat, seemingly asleep.

"What is this, Ricky?"

He closed his hand over the stick shift. "It's a Hurst T-handle four speed."

"I mean, who's *that?*" She wanted to throttle the woman but there was only one door on this side. Talisha would've had to drag Ricky out of the driver's seat to get at her. "Hey you!" She stuck her head in the window. "Who the hell are you?"

"A posi rear axel," said Ricky.

The woman stirred.

"There's nobody but you, 'Sha," he said.

When the woman raised her face into the dim glow of the dome light, Talisha could see it was true. It was her, like a double or something. She was dressed in shimmer tights and a zebra print halter top, clothes that Talisha had thrown out years ago. She looked to be wearing Talisha's favorite pink lipstick, "Baby Kiss."

"So get in." Ricky reached across to the passenger door and opened it.

"And do what?"

Ricky leered and stepped on the gas. Three hundred and sixty-six horses screamed.

Talisha gave him her back and strode down the line of cars. But there was no escape. He called to her from every car. "1990 Jaguar XJS! 1929 Duesenberg J Murphy Roadster! 1952 DeSoto FireDome!"

As she passed an enormous boxy sedan with tiny windshields, he honked the horn. It startled her and she jumped.

"1932 Chrysler CL Custom Imperial," he said. "Oilite squeak-proof springs. Double drop girder truss . . ."

"Stop it, Ricky."

He opened the door and got out of the car. "Why did you swallow that pill, 'Sha?"

"So I could tell you to go suck cactus."

"You could've done that at the apartment." Now he was wearing a gray, one-button cutaway tuxedo with a lavender vest and matching four-in-hand tie. "You wanted to see what I was doing, didn't you?" He crossed the front of the car, brushing a finger along the elaborate chrome grill.

"And now I have, thanks so much." But she hesitated. "Who's dressing you, anyway?" she said.

"You like?" He struck a pose and then turned around slowly to give her the full effect. "I uploaded a fashion bug." He opened the rear passenger door. "You haven't seen it all, Talisha. Come look."

She heard the sleeping closet door open and the real Ricky tiptoed in. He didn't turn on the lights.

"Internal hydraulic brakes," said the Ricky in the mech-dream. "All steel body. Floating power engine mountings."

The old box springs of their bed creaked as Ricky lay down. He didn't touch her but she could sense his nearness by the sag of the mattress. "Please Talisha," he whispered. "Let me show you."

Talisha saw her double lounging on the back seat in a pink felt smoking jacket over a plum crepe gown. Her face was partially obscured by the netting draped from her shrimp-colored pillbox hat and the plume of smoke from the Chesterfield cigarette in her left hand. Talisha had never smoked before and never would. On the seat next to the double was a wicker bassinet. When the baby gurgled, Talisha felt like she'd been slapped.

"Whose is that?"

"Ours." Ricky beamed at her.

"Yours, you mean."

"I know you've been wanting to have a kid." He reached past her and rubbed his knuckle against the baby's cheek. "It's a little boy. So what should we name it?"

"How the fuck should I know. Ask *her*."

For a second the two Talishas stared at each other. Then the double rolled her window down and flipped her cigarette out at The Dark Side Of Town.

"She doesn't speak," said Ricky. "She's just a place holder."

"This is sick." Talisha shook her head. "It's not real, Ricky. Nothing here is. It's all inside your head."

"Sure, and now it's inside your head too. That's the point. Two more pills and you'll lock in to the servers at Werefolk."

She gazed at him in astonishment and horror.

"What do you think I've been doing here, 'Sha? Getting this place ready for you."

Talisha turned and ran back the way she had come.

Ricky called after her. "It's the only way for people like us."

"But I don't want to live in a car." Talisha said as she rolled onto her side. Ricky was watching her, his eyes bright in the gloom of the sleeping closet. "Not even in a whole fleet of cars." She reached across the bed and touched his arm.

"Then don't," said Ricky.

The biggest car she had ever seen edged out of the line, blocking her way. She heard the hum of an electric motor and then Ricky stuck his head through a hole in the roof. "2005 Ford Excursion XLT Premium with optional moonroof. It has a V-10 engine, 310 horses."

"What do you mean, *don't?*" Talisha said.

He pulled the SUV up beside her. Talisha was wearing a fawn-colored fleece jacket, twill khakis, and a lavender turtleneck, clothes she had never owned before in her life. She opened the front passenger door and looked in.

"Rear seat DVD with a twelve inch LCD," said Ricky. "Ten cup holders."

The Excursion was as huge on the inside as it looked from the outside, but it still wasn't big enough to live in. There were three rows of two-toned leather seats. The baby was strapped into a rear-facing car seat behind Ricky. The double was gone.

"Want to go for a spin?" Ricky's face shone in the light of the instrument console.

They cruised The Dark Side Of Town, their headlights illuminating blank facades and empty lots. "I'm not ready for sun," said Ricky. "In the daylight, all the holes would show. But now that you're here, more stuff will get done. Here it is." He pressed a button on the dash and a garage door began to open. "I haven't done any decorating yet." He pulled into the middle bay of a three car garage. The other two bays were empty.

Talisha slid across the bed and gave Ricky a tentative caress. He whooped and pulled her on top of him as he shut the Excursion off. Talisha stepped down from the car and took in the garage.

Her garage. The walls were white. The white steel door that opened into the house was up two steps to the left. The garage was nice, but way too plain. Ricky kissed Talisha and she ran her tongue along the edges of his front teeth as she traced the spot on the garage wall where the window ought to be with her long, pretty fingers. A nine-light Prairie Style double hung with real wood grilles shimmered into existence. Yes, that was better, but not quite there yet. Her window needed some curtains, say chintz. With big yellow roses.

"It's a garage, 'Sha." said Ricky. "Who hangs curtains in a garage?" He fumbled at the front snap of Talisha's pants. He was never very good at undressing her.

"We do," Talisha said, but she changed the pattern to little white daisies on a field of blue. It was easy, like playing the flute or piano or something.

Ricky unbuckled the harness on the car seat and slid Talisha's pants over her hips and hefted the baby. "Ready for the tour?" he said.

"Ed." Talisha held out her arms for their son. "We'll call him Ed."

for Janis Ian

The Leila Torn Show

*T*HE LEILA TORN SHOW WAS NERVOUS AS SHE SUR-
veyed the audience on the studio monitor, trying to get a feel for
their mood. When her band played her theme song as Slappy
O'Toole stepped onto the set for the pre-show warm up, their
fanfare was ragged. Chill, the band leader, glared at Bebop, the
trumpet player and Bebop stared at his shoes. *The Leila Torn Show*
could see the studio audience shifting uncomfortably in their seats.
She winced as Slappy's jokes bounced off them. Maybe they were
just tired. Or hearing-impaired. Or Estonian. A bead of sweat glis-
tened just below Slappy's receding hairline.

The Leila Torn Show had known all along that there would be a
huge letdown after last week's episode, when she had killed off her
main character. But she had to push on. If she could just hold her
own through tonight, she'd be all right.

Her content providers were already looking ahead. In the comedy segment of next week's episode, they wanted to send someone
to the dentist. The ceepees hadn't decided who it would be yet,
although Slappy had already put in his bid. *The Leila Torn Show* felt
sorry for him; he was in just one scene this week and he had only
two lines, a joke about the weather. Her staff demographer had
explained to him that his numbers skewed old and fat. Grandmas

with deep fryers wrote him fan email but they didn't buy enough upscale product.

The ceepees were pitching her a waiting room scene for the dentist episode that would feature two or three oddballs.

"Odd but wacky," Cass said.

"In a surreal way," said Graves, the head content provider.

Then would come a teeth-cleaning scene. Margo Rain, the guest talent, was to play the chatty hygienist. She'd go blonde, of course, and pump up her boobs a cup size. And the hemline of her uniform dress would be short as a sinner's memory. "She'll stop the eighteen to twenty-five-year-old males in mid-click," said Graves. "Remotes will fall from their trembling hands." But it wouldn't do to stereotype Margo Rain. After all, she was a legitimate actress, not bound to any one show. She had the complete works of Ibsen loaded into her memory. Euripides. Edward Albee. *The Leila Torn Show* was courting respect this season. She was tired of going for the cheap laugh.

"Thing is, I can't help the way I look," Slappy told the audience as he wiped his forehead with a limp handkerchief. "Me, I've always been hard on the eye, so you might say." He puffed out his cheeks. "I mean, I was so ugly as a kid that I had to trick or treat over the phone."

A ripple passed through the first four rows of the studio but died there. *The Leila Torn Show* snorted in disgust. The studio audience was still breathing, but that seemed to be all they were capable of at the moment.

The ceepees were proposing a classic complication for the crime segment of next week's episode. After one of the talent—probably not poor Slappy—finished getting his teeth cleaned, he would grab his trench coat and leave. Only he'd get the wrong coat, one belonging to a corrupt, wacky aide to a Congresswoman. The Congresswoman would also be played by Margo Rain. The wacky, corrupt aide intended to sell documents to the tabloid press proving that the Congresswoman had had an illegal personality boost. The talent with the clean teeth would eventually turn those papers over to Leila.

Or rather, the new Leila.

"Sure, I've put on a few pounds since the show started—I don't deny it. Hey, I've got the only car in town with stretch marks." Slappy clapped his hands to his paunch and bugged out his eyes hopefully, but the studio stayed as quiet as a snowfall.

The aide would then be poisoned and the Congresswoman

would be accused of the murder, which would make this a case for Leila's law firm. Slappy currently worked as her chauffeur, although in the first few seasons, when he had been younger and slimmer, he had been her sidekick. He was always campaigning for more to do in the crime segments. Sometimes he got to cover the back entrance when Leila kicked in the front door of the murderer's house. Mostly he just got the plot explained to him.

"And when I get home, it's the same. My wife says that I'm as useless as rubber lips on a woodpecker." Slappy's wife had been killed in Season Seven, although as far as *The Leila Torn Show* knew, he might have remarried in dreamspace. He clapped a hand over his eyes, waited a beat and then spread his fingers and peeked shyly through at the studio audience. She could barely stand to watch her oldest talent, now the sole survivor from the original cast, demean himself this way. But there wasn't much else he could do for her these days.

In next week's fantasy segment, Lucifer would stop the action as usual, just as the jury was about to return its verdict. The ceepees hadn't yet worked out what deal the devil would offer the Congresswoman for an acquittal. Cass was pitching a commitment to lower the voting age to thirteen, so they could cameo one of those teens from *Rock Zombie High* that everyone was talking about. Graves was holding out for a yes vote on equal rights for dogs; then they could cross-promote with the ongoing puppynappy series on *The Daily Now*.

Slappy gave up on the studio audience. He smeared a grin onto his round face and gave them a broad, over-the-head wave. "Well, I'm glad you decided to stay, because we have another great show for you coming right up. Our guest tonight is Kent Turnabout from *Candy Asteroid*." Slappy nodded, waiting for the sleepy applause to die down. "I know you're really going to like this episode, folks, because I'm hardly in it at all."

Some lackwit in the back row gave him two sarcastic claps.

"Thanks, Mom." Slappy turned to the band. "How about a little vanishing music, Chill?" The band struck up "Turn Left on Lonely Street" and Slappy trotted into the wings.

The assistant whip, Herb Katz, gave him a sympathetic pat on the back. "Tough crowd tonight."

"I've seen happier gravestones." He pulled off his tie. "You make any decisions about the dentist skit next week?" He started to unbutton his shirt.

The Leila Torn Show decided it would be a kindness to break the bad news to Slappy then and there. "I think we're going to give it to Jay," said Herb. "He's a good fit, don't you think?" J. Timson Traylor was Leila's landlord, a know-it-all and a bit of a prig. "He can play grouchy in the waiting room scene and everyone will love it when Margo shuts him up by sticking a mirror and that little pointy thing into his mouth."

"A scaler," said Slappy. "It's called a scaler."

"If you say so." Herb's face went blank. "Nobody is going to know that's what it's called, Slap."

"I do." He dropped his shirt on the floor. "Jay will." A clothes snake slithered toward it. "I'll give it to the ceepees." The snake unhinged its jaw and swallowed the shirt. "Maybe they can tweak a gag out of it."

"Tell them to have Margo stick him with it."

Slappy stepped out of his pants and waved over his shoulder as he headed for the ceepees' den. *The Leila Torn Show* was grateful to have talent who still cared about her as much as Slappy O'Toole. He was a real team player. Of course, he had to be. He wasn't ever going to be spun off to a show of his own. As the snake ate Slappy's pants, she decided to have her ceepees write him a new warm-up set. Something less personal. Maybe about robots. Or Chinese food.

Herb Katz trudged down to the prop room and opened Anita Bright's closet. She shivered as the florescent light penetrated her dreamspace.

"Thirty minutes, Anita," said Herb. "Time to get dressed."

Anita growled and stretched. She was naked; most of the talent waited for their calls in the nude. It made costume changes go faster. Two clothes snakes coiled by the makeup table just outside the closet, waiting to disgorge Anita's underwear and blouse and the indigo Jacquard pantsuit she would wear in the crime scene. Anita was a detective working out of Homicide, who was Leila's nemesis and sometime lover. Old Leila. She had a delicious body; there was no question that appropriate curves had always been part of the show's appeal. But all that taut, creamy skin did nothing for Herb Katz, who was happily married to Chill Jensen, the band leader in dreamspace, where her talent lived when they weren't doing the show.

"How's the house?" said Anita, taking a seat at the makeup table.

"A freezer filled with mom and popsicles," said Herb. "Slappy barely got out alive."

"He needs better lines." Anita picked up the bra the snake had coughed into her lap. "We all do." She slipped it on.

"And the ceepees say they need fresh talent."

"Ceepees come and go," she said bitterly. "This cast has been earning the ratings for seventeen seasons."

"Seventeen is a lifetime in dog years."

In the studio overhead, Kent Turnabout was getting the first big laughs of the episode. The ceepees had him playing a funeral director, newly arrived from Mars, who hadn't quite adjusted to Earth's gravity. He flopped unexpectedly into mourners' laps, almost knocked Leila's closed coffin off its stand and then tried to apologize to it. The laughter pattered against the ceiling of the prop room like rain. "That sounds promising," said Herb.

The Leila Torn Show was relieved that the studio audience was finally reacting, even if it was only because of Turnabout's frenetic mugging. Sensing that he had to carry the comedy segment pretty much by himself, he buzzed around the set like the world's most smarmy fly. In comparison, her own talent seemed about as animated as office furniture. Still in shock over Leila's death, they offered him straight lines at arm's length and watched bleakly as he snatched laughs from their limp grasp. Turnabout was only the third male lead on *Candy Asteroid* but he was one of the hottest talents on the Allview. He could pop a smile out of a meter maid just by arching an eyebrow. Already there was talk of spinning him off into his own show.

"The only reason they're laughing," said Anita, "is because the man is a lightweight. He hasn't got the brains that God gave to smoke. I swear, if he even looks sideways at the cameras while I'm testifying, I'm coming off the stand to kick the grin off his silly face."

"Easy, girl," said Herb. "Everyone agreed that we needed some fluff after last week. And he'll pull millions of stupids in."

Anita glared at him in the mirror. "I thought we were leaving the stupids to *Breakfast with the Blockheads*." She slithered into her slip. When she looked up again, he was off rousting the rest of the crime segment talent out of dreamspace.

The Leila Torn Show had known that killing her lead off would make for trouble with her talent as soon as Leila had suggested it. But over the five episode arc that had concluded last week, her ratings had shot back almost to where they had been in her glory days. She felt as powerful as she had ever been, ready to wrestle with the Allview for a slot higher up on the main menu, more cross promotion with other shows, better guest stars, and pricier audience giveaways. But these next few episodes were key. She had to hold her rediscovered audience after seventeen years of pratfalls and stabbings and all-expense paid vacations to the moon.

Anita shrugged into the jacket of her pantsuit and slipped on her matte black flats. She turned away from the full length mirror that she shared with Parthia Lukacz and looked over her shoulder at herself in the mirror. She tilted first one shoulder down and then the other, pursed her lips and thought pillow thoughts. She had been hoping to catch up with Slappy in dreamspace to ease his pain but she hadn't been able to find him, which was strange. He was the only one of the cast with a soul, in her opinion. Maybe they could steal a few private moments here in the studio. The possibility titillated her. She knew she wasn't supposed to do all that much in reality except be on the show. If she wanted to make her own decisions, she could choose in dreamspace. But dreamspace was so pale and the studio was so vivid. If she and Slappy . . .

The Leila Torn Show squashed that dangerous thought flat and sent Anita to check the new Leila.

The new Leila was the daughter of the old Leila's evil twin, Nia, who was introduced in Season Four. The old Leila had barely had time to have sex, much less give birth and raise children. She was too busy solving murders and contending with the devil for the souls of the guest stars. Her twin Nia, on the other hand, had enjoyed plenty of leisure when she wasn't corrupting mayors or managing her international crime cartel. Nia had shielded her daughter from that part of her life, however. In fact, the ceepees hadn't even realized that Nia had a daughter until Season Fifteen. At the climax of last week's episode, the old Leila had summoned the last of her strength to tell the new Leila of Nia's nefarious doings. And then she died of the slow-acting poison that a mysterious someone had slipped her in an episode five weeks earlier. *The Leila Torn Show* had killed her lead talent off despite the biggest audience of the season, 87% of which had clicked a preference for the old Leila to save herself. In last week's fantasy segment, the devil had offered her a miracle cure in exchange for leaving the new Leila in her mother's malevolent clutches. This, of course, was something the old Leila could never do. *The Leila Torn Show* knew it was possibly foolhardy to go up against her audience like that, but that was the kind of show she was. People would either have to accept her or click on. And nobody but *The Leila Torn Show* would ever know how much it hurt to let her poor, brave Leila sacrifice herself for the good of the show.

Now she had to help the new Leila sell this plot twist to the hundred million customers of the Allview. *The Leila Torn Show* was by no means certain that she was up to the task, which is why she'd asked Anita to watch out for her.

The new Leila had inherited the old Leila's dressing room and had remade it to her own tastes. The old Leila liked hard surfaces that showed their years. There had been rust on the overhead beams and her Napoleon IV mirror had needed resilvering. This Leila was a fan of butterflies. The wallscape showed a tropical rainforest swarming with Longwings and Julias and Swallowtails and Blue Waves. The mirror was in the shape of a Gulf Frittilary and was lit by glowworms. Reflected in it was the face of the new lead of *The Leila Torn Show*. Her eyes were haunted and when she saw Anita her mouth puckered into a walnut. Anita was certain then that this episode was about to plunge off a cliff but she was talent. It was her role here to underplay her feelings, show confidence in the new Leila that she didn't feel.

"Ready for your big debut?" she said brightly.

"There were supposed to be raisins," said Leila stiffly. "I specifically asked Herb for raisins."

Anita glanced at the bowl of Muscat raisins on the dressing table, dark as garnets. Leila followed her gaze and then with a screech of frustration swept the bowl onto the floor, shattering it.

"I said golden raisins!" She bounced on her chair twice. "I thought we spoke English on this show."

Anita took a breath. "We all get the jitters, Leila." Then another, longer breath. "I remember my first episode . . ."

"I didn't upload my part." She regarded herself with grim satisfaction in the butterfly mirror, as if she had just issued some kind of artistic manifesto.

Anita clamped her teeth together so hard she thought she might shatter a molar. *The good of the show*, she told herself. "Well then," she said carefully, "since there's no time for you to dip into dreamspace to catch yourself up, the whips will have to feed you lines through your earstone." Anita tried to imagine how a talent could turn into a stupid. "Don't worry, they do that all the time with last minute rewrites."

"I did it on purpose, you know. I'm going to give a cold reading." She emphasized *cold* and *reading* as if these were terms of art that Anita might not be familiar with. "That way whatever I say will sound like I just made it up."

"Like you just . . . ? But you're on in ten minutes with Turnabout." Anita was so taken aback that she spoke before she realized what she was saying. "He'll stick his tongue into your ear and then tuck you into his back pocket, if you don't know what you're doing."

"He wouldn't." Leila's eyes went wide. "He came to visit me

yesterday in dreamspace. He seemed so nice. He brought me a puppy."

"*Kent Turnabout?*"

Leila spun away from the mirror to face Anita. "You all hate me because I'm not her." Then she melted into tears. "I can't do this. I'm not a talent. I was going to be a pet groomer." She picked up a brush imprinted with the bright yellows of the Golden Angelwing butterfly. "I don't know anything about solving murders and I'm scared of the devil."

"Listen, Leila. You have to pull yourself together. We're all depending on you. You're the lead now."

"I don't want to be the lead!" She brushed her hair furiously. "I want raisins."

It was all Anita could do to keep from slapping her. If there was one thing that all the talent in the cast had yearned for over the years, it was to be spun off to a show of their own. Anita had conceived any number of elaborate sets for *Love, Anita* in dreamspace. Yet like everything else in dreamspace, it wasn't good enough. Dreamspace was her refuge but she longed for the reality of *The Leila Torn Show* and the Allview. Now this brat was handed the coveted prize of the lead on a show and all she could think of was to push it away?

Anita could feel her fingernails stabbing her palm but her voice was steady. "What would your aunt say if she could hear you now?"

"She's dead. The show killed her."

"She offered to die so the rest of us could go on." She put a hand on Leila's hot, wet cheek and turned her head so that their eyes met. "Doesn't that mean anything to you?"

"Of course it does. I loved Leila too." She shook herself free. "But why won't anybody listen to me? What if I can't *be* her?"

There was a knock at the door; Herb Katz cracked it open. "Fifteen minutes, Leila," he called, and then stuck his head in. He was neither surprised to find Anita in the room nor alarmed to see Leila in tears. "Are you two girls having a heart-to-heart?"

"We can't." Leila swiped at the corner of her eye. "We're one heart shy."

Anita and Herb exchanged glances. "You'll be fine, Leila." Herb touched a finger to his forehead. "Fifteen minutes."

The Leila Torn Show wasn't so sure. The way this episode was going so far, she wondered if she might have made a mistake. Had she betrayed herself just to eke out a few limp last episodes? How many shows survived the death of the lead? Watching Kent Turnabout chew up her talent in the comedy segment made her wish she had lured some hot second lead from another show to replace Leila. Or maybe a strong pitch might have enticed Margo Rain to become her lead, instead of just signing on for a guest shot. She would even have considered calling herself *The Margo Rain Show*. After all, what was in a name?

The Leila Torn Show was so depressed that she turned away from the studio for the first time ever while an episode was live. The whips could run the show without her. Leila would either score or she wouldn't. The cast would either rally or not. Her audience would either stay or click elsewhere. All she could do now was watch anyway, just like the millions of customers of the Allview. But *The Leila Torn Show* could not bear to look at how far she had fallen, so instead she ghosted back into her archives.

Critics maintained that her best seasons were the First and Second, the Eighth, when she first introduced the comic segment and the Twelfth, Thirteenth, and Fourteenth, when Graves's inspired casting of Lucifer for the fantasy segment had vaulted them to the top of the Allview menu. But *The Leila Torn Show*'s favorite season was the Third, when she was a straight crime show and the plots were all fresh. The cast had been different then, full of ambition and wisecracks. Leila had been a P. I. going to law school at night. Slappy had been Slick, thirty pounds thinner, an ex-con turned P. I. who was sexy and funny and quick with his fists. He and Leila had had an affair in Season Two that Slick never really got over, but in Season Three, their banter suggested they might still get back together. In those days, Anita Bright was a cop on a mission to make detective and maybe leap to her own show; she had no use for Leila and wasn't afraid to let the world know it. Leila still had a roommate in Season Three: Meg Wordsworth, a reporter for *Watch This*, who had a knack of being in the right place at the right time, mostly because she was always tagging along with Leila on her cases. Tom Rocket had not yet left the law firm where Leila worked to go to outer space. And of course, back then Leila was in almost every scene; she *was The Leila Torn Show*.

But what always drew her back to Season Three was Leo No, Leila's criminal nemesis for ten different episodes. Although she had put several of his lieutenants behind bars—and two into the morgue—he always managed to skip free just when she thought she had him. He sent her a different playing card—all hearts, starting with the deuce—as a taunt at the conclusion of each of his Season Three episodes. *The Leila Torn Show* still didn't understand why

Graves had refused to let Leila capture him and why the Leo No arc stopped at the jack of hearts. But then she didn't understand ceepees; what they did seemed equal parts mendacity and black magic. In the last episode of Season Three, Meg had reported that No had died in the terrorist nuking of Geneva; the cast believed that it was just a ceepee tease for Season Four. But then, in the second episode of that season, Meg had been kidnapped and held hostage until she was executed in the cliffhanger last episode. After that, the ceepees never got around to raising Leila's first archenemy from the dead.

Leila had come closest to Leo No in the jack of hearts episode, in which she was representing the wife of a psychiatrist played by the late Dame Hillary Winterberry. The payoff scene was set among the dressing rooms of a Midnight on Main menswear store, in which Leila had to go from stall to stall, searching for the killer. *The Leila Torn Show* knew it was dangerous to spend too much time looking at reruns, but in her dispirited state, she couldn't seem to help herself.

INT. STORE/SWINGING HALF DOORS
                    SLICK
(*draws gun*)
In there?

                    LEILA
Yes. But there isn't going to be any gunplay, loverboy. This is No's accountant, not his muscle.
                    SLICK
You willing to bet your life on that?
                    LEILA
Why not? I like the odds. (*beat*) But if I lose you can keep my ashes under the bed.
(*pushes through doors*)
INT. STORE/DRESSING ROOM CORRIDOR
                    LEILA
Lester?

            (*pulls aside first curtain*)
INT. STORE/DRESSING ROOM STALL/CUSTOMER IN BOXERS
                    CUSTOMER
No Lester in here, babe. But there's room for you.
                    LEILA
Sorry. I'm looking for my son. He's supposed to be trying on his prom tux.

(*closes curtain*)

(*aside*) Boxers. Not my type.

INT. STORE/DRESSING ROOM CORRIDOR

LEILA

Oh Lester, honey?

(*pulls aside second curtain*)

INT. STORE/DRESSING ROOM STALL/THE DEVIL IN SILK TOKAJER SUIT

THE DEVIL

Try two stalls down.

THE LEILA TORN SHOW

You! But you were never in this episode! (*beat*) Wait, *you* were Leo No?

THE DEVIL

Me? Too small a role. (*beat*) Besides, I hate being typecast.

THE LEILA TORN SHOW

How did you get into my archive? What is this?

THE DEVIL

(*spreads his hands*)

The usual. I'm here to offer you a proposition.

INT. STORE/DRESSING ROOM STALL/CLOSEUP: THE LEILA TORN SHOW

THE LEILA TORN SHOW

No.

INT. STORE/DRESSING ROOM CORRIDOR/ANGLE

THE DEVIL

No? Not even interested in hearing the terms?

THE LEILA TORN SHOW

I'm not talent. I'm the show.

THE DEVIL

You think, you feel, you enjoy and suffer. My, how you suffer. I believe we have a basis for a transaction. (*beat*) Just out of curiosity, how many more years would you want?

THE LEILA TORN SHOW

Years?

THE DEVIL

If this new lead doesn't work out, you've probably got less than a handful of episodes left before the Allview shuts you down.

INT. STORE/DRESSING ROOM STALL/CLOSEUP: THE LEILA TORN SHOW

THE LEILA TORN SHOW

You can give me years?

INT. STORE/DRESSING ROOM STALL/CLOSEUP: THE DEVIL
THE DEVIL
Years.
INT. STORE/DRESSING ROOM STALL/ANGLE
THE LEILA TORN SHOW
This is a joke the ceepees are playing on me. You can't make that something like that happen. You're just talent.
THE DEVIL
No, Lucifer is just talent. I'm the devil, sister, the real deal. I'm offering you years because when I get you, I get the rest of the cast all at once. I'm tired of collecting your people piecemeal. I can extend myself for a package deal.
INT. STORE/DRESSING ROOM STALL/NEW ANGLE
THE LEILA TORN SHOW
My people?
THE DEVIL
Ever wonder how Graves got to be head ceepee? Why Jay is written into every segment?
THE LEILA TORN SHOW
I don't believe you've been talking to my talent. I'd know about it.
THE DEVIL
Why? You're not God. You're just a show. (*beat*) Care to deal?
THE LEILA TORN SHOW
(*backing away*)
No. Get away from me.
THE DEVIL
That's what they all say—at first. Tell you what . . . I'll start things rolling in your direction and then come back in a while for your final answer. Meanwhile, if you don't mind . . .
(*pulls curtain closed*)

"Has anyone seen Slappy?" Herb Katz slipped into the Green Room. Anita Bright, Parthia Lukacz, and J. Timson Traylor glanced up from their game of Hearts. "I checked everywhere: backstage, his closet, makeup, the john, the ceepee's den. He missed the ten minute call and now he's about to miss his cue."

"Well, he hasn't been with us," said Parthia, the assistant D. A. who Leila regularly skunked in court. "If we had a fourth, we could play bridge."

"Something's wrong," said Anita, coming out of her chair.

Traylor put his hand on her arm. "And you're not the one to put it right." He tugged her back onto her seat. "We're playing a hand here."

The Leila Torn Show could see that Traylor was trying to shoot the moon. If he could lull Parthia into dumping her queen of spades onto his king, he'd have it.

"He's right, Anita," said Herb. "You stay put or you'll miss your cue."

"Besides," continued Traylor, "Turnabout will skip right by Slappy's lines if he gets the chance. All Slappy has tonight is a weather report."

"Bastard Turnabout is making this episode up as he goes," grumbled Parthia. She put her hand on the queen of spades, jiggled it thoughtfully and then pulled the ten instead. "And Leila, our new leading doormat, is letting him walk all over her."

"Can you believe he had the balls to steal some of her lines before she could spit them out?" said Traylor.

"Maybe he'll start questioning witnesses once we go to trial." Parthia raised her hand and spoke in her most outraged courtroom bark. "Your honor, I object. Counsel for the defense is irrelevant, immaterial, and catatonic."

Traylor chuckled. Anita opened her mouth to suggest that Herb check for Slappy outside the stage door that opened onto Tomcat Alley but Herb Katz had already vanished. Sometimes it seemed to her as though the whips had the ability to pass through walls.

The Leila Torn Show was disturbed by Slappy's disappearance. She began a quick inventory of the building but couldn't see him anywhere. He must have left, as impossible as that seemed. It only confirmed what the devil has said to her, that her cast, her whips, her band, even her ceepees could keep secrets from her. Free will was fine in dreamspace but it had no place in the studio.

"Torn?" said the Allview's show-to-show messaging system. It overrode all *The Leila Torn Show*'s other inputs; she could no more ignore it than she could a lightning strike. "Rocket here."

Rocket Law was where Tom Rocket had finally landed after the Allview had lifted him from her at the end of Season Five. Tom had guested everywhere while the Allview developed a show for him. *Rocket Law* followed the adventures of a ragtag limited partnership of defense attorneys who flitted around the galaxy in their starship *Queen of Hearts* righting wrongs, bending alien statutes, and having affairs. While it had never quite reached the top of the Allview menu, it was a solid second tier show, which consistently delivered a high attention quotient.

"Rocket, I'm live right now," said *The Leila Torn Show*. "Can this wait?"

"And I'm watching you right now," said *Rocket Law*. "The episode is a bust."

The Leila Torn Show bit back her anger. "It's just Turnabout." When had she ever called *Rocket Law* to criticize his stupid lawyer tricks? "He's too big for the part."

"No, it's your lead, Torn. You dropped a mouse in the lion's den."

"Since when did you grow your critic's horns?"

"Since never. I'm talking numbers, not art."

The Leila Torn Show had been afraid to check but there was no getting around it now that she had been directly challenged by another show. According to the instants, she'd been hemorrhaging ratings at about a point a minute even since Leila had made her first appearance.

"I'm busy, Rocket," she said. "Skip to the payoff."

"I'll take this new Leila off your hands. My ceepees have come up with a great multi-episode plot line. Do you know who her father is?"

The Leila Torn Show consulted Graves and the other ceepees. "No. Nia never revealed who the father was."

"Well, Tom Rocket tells me that it's probably him. So now my ceepees are saying we should bring her aboard the *Queen of Hearts*. The Delalo are trying to get back at Tom for breaking the Molybdenum Treaty and we're having it that they've implanted a personality worm in Leila, which explains why she's such a stiff. I'm offering a crossover plot for the next two episodes. My ceepees get veto power over yours—I don't do boob jokes on my show. After that Leila joins my cast and I'll send Miriel Six over to you. She wants to settle down and have her puppies."

Miriel Six was only *Rocket Law*'s third female lead, but she was one of the sexiest dogs on the Allview.

"Miriel Six isn't a lead."

"Neither is the mouse you've got now. You're the show so it's your call, but you could go with guest leads until you find your girl. Or give that Anita Bright her shot; she's waited long enough."

"You're right, Rocket. I *am* the show."

"Don't get all huffy. And another thing, Tom asked if you wanted to send Slick O'Toole over too. I'll throw in some cross-promo. Have one of your talent give him a shout every few episodes, get him up to speed with what's happening back on Earth."

"You want *Slappy*?"

"Apparently he and Tommy were pals in your dreamspace. Anyway, think it over. We can talk again. By the way, you're down another three points." He clicked off.

As soon as *Rocket Law* released his hold on her head, the sounds and sights of the studio swarmed in once again on *The Leila Torn Show*. For better or worse, the episode was almost over. Lucifer was working the studio audience, looking to give away an American Cookhouse complete kitchen makeover just before the commercial break leading into the denouement. "Is there a Miss Angelina Bandoli in the house?" he called. "Angelina Bandoli?" *The Leila Torn Show* read him down to his neurons and confirmed that he was nothing but talent.

A petite, silver-haired woman in a housedress decorated with blue daisies levitated out of her seat with a squeal of joy.

"I hear you, mother." Lucifer charged up the aisle, holding the microphone in front of him like a knight with his lance. "Angelina, Angelina? Isn't that Italian for *angel*? Not sure I can do business with your kind."

The studio audience groaned in frustration.

Lucifer shook his head good-naturedly to reassure them he was just kidding. Once he called out a name, everyone knew it was a done deal. "So mother, it says here you've had a bad year." He thrust the mike at her and she rattled off a sad and slightly incoherent tale of hip replacement, multiple power failures, dead clownfish, and a stove fire. There were only forty-five seconds left before the commercial when he interrupted her.

"I'm satisfied." He turned to the camera and addressed the customers at home. "Are you satisfied?"

The studio audience replied as one. "We're *satisfied.*"

Lucifer turned back to Angelina Bandoli. "So mother, you're prepared to make a deal with the devil for state-of-the-art kitchen appliances from the American Cookhouse collection?"

Angelina glanced down at her empty seat, shy as a ten-year-old anticipating her first kiss.

Lucifer put an arm around her shoulder and leered into the camera. "And what are you willing to trade for this fabulous prize?"

"Stop!" The voice exploded from the wings, stage left. The curtain shivered and Slappy O'Toole stepped into the lights, a gun in his hand and a wildness in his eyes that *The Leila Torn Show* hadn't seen in years. "Stop this now."

Backstage, Herb Katz murmured, "Hold the commercial until I say."

"This is all wrong," said Slappy, trudging downstage toward the audience, the gun dangling like an afterthought. "Wrong, wrong, wrong." He called out to Lucifer. "We can't go on like this. We've ruined this show, all of us. Made it a joke."

The stage right curtains billowed and Kent Turnabout skipped onto the stage. *The Leila Torn Show* couldn't read her guest star as well as she could read Slappy but she knew if there were improvising going on, Turnabout would try to be part of it.

"That's right!" Turnabout danced around Slappy twice and then put an arm on his shoulder. "It's all a big joke now." His voice bounced mightily off the last row of the house. "I watched Leila when I was just a kid. I used to cheer when she caught the killer." He pointed at the people in the front row. "You good folks did too, right?" The audience murmured, uncertain whether they were in the comedy or the crime segment of the show. "In the old days there was justice," he said. "Now there are dishwashers."

Slappy shook Kent Turnabout off and pointed the gun at him. "You're what's wrong with this show, asshole."

The studio audience gasped.

The Leila Torn Show hadn't seen that gun since Season Seven, when Slick's wife had been murdered. When Slick had become Slappy. Now, ten years later, his arm trembled under its weight. "Leila would have never let the likes of you on when she was alive."

"Poor old Slippy." Turnabout stepped three paces back, made a gun of his thumb and forefinger and aimed at him. "Maybe you're what's wrong with this show. You're not funny anymore. That's why Leila put you on the shelf." He went up on tiptoes to place an imaginary Slappy on the highest shelf he could reach, making a noise like a slide whistle.

The Leila Torn Show guessed that stupids all over the world were peeing their pants with laughter.

Slappy considered, then nodded. "You're right," he said and put the gun to his temple. "I am just about done."

The house went quiet. Then a woman, maybe Angelina Bandoli, started to weep. Everyone was watching Slappy.

Except for Kent Turnabout, who was not about to be upstaged by a sad, fat, old ex-P. I. "You may be done, Mr. Sloppy," he called brightly, "but I'm not." He bounded across the stage like a deer on fire, snatched the gun from Slappy and put it to his own head.

"He thinks it's just a prop," Herb Katz's voice rang in every earstone. "Please God, somebody tell him that thing might be loaded."

The studio audience was just beginning to clap when he pulled the trigger. The gun fired with a roar like hell cracking open.

"Curtain!" shouted Herb Katz. "Lower the goddamn curtain."

But it was Chill Jensen who saved the day. The band leader called out "Star-Spangled Banner," tapped his baton and as soon as the band began to play the studio audience stood and sang along. The house was a little shaky but the customers at home couldn't smell the cordite or see the finger of blood poking from beneath the curtain. After they finished with the national anthem, Chill called for *The Leila Torn Show* theme song. The house lights came up and the audience stood and shuffled out, muttering in confusion.

The ceepees boiled out of their den to see the corpse for themselves. The band left their instruments on the bandstand and joined the cast which lingered in the wings, waiting for *The Leila Torn Show* to do something, say anything. But she was speechless in the shock of the moment. She kept telling herself that what had happened had nothing to do with her. It was the devil's work. She had asked for none of it.

Then the cops from *Protect and Defend* showed up, and sent everyone back to their dressing rooms and offices. Anita led Slappy back to the Green Room and sat with him there, holding his hand. To distract him, she put on one of his favorite episodes from Season Two, the one where he found the sailboat in the swimming pool. Many of the talent jumped straight into dreamspace while they waited to give their statements, momentarily safe from the rough and tumble of reality. Meanwhile, the cops went about their jobs with grim efficiency, although clearly *Protect and Defend* was jubilant at the chance to crossover into what promised to be a ratings bonanza.

Finally Graves shook *The Leila Torn Show* out of her lethargy. "We've got messages," he said. "Hundreds of them."

The Leila Torn Show scanned them quickly, and then left all but one for her ceepees to handle.

"I loved it," breathed Margo Rain. "Every minute of it. I've never seen a show blow itself up like that. And two weeks in a row. You're so brave. I'm very excited now to be on next week. You do have something special for me, no? Whatever you want, I'm yours."

The Leila Torn Show considered. In her heart, she believed that she hadn't agreed to anything. And she had to think of the good of the show.

"I have a proposition for you, Margo," she said.

Mother

LES TRIED NOT TO THINK ABOUT THE BABY. IT'D had that swampy cough for two days. Now its temperature was a hundred and one. Was that dangerous? She didn't know. Probably have to bring it to a doctor or maybe even a hospital. She stood on the pedals as her cart climbed Deacon Parker Road. Wouldn't be cheap. Have to temp somewhere to pay the bill. Cost her two days, maybe more, assuming anyone would hire a boo living out of a cart.

She hated the baby.

Birth Control said the baby's name was Gary. The people there were as smothery as the ones on the moon. Should be her decision what to call the son of a bitch. When she had a baby of her own, Gary was the last thing she'd name it. Les would call her baby Shithead Bleeding Motherfucker before she'd call it Gary. She knew it was probably points off that she couldn't think of the baby by its Birth Control name. When she took it to the doctor, she'd have to say its name. A mother didn't call her kid, *it* or *the baby*. She wondered whether the judge at Birth Control would certify her fit to mother, if he knew how Les felt about this one. She'd heard they could see inside your head now. Just like the aliens.

Gary, she thought. Poor little Gary.

If she didn't pedal fast enough, little flying bugs would catch up to her cart. Didn't bite, but they buzzed into her eyes and up her nose. She kept batting at them. They were too stupid to live. On the moon, there weren't any bugs. But she wasn't on the moon and she could never go back. Not knowing what she knew. The aliens had seen to that. Les's mother had figured them out, so they killed her and sent Les down. Made her mad, how stupid people were. The aliens said they had come to help but what they really wanted was to wipe everyone out. First they'd take care of the women. Which meant the end of men too—not that Les would miss *them* much. Then the only ones left would be little girly snips that owed everything to the fucking aliens.

That's why she had to have babies of her own. Lots of babies.

It was a warm, spring afternoon. If she pulled the cowling down to protect herself from the little flying bugs, she'd start to sweat from pedaling. Sky was blue and cloudless and she could see the moon making a mocking silver face at her. Knees didn't hurt that much. Getting used to Earth gravity. She pedaled faster because she was still in Massachusetts. Would be at least another week before she got to Portsmouth, especially if she stopped for the baby. She'd be twenty-eight-years old on May third. Maybe her father, who she had never met, would give her a birthday present. *Hi, Dad, I'm home from the moon. How about a nice fat cash card?* She wouldn't have to get married then. She could stay on the road. Nobody understood that Les loved her cart. She *liked* being a boo.

If she were married, they'd let her have her babies. Sure, just like that. Bonus points for being married. But they couldn't make her sleep with men if she didn't want to. Or with aliens. Or dogs. No, they couldn't make her live in a house or work a steady job or bathe more than once a week, like a good fucking clem. It was the law. If she wanted to have a baby or two or ten, all she had to do was take care of the Birth Control's baby. Finish their training to be certified a mother. She had it all figured out.

Except she could hear the baby crying. Hear it even though it was in the trunk, smothered in the sleeping bag. "Shut up," she muttered and squeezed the handlebars until her knuckles went white. For ten more minutes she pedaled, telling herself the little asshole would go back to sleep. Its yelping made her squirrelly. Finally she pulled over and opened the trunk.

She took a bottle of formula from the crate and shook it warm. For a while, she couldn't find the mouth peripheral. It had slid under her mother's ashes. She untangled the cord and snapped it to the baby's I/O port. Opened the baby.

For a change it stopped crying when it saw her. The fever hadn't gone up, but it hadn't gone down either. Its eyes were shiny. Of course, the poop light was blinking. She had to change the little shitbag before she could feed it. She peeled a nap off the roll, leaned out of the trunk and stuffed it into the mouth. The baby gave Les a noseful of stink as the mouth processed the nap. Shreds drifted to the ground like paper snow. The pix showed babyshit that was runny and as green as pond scum.

Les stretched a nipple onto the bottle of formula and stuck the bottle into the mouth. The mouth began to process it with moist sucking sounds. She held it there, leaning out of the trunk while the spent formula dribbled onto the ground. Most parents fed their Birth Control babies over a sink or a toilet. Mother Nature was Les's toilet.

Back in February, Les had tried holding a cup under the mouth to catch the formula. She knew mouths put some nastiness into spent formula to keep parents from reusing it. A Birth Control baby was supposed to cost what a real baby cost. Part of the training. But Les had been too hungry to care. Stuff tasted like liquid cardboard, but that was all right. Filled her belly and she'd kept it down. But it gave her nightmares for two days. The kind of nightmare where the aliens cut her nipples off and her jaw clenched so hard that her teeth shattered as she slid down razor wire. Ever since, she had let what came out of the mouth alone. She had *that* all figured out.

Formula was about two dollars for a two hundred milliliter self-warming bottle. The baby needed three a day. Four if it spat out the oatmeal, which it better never do again. That was forty-two dollars a week. Naps were another eleven a week. She had just eighty-seven dollars and thirty-seven cents left on her cash card. She was at least a week away from Portsmouth. *Her* lunch would be a belly full of water and a slice of spun cheese.

When the baby finished eating, Les unplugged the mouth. The baby just lolled on its screen, paying no attention to her. They said she was supposed to talk to it, but she never knew what to say.

"Go back to sleep, you dumb little fuck."

The pallid glow of the pix reminded her of when she hid in her mother's locker on the moon for two days. Took that long for the squirrelly men to find her. Took a minute for them to tell her about the accident.

She put everything away and climbed back onto the saddle of the cart. Changed the pix in the center of the steering wheel from Newsmelt to a map. Les loved maps. They made her feel free, like she had escaped all the traps the aliens had set. Sometimes at night she would fall into her maps for hours, plotting a course for the next day. So many ways to go. She would've lived in a map if she could. She wouldn't have minded being flat. According to the map genie, she was at the intersection of Deacon Parker Road and Route 10, which GPSed to N 42° 40.587' W 72° 29.761'. If she didn't cross the Connecticut River soon, she'd have to go all the way north to Brattleboro, Vermont. She had told the genie to keep her off big roads and away from cities, but that was too long a detour. So she figured she had to cross in Northfield. There were two choices, the Route 10 Bridge and the Schell Bridge. She decided on the Schell Bridge because it was named after someone. To get to it, she'd have to pass by places called Hell's Kitchen and Satan's Kingdom. Maybe the devil would invite her to dinner.

A stupid little flying bug bounced off her ear.

She never saw the devil. Talked to a cop instead. Came up behind her on Route 142 and just hung on her tail at fifteen kilometers an hour. Maybe they didn't see many boos this far up in Massachusetts. Clems thought all boos were the same. Thought they were lazy. Thought they were anti-social. A lot of clems thought they were crazy. But Les wasn't breaking any laws, that she knew of. The gun wasn't loaded. Didn't even own ammunition.

She pulled over, slid off the saddle and walked back toward the cop. He let his car roll to a stop. It was an electric, quiet as the inside of Mom's locker. Said *Town of Mount Hermon, Massachusetts* on the door.

Cop lowered his window. "Afternoon, ma'am."

"You know, I used to live on the moon." Les pointed. "The Mare Nubium, right at the bottom of its mouth there."

"That so?" Cop didn't look.

"We don't have police on the moon. You know why?"

Cop waited.

"Because the moon kills you her own self if you break her rules."

Cop squinted at her, as if she had feathers coming out of her nose.

"Look," she said, "I've got everything I own in this cart. Take us about ten minutes to sort through. You want to see?"

Cop shrugged. "No, ma'am."

Les was relieved. Didn't want to be explaining about the baby. "Then why are you following me?"

"You're one of those boos we heard of. You don't live anywhere."

I'm a boo, she thought, and you're the mudhugging clem of all time. "I'm traveling," she said. "That's all."

"Where are you going, ma'am?"

"I'm hoping for Northfield tonight. Portsmouth, New Hampshire, eventually. I've got family there."

"That so?" Cop made no move to write her up. Acted as if he had nothing better to do than sit and chat with her. Only he didn't have anything to say.

"Tell you what I'm going to do." She pictured the map. "In a little while, I take a right onto River Road. I follow it to the end and take a left onto Caldwell. I stay on Caldwell until I get to East Northfield Road, where I take a right. In two tenths of a mile, I cross over the Schell Bridge and I'm in Northfield. That make any sense to you?"

Cop leaned out the window. "I bet you met some of those aliens up there on the moon."

"A few." She couldn't tell what he wanted her to say.

"Did they stink?"

The little bugs had caught up to her again. "They had a smell, sure." She waved some toward the cop.

"I've heard that." He pulled his head back into the car like a turtle. "Do you ever get lonely," cop said, "pedaling that thing around all by yourself?"

Les got that crinkle in the back of her neck but she didn't want to do anything bad. Not until she was finished with the baby. "No." She gave him a shriveled little laugh. "I'm my own company."

"I'll bet you are." Cop wasn't smiling.

"It's getting buggy," she said. "I've got to go."

Les didn't look back and he didn't stop her. She swung onto the saddle and started pedaling the cart. Spotted him in the rear view. He was following as if nothing had happened. Probably had his hand between his legs. Les turned herself into a pedaling machine. There was steel in her calves. She flew down the road. Nothing like homicidal rage to add a couple of klicks an hour. They always did this to her, men and their fucking attitudes. Fucking her over. She imagined the sound he'd make if she shoved his stumpy fingers between her spokes. His dick too, only there probably wasn't enough of it. All of a sudden he's interested in aliens? He didn't know shit. Les knew. They were smart, the aliens, and clems like the cop were bone stupid. Sure, the aliens shared some of their tech and said all the right things about not fucking with human culture.

Except they were offering immortality to pre-pubescent girls only. So when all the little girls got snipped, there would be no one to have the babies. How hard was that to figure out?

Cop bastard followed her all the way to the river.

There were no women doctors in Northfield. At least, none that the search genie could find. Twelve hundred clems living in a town that could house three thousand. No wonder there weren't any woman doctors. Les was in no mood to put herself in another man's power. Except the god damn baby's temperature was one hundred and two. She zoomed on his face. Spots on both cheeks, the color of the blush on a peach.

Les was still a little sticky from escaping the cop. Parked in front of the clinic on Woodruff Way. The doctor had better be in or something bad was going to happen. Maybe she'd go looking for ammunition. It was a sweet gun she'd hidden next to the wheel well. Ruger AP11 recoil-operated autoloader. Les hurled the sleeping bag against the side of the cart and grabbed the baby.

The receptionist made her wait almost an hour because she wouldn't fill out any forms. Les told her she didn't have to. It was the law. All Les had to do was give her ID number. She had it all figured out. The receptionist didn't like that. But then Les didn't like the receptionist. A cancer of a woman with an overdose of blonde hair. Les didn't like having an ID number, either. What she wanted was to be invisible to the computers. The aliens could see into computers. She had figured that one out too. In other countries, ordinary folks could be invisible. Brazil. Egypt. Uzbekistan. But not in the U S of A. Here you had to be a boo. Live on the road. Fine with Les.

Finally they let her into Dr. Majumdar's office. On one wall was a collection of old clocks. They tocked and clacked and whirred insults at her. She was wasting his time, they said. They said he had diplomas from the University of Wisconsin and the Medical School of Tufts University. Busy man. A clem, with a house and a dishwasher and a queen-sized bed. A pixwall behind his desk showed a home vid of India. A little girl wandered through empty stone temples. Whoever had shot her had a nervous eye. Not a book in the room.

"Ms. Isenberg?" The doctor blanked his desktop pix. Rose from his chair. "What seems to be the problem?" He was too busy to come around the desk to greet her.

It wasn't that Les didn't like the way men looked. She did. She just didn't want to sleep with them. This one was easy on the eye. Slim with the posture of an oak. Good cheek bones, handsome in a dark way. Bonus points for the gray hair at the temples. She'd need sperm someday, when they certified her to have her babies. Sure, she'd probably get it from the Birth Control bank. But Doctor Majumdar had genes worth passing on. She pictured herself milking the spew out of him like a cow. She smiled, catching it in a silver cup.

"It's poor little Gary." She leaned across the desk to hand him the baby. "He's sick."

He took the baby from her but did not open it. There was a greasy smudge on the outside. Chain oil, maybe. Maybe a fried chicken fingerprint. Dr. Majumdar pulled a tissue from the desk drawer and wiped the baby's cover. Dropped the tissue into a woven basket. Les should have scrubbed the baby down with ammonia. Points off for sure. He sat, opened the baby and studied its welcome screen.

Les sat opposite him but couldn't keep still. Her nerves sang.

He tapped though various screens, checking records, making choices. Even though his face showed nothing, he was judging her. She could tell. The baby coughed up green mud. Then it cried. The tinny speakers made its voice squeak like a bad bearing.

"Ms. Isenberg," said Dr. Majumdar, "the minimum daily requirements for a child this age are at least three meals of at least four hundred calories. . . ."

"He ate this morning, a whole bowl of oatmeal."

". . . with an interval of not more than eight hours between daytime meals."

"We've been on the road all day."

"Even so. And he needs liquids at regular intervals. Juice. Milk. Water. Does he cry a lot?"

"Some." Wasn't about to tell him that it cried all the time.

He glanced up at her. "Why have you applied for a parenting permit, Ms. Isenberg?"

"Nobody's having babies anymore." The nerves in her leg were singing so loud that her left foot tapped. "I'm different."

"It won't be easy in your circumstances."

"Nothing is easy."

"I'm sure." He nodded and closed the baby. "I've entered a record of this visit in your baby's medical file. Gary has Selkirk's pneumonia. Don't worry, we've caught it in plenty of time. You may have heard that Selkirk's is caused by a new strain of pneumococcus that is resistant to first generation antibiotics. I'm afraid I have to prescribe Difloxcid, one of the oxazolidinones."

"You're afraid?"

"It's very expensive, about thirty dollars a day. He'll need to take it for ten days."

Three hundred dollars. Two days lost, maybe more. The back of her neck crinkled. She pictured herself bashing Dr. Majumdar's head in with the baby. That would get her on Newsmelt for sure. Top of the welcome screen. He knew she didn't have insurance. Insurance puts you into too many databases. Wasn't fair. The baby was a fucking simulation. Nothing about it was real, except the time and money it took her to take care of it. Then she realized what was happening. The aliens were trying to blow her up. If she didn't pass the training then Birth Control would never let her have babies of her own. The cop and the doctor and the Birth Control judge, all of them in on it. She had it all figured out now.

"Can I ask you a question, Doctor?"

He frowned. "I suppose."

"What do you think the aliens are up to?"

"I beg your pardon?"

"Take that little girl there." She pointed at the pix behind the desk. "Let me guess—your daughter is an only child?"

He turned around to look at the pix. The little girl was sitting at the edge of a swimming pool, dangling her legs in the water. Behind her was a white building with a lot of domed towers.

"Ms. Isenberg . . ."

"Suppose she wants to get snipped? Live forever? What if all the little girls in the world get snipped?"

"It won't happen." He faced her again. "Less than five percent choose . . ."

"It was two percent back when I was on the moon. And the birth rate was way down even before the aliens came."

He raised his hand to stop her. "You were on the moon?"

She leaned across the desk and slapped his hand down. "It's poison, Doctor. The aliens slipped us slow-acting poison." She saw the shadow of fear on his face. She could tell he was not often afraid.

"You can't be from the moon. They quarantined everyone after the accident at Tycho."

"Wasn't an accident. They've been waving lies at you, Doctor, and you're too scared to do anything but salute. The aliens know exactly what kind of humans they want living here and it isn't us.

Which is why you need me. I just want to bring life into the world. So why make me jump through hoops?"

"It's hard work being a parent." He made a twitchy pass over the desktop and all the pixes lit up. "Not everyone can do it."

"So my babies will be a little wild. At least, I'm going to have babies. Your little girlie snip sure as hell isn't." She guessed he had called for help. That was all right. Slapping him had smoothed the crinkle. Nothing bad had to happen just yet. Dr. Majumdar wasn't the real problem. He was just a man. "Be careful, Doctor." Les tucked the baby under her arm. "Your clocks are ticking."

She shot out of her chair, deliberately knocking it over. He jumped. That made her feel better about the visit. It helped that clems were scared of her. She kicked the overturned chair out of her way. All right, then. She'd get the baby its fucking medicine. Finish her training and then make the Birth Control judge let her have her babies. Girl babies, who would grow up to hate aliens and men. What her mother would have wanted.

Les was the only one now who could save the world. She had it all figured out.

Dividing the Sustain

BEEN WATANABE DECIDED TO BECOME GAY TWO days before his one hundred and thirty-second birthday. The colony ship had been outbound for almost a year of subjective time and the captain still could not say when they might make planetfall. Everyone said that dividing the sustain between the folded dimensions was more art than science, but what Been wanted now was a schedule, not a sketch. He couldn't wait any longer to recast himself as a homosexual because he worried that he might go stale and lose his mind.

He'd been comfortable—too comfortable—hunkered among the colonists aboard the slipship *Nine Ball*, two thousand, three hundred and forty-seven lumps, not one of whom had an edge sharp enough to cut butter. The lumps were all well under a century old and so had never needed to be recast. In moments of weakness—in line for the sixth lunch seating, say, or toward the yawning climax of the daily harmony circle—Been worried that he was becoming a lump himself. Sometimes as the pacifiers nattered on about duty and diligence, he could almost imagine what it might feel like to pass through Immigration someday and actually be looking forward to planting beans or selling hats or running a botloader. It was an alarming daydream for a soon-to-be hundred and thirty-two-year-old mindsync courier carrying a confidential personality transplant to the Consensualist colony on Little Chin.

Sandor, Nelly, and Zola, his podmates on the ship, did not greet his decision to recast as a homosexual with much enthusiasm. To become full-fledged Consensualists, the colonists had agreed to a personality dampening that would smooth away the sharper edges of their individuality. The treatment chilled passion into fondness, anger into simple annoyance. To get Been a berth on the *Nine Ball*, his client had provided forged records showing he'd had the treatment, had invented as well a resume as a genetic agronomist. But poor Sandor had certainly been dampened. In his own diffident way, he made it clear that he had no intention of redirecting what little sex drive he could muster toward Been. And presumably once he was gay, Been would not be spending any time in the sleep hutch that Nelly and Zola shared. The two women in Been's pod had their own sexual arrangement. They would occasionally invite either Been or Sandor to their hutch, although spending the night with the two of them was more work than swimming the Straits of Sweven in a spacesuit. It took Been hours to recover, while Sandor was usually pale and wobbly for a day afterward. If Been became gay, it would put a fatal kink in the sexual consensus of their pod.

Which was his plan exactly.

"I'm going to ask you a question," said Sandor, "and I want you to consider it in the spirit in which I am posing it, that is, without malice and with a genuine fondness for you as a person."

"Are you asking him or making a speech?" Nelly had wrapped herself in her comfort rug so that only her head showed.

"Did you want to handle this?" Sandor clutched his mug of coffee as if worried that it might wrench itself out of his grasp and fly at someone. "No, I didn't think so." Been could tell how upset the others were by the way they were letting their manners slip. The three of them ought to report themselves to their harmony circles, but Been knew they wouldn't. "Well then, Been," said Sandor, "how do you see yourself functioning as a member of our pod if you adopt this new sexual orientation? Because, forgive me for being frank, but it seems to me that this unilateral action on your part is not in harmony with the principles of Consensualism." He took a careful sip from the mug.

"I don't understand." Been pushed off the couch. "I've been living with you since we left orbit around Nonny's Home." In four quick steps, he had paced from one end of the common room to the other. "Have I been doing something all this time that bothered you?"

"Beenie," said Zola, "this pod has as much need for a gay man as we have for a singing kangaroo." She grinned at him from the tiny food prep bay as she melted her own coffee cup back into the counter. "We just wonder why you aren't thinking about that."

"Is that all I am to you, a hard cock?"

"No," said Zola. "You're also a tongue."

"And clever fingers." Nelly sounded wistful.

"I do more than just pop into bed whenever you two call," said Been. "Who asks all the questions? Suggests shows to watch, books to read? Who tells the most entertaining lies?"

He saw Sandor and Zola exchange glances. They would probably be relieved not to be fooled by any more of Been's entertaining lies.

Nelly just sighed. "It isn't as if you're about to go stale or anything. What are you, eighty-two? Eighty-three? You've got decades before you have to recast yourself."

Of course, Been had lied about his age, not merely for entertainment value, but in order to be accepted as a Consensualist. He slumped against the wall, closed his eyes and tried not to smile. He already knew he'd be leaving the pod. He just needed to make sure that, when his podmates reached consensus, *they* were the ones to ask him to go. That way Zola would feel obligated to help him find a new place to stay until the *Nine Ball* reached Little Chin. Been knew that no other pod would take him at this late date. There were two gay pods on the *Nine Ball*, but one was notoriously overcrowded and for the last few weeks Been had been busy annoying a key member of the other. Been's plan required that he move in with Zola's friend, Ilona Quellan, the captain's ex-wife. Been thought he might be in love with Ilona, even though they had never even been introduced, but becoming a homosexual would solve that problem nicely.

"So what do we do now?" he said.

"Homosexual?" said Zelmet Emsley's talking head. "Sure, it's just a straightforward recompilation." He settled onto a chair behind the intake counter in BioCore Receiving. The lightboard on top of the counter shimmered to consciousness and began to sing as he waggled his hand over it.

"As I remember, most of it is at chromosome seven, region 7q36," Emsley tapped through a series of files. "Right, and chromosome eight, region 8p12. *Hmm.* I'll need to tweak chromosome ten at 10q26." He wiped the lightboard with a dismissive wave. "Outpatient procedure, check in tomorrow after lunch and you can eat dinner first shift. Should take the sprites five or six days to spread to all your cells and that's it, since you don't need to grow anything you don't already have." Emsley's talking head fixed Been with an officious stare. "But why do it at all?" His eyes bulged, suddenly as big as plums. "*Hmm?*" Even his thinking head blinked itself awake and squinted in Been's general direction. "Trouble back in the pod?"

Strictly speaking, Been's reasons for wanting to switch his sexual orientation were none of Emsley's business. Zelmet Emsley wasn't a colonist. He was crew, the *Nine Ball*'s First Bioengineer; it was his job to look after the health of the colonists. This included performing re-embodiments if requested, assuming that they posed no harm to anyone and did not make unreasonable demands on the resources of the BioCore. But Been was determined to be diplomatic with Emsley. In his decades of experience traveling on slipships dividing the sustain, he had learned the hard way that it never paid to provoke the crew.

"No, no trouble." Uninvited, Been sat down on the float across the desk from Emsley. It settled toward the deck briefly, before bearing up under his weight. "The thing is that Friday is my birthday and . . . well . . . I'm afraid I under-reported my age. I'm actually going to be a hundred and thirty-two. Born on April 11, 2351. On Titan—that's a moon you've probably never heard of back in the First System. Only eight and a half AU from Earth. Practically next door to the home world although I never did make it there. Somebody said the Captain hails from Earth, or is that just a rumor? Because that would practically make us neighbors. How come we never see him—Captain Quellan, I mean? He's not virtual, is he?"

"You see him every day on the lightboards." Both of Emsley's heads gazed at him sternly. "This is a colonial transport, Mr. Watanabe, not a cruise ship. The captain keeps a lean crew and likes to make sure things are done right, which means he's too busy to be socializing with passengers."

"My friends call me Been." He pushed at the deck and the float bobbed and swung away from the counter. "Right, I understand he's busy. So anyway, I'm a hundred and thirty-two and feel like I might be going a little stale so I'm thinking it's time for a recast."

"I take it you had some reason to claim that you were fifty years younger than you actually are?" Emsley seemed more amused that annoyed at Been's confession. "You've deceived us, Mr. Watanabe."

"Not you, so much as Henk Krall and Lars Benzonia." On another ship bound for a different planet, this might have been a serious matter. But the *Nine Ball* was no luxury liner and Been suspected that he wasn't the only one on board who had misrepresented himself. Zola, for example, seemed rather an unlikely Consensualist.

"*Hmm*," said Emsley. "I thought you people were against changing personalities."

"We're not against it, we're just supposed to get consensus on it and that's hard. Can you keep a secret?"

Emsley pointed at the lightboard and the hatch to BioCore slid shut. "Try me."

"I'm not so sure I am a Consensualist anymore."

"Mr. Watanabe, we're bound for a colony that is almost entirely Consensual."

"Been," he said. "I guess that will make me someone special, won't it? Actually, at first I was wondering if I shouldn't recast as a woman but then I thought that it would be too much trouble in too short a time. I mean we *are* going to make planetfall soon, aren't we? The captain's first estimate was that it would take just eight months to divide the sustain."

"Trouble, yes," As Emsley tilted his chair against the bulkhead of the BioCore, the seatback cracked under the strain, reformed, and then knit itself together to take his weight. His thinking head rested against his talking head.

"You've been recast," said Been, "am I right?"

"Three times."

"How long did you wait for your first?"

"I was a hundred and forty-one when I had my personality transplant. At two hundred and thirteen, I became a heterosexual. And I was three hundred and four when I got this." He tapped the temple of his thinking head.

There were only so many times a human could be recast before going stale and each had to be more radical than the last. Oak Suellentrop was currently the oldest living human. At four hundred and sixty-two, he had been recast seven times, most recently as a floating bladder that cruised the jet streams in the upper atmosphere of Jupiter.

"Well, the thing is," said Been, "my grandmother went prematurely stale. We didn't realize how far gone she was until it was too late. We tried everything—transplant, bodymods, transgendering, total re-embodiment—to shake her out of it." He let his voice go husky out of respect for this fictitious grandmother; Been had never known his real one. "She lived to be two hundred and eight but for the last sixty years all she wanted to do was watch old-fashioned porn and look up at Saturn." Been pounded his fist into his open hand. "So yes, I'm a little nervous. Ready to embrace paradigm shift and grab a new point of view. Give me that electric kiss of anxiety and 'Happy birthday, Been!' "

"You could grow another head," said Emsley.

"I suppose." Been looked thoughtful, as he pretended to consider the possibility. "But that would be at least as much trouble as becoming a woman, wouldn't it? Besides, what would I put in it? I don't think I'm smart enough to have more than one head. I mean, look at you. How much extra storage do you have up there, anyway?"

Emsley perked up. Like most people who had opted for radical bodymod in a late recasting, he was clearly proud of what he'd had done. He unfixed his shirt so that Been could admire the astonishing breadth of his clavical bridge and the bulge where his spinal cord split in two. His thinking head was smaller than his talking head and had only a vestigial mouth and smudge of a nose. It sat low on its own stubby neck and seemed not to have much range of motion.

"People used to think that symmetry was the key to beauty." Emsley twisted his talking head to admire his thinking head. "But in my experience women are just fascinated by asymmetry."

"I was hoping to be gay," Been said.

Although it didn't open its eyes, Emsley's thinking head scowled. A flicker of embarrassment passed across the features of the talking head at being caught celebrating himself so thoroughly. "Yes, of course."

"Are there side effects I should know about?" Been pushed at the deck and the float drifted a few centimeters closer to the counter. "I heard there were changes in the brain."

Emsley shrugged. "The interstitial nucleus of your anterior hypothalamus will shrink over time, but no one will be able to tell that unless they peel your brain as part of a total re-embodiment. The pheromone palette in your sweat will change. The people who you live with who are used to the way you smell might tell you that something's different, without knowing what exactly."

"Doesn't sound so bad."

As Emsley leaned forward, his chair cracked once again and recurved around him. "In some ways, sexual reorientation is the most subtle of all possible recastings. Your sexuality, however you decide to express it, does not reside solely in your DNA. It's in your brain, your genitals, your memory, your image of yourself, and your personality. Yes, we can manipulate nature but there is also nurture to consider. I was gay for more than two centuries and I was still having great sex with men some forty years after I became genetically straight. Just as you will have a hundred and something years of heterosexual nurture to deal with if you become gay."

"Thirty-two." He bounced off the float. "A hundred and thirty-two. My birthday is Friday, can you do it before then?"

Emsley never got the chance to answer. The high-pitched wail of a child in pain filled the passageway just outside BioCore Receiving. The hatch slid aside revealing two dazed colonists carrying a very pale boy, who was maybe five or six. His right hand was wrapped in a bloody towel.

"There." Emsley pointed to the float where Been had just been sitting and they set the boy down on it. Been pressed himself against the rear bulkhead to keep out of the way.

The boy tried to curl into himself around the wounded hand but the bioengineer gently rolled him onto his back. "What is this then?" Emsley's manner was so cool he might have been asking the time.

"The boys got into the air vent somehow and Joss stuck his hand into a fan," said the man, whom Been took to be the dad. "It was dark."

The expressions on Emsley's faces were calm but alert as he pushed the boy's hair aside. "Boys," he said, as he painted sensor sprites onto the pallid forehead with his medfinger. Been could hear the lightboard begin to sing the boy's vital signs. "Why is it always boys?"

"It's my fault," said the woman, probably the mom. She sniffed but did not cry.

"Our fault," said the dad.

"Yes, you're right," she said miserably.

"Let's make Joss comfortable." Been heard hissing as Emsley pressed the medfinger to the boy's temple. Joss immediately went limp. Emsley closed the boy's eyes and unwrapped the towel. "Oh dear," he said. Blood spattered onto the float. "Were you able to find any of the fingers?"

The dad was already offering him a blood-smeared baggie containing the severed fingers.

Emsley held it up to the brightly illuminated overhead. "*Hmm*," he said. "Too mangled." He dropped the baggie into the trash. The mom gave off a strangled *yip* of protest as the lid closed for incineration.

"Don't worry." Zelmet Emsley smiled at the boy's parents. "We'll grow him better ones." As he maneuvered himself behind the float to push it into the BioCore, he noticed Been still squeezed against the bulkhead. "Ah, Been. I'll see you Thursday, then?"

Been didn't know exactly who had bought the personality transplant that he was carrying in his mindsync, but that was often the case in his line of work. Besides, it all was perfectly legal. Everyone had the right to be recast, especially when there was a possibility that the client might go stale. Of course, the citizens of Little Chin could ostracize anyone who was recast without consensus approval. Been suspected that he was working for one of the leaders of the colony, which was why the client had paid extra for covert delivery. Been's problem was that he had no idea where he was supposed to download the transplant. His contact on Nonny's Home had never shown up. There had been no final briefing. With a one-way ticket, false ID, the transplant, and a third of his fee in hand, Been had chosen at the last minute to continue on to Little Chin in the hopes that the client would contact him there.

But as the year aboard the slipship dragged by, he had come to regard his decision as foolhardy. How was he supposed to make delivery while remaining under cover? Sneak up on Lars Benzonia, Acoa Renkl, and Elma Stitch and ask if they were going stale? And if he couldn't connect, he might be stuck on Little Chin with a personality transplant that only his client could unlock. His partial fee would pay for a ticket to someplace else, but probably nowhere he wanted to go. Meanwhile, the Consensualists would surely shun him once they found out that he barely knew the difference between agronomy and astronomy. Been needed a backup plan. He was sure that if he could only get a chance to talk to Harlen Quellan, captain and owner of the *Nine Ball*, he'd be able to strike some kind of deal for transport back to Nonny's Home. He could offer partial payment and then join the crew to work his passage back. Once he was home, he could either insist on being paid in full or else return the personality transplant to AllSelf for a salvage fee. But first he had to see Harlen Quellan and the captain had proven impossible to see.

"Been Watanabe," Zola said over the din of the second seating for breakfast, "this is Ilona Quellan."

Zola had been standing between Been and Ilona. Now she stepped back so that he had an unobstructed view. Ilona sat by herself, as was her custom. She glanced up warily from a bowl of steamed rice, a short stack of pancakes spread with butter, a filet of lightmeat, and half a grapefruit. Zola seemed to expect Been and Ilona would shake hands, but Been sensed that this was not an intimacy the pregnant woman would welcome. Instead he circled to the other side of the long table, put his bowl of Figs 'N Flakes down and sat opposite her, fighting the absurd attraction he had felt ever since he had first seen this unhappy woman.

"Hello, Been Watanabe," she said. "I understand you want something of us?"

Been touched his forefinger and middle finger to his eyes, nose, and lips before turning them toward Ilona. "Hello, Ilona Quellan. Tomorrow is my birthday."

"Happy birthday to you then, sir." She spread a hand over her huge belly. "This baby and I rejoice that you continue to exist."

The rest of Been's pod settled around the two of them. Zola inserted herself next to Ilona and introduced her to Sandor and Nelly. She had met Ilona at the Arachnophiliac's Meetup and had twice taken care of Ilona's marbled spider Rags while Ilona was getting the baby re-embodied. Rags was an *araneus marmoreus* that daily filled her terrarium with webs of hypnotic complexity.

There was a long moment when nobody had anything to say. Zola and Nelly perched expectantly at the edges of their chairs. Sandor began to eat. Ilona gazed at Been, apparently waiting for him to answer her original question. Been smiled back.

There was nothing remarkable about Ilona Quellan, other than that she was extremely pregnant. She was a small woman, and her belly was so huge that the baby almost seemed to be more of her than she was of herself. She had fine features: subtle lips, steep eyebrows. Her black hair had highlights of gray. She looked tired, but that was only to be expected. She had been pregnant with her son for more than three years, if the rumors were to be believed. The babyface medallion that hung around her neck showed the baby to be asleep.

If he tried, Been could look at Ilona critically. For example, no one could miss her constant scowl. Been could count the wrinkles and hear the mistrust in her voice and sense the wall she had built around herself to keep the world away. But he didn't care; he imagined smoothing her wrinkles with his kisses and climbing the wall to win her heart. Of course, he had nursed his impossible infatuation from a distance because he was afraid of where it might leave him. She was the captain's ex, pregnant, sad, unattainable, and aloof. Been had had many slipship romances, but never a secret obsession. It was so unlike him; he was at once delighted and alarmed.

Zola kicked Been under the table. He glanced over at her and she twitched her head toward Ilona. Sandor had his nose in a plate of eggs but Nelly had pushed back from the table, too nervous to eat. Been could tell that the women in his pod were going to start speaking for him if he didn't speak for himself.

"For my birthday," he said, "I decided to give myself a present. I'm going to be gay. Zelmet Emsley has already programmed the sprites; I'm getting them later today."

"And what made you decide this, Been?" said Ilona.

"I've never been gay." He shrugged. "I've never really been anyone but myself. Rather boring, wouldn't you say? And I suppose I'm worried about going stale."

"At your age?" Sandor grunted in disbelief.

"We all go stale eventually," said Ilona. "Immortality is for turtles."

"Ilona is an authority on creative discomfort," Zola broke in. They had all agreed that this was their best and maybe only chance to move Been out of the pod now that they were sure he was going to become gay. Zola wasn't going to let Been ruin it. "You should see what she has done with her cabin. It's like a maze."

Nelly nodded vigorously. "Zola told me that just finding the couch made her feel smarter." Her enthusiasm had an edge of desperation. "No one could ever go stale there."

"I'd very much like to see it," said Been.

Ilona nodded and then poured syrup over her pancakes, her fish, and her grapefruit. Zola and Nelly began to eat as well, as if something had just been settled, although Been wasn't sure what.

Zola said, "I really appreciate this, Ilona."

"Appreciate what?" Ilona teased a sliver from the filet with her chopsticks. "Don't assume, Zola. What do you imagine I'm doing?"

"You're talking to us," said Been.

"You're here. It would be impolite to do otherwise." Her smile was chilly. With a wrench, Been realized that he was wasting his time trying to charm her. Ilona Quellan would never willingly disrupt her life by letting him move in to the spare hutch in her cabin.

At that moment, the babyface lit up. The eyes on the medallion blinked several times, awash in a blue glow. They took in the people gathered at the table. Nelly gave the babyface an uncertain smile; many of the colonists were spooked by the long unborn baby Quellan. Zola waved. Finally the babyface noticed Been.

"Hullo, baby," Been said. "You're very lucky to have such a devoted mother."

The babyface regarded him with blue seriousness.

"And a famous father, captain of this marvelous slipship."

Zola gasped. Not only had she warned Been not to mention Ilona's ex but the pod had reached consensus that he shouldn't. Harlen Quellan was the reason Ilona still suffered through her endless pregnancy. After the divorce, she had refused to give birth to their son until Harlen agreed to honor a pre-nuptial agreement giving her a third of their joint assets, which included the *Nine Ball.*

A shadow passed over Ilona's features. "This baby doesn't speak to strangers, sir."

"Really? I'm very good with children." Been spoke with an easy obliviousness. "You know, I'm still hoping to meet your husband someday, Ilona. We've been a year aboard and I've only seen him on the lightboards, never in the flesh. That's odd, don't you think? It's not that big a ship." He peered into the babyface. "If your father has visitation rights, baby, would you put in the good word?"

The little mouth on the babyface twisted. "Googoo, gah, gah, gah."

Ilona's head dropped so that her chin rested against the babyface. She covered her mouth with her hand and murmured to it. The babyface blurbled back. As this went on, Been was pleased to see that mother and baby were arguing.

As one, Been and his entire pod leaned toward Ilona Quellan, hoping to catch some of the conversation. The rumors were that that baby Quellan had long since achieved consciousness in the womb, but nobody knew what it did with it.

Finally Ilona let her hand fall to her side. She gave Been a prickly glare. "On your birthday," she said, "there is to be a party?" The babyface was watching him intently.

The question caught Been by surprise. He glanced at his pod-mates, but they just gawked back at him like he had sprouted another ear.

"Not that I know of," he admitted.

"It doesn't speak well of you, Been Watanabe, that no one cares to celebrate your birthday. These people, for instance." She gestured at Zola, Nelly, and Sandor. "Zola tells me you have been living together for the past year."

Zola shook herself. "We think Been is wonderful. Isn't that right?"

"Yes."

"Of course."

"And we support his decision to . . . um . . . change himself," said Nelly. "Definitely."

Consensus on this subject was also enthusiastically confirmed.

"It's just that he doesn't quite fit. . . ."

Ilona interrupted before Sandor could finish. "This baby thinks your friend should have a birthday party." She pushed her chair back and stood up with difficulty, her belly barely clearing the edge of the table. "If there is a party, this baby would like you to invite both it and its father." She rested her hands on the table wearily. "I can't speak for Captain Quellan, but I can assure you that that this baby would be certain to attend."

Throwing a party on the *Nine Ball* was so complicated that very few of the colonists had managed it. Members of a single pod could gather easily enough in their common room, and they might invite a few guests, depending on whether they could reach consensus about intruding into one another's personal space. But if more than one pod wanted to socialize, it would have to be in public space, which was at a premium on the *Nine Ball*. The AgCore had room enough, but was not particularly party-friendly. There was a pungent iron stink in the abattoir where Molly, the *Nine Ball*'s amiable fatling, sloughed off slabs of her living light and darkmeat. And the CO_2 in the greenhouse ran to 6% — good for the hydroponic plants, fatal for parties. There wasn't much open space in the library. The virtuality shells lining the VRCore were ninety percent singles and ten percent doubles. The cafeteria was in continuous use, with the eighth seating for any given meal being immediately followed by the first seating of the next meal. When the two meeting rooms weren't booked by one of the colonists' sixteen Infrastructure Planning Groups or the harmony circles, they were being used by the various meetups which had formed during the run to Little Chin. These ranged from Amateur Astronomy to Zen League Baseball. The Space-Friendly Pet Meetup alone had a dozen subsections: spiders, ants, pretters, frogs, turtles, snakes, mice, gerbils, hamsters, ferrets, squee, and birds.

The other complication with throwing a party was drawing up a guest list. In a society where everyone was friendly but nobody was much of a friend, how were Been's podmates to decide who to invite to his birthday party? For there *was* going to be a party, and in a most unusual place. To the general astonishment of all aboard, even the crew, Captain Harlen Quellan himself had offered the ControlCore for Been's birthday party. It was widely assumed, at least among the colonists, that this meant that the captain would be making his first public appearance of the run. The guest list Been and his podmates finally decided upon was an odd mix of crew and colonists—especially odd because these two groups did not usually have much to do with one another. The colonists regarded the crew as outrageously idiosyncratic; almost all of them had been recast with custom bio or mechmods. Crew could be quarrelsome and vulgar. They held grudges. Sometimes they solved problems by screaming at one another.

The crew thought the colonists were boring.

The colonists who attended Been's party were Tedia Grossman, Grel Laconia, and Ydt, whom Been knew from the Artful Exaggerators Meetup. They were some of the worst liars he had ever met, but for Consensualists, they were fair company. Gala Lysenko, Beth Fauziah, and Foxcroft Allez came from the Future Farmers Meetup. They had spent the last few months subjective trying to get Been to reveal what wonder food was stowed in the CargoCore. Been had hinted and dodged for months, since his credentials as a genetic agronomist were nothing but well-crafted lies. He didn't even like vegetables. Dizzy and Henk Krall, who were subsidizing the run to Little Chin, had invited themselves, no doubt to protect their interests. And of course, Nelly, Zola, and Sandor were there, hoping that the party might somehow help them move their superfluous podmate out. From the crew, aside from Harlen Quellan, baby Quellan, and of course, his mother—invitations went to Matty, Ment, and Vron Zink, who were the factors in charge of dividing the sustain so that the *Nine Ball* could slip through the folded dimensions. Everyone was eager to hear the Zinks' latest estimate of when the slipship would arrive at Little Chin. Zelmet Emsley was invited, as well Kinsella Frecktone, who managed the *Nine Ball*'s AgCore and was presumably a professional colleague of Been's, although they had hardly spoken since leaving Nonny's Home. Nobody could quite figure out why Kastor maven Lodse, the assistant cargo steward, was on the guest list.

Been rode the lift to the frontmost level of the *Nine Ball* with Nelly and Sandor; Zola had volunteered to bring the birthday cake from the cafeteria. Been was feeling a little flushed; Zelmet Emsley's sprites had been having their way with his genome for not quite a day now. He worried that his skin was getting tighter; he could almost feel his fingerprints.

The lift hatch slid away and he was gazing into the dazzle of the ControlCore's lightboards.

"Hmm." Zelmet Emsley sounded as if he were a swarm of bees.
"Here's the man of the hour."

Been blinked, distracted by the way the lightboards were singing
their status reports.

"We're here, Been," hissed Nelly. "Step off." When she nudged
Been in the small of the back, her knuckle pricked him like a knife
and he felt a surge of terror. How long had he been paralyzed by the
sights and sounds of ControlCore? Sandor had a hand clamped over
the shivering lift hatch to keep it from closing. Been realized then
that he was having an unexpected reaction to the sprites. Adrenaline
skittered through him and brain cells that had too long been dor-
mant began to fire. He had to get in control of himself. This might
be his chance to talk to Harlen Quellan.

"Is the captain here?" said Been.

When Emsley's thinking head grimaced, it looked like its face
was pressed against a window. "Not yet," said his talking head.

Been let Gala and Beth peel him away from Emsley. They
wanted him to see how Kastor maven Lodse could pull up real time
images of any single cargo container on board and then inspect
their contents virtually.

"So that means you can tell us what's in any container?" Gala
rested a hand lightly on Lodse's shoulder. "Say, for example"—she
shot Been a mischievous grin—"Y7R in cold locker three?"

Lodse gestured at the lightboard. It sang back to him and then a
green Lifetec container appeared on it. "Could." He nodded at the
lightboard. "But won't. Not my job. My job is getting stuff from here
to there."

"Please, Kastor. We've heard rumors that we're carrying some
revolutionary new seed stock that could save Little Chin." Now
Beth was testing Been to see if he would react.

Been thought he could see malice curling off her smile like
smoke. "We're planting seed, Beth, not rumors."

"You won't talk to us, Been Watanabe, so now we're not talking
to you." Gala closed her hand on Lodse's shoulder. "What about it,
Kastor? Aren't you interested?"

"Not really." Lodse waved at the lightboard and it went back to
the default overview of the CargoCore. "To us, cargo is nothing but
bins, barrels, and bulbs. Some of them have to be kept warm, some
cold. Some of them need to breathe, others want to be airtight. All
we care about is whether someone is coming to sign for them at the
end of the run."

More people arrived at the party and then Gala and Beth were gone and a drunken Henk Krall was leaning against him so hard that Been had to brace himself to keep from pitching backward. At first Been thought Henk might be flirting with him, but then the conversation turned rancid.

"I'm sorry to say, Been, that there have been some who question whether you are truly committed to Consensualism." Henk's voice slurred and he added a couple of unnecessary syllables to *Consenualism*. "I intend to bring this problem to Lars Benzonia once we make planetfall. You are a serious disappointment."

Been looked to Dizzy to pull her drunken husband off him but she just shook her head. "Henk, I'm wondering if Been's personality dampening might not have been completely effective," she said. "Do you think that's possible, Been dear? Might that be why you are taking such drastic steps?"

"Have taken." Been stepped away from Henk suddenly and when the old man lost his balance, Been danced him to a bulkhead and parked him against it. "You want to see drastic steps?" he called out to the room. Dizzy watched, astonished, as he continued to dance away from Henk. "*Draa*-astic steps, *fan*-tastic steps," he crooned and caught a smirking Kinsella Frecktone up in his arms; he fit there like the key to Been's lock. Been wondered if Emsley might not have been wrong and he had become fully gay overnight. "Come with me, darling, and together we'll take enthusi-*ass*-stic steps to the stars." Been swung him into a cross body lead and Kinsella actually followed along for a few beats.

Then a lot of people were laughing and Been was laughing too and someone gave him something dangerous to drink and he took a sip that looked bigger than it was and when no one was looking, he spilled the rest into a trash container just before he fell in with the Zinks.

"So when are you going to post a hard estimate for planetfall?" Been could never tell Matty from Vron Zink, especially when their datacords were melded together. The brothers were wide, dark, grim men with breath bad enough to make engineers flinch. They never got jokes, no matter how obvious the telling. Their niece Ment was younger and blonder. She had come aboard the *Nine Ball* to learn the family trade.

"The sustain has been very folded tight," said the brothers, speaking in unison as they always did when they were sharing mind.

Young Ment Zink wandered over, as if sensing that her uncles were talking business. The segmented datacord began to uncoil from around her neck. "Want me to meld too?" she said to her uncles.

"Not necessary," they said. "We have enough processing capacity for this conversation."

Ment wound her datacord back behind her hair in disappointment. "Happy birthday, Mr. Been Watanabe," she said. "This is quite a coup. What do you know about the captain that we don't?"

"Never met the man."

"He's asking that we'll make planetfall when," said the uncles.

"I'd say we have at least two scant folds to slip through," said Ment.

"Tomorrow," said the uncles. "Or the after day."

"Tomorrow?" said Been. "You mean tomorrow ship subjective tomorrow?"

"No, standard tomorrow," said Ment. "In the broad dimensions. They must be thinking in real time."

"So what's that going to be in ship subjective time?"

"We pass currently twenty-three ship subjective days for each standard day," said the brothers, "but the sustain very crunches our subjective space-time fast."

Ment polished the tip of her datacord with her thumb. "This is all probability-driven, but it's most likely we'll reach one-to-one subjective-to-standard time in under two weeks."

"But two weeks is also error margin," said the uncles.

"Two weeks subjective?" It had always made Been dizzy when he thought about time dilation in the sustain of the six folded dimensions, so he didn't.

"Subjective, yes," said Ment. "And when we close the sustain we should be just a day from planetfall."

Been shut his eyes and tried not to look stupid.

"But what will we find there?" Zola had her arm tight around Nelly and was playing nervously with the ends of her podmate's hair. Been was in the midst of a knot of colonists. He couldn't see the Zinks anywhere.

"Ydt claims that the colony on Little Chin voted to dissolve," said Nelly.

"He heard it from the captain."

"Actually, the crew heard it from the captain. I had it from Kastor maven Lodse."

"Lars Benzonia has gone stale because the teachers blocked consensus on a recast." Foxcroft Allez cheeks were flushed. "There's nobody to lead them."

"Us," said Nelly.

Ydt peeked over her shoulder. "Everyone on Little Chin will cram onto the *Nine Ball*. Once we get pushed off, they'll come swarming. Captain booked the entire colony yesterday."

"Is he here?" Foxcroft glanced around the ControlCore.

"Not yet."

"He can't possibly have heard any such thing." Now that Been had to think about subjective and standard time again, it filled his head with fizz. "We're still dividing the sustain, Ydt. No message can get from the broad dimensions to the folded dimensions because of time dilation."

"Go ask Kastor if you don't believe me," said Ydt.

Sandor turned to look for the cargo steward.

"Don't make a fool of yourself." Been caught Sandor by the arm. "I don't know how you can step onto a slipship without learning the first thing about interdimensional physics."

"It isn't true?" Nelly slumped against Zola in relief.

"It *could* be true." Ydt beamed at his fellow colonists. "That's the beauty of it. We just have no way of knowing."

Been poked Ydt in the chest. "Ever think of trying out for the Artful Exaggerators, Ydt?"

Ydt grinned and poked him back. "I recruited *you* to the Exaggerators, Watanabe."

"My point exactly."

"You're hot, Been," Zelmet Emsley traced a medfinger just under Been's hairline. "Your temperature is 39.3° Maybe you should go back to your hutch to rest?"

"Is the captain here yet?" said Been.

"At least sit down."

"*Happy birthday to you, happy birthday to you, happy birthday dear . . .*"

Been found that he was holding a plate with a slab of spice cake with a light green frosting that rippled like waves on a pond. On top of the frosting floated the dark green letters *p*, *y*, and *B*.

Ilona's huge belly was hard as a fist. It bumped against him as she went up on tiptoes to whisper into his ear.

"Harlen put you up to this." Her voice tickled him. "He's using you to harass me. Make me let him go."

"But I've never even met the captain," said Been.

Her face was too close to his. "That doesn't mean anything." Been could feel her anger burning his cheek. He wondered what would happen if he kissed her. No part of her personality had been dampened: she'd probably punch him.

"Is the captain here?"

She snorted.

"There's a secret, isn't there?"

"There are always secrets." Her hand rested on the shelf of her belly. "Come down to my cabin," she said. "He wants to see you."

Zola had been right, Been thought. The common room of Ilona Quellan's cabin was a showcase for the creative discomfort style of interior design. Her deckscape pitched and changed levels without warning, but at least it didn't move. Panels of varying solidity slowly dripped from the overhead or melted back into the deckscape. They were not hard to avoid, but the point was that they had to be avoided. Mobile floodlights crawled across the overhead and down the bulkheads. The furniture was snug enough: a wide, parti-colored couch, a scatter of low and high chairs. Three hutches, a food prep bay, and a head opened onto the common room. The hatch to each of the sleep hutches was a lightboard showing scenes from old 3D vids or alien landscapes. They rotated 90° at random intervals so that Been had to lean over and cock his head to make sense of them. Been knew that the research showed that people who moved into a challenging environment showed measurable gains in intelligence and lived years and even decades longer without needing to be recast. But he had no interest in spending his life fighting his way through an obstacle course every night just to climb into bed.

However, he could put up with it for a couple of weeks, assuming the Zinks had estimated planetfall accurately. "It's an amazing place you have here," he said.

Ilona sprawled on the couch with two pillows under her head and one between her legs. She had changed into a pair of loose silk pajamas, the top of which crept up her belly, showing a grin of white skin.

"I used to be beautiful," she said.

Been didn't hesitate. "You still are."

"Please." She pushed a hand at him wearily. "Throw away the script if you're going to live here."

"Am I going to live here?" He stepped around a tumescent panel and pulled up a chair to face her.

"He said to me, 'I'll give you the stars for a wedding present.' And I was too young to realize that was one of the oldest scripts ever written."

"How old are you now?"

She considered. "A hundred and forty-one? Forty-two? No, forty-one."

"And never been recast?"

"I'm pregnant, Been. I've been pregnant for twenty-nine months. That's all the recasting I can stand for the moment." She nodded at the meter-wide yellow panel beginning to dribble from the overhead; in an hour they wouldn't be able to see one another. "And I live here. In this 'amazing place' as you say. Tell me that's not from a script." She pleaded with the overhead. "Can't anyone come up with some new lines?"

In Been's experience, that was the kind of thing that people going stale said. Ilona was silent for a moment. Then her eyes fluttered shut. But the babyface was awake and watching him. The medallion had slipped on its chain and was resting against Ilona's left breast.

"How does it feel to be gay?" said Ilona. Her eyes remained closed.

"It doesn't feel like anything at all," said Been. "I was a little dizzy back at the party, but that's because I still have sprites swarming me. Zelmet Emsley claims that becoming gay is a pretty subtle recasting. I won't feel the full effect for months. Or even years."

She propped herself up on an elbow. "So did you have an active sex life when you were straight? I'll bet Zola is a handful and a half."

"You'd win that one."

"And you?"

"I didn't get any complaints."

"Means nothing." Her laugh was bitter; it left a bad taste in Been's mouth. "Men complain. Women settle."

"I'm not sure that's right," he said.

She let her head drop and her eyes shut again. Several long minutes passed. Been was tired too and he was feeling frustrated. He liked watching Ilona drowse but she'd said that Harlen Quellan wanted to speak to him. Where was he?

"Time?" He raised his voice, hoping to wake her up.

The lightboard hatch nearest him went into clock mode: 02:31:12, 02:31:13, 02:31:14. It was later than he'd thought.

The babyface was smiling at him now. Been stood, walked uphill to the couch and leaned close. "Where's your daddy, baby?"

"Grrl, goo," said the babyface.

He tried to do the math. If Ilona's baby had been actually born at nine months, that would mean it would be twenty months old now. What could babies do at twenty months? Talk? Walk? But then Zola had said that the baby had been re-embodied several times to keep it from being born. What was it thinking there inside her?

Other than having been an infant a hundred and thirty-two years ago, Been hadn't had a lot of experience with babies. He had spent most of the last seventy years subjective ferrying personalities to the Thousand Worlds on slipships.

"So Been, you had an active sex life as a heterosexual," murmured Ilona, her eyes still shut, "and you're too new at homosexuality for it to have taken. Have I got that right? Is that why you're staring at my chest?"

"Ilona!" The clock on the lightboard disappeared and was replaced by an image of Harlen Quellan. "Don't start."

She sat up abruptly, the babyface banging against her belly. "Why? Just because I'm pregnant, I'm not allowed to want sex? It's been almost three years, you bastard."

Been thought it cruelly unfair that he had to choose between hearing more about Ilona's desires and meeting Harlen Quellan. The captain now presented himself, not quite life sized, on all five of Ilona's hatches. He appeared to be floating weightlessly in some private corner of his slipship, beyond the sway of artificial gravity. Harlen Quellan could have been fifty, one hundred and fifty, or three hundred and fifty. His skin was smooth and glossy, his hair green as a dream. He wore his dress uniform as if he had been born in it, the silver captain's bars on his jacket catching the light, his pants with razor creases, dazzling white foot and hand gloves. He'd had his datacord grafted to his coccyx like a tail and it switched back and forth as he spoke. He was too perfect by half in Been's estimation; nobody real looked that good.

"I'm sorry that I didn't make it to your birthday party, Mr. Watanabe, but the press of ship's business keeps me busy."

"Continuously, Captain?" said Been. "For the entire run?"

He bowed stiffly. "I'm here now, sir."

"I was hoping I might talk to you alone, Captain."

"But there is no alone on my ship." He gestured at the cabin expansively. "Every cubic millimeter is under surveillance. The crew must see everywhere always. That's our job."

"I think he means me, Harlen. Go ahead, you two can conspire together." Ilona heaved herself off the couch. "I need to use the bathroom anyway."

Been waited until the hatch to the head slid shut. "I've been wanting to talk to you, Captain."

"Yes, Mr. Watanabe," he said dryly. "Forty-seven messages sent by you, all of them ignored by me. You've asked every member of my crew about me. You are now pestering my ex-wife. And you've had the god-damned nerve to try to speak to my unborn son."

"So it's a boy then?"

"Sir, I've been observing you for months now. What I've noticed is that you are adept at steering conversations just where you want them to go. You flatter, sir, and cajole and you will craft a lie whenever it's convenient. I have a ship to run and have no time for such diversions, god damn it, so let me get to the point." He aimed a long foretoe at Been. "What is the expected rate of gene flow from transgenic corn plants to their wild-type cultivars?"

Been felt as if there were a rope tightening at his throat. "I beg your pardon?" He choked on the words.

"How do you use fluorescence quenching to monitor changes in carotenoid levels in living plants?"

He was suddenly dizzy and knew it had nothing to do with sprites.

"Of course, agronomy is a vast field," said the captain. "Maybe these questions are too esoteric. In that case, what is the iron component of the synthetic hydroxyapatites we use in the *Nine Ball*'s AgCore?"

Been sagged onto a chair. "What do you want?"

Harlen Quellan's image began drifting from the vertical to the horizontal. "Two days ago you told Zelmet Emsley that you're no longer sure that you're a Consensualist. I say that you never were one. Neither are you a god-damned genetic agronomist. Yet when you passed through Immigration on Nonny's Home, you gave a sworn statement to that effect. It is one thing to lie to these colonists, sir. It is quite another to commit perjury to planetary authorities."

"I've been on several dozen slipships in my life, Captain, and not one of them had a passenger manifest that could stand close scrutiny."

"Several dozen, Mr. Watanabe? Not many agronomists are so well traveled." Harlen Quellan smiled grimly. "My friend Zelmet ran a scan on your brain while you were in our BioCore. I believe he forgot to ask your permission. My apologies. I assume it would not surprise you to know that you have a mindsync with a capacity of twenty-two exabytes embedded in your cerebrum. Clearly, sir, you are a courier. What information are you carrying to Little Chin?"

"Personality transplant."

"For?"

Been spread his hands and shrugged.

"Yes. Discretion would be part of your contract." Harlen

Quellan's tail lashed impatiently. "Well, this is my fifth run to Chin. I can think of several people there who have both the need and the resources for such a recasting." He laughed. "Consensualism is for the young and foolish, Mr. Watanabe. Not for the likes of you and me." His datacord coiled around something offscreen and he drifted off the lightboard until only his gloved feet showed. "I'll respect your privacy for now, sir, and that of your client," he called. "But god damn it, you had better respect mine as well."

"I don't want to go back to live in my old pod."

"So I understand. You can move in with Ilona. I'm ordering it now." He pushed himself back onto the lightboard. "I take it that was your plan all along?"

Been could not help but grin.

"Well, you've succeeded, sir." He saluted Been. "My compliments."

"If you have a minute, Captain, there's a business matter I'd like to discuss."

"A minute is what I don't have just now, Mr. Watanabe." Harlen Quellan shook his head. "You have already taken too much of my time."

"Maybe later then?"

"Ilona!" Harlen Quellan's image knocked on the hatch to the head. "Are you all right?"

Been heard the toilet swoosh.

"Ilona is difficult enough as it is, sir." Harlen Quellan wagged his foretoe at Been. "Don't make my life with her any harder."

The hatch slid open. Ilona Quellan curled a hand around the threshhold on either side and pulled herself through. "So," she said, "what did I miss?"

The common name for Rags, Ilona's pet spider, was a marbled orb-weaver. She was about two centimeters long and ate hapless and wingless fruit flies which Ilona raised in a jar next to her terrarium. Rags had a blindingly orange cephalothorax and black-and-orange banded legs. Her huge cream-colored abdomen was marked with a black pattern that looked like two faces screaming in pain. The spider reminded Been a little of Ilona herself, with her outsized belly and the babyface hanging around her neck, but he knew better than to remark on this.

While he couldn't see his way to doting on Rags quite the way Ilona did, he did become fascinated by the spider's web-building. She made one almost every day, eating the old one so that she could build anew. In nature, Ilona said, Rags would release a line of her webbing into the wind and wherever it caught she would pull it tight. In the terrarium she walked her first line from one end of the glass to the other. She would cross the center of the horizontal line and spin a web straight down, pulling it into a Y shape. She would then spin many radii of non-sticky structural webbing before finally finishing her structure with spirals of sticky capture silk. Ilona usually dropped live fruit flies directly onto the web for Rags, although sometimes she just let them loose in the terrarium to find their own path to doom. Occasionally when Rags built a particularly beautiful web, Ilona would fetch her pet out of the terrarium and spray the web with some gaily colored fixative, so she could save it to a scrapbook. The next day Rags would get an extra fruit fly.

Been got his first look at Ilona's scrapbook four days after he'd moved in. She had been brusque at first, treating Been as if he were some naïve colonist. Been wasn't sure how much Harlen Quellan might have told her about him and he saw no need to reveal his secrets to her unnecessarily. But he made no pretense to belief in Consensualism and, if she had been paying any attention at all, she would have noticed that many of the colonists had stopped treating Been as one of their own. This was no doubt because Henk Krall had been lobbying to ban Been from the Little Chin consensus once they arrived, for being recast without permission and for other acts of egregious individuality. Of course, only Lars Benzonia himself, founder of Little Chin, could call for a consensus on ostracism, but Krall was busy laying the groundwork.

Lars Benzonia had first developed the principles of Consensualism while a young man working his way across the Thousand Worlds as an itinerant biographer. It wasn't until he was hired to write the biography of Gween Renkl, one of the richest women on Nortroon, that he got the chance to put his philosophy into practice. He struck up a friendship with Gween's son, Acoa Renkl, who stood to inherit his mother's fortune, but had no idea what to do with it. Lars Benzonia gave Acoa Renkl his mission in life: to help spread the harmony of collective thinking throughout the galaxy. The galaxy had not been overly impressed with Consensualism, however, especially after so many of its elders had gone stale waiting for a consensus to form around their recastings. But a century after Lars Benzonia and Acoa Renkl had first met, there were still enough Consensualists to populate a colony on the world Renkl had bought for his friend.

On the sixth day Ilona finally stopped smirking as Been stumbled through her common room in creative discomfort. It was right after he tripped over a panel that had not quite finished melting into the deckscape and crashed into one of her low chairs, crushing it utterly. He rolled off the wreckage, and stared at the eight-centimeter gash in his forearm. His blood was pooling in a deck pocket. She grudgingly went with him to BioCore and remained while Zelmet Emsley painted artificial skin onto the cut. Emsley also took the opportunity to run a DNA scan; he pronounced Been completely homosexual. Been did not know quite what to make of this since living with Ilona had only fueled his secret infatuation.

Even before he had moved into her spare hutch, Been had observed that Ilona was on edgy terms with the crew, who sided with their captain in the dispute between the Quellans. However she was very friendly with Emsley. They chatted easily. She made fun of the colonists; he filled her in on the latest ship's gossip. When he asked after Rags, Been realized that Emsley had one of Rags's webs framed on the bulkhead behind the intake counter.

"Is she ready for another Rich?" Emsley's talking head was grinning.

Ilona shrugged. "I'm not having any sex, so neither is she."

"Rich?" said Been.

"Zelmet keeps a couple of dozen male orbweavers on ice. I call them all Rich. Every so often we thaw one out and show Rags a good time."

"*Hmm.* I have my doubts as to whether spiders enjoy mating," said Emsley. "I would imagine that pleasure was reserved for vertebrates."

"He keeps her egg cases on ice too. If we make planetfall on a terraformed world, I thaw them out and set them free."

"Speaking of reproduction, don't forget you're due to have the baby re-embodied." Emsley's thinking head was simpering at Ilona's babyface, trying to make it laugh. "You almost put it off too long last time. If you go into labor, my hands are tied."

"I know, I know," she said wearily.

They parted as they left the BioCore. Ilona wanted to be alone and went off to the VRCore. Been was considering whether to lift down to the library to read up on the life cycle of orbweavers when he ran into Nelly. He accepted her invitation to catch the fourth lunch seating.

"So do you miss me?" Been rolled a wad of drigi noodles onto his fork.

"Of course we do, Beenie." She reached across the table to

touch his hand. "We had Sandor in the other night and . . . well
. . ." She made a lemon face and laughed. "He tries, he really does.
Of course, when we get to Little Chin, things are bound to change.
There will be lots of trades and turnover. Some of our pods will
probably break up and new ones will form. You'll find your place."

Been let that go by without comment.

"And pay no attention to Henk Krall." She leaned forward and
lowered her voice. "If you ask me, he should stop talking about how
you got recast and think about doing it himself. Zola claims he's
already half stale."

"I'm not worried."

"Your friend was so bad the other night at your birthday party."
She sipped darkmeat broth out of a cup.

"My friend?"

"The one with the name. Ydt? He really had us scared, pretending that the colony was going to disband because Lars Benzonia was
stale. I was ready to stick my head out of the airlock. I can't believe
you actually practice lying in that meetup."

"It's actually harder to tell the truth." As soon as he said it, he
realized that it was true. Been had been surprising himself lately.

Nelly laughed. "How's it going with Ilona? Zola says she's all
right, but she makes me itch. I mean, it's not only the captain she's
holding hostage, but it's her own baby too."

"We get along all right, I suppose. I like her, although she's not
the friendliest person I've ever roomed with. It's just that she's lonely
and that's made her hard."

"Well, you're good company. Cheer her up. Tell her some of
your lies."

Been had no chance to cheer Ilona up either that day or the next.
She seemed preoccupied, absent even when she sprawled across
from him in their common room. It wasn't until late on the eighth
day that she appeared in the threshold of his hutch and said that she
couldn't sleep. She was going to the cafeteria to catch the end of the
sixth dinner seating. Did he want anything? He saw that it was only
23:12 and said that he'd go with her for a snack.

"It's such an old story," she said. "It's embarrassing, actually."
Her hands were wrapped around a mug of coffee. The cafeteria was
only about a third full at the end of the day and they were sitting
alone at a corner table. "When we talked about the pregnancy, I
thought it might bring us together. I was feeling like the backup
wife." She made a strangled sound that might have been a laugh.

"No, not even." She counted on her fingers. "Ship first, crew second, passengers third, Ilona a distant fourth."

Been gave her a sympathetic groan and dipped his spoon into his salak yogurt.

"Nobody can force me to have this baby," she said. "He tried to take me to court on Kenning and they laughed him right onto the street. The law is that the baby is me until it's born and Harlen Quellan can't make me do anything to myself."

"Why do you always call the baby it? He's a boy, no?"

"Of course it's a boy!" She spoke so fiercely that the babyface woke up and cast its pale blue light onto her hands.

"We don't have to talk about this if it upsets you."

"It doesn't, Been; we're divorced." She ran a finger around the rim of her cup. "After I was pregnant I found out that he'd been sleeping with Kinder Shwaa. He said it had been over months before, but still. He hired *her* to replace *me* in the cafeteria after we got married. The sexy first steward on a slipship. Orgasms in space! Another cliché, straight out of cheap VR comix. I made him fire her." She stood up. "I'm done here." She hadn't drunk any of the coffee.

She calmed down by the time they were walking down the companionway to their cabin. "I know I'm going to have this baby someday. Harlen knows it too. He's just determined that it's going to be on his terms and not mine. He's the captain so he expects to get his way."

"I heard you want part of the ship as a settlement."

"It's not about the money." She paused at the hatch. "Well, it is, but what probably scared him more was when I said I wanted my share so I could sell to Transtellar." The hatch slid away. Been followed her into their common room. "He worked over a century for them so he could own a ship without any partners. And he hates Transtellar." She noticed her reflection in one of the blank lightboards and shuddered. "Scenery," she cried. "Show me scenery." All the boards lit up with images of the salt castles on Blimmey. "Okay, I was hot and so I didn't begin the divorce negotiations in the best way. It was a stupid thing to say. Things spun down after that."

"He worked for Transtellar for a century? How old is he?"

"I forget. Over three hundred and fifty." She settled gingerly onto the couch. "He's been recast four times." Been was about to sit in one of the chairs but she tapped her hand on the cushion beside her. "Do me a favor," she said.

He almost hit his head on a descending panel but managed to

slide in next to her. The babyface was gazing at him as if it were frightened.

Ilona noticed Been looking at the babyface and not at her. She picked it up and turned it so she could see it. "I'm not going to be your mother," she told it. "I don't want to be around you at all. Let the crew take care of you."

Despite himself, Been was aghast. "You sound like you hate it." Having Ilona and Harlen Quellan for parents wasn't their baby's fault.

She let the babyface fall back around her neck. "It knows that I do. But it's part of me." She caught his gaze and seemed to sense his shock. "There's so much you don't understand."

Been chuckled bitterly. "I'm beginning to realize that."

"I've lost everything," she said. "I have nothing."

At that moment Been felt as if he were outside himself, looking in. None of his feelings for Ilona made sense. Before he'd become gay, that would have been reason enough to bolt off the couch and run for his hutch. He was a mindsync courier; he'd spent most of his life buried in the sustain with strangers. But after a year of enduring the pale emotions of the colonists, he felt irresistibly drawn to this woman, who was burning with anger and need. He'd never been a particularly sympathetic to others, but now he was experiencing Ilona's anguish as if it were his own. And maybe that was the real reason why he stretched his hand out and brushed the back of hers. He was one hundred and thirty-two years old and he was certain that he had never felt so deeply about anyone ever before.

"Is there something I can do?"

"There's another line I've heard too many times." She slumped against the back of the couch and stared up at him. "Oh, come on, Been. You're gay."

"Not very. And you're very pregnant. Now that we've covered the obvious, I'd like to kiss you."

She looked dubious. "Is that all?"

He kissed her lightly on the lips but then pulled back, as if tasting her flavor to see if he liked it. "Not really."

"Do you know what you're doing?"

"I do," said Been. "Are you trying to talk me out of it?"

"No."

He touched the side of her face and she leaned hungrily into his caress. He said, "I'll be careful."

"No," she said. "Don't do that. I'm through being careful."

Been reached around the back of her neck and pulled the chain with the babyface over her head. "Go to sleep, baby." He tucked it between the cushions of the couch.

"He'll be watching," said Ilona. "Harlen."

Been saluted the overhead.

"That won't bother you?"

"It will," he said. "But not so you'll notice." He tugged at the hem of her blouse and slid it slowly over her belly. She raised her arms as if in surrender and he pulled the blouse up and over and dropped it onto a panel melting into the floor. Her skin was so pale and so taut that he could see traceries of blue veins beneath it.

"He put you here to punish me, didn't he?" said Ilona. "To make me uncomfortable? Is that what this is?"

"I wanted to be here from the moment I first saw you." Been rested his hands on her shoulders and met her gaze full on. "Right here." He grinned. "Well, maybe a little closer."

"Thank you." She was breathing into his mouth when she said it. Her breath was so sweet. "Thank you very much."

It was not the most physically pleasurable lovemaking Been had ever had and it was certainly not easy. Ilona could never find a comfortable position for very long and he had trouble keeping his penis in her. But it was tender and funny and at the end he wasn't careful at all.

Afterward he lay spooned against her back, his arms draped over her belly. He was playing with the short hairs on her neck when the entire *Nine Ball* gonged as if struck by an enormous hammer.

"What was that?" Ilona started awake.

"The earth moved," said Been. "Only I think it came a little late."

"They're closing the sustain," she said.

"Good morning, ladies and gentlemen." Captain Harlen Quellan appeared on all five lightboards in his dress uniform. He did not appear to notice that this particular lady and gentleman were naked. "Some of you may have been startled by the bump a few minutes ago. There is nothing to worry about. We are approaching one-to-one ship subjective to galactic standard time and are beginning to close the sustain."

"Oh, Been," said Ilona.

He squeezed her. He could hear applause echoing down the companionways.

"It's possible that there will be a few more such mild bumps," said Harlen Quellan.

"Been, it's wet here."

"So I would encourage all of you . . ." The captain's image froze in mid-sentence, his mouth still open as if he were surprised that he had nothing more to say.

Ilona heaved herself to a sitting position, grabbed at Been's hand and pressed it to the cushion where she had been lying. He felt a wet spot not quite the size of his palm. "It *is* wet," he said.

"Get the float!" she cried and bolted for the head. "Get Zelmet."

"Nice timing," Emsley said, as Ilona came out of the head, her face ashen. "Contractions?"

She nodded.

Everything happened at once and for some reason Been found himself at the center of it, right by Ilona's side. Zelmet Emsley had come with the float and Brend Diosia, the *Nine Ball*'s Second Bioengineer. They loaded Ilona onto it. As they were dodging her through the obstacles in the common room, Ilona reached out and grabbed Been's wrist. He lurched toward her and almost upended the float.

"I want him," she said to Emsley.

"Easy, Ilona," said Brend Diosia. "All you have to do is ask. It's your party."

As Brend pushed the float down the companionway, Zelmet Emsley took Ilona's vital signs with his medfinger. Both of his heads watched the lightboard at the end of the float. "*Hmm.*" Once again, Been was struck by his cool detachment. "I see you had sex."

"Yes," said Been.

"Vaginal intercourse?"

Ilona moaned.

"With an ejaculation."

"I did," Been said.

"Well, that's one way. Did you know, Been, that your semen contains some prostaglandins? This is the same family of unsaturated carboxylic acids we use to induce labor. And if Ilona had an orgasm, she would now be producing oxytocin, the hormone that causes contractions. Orgasm, Ilona?"

"Yes," she said through clenched teeth.

Emsley patted her arm. "Good for you."

"But that's not a reliable way to induce labor," said Brend.

"No." Emsley had removed the tip of his left medfinger and replaced it with a tip that was several centimeters longer, "but it passes the time." He tapped his two medfingers together, the short to the base of the long and nodded. "I'm going to give you the spinal block now, Ilona. This is all going to go just as we discussed. We're going to place a urinary catheter into your bladder, we're going to shave a little of your pubic hair so we can make the incision. You said you wanted to watch the operation so we won't cover you."

"Operation?" said Been.

"She has to have a Caesarian section," said Brend. "The head is too big." The hatch to BioCore Receiving slid away and they whisked the float past the intake counter and into the BioCore itself. The captain was still frozen in mid-sentence on the lightboard in Receiving. Been thought maybe he ought to be worrying whether something was wrong with the ship, but at the moment he had other problems.

When Ilona had been prepped and Been, Zelmet Emsley, and Brend Diosia were scrubbed, Emsley turned to Been. "We're going to start now. You hold her hand, that's what she brought you here for. This isn't going to take long, but if you feel a little faint, you can sit on this chair." He kicked a stool next to the float. "Shall we, Brend?"

Been watched with no little horror as Emsley skived a twenty-five centimeter incision through the skin of Ilona's abdomen. The skive coated the incision with dermslix, so there was no bleeding. He continued to cut through several layers of tissue and then suddenly a stream of clear fluid came blurbling out of the incision. Emsley waited while Brend suctioned it up. "We're into the uterus, Ilona. You didn't lose all that much amniotic fluid when your membrane broke, so we're cleaning it up. Not much longer now."

"Do it." Ilona was squeezing Been's hand so hard that the tips of his fingers were tingling.

Emsley reached through the incision and felt around for a grip. As he did, his thinking head turned to Been and winked. "Got it. Brend, forceps on the incision." Brend Diosia clamped the cut in Ilona's abdomen open wide as Emsley pulled the struggling baby out.

It was astonishingly ugly, covered with blood and amniotic fluid and a waxy white coating. But Been was certain that it was misshapen as well. The head was so huge that the little, pink squirming body seemed like a useless appendage. And it had a tail that was thick as Been's finger and some thirty centimeters long.

Been didn't recognize the baby's face at first.

"God damn it, Ilona," squeaked a voice as thin as a spider's web. "Took you long enough. Don't you know I've got a ship to run? And we've got to close the god-damned sustain."

*   *   *

On most planets of the Thousand Worlds, Captain Harlen Quellan might have been fined or stripped of his pilot's license or even sentenced to serve a term of incarceration in a rehabilitation VR for dereliction of duty, had the proper authorities been alerted. While re-embodied as a fetus, he was only intermittently available to command his slipship using the babyface. Originally the Quellans had planned for Ilona to be pregnant while the *Nine Ball* was in drydock. But the divorce had wrecked everything. When the time had come to honor their next transport contract, the Quellans had to come to an accommodation with one another, or risk losing the *Nine Ball* to their creditors. So Harlen Quellan created a virtual captain to cover for him whenever Ilona decided to make it impossible to connect to the ship through the babyface. Each had sought to get what they wanted by making the other miserable. All of the crew knew that Ilona was pregnant with her ex-husband but no one else did. Except, that is, for Been Watanabe, the sole outside witness to the birth of Harlen Quellan. He had his own reasons for keeping the Quellans' secret.

The consensus of the colonists on Little Chin, as well as the new arrivals from the *Nine Ball*, was that Lars Benzonia should accept the personality transplant that Been had carried from Nonny's Home. The entire colony had been shocked to learn that Acoa Renkl, Benzonia's most trusted advisor, had secretly contracted to have the transplant delivered to him against consensus. However, Renkl had gone clearly and irretrievably stale while he waited, throwing the Consensualists into a panic that their founder might succumb as well. So Lars Benzonia was quickly recast. For saving the mind of the First Consensualist, the grateful citizens of Little Chin voted the heroic mindsync courier a tract of forty hectares of prime bottomland along the Thalo River in the Tenderland District.

In the decades following his first personality transplant, it was said that Lars Benzonia became less dogmatic about the primacy of the consensus over the individual. Some point to the career of Zola Molendez, who in 2514 was named Pacifier Select, as another key factor in the reform of Consensualism. In any event, the fortunes of the colony soared.

As did those of Been Watanabe, formerly a mindsync courier, currently in the interstellar export/import business, specializing in hats. Caps, snoods, crowns, shuffs, turbans, fedoras, tricornes, kimberlys, bowlers, bonnets, toppers, helmets, and toques—as a young man Been had never realized how many citizens of the Thousand Worlds felt the need to cover their heads. He and Ilona had been able to set themselves up in the hat business, thanks to the income

from Been's holdings on Little Chin and the regular payments
Harlen Quellan made to Ilona as part of the final divorce settlement. He was buying back her one-quarter share of the *Nine Ball*
over time.

Whenever he was on Nonny's Home, Harlen Quellan liked to
drop in on Been and Ilona to make a payment in person. Ilona
maintained that he was hoping to find them split up, but Harlen
Quellan claimed he just wanted to set eyes once again upon "the
luckiest god-damned bastard ever to book passage on my ship."
They watched him now from the porch of their house as he strode
down their front walk to his hover. He swerved to tousle their daughter Benk's hair but she slapped his hand away. Little Benk was busy
teaching Rags's great-great-great-spiderlings to dance. And she was
her mother's daughter.

"After all these years, I still don't understand why you did it."
Been slid his arm around Ilona's waist.

"What?"

"You were pregnant with your own husband, Ilona!"

She giggled. "Ssh! He'll hear you."

Harlen Quellan turned to wave a last goodbye and then folded
himself through the hover door.

"Good." Been waved back and gave him the most insincere
smile he could muster. "Maybe he'll take offense and stop coming
around."

"It was his fifth recasting," she said as they watched their daughter twirl around twice and then drop to hands and knees, so she
could press her face against the terrarium to instruct her spiderlings.
"He needed to go radical. And I didn't want to be married to a mino-
taur or a wheelie." She sighed. "Mostly it was because I loved him."

"You mean you *thought* you loved him."

She shook her head. "No, I really did." She leaned into him.
"Does that still bother you?"

Been considered. "A little." He knew it had all happened a long
time ago. He tried to remember what his life had been like before
he'd become gay. It was hard, but he knew one thing for certain. He
had never really been in love. "But not so you'd notice."

As Harlen Quellan's hover lifted straight off the landing pad and
shot into the creamy sky of Nonny's Home, Been gave a low whistle.

"What are you thinking?" said Ilona.

"I'm thinking . . ." He chuckled. ". . . that I'll never have to
divide the sustain again."

The Edge of Nowhere

LORRAINE CARRAWAY SCOWLED AT THE DOGS THROUGH the plate glass window of the Casa de la Laughing Cookie and Very Memorial Library. The dogs squatted in a row next to the book drop, acting as if they owned the sidewalk. There were three of them, grand in their bowler hats and paisley vests and bow ties. They were like no dogs Rain had ever seen before. One of them wore a gold watch on its collar, which was pure affectation since it couldn't possibly see the dial. Bad dogs, she was certain of that, recreated out of rust and dead tires and old Coke bottles by the cognisphere and then dispatched to Nowhere to spy on the real people and cause at least three different kinds of trouble.

Will turned a page in his loose-leaf binder. "They still out there?" He glanced up at her, his No. 2 pencil poised over a blank page.

"What the hell do they think they're doing?" Rain made brushing motions just under the windowsill. "Go away. Scram!"

"Scram?" said Will. "Is scram a word?"

Will had been writing *The Great American Novel* ever since he had stopped trying to prove Fermat's Last Theorem. Before that he had been in training to run a sub four-minute mile. She'd had to explain to him that the mile was a measure of distance, like the cubit or the fathom or the meter. Rain had several books about ancient measurement in the Very Memorial Library and Will had borrowed them to lay out a course to practice on. They'd known each other since the week after Will had been revived, but they had first had sex during his running phase. It turned out that runners made wonderfully energetic lovers—especially nineteen-year-old runners. She had been there to time his personal best at 4:21:15. But now he was up to Chapter Eleven of *The Great American Novel*. He had taken on the project after Rain assured him that the great American novel had yet to be written. These days, not many people were going for it.

"Where do dogs like that come from, anyway?" Will said.

"Don't be asking her about dogs," called Fast Eddie from his cookie lab. "Rain hates all dogs, don't you know?"

Rain was going to deny this, but the Casa de la Laughing Cookie was Fast Eddie's shop. Since he let her keep her books in the broken meat locker and call it a library, she tried not to give him any headaches. Of course, Rain didn't *hate* dogs, it was just that she had no use for their smell, their turds hidden in lawns, or the way they tried to lick her face with their slimy tongues. Of course, this bunch wasn't the same as the dim-witted dogs people kept around town. They were obviously creatures of the cognisphere; she expected that they would be better behaved.

Will came up beside her. "I'm thinking the liver-colored one with the ears is a bloodhound." He nodded at the big dog with the watch on its collar. "The others look like terriers of some sort. They've got a pointer's skull and the short, powerful legs. Feisty dogs, killers actually. Fox hunters used to carry terriers in their saddlebags and when their hounds cornered the poor fox, they'd release the terriers to finish him off."

"How do you know that?" said Rain, suddenly afraid that there would be dogs in *The Great American Novel*.

"Read it somewhere." He considered. "Jane Austen? Evelyn Waugh?"

At that moment, the bloodhound raised his snout. Rain got the impression that he was sniffing the air. He stared through the front window at . . . who? Rain? Will? Some signal passed between the dogs then, because they all stood. One of the terriers reared up on its hind legs and batted the door handle. Rain ducked from Will's side and retreated to the safety of her desk.

"I'm betting they're not here to buy happy crumbs." Will scratched behind his ear with the rubber eraser on his pencil.

The terrier released the latch on the second try and the door swung open. The shop bell tinkled as the dogs entered. Fast Eddie slid out of the lab, wiping his hands on his apron. He stood behind the display case that held several dozen lead crystal trays filled with artfully broken psychotropic cookies. Rain hoped that he'd come to lend her moral support and not just to see if the dogs wanted his baked goods. The terriers deployed themselves just inside the door, as if to prevent anyone from leaving. Will stooped to shake the paw of the dog nearest him.

"Are you an Airedale or a Welsh?" he said.

"Never mind that now," said the dog.

The bloodhound padded up to Rain, who was glad to have the desk between them. She got a distinct whiff of damp fur and dried spit as he approached. She wrinkled her nose and wondered what she smelled like to him.

The bloodhound heaved his bulk onto his hind legs. He took two shaky steps toward her and then his forepaws were scrabbling against the top of her desk. The dark pads unfolded into thick, clawed fingers; instead of a dew claw, the thing had a thumb. "I'm looking for a book," said the dog. His bowler hat tipped precariously. "My name is Baskerville."

Rain frowned at the scratches the dog's claws made on her desktop. "Well, you've got *that* wrong." She leaned back in her chair to get away from its breath. "Baskerville wasn't the hound's name. Sir Charles Baskerville was Sherlock Holmes's *client*."

"You may recall that Sir Charles was frightened to death by the hound well before Dr. Mortimer called on Holmes," Baskerville said. He had a voice like a kettle drum. "The client was actually his nephew, Sir Henry."

Rain chewed at her lower lip. "Dogs don't wear hats." She didn't care to be contradicted by some clumsy artifact of the cognisphere. "Or ties. Are you even real?"

"Rather a rude question, don't you think?" Baskerville regarded her with sorrowful, melted-chocolate eyes. "Are *you* real?"

The dog was right; this was the one thing the residents of Nowhere never asked. "I don't have your damn book." Rain opened the top drawer of the desk, the one where she threw all her loose junk. It was a way to keep the dog from seeing her embarrassment.

"How do you know?" he said reasonably. "I haven't told you what it is."

She sorted through the contents of the drawer as if searching for something. She moved the dental floss, destiny dice, blank catalog cards, a tape measure, her father's medals, the two dead watches, and finally picked out a bottle of ink and the Waterman 1897 Eyedropper fountain pen that Will had given her to make up for the fight they'd had about the laundry. The dog waited politely. "Well?" She unscrewed the lid of the ink bottle.

"It's called *The Last President,*" said Baskerville. "I'm afraid I don't know the author."

Rain felt the blood drain from her face. *The Last President* had been Will's working title for the book, just before he had started calling it *The Great American Novel*. She dipped the nib of the fountain pen into the ink bottle, pulled the filling lever and then wiped the nip on a tissue. "Never heard of it," she said as she wrote *Last Prez??* in her daybook. She glanced over at Will, and caught him squirming on his chair. He looked as if his pockets were full of crickets. "Fiction or non-fiction?"

"Fiction."

She wrote that down. "Short stories or a novel?"

"I'm not sure. A novel, I think."

The shop bell tinkled as Mrs. Snopes cracked the door open. She hesitated when she bumped one of the terriers. "Is something wrong?" she said, not taking her hand from the handle.

"Right as nails," said Fast Eddie. "Come in, Helen, good to see you. These folks are here for Rain. The big one is Mr. Baskerville and—I'm sorry I didn't catch your names." He gave the terriers a welcoming smile. Fast Eddie had become the friendliest man in Nowhere ever since his wife had stepped off the edge of town and disappeared.

"Spot," said one.

"Rover," said the other.

"Folks?" muttered Mrs. Snopes. "Dogs is what I call 'em." She inhaled, twisted her torso, and squeezed between the two terriers. Mrs. Snopes was very limber; she taught swing yoga at the Town Hall Monday, Tuesday, and Thursday nights from 6-7:30. "I've got a taste for some crumbs of your banana oatmeal bar," she said. "That last one laid me out for the better part of an afternoon. How are they breaking today, Eddie?"

"Let's just see." He set a tray on the top of the display case and pulled on a glove to sort through the broken cookies.

"You are Lorraine Carraway?" said Baskerville.

"That's her name, you bet." Will broke in impulsively. "But she hates it." He crumpled the loose-leaf page he had been writing on, tossed it at the trashcan and missed. "Call her Rain."

Rain bristled. She didn't hate her name; she just didn't believe in it.

"And you are?" said the bloodhound. His lips curled away from pointed teeth and black gums in a grotesque parody of a smile.

"Willy Werther, but everyone calls me Will."

"I see you are supplied with pencil and paper, young Will. Are you a writer?"

"Me? Oh, no. No." He feigned a yawn. "Well, sort of." For a moment, Rain was certain that he was going to blurt out that *he* was the author of *The Last President*. She wasn't sure why she thought that would be a bad idea, but she did. "I . . . uh . . ." Now that Will had Baskerville's attention, he didn't seem to know what to do with it. "I've been trying to remember jokes for Eddie to tell at church," he said. "Want to hear one?" Fast Eddie and Mrs. Snopes glanced up from their cookie deliberations. "Okay then, how do you keep your dog from digging in the garden?"

"I don't know, Will." Rain just wanted him to shut up. "How?"

"Take away his shovel." Will looked from Baskerville to Rain and then to Fast Eddie. "No?"

"No." Eddie, who had just become a deacon in the Temple of the Eternal Smile, shook his head. "God likes her jokes to be funny."

"Funny." Will nodded. "Got it. So what's this book about anyway, Mr. B?"

"Will, I just don't know," said the bloodhound. "That's why I'd like to read it." Baskerville turned and yipped over his shoulder. Rover trotted to him and the bloodhound dropped onto all fours. Rain couldn't see what passed between them because the desk blocked her view but when Baskerville heaved himself upright again he was holding a brass dog whistle in his paw. He dropped it, clattering, on the desktop in front of Rain.

"When you find the book, Rain," said Baskerville, "give us a call."

Rain didn't like it that Baskerville just assumed that she would take on the search. "Wait a minute," she said. "Why do you need me to look for it? You're part of the cognisphere, right? You already *know* everything."

"We have access to everything," said Baskerville. "Retrieval is another matter." He growled at Spot. The shop bell tinkled as he opened the door. "I look forward to hearing from you, Rain. Will, it was a pleasure to meet you." The bloodhound nodded at Fast Eddie and Mrs. Snopes, but they paid him no attention. Their heads were bent over the tray of crumbs. Baskerville left the shop, claws clicking against the gray linoleum. The terriers followed him out.

"Nice dogs." Will affected an unconcerned saunter as he crossed the room, although he flew the last few steps. "My book, Rain!" he whispered, his voice thick. With what? Fear? Pride?

"Is it?" Rain had yet to read a word of *The Great American Novel*; Will claimed it was too rough to show. Although she could imagine that this might be true, she couldn't help but resent being shut out. She offered him the whistle. "So call them."

"What are you saying?" He shrank back, as if mere proximity to the whistle might shrivel his soul. "They're from . . ." He pointed through the window toward the precipitous edge of the mesa on which Nowhere perched. ". . . out there."

Nobody knew where the cognisphere was located exactly, or even if it occupied physical space at all. "All right then, don't." Rain shrugged and pocketed the whistle.

Will seemed disappointed in her. He obviously had three hundred things he wanted to say—and she was supposed to listen. He had always been an excitable boy, although Rain hadn't seen him this wound up since the first time they had made love. But this was neither the time nor the place for feverish speculation. She put a finger to her lips and nodded toward the cookie counter.

Mrs. Snopes picked out a four gram, elongated piece of banana oatmeal cookie ornamented with cream and cinnamon hallucinogenic sprinkles. She paid for it with the story of how her sister Melva had run away from home when she was eleven and they had found her two days later sleeping in the neighbor's tree house. They had heard the story before, but not the part about the hair dryer. Fast Eddie earned an audience credit on the Barrows's Memory Exchange but the cognisphere deposited an extra quarter point into Mrs. Snopes's account for the new detail, according the Laughing Cookie's MemEx register. Afterward, Fast Eddie insisted that Rain admire the banana oatmeal crumb before he wrapped it up for Mrs. Snopes. Rain had to agree it was quite striking. She said it reminded her of Emily Dickinson.

They closed the Very Memorial Library early. Usually after work, Will and Rain swept some of Eddie's cookie dust into a baggie and went looking for a spot to picnic. Their favorites were the overlook at the southwestern edge of town and the roof of the Button Factory, although on a hot day they also liked the mossy coolness of the abandoned fallout shelter.

But not this unhappy day. Almost as soon as they stepped onto Onion Street, they were fighting. *First she* suggested that Will show her his book. *Then he* said not yet and asked if she had any idea why the dogs were asking about it. *Then she* said no—perhaps a jot too emphatically—*because he* apparently understood her to be puzzled as to why dogs should care about a nobody like him. *Then he* wondered aloud if maybe she wasn't just a little jealous, *which she* said was a dumb thing to say, *which he* took exactly the wrong way.

Will informed her icily that he was going home because he needed to make changes to Chapter Four. Alarmed at how their row had escalated, Rain suggested that maybe they could meet later. He just shrugged and turned away. Stung, she watched him jog down Onion Street.

Later, maybe—being together with Will had never sounded so contingent.

Rain decided to blame the dogs. It was hard enough staying sane here in Nowhere, finding the courage each day not to step off the edge. They didn't need yet another cancerous mystery eating at their lives. And Will was just a kid, she reminded herself. Nineteen, male, impulsive, too smart for his own good, but years from being wise. Of course he was entitled to his moods. She'd always waited him out before, because even though he made her toes curl in frustration sometimes, she did love the boy.

In the meantime, there was no way around it: she'd have to ask Chance Conrad about *The Last President*. She took a right onto Abbey Road, nodding curtly at the passersby. She knew what most people thought about her: that she was impatient and bitter and that she preferred books to people. Of course, they were all wrong, but she had given up trying to explain herself. She ignored Bingo Finn slouching in the entrance to Goriot's Pachinko Palazzo and hurried past Linton's Fruit and Daily Spectator, the Prynne Building, and the drunks at the outdoor tables in front of the Sunspot. She noticed with annoyance that the Drew Barrymore version of *The Wizard of Oz* was playing for another week at the Ziegfowl Feelies. At Uncle Buddy's she took a right, then a left onto Fairview which dead ended in the grassy bulk of the Barrow.

Everything in Nowhere had come out of the Barrow: Rain's fountain pen, the books in the Very Memorial Library, Will's endless packs of blank, loose-leaf paper, Fast Eddie's crystal trays and Mrs. Snopes's yoga mats. And of course, all the people.

The last thing Rain remembered about the world was falling asleep in her husband Roger's arms. It had been a warm night in May, 2009. Roger had worked late so they had ordered a sausage and green pepper pizza and had watched the last half hour of *The African Queen* before they went to bed. It was *so* romantic, even if

Nicholson and Garbo were old. She could remember Roger doing his atrocious Nicholson imitation while he brushed his teeth. They had cuddled briefly in the dark but he said he was too tired to make love. They must have kissed good night—yes, no doubt a long and tender last kiss. One of the things she hated most about Nowhere was that she couldn't remember any of Roger's kisses or his face or what he looked like naked. He was just a warm, pale, friendly blur. Some people in Nowhere said it was a mercy that nobody could remember the ones they had loved in the world. Rain was not one of those people.

Will said that the last thing he remembered was falling asleep in his *Nintendo and American Culture* class at Northern Arizona University in the fall of 2023. He could recall everything about the two sexual conquests he had managed in his brief time in the world—Talley Lotterhand and Paula Herbst—but then by his own admission he had never really been in love.

The Barrow was a warehouse buried under the mesa. Rain climbed down to the loading dock and knocked on the sectional steel door. After a few moments she heard the whine of an electric motor as the door clattered up on its tracks. Chance Conrad stood just inside, blinking in the afternoon sunlight. He was a handsome, graying man, who balanced a receding hairline with a delicate beard. Although he had a light step and an easy manner, the skin under his eyes was dark and pouchy. Some said this was because Chance didn't sleep much since he was so busy managing the Barrow. Others maintained that he didn't sleep at all, because he hadn't been revived like the rest of the residents of Nowhere. He was a construct of the cognisphere. It stood to reason, people said. How could anyone with a name like Chance Conrad be real?

"Lorraine!" he said. "And here I was about to write this day off as a total loss." He put his hand on her shoulder and urged her through the entrance. "Come, come in." Chance had no use for daylight; that was another strike against his being real. Once the Barrow was safely locked down again he relaxed. "So," he said, "here we are, just the two of us. I'm hoping this means you've finally dumped the boy genius?"

Rain had long since learned that the best way to deflect Chance's relentless flirting was just to ignore it. As far as she knew, he had never taken a lover. She took a deep breath and counted to five. *Unu, du, tri, kvar, kvin.* The air in the Barrow had the familiar damp weight she remembered from when she first woke up at Nowhere; it settled into Rain's lungs like a cold. Before her were crates and jars and barrels and boxes of goods that the people of Nowhere had asked the cognisphere to recreate. Later that night Ferdie Raskolnikov and his crew would load the lot onto trucks for delivery around town tomorrow.

"What's this?" Rain bent to examine a wide-bladed shovel cast with a solid steel handle. It was so heavy that she could barely lift it.

"Shelly Castorp thinks she's planting daffodils with this." Chance shook his head. "I told her that the handles of garden tools were always made of wood but she claims her father had a shovel just like that one." He shook his head. "The specific gravity of steel is 7.80 grams per cubic centimeter, you know."

"Oh?" When Rain let the handle go, the shovel clanged against the cement floor. "Can we grow daffodils?"

"We'll see." Chance muscled the shovel back into place on its pallet. He probably didn't appreciate her handling other people's orders. "I'm racking my brains trying to remember if I've got something here for you. But I don't, do I?"

"How about those binoculars I keep asking for?"

"I send the requests. . . ." He spread his hands. "They all bounce." The corners of his mouth twitched. "So is this about us? At long last?"

"I'm just looking for a book, Chance. A novel."

"Oh," he said, crestfallen. "Better come to the office."

Normally if Rain wanted to add a book to the Very Memorial Library, she'd call Chance and put in an order. Retrieving books was usually no problem for the collective intelligence of humanity, which had uploaded itself into the cognisphere sometime in the late Twenty-third Century. All it needed was an author and title. Failing that, a plot description or even just a memorable line might suffice for the cognisphere to perform a plausible, if not completely accurate, reconstruction of some lost text. In fact, depending on the quality of the description, the cognisphere would recreate a version of pretty much anything the citizens of Nowhere could remember from the world.

Exactly how it accomplished this, and more important, why it bothered, was a mystery.

Chance's office was tucked into the rear of the Barrow, next to the crèche. On the way, they passed the Big Board of the MemEx, which tracked audience and storyteller accounts for all the residents of Nowhere and sorted and cataloged the accumulated memories. Chance stopped by the crèche to check the vitals of Rahim Aziz, who was destined to become the newest citizen of Nowhere, thus bringing the population back up to the standard 853. Rahim was to be an elderly man with a crown of snowy white hair surrounding an oval bald spot. He was replacing Lucy Panza, the tennis pro and Town Calligrapher, who had gone missing two weeks ago and was presumed to have thrown herself over the edge without telling anyone.

"Old Aziz isn't quite as easy on the eye as you were," said Chance, who never failed to remind Rain that he had seen her naked during her revival. Rahim floated on his back in a clear tube filled with a yellow, serous fluid. He had a bit of a paunch and the skin of his legs and under his arms was wrinkled. Rain noted with distaste that he had a penis tattoo of an elephant.

"When will you decant him?"

Chance rubbed a thumb across a readout shells built into the wall of the crèche. "Tomorrow, maybe." The shells meant nothing to Rain. "Tuesday at the latest."

Chance Conrad's office was not so much decorated as over-stuffed. Dolls and crystal and tools and fossils and clocks jostled across shelves and the tops of cabinets and chests. The walls were covered with pix from feelies made after Rain's time in the world, although she had seen some of them at the Ziegfowl. She recognized Oud's *Birthdeath*, Marette de Valois in full fetish from *Time StRanger* and the wedding cake scene from *Two of Neala*.

"So this is about a novel then?" Chance moved behind his desk but did not sit down. "Called?" He waved a hand over his desktop and its eye winked at him.

"*The Last President*." Rain sat in the chair opposite him.

"Precedent as in a time-honored custom, or President as in Marie Louka?"

"The latter."

He chuckled. "You know, you're the only person in this town who would say *the latter*. I love that. Would you have my baby?"

"No."

"Marry me?"

"Uh-uh."

"Sleep with me?"

"*Chance.*"

He sighed. "Who's the author?"

"I don't know."

"You don't know?" Chance rubbed under his eyes with the heels of his hands. "You're sure about that? You wouldn't care to take a wild guess? Last name begins with the letter . . . what? A through K? L through Z?"

"Sorry."

He stepped from behind the desk and his desktop shut its eye. "Well, the damn doggie didn't know either, which is why I couldn't help him."

Rain groaned. "He's been here already?"

"Him and a couple of his pooch pals." Chance opened the igloo which stood humming beside the door. "Cooler?" He pulled out a frosty pitcher filled with something thick and glaucous. "It's just broccoli nectar and a little ethanol-style vodka."

Rain shook her head. "But that doesn't make sense." She could hear the whine in her voice. "They're agents of the cognisphere, right? And you access the cognisphere. Why would it ask you to ask itself?"

"Exactly." Chance closed the door and locked it. This struck Rain as odd; maybe he was afraid that Ferdie Raskolnikov would barge in on them. "Things have been loopy here lately," he said. "You should see some of the mistakes we've had to send back." He poured broccoli cocktail for himself. It oozed from the pitcher and landed in his coffee mug with a thick *plop*. "I've spent all afternoon trying to convince myself that the dogs are some kind of a work-around, maybe to jog some lost data loose from the MemEx." He replaced the pitcher in the igloo and settled onto the chair behind his desk. "But now you show up and I'm wondering: Why is Rain asking me for this book?"

She frowned. "I ask you for all my books."

He considered for a moment, tapping the finger against his forehead and then pointed at her. "Let me tell you a story." Rain started to object that she had neither goods nor services to offer him in return and she had just drained her MemEx account to dry spit, but he silenced her with a wave. "No, this one is free." He took a sip of liquid broccoli. "An audience credit unencumbered, offered to the woman of my dreams."

She stuck out her tongue.

"Why does this place exist?" he asked.

"The Barrow?"

"Nowhere."

"Ah, eschatology." She laughed bitterly. "Well, Father Samsa claims this is the afterlife, although I'll be damned if I know whether it's heaven or hell."

"I know you don't believe *that*," said Chance. "So then this is some game that the cognisphere is playing? We're virtual chess persons?"

Rain shrugged.

"What happens when we step off the edge?"

"Nobody knows." Just then a cacophony of clocks yawped, pinged, buzzed in six o'clock. "This isn't much of a story, Chance."

"Patience, love. So you think the cognisphere recreated us for a reason?"

"Maybe. Okay, sure." A huge spider with eight paintbrush legs shook itself and stretched on a teak cabinet. "We're in a zoo. A museum."

"Or maybe some kind of primitive backup. The cognisphere keeps us around because there's a chance that it might fail, go crazy—I don't know. If that happened, we could start over."

"Except we'd all die without the cognisphere." The spider stepped onto the wall and picked its way toward the nearest corner. "And nobody's made any babies that I know of. We're not exactly Adam and Eve material, Chance."

"But that's damn scary, no? Makes the case that none of us is real."

Rain liked him better when he was trying to coax her into bed. "Enough." She pushed her chair back and started to get up.

"Okay, okay." He held up his hands in surrender. "Story time. When I was a kid, I used to collect meanies."

"Meanies?" She settled back down.

"Probably after your time. They were bots, about so big." He held forefinger and thumb a couple of centimeters apart. "Little fighting toys. There were gorilla meanies and ghoul meanies and Nazi meanies and demon meanies and dino meanies. Fifty-two in all, one for every week of the year. You set them loose in the meanie arena and they would try to kill one another. If they died, they'd shut down for twenty-four hours. Now if meanies fought one on one, they would always draw. But when you formed them into teams, their powers combined in different ways. For instance, a ghoul and Nazi team could defeat any other team of two—except the dino and yeti. For the better part of a year, I rushed home from school every day to play with the things. I kept trying combinations until I could pretty much predict the outcome of every battle. Then I lost interest."

"Speaking of losing interest," said Rain, who was distracted by the spider decorating the corner of Chance's office in traceries of blue and green.

"I'm getting there." He shifted uncomfortably in his chair, and took another sip from the mug. "So a couple of years go by and I'm twelve now. One night I'm in my room and I hear this squeaking coming from under my bed. I pull out the old meanie arena, which has been gathering dust all this time and I see that a mouse has blundered into it and is being attacked by a squad of meanies. And just like that I'm fascinated with them all over again. For weeks I drop crickets and frogs and garter snakes into the arena and watch them try to survive."

"That's sick."

"No question. But then boys can't help themselves when it comes to mindless cruelty. Anyway, it didn't last. The wildlife was too hard on the poor little bots." He drained the last of the broccoli. "But the point is that I got bored playing with a closed set of meanies. Even though I hadn't actually tried all possible combinations, after a while I could see that nothing much new was ever going to happen. But then the mouse changed everything." He leaned forward across the desk. "So let me propose a thought experiment to you, my lovely Lorraine. This mysterious novel that everyone is so eager to find? What if the last name of the author began with the letter . . ." He paused and then seemed to pluck something out of the air. "Oh, let's say 'W'."

Rain started.

"And just for the sake of argument, let's suppose that the first name also begins with 'W' . . . Ah, I see from your expression that this thought has also occurred to you."

"It's not him," said Rain. "He was revived at nineteen; he's just a kid. Why would the cognisphere care anything about him?"

"Because he's the mouse in our sad, little arena. He isn't simply recycling memories of the world like the rest of us. The novel your doggies are looking for doesn't exist in the cognisphere, never did. Because it's being written right here, right now. Maybe imagination is in short supply wherever the doggies come from. Lord knows there isn't a hell of a lot of it in Nowhere."

Rain would have liked to deny it, but she could feel the insult sticking to her. "How do you know he's writing a novel?"

"I supply the paper, Rain. Reams and reams of it. Besides, this may be hell, as Father Samsa insists, but it's also a small town. We meddle in each other's business, what else is there to do?" His voice softened; Rain thought that if Chance ever did take a lover, this would be how he might speak to her. "Is the book any good? Because if it is, I'd like to read it."

"I don't know." At that moment, Rain felt a drop of something cold hit the back of her hand. There was a dot the color of sky on her knuckle. She looked up at the spider hanging from the ceiling on an azure thread. "He doesn't show it to me. Your toy is dripping."

"Really?" Chance came around the desk. "A woman of your considerable charms is taking no for an answer?" He reached up and cradled the spider into his arms. "Go get him, Rain, you don't want to keep your mouse waiting." He carried it to the teak cabinet.

Rain rubbed at the blue spot on her hand but the stain had penetrated her skin. She couldn't even smudge it.

But Will wasn't waiting, at least not for Rain. She stopped by their apartment but he wasn't there and he hadn't left a note. Neither was he at the Button Factory nor Queequeg's Kava Cave. She looked in at the Laughing Cookie just as Fast Eddie was locking up. No Will. She finally tracked Will down at the overlook, by the blue picnic table under the chestnut trees.

Normally they came here for the view, which was spectacular. A field of wildflowers, tidy-tips and mullein and tickseed and bindweed, sloped steeply down to the edge of the mesa. But Will was paying no attention to the scenery. He had scattered a stack of five loose-leaf binders across the table; the whole of *The Great American Novel* or *The Last President* or whatever the hell it was called. Three of the binders were open. He was reading—but apparently not writing in—a fourth. A No. 2 pencil was tucked behind his ear. Something about Will's body language disturbed Rain. He usually sprawled awkwardly wherever he came to rest, a giraffe trying to settle on a hammock. Now he was gathered into himself, hunched over the binder like an old man. Rain came up behind him and kneaded his shoulders for a moment.

He leaned back and sighed.

"Sorry about this afternoon." She bent to nibble his ear. "Have you eaten?"

"No." He kissed the air in front of him but did not look at her.

She peeked at the loose-leaf page in front of him and tried to decipher the handwriting, which was not quite as legible as an EEG chart. . . . *knelt before the coffin, her eyes wide in the dim holy light of the cathedral. His face was wavy* . . . No, thought Rain straightening up before he suspected that she was reading. Not *wavy*. *Waxy*. "Beautiful evening," she said.

Will shut the binder he had been reading and gazed distractedly toward the horizon.

Rain had not been completely honest with Chance. It was true that Will hadn't shown her the novel, but she *had* read some of it.

She had stolen glimpses over his shoulder or read upside down when she was sitting across from him. Then there was the one guilty afternoon when she had come back to their apartment and gobbled up pages 34-52 before her conscience mastered her curiosity. The long passage had taken place in a bunker during one of the Resource Wars. The President of Great America, Lawrence Goodman, had been reminiscing with his former mistress and current National Security Advisor, Rebecca Santorino, about Akron, where they had first fallen in love years ago and which had just been obliterated in retaliation for an American strike on Zhengzhou. Two pages later they were thrashing on the president's bed and ripping each other's clothes off. Rain had begun this part with great interest, hoping to gain new insight into Will's sexual tastes, but had closed the binder uneasily just as the President was tying his lover to the Louis XVI armoire with silk Atura neckties.

Will closed the other open binders and stacked all five into a pile. Then he pulled the pencil from behind his ear, snapped it in two, and let the pieces roll out of his hand under the picnic table. He gave her an odd, lopsided smile.

"Will, what's the matter?" Rain stared. "Are you okay?"

In response, he pulled a baggie of cookie dust from his shirt pocket and jiggled it.

"Here?" she said, coloring. "In plain sight?" Usually they hid out when they were eating dust, at least until they weathered the first rush. The Cocoa Peanut Butter Chunk made them giggly and not a little stupid. Macaroon Sandies often hit Rain like powdered lust.

"There's no one to see." Will licked his forefinger and stuck it into the bag. "Besides, what if there was?" He extended the finger toward her, the tip and nail coated with the parti-colored powder. "Does anyone here care what we do?"

She considered telling him then what Chance Conrad had said about small towns but she could see that Will was having a mood. So she just opened her mouth and obediently stuck her tongue out. As he rotated the finger across the middle of her tongue, she tasted the sweet, spicy grit. She closed her mouth on the finger and he pulled it slowly through her lips.

"Now you," she said, reaching for the baggie. They always fed each other cookie dust.

Rain and Will sat on the tabletop with their feet on the seat, facing the slope that led down to the edge of Nowhere. The world beneath the impossibly high cliff was impossibly flat, but this was still Rain's favorite lookout, even if it was probably an illusion. The land stretched out in a kind of grid with rectangles in every color of green: the brooding green of forests, the dreaming green of fields under cultivation, and the confused gray-green of scrub land. Dividing the rectangles were ribbons the color of wet sand. Rain liked to think they were roads, although she had never spotted any traffic on them. She reached for Will's hand and he closed it around hers. He was right: she didn't care if anyone saw them together like this. His skin was warm and rough. As she rubbed her finger over the back of his hand, she thought she could make out a faded blue spot. But maybe it was a trick of the twilight, or a cookie hallucination.

The rectangles and the ribbons of the land to the southwest had always reminded her of something, but she had never quite been able to figure out what. Now as Eddie's magic cookie dust sparked through her bloodstream, and she felt Will's warm hand in hers, she thought of a trip she had taken with her father when she was a just a kid to a museum in an old city called Manhilton, that got blown up afterward. In the museum were very old pix that just hung on the wall and mostly didn't do anything, and she remembered taking a cab to get there and the cab had asked what her name was but she wouldn't tell it so it called her *little girl* which she didn't like because she was seven already, and the museum had escalators that whispered music, and there was one really, really big room filled with pix of all blurry water lilies, and outside in a sculpture garden there were statues made of metal and rocks but there were no flowers because it was cold so she and Dad didn't stay out there very long and inside again were lots of pix of women with three eyes and too many corners and then some wide blue men blocked her view of the Mona Lisa so she never really saw that one, which everyone said later was supposed to be so special but one she did see and remembered now was a pix of a grid that had colored rectangles and with ribbons of red and yellow separating them, and she asked her Dad if it was a map of the museum and he laughed down at her because her Dad was so tall, tall as any statue and he said the pix wasn't a map, it was a *mondrian* and she asked him what a *mondrian* was and then he laughed again and she laughed and it was so easy to laugh in those days and Will was laughing too.

"I want to go down there." He laughed as he pointed down at the mondrian which stretched into the rosy distance.

"There?" Rain didn't understand; the best part of her was still in the museum with her father. "Why?"

"Because there are people living there. Must be why Chance

won't give out binoculars or telescopes." He let go of her hand. "Because it's not here."

"You're going to step over the edge?" Her voice rose in alarm.

"No, silly." He leapt up, stood on the tabletop and raised his arms to the sky. "I'm going to climb down."

"But that's the same thing."

"No, it isn't. I'll show you." He slid off the picnic table and started toward the thicket of scruffy evergreens and brambles that had overgrown the edge of Nowhere. He walked along this tangle until he came to a bit of blue rag tied to a branch, glanced over his shoulder to see if she was still with him and then wriggled into the scrub. Rain followed.

They emerged into a tiny clearing. She sidled beside him and he slipped an arm around her waist to brace her. The cliff was steep here but not sheer. She could make out a narrow, dirt track that switched back through scree and stunted fir. Maybe a mountain goat could negotiate it, if there were any mountain goats. But a single misstep would send Will plunging headlong. And then there was the Drop. Everyone knew about the Drop. They traded stories about it all the time. Scary stories. She was about to ask him why, if there were people down there, they hadn't climbed up for a visit, when he kicked a stone over the edge. They watched it bounce straight down and disappear over a ledge.

"Lucy Panza showed me this," said Will, his face flushed with excitement.

Rain wondered when he'd had time to go exploring the edge with Lucy Panza. "But she stepped over the edge."

"No," he said. "She didn't."

She considered the awful slope for a moment and shuddered. "I'm not going down there, Will."

He continued peering down the dirt track. "I know," he said.

The calm with which he said it was like a slap in the face. She stared at him, speechless, until he finally met her gaze. "I'll come back for you." He gave her the goofy, apologetic grin he always summoned up when he upset her. "I'll make sure the path is safe and I'll make all kinds of friends down at the bottom and when the time is right, I'll be back."

"But what about your book?"

He blew a dismissive breath between his lips. "I'm all set with that."

"It's finished?"

"It's crap, Rain." His voice was flat. "I'm not wasting any more time writing about some stupid made-up president. There are no more presidents. And how can anyone write the Great American novel when there is no more America?" He caught his breath. "Sorry," he said. "I know that's what you wanted me to do." He gave her a sour smile. "You're welcome to read it if you want. Or hand it over to the dogs. That should be good for a laugh." Then he pulled her into his arms and kissed her.

Of course Rain kissed him back. She wanted to drag him down on top of her and rip his clothes off, although there really wasn't enough room here to make love. She would even have let him take her on the picnic table, *tie her* to the damn table, if that's what he had wanted. But his wasn't the kind of kiss that started anything.

"So I'm coming back, I promise," he murmured into her ear. "Just tell everyone that you're waiting for me."

"Wait a minute." She twisted away from him. "You're going now? It's almost dark. We just ate cookie dust." She couldn't believe he was serious. This was such a typical boneheaded-Will-stunt he was pulling. "Come home, honey," she said. "Get some sleep. Things might look different in the morning."

He stroked her hair. "I've got at least another hour of light," he said. "Believe me, I've thought about this a long time, Rain." Then he brushed his finger against her lips. "I love you."

He took a step over the edge and another. He had gone about a dozen meters before his feet went out from beneath him and he fell backward, skidding on his rear end and clutching at the scrub. But he caught himself almost immediately and looked up at her, his face pale as the moon. "Oops!" he called cheerfully.

Rain stood at the edge of the cliff long after she could no longer see him. She was hoping that he'd come to a dead end and have to turn back. The sun was painting the horizon with fire by the time she fetched Will's binders to the edge of Nowhere. She opened one after another and shook the pages free. They fluttered into the twilight like an exaltation of larks. A few landed briefly on the path before launching themselves again into the breeze and following their creator out of her life. When all the pages had disappeared, Rain took the whistle that the dogs had given her and hurled it as far into the mondrian as she could.

Only then did she let herself cry. She thought she deserved it.

Rain found her way through the gathering darkness back to the apartment over Vronsky's Laundromat and Monkeyfilter Bowladrome. She put some Szechwan lasagna into the microwave and pushed it around her plate for a while, but she was too numb to be hungry. She would have gone to the eight o'clock show at the Ziegfowl just to get out, but she was mortally tired of *The Wizard of Oz*, no matter whom the cognisphere recast in it. The apartment depressed her. The problem, she decided, was that she was surrounded by Will's stuff; she'd have to move it somewhere out of sight.

She placed a short stack of college-lined, loose-leaf paper and four unopened reams in a box next to *The Awakening, The Big Snooze,* and *Drinking the Snow.* Will had borrowed the novels from the Very Memorial Library but had made way too many marginal notes in them for her to return them to the stacks. Rain would have to order new ones from Chance in the Barrow. She threw his Buffalo Soldiers warm-up jacket on top of several dusty pairs of Adidas Kloud Nine running shoes. Will's dresser drawers produced eight pairs of white socks, two black, a half dozen gray jockey shorts, three pairs of jeans, and a stack of T-shirts sporting pix of Panafrican shoutcast bands. At the bottom of the sock drawer, Rain discovered flash editions of *Superheterodyne Adventure Stories 2020-26* and *The Complete Idiot's Guide to Fetish.* She pulled his mustard collection and climkies and homebrew off the kitchen shelves.

And that was all it took to put Will out of her life. She shouldn't have been surprised. After all, they had only lived together for just over a year.

She was trying to talk herself into throwing the lot of it out the next morning when the doorglass blinked. She glanced at the clock. Who did she know that would come visiting at 10:30 at night? When she opened the door, Baskerville, Rover, and Spot looked up at her.

"You found the book?" The bloodhound's bowtie was crooked.

Beneath her, Rain could hear the rumble and clatter of the bowling lanes. "There is no book."

"May we come in?"

"No."

"You threw the whistle off the edge," said Baskerville.

As if on signal, the two terriers sat. They looked to Rain as if they were settling in for a stay. "Where's Will?" said Rover.

She wanted to kick the door shut hard enough to knock their bowler hats off, but the terrier's question took her breath away. If the cognisphere had lost track of Will, then maybe he wasn't . . . maybe he was . . . "I hate dogs," she said. "Maybe I forgot to mention that?"

Baskerville regarded her with his solemn, chocolate eyes and said nothing.

The terrier's hind leg scratched at his flank. "Has something happened to him?" he asked.

"Stop it!" Rain stomped her foot on the doorsill and all three dogs jumped. "You want a story and I want information. Deal?"

The dogs thought it over, then Rover got up and licked her hand.

"Okay, story." But at that moment, Rain's throat seemed to close, as if she had tried to swallow the page of a book. *Will was gone.* If she said it aloud, it would become just another story on the MemEx. But she had to know. "M-My boyfriend climbed over the edge a couple of hours ago trying to find a way down the cliff. I pitched the goddamn novel he was writing after him. The end."

"But what does this have to do with *The Last President?*"

"That was the name of his book. Used to be. Once." She was out of breath. "Okay, you got story. Now you owe me some god-damn truth. He's dead, right? You've absorbed him already."

Rover started to say, "I'm afraid that we have no knowledge of . . ." But she didn't give the dog a chance to finish; she slammed the door.

She decided then not to throw Will's things out. She dragged them all into the bedroom closet and covered the pile with the electric blanket. She made one more pass around the apartment to make sure she had everything. Then she decided to make a grocery list so she could stop at Cereno's on the way home from work tomorrow. That's when she discovered that she had nothing to write on. She gave herself permission to retrieve a couple of pages of Will's paper from the closet—just this once. As long as she was writing the list, she didn't have to think about Will on the cliff or the dogs in the hall. She cracked the apartment door just enough to see that all three of them were still there, heads on paws, asleep. Spot's ear twitched but he didn't wake up. She sat on the couch with the silence ringing in her ears until she got up and muscled the dresser over to block the closet where she had put Will's stuff. She thought about brushing her teeth and trying for sleep but she knew that would be a waste of time. She was browsing the books on her bookshelf, all of which she had long since read to tatters, when the phone squawked.

Rain was sure it was the dogs calling, but decided to pick up just in case.

"Lorraine Carraway?"

Rain recognized Sheriff Renfield's drawl and was immediately annoyed. He was one of her best customers—an avid Georgette Heyer fan—and knew better than to call her by her proper name.

"Speaking, Beej. What's up?"

"There's been some trouble down to the Laughing Cookie." He was slurring words. He pronounced *There is* as *Thersh*.

"Trouble?"

"Fast Eddie said you had dogs in the store today. Dogs with hats."

"What kind of trouble, Beej? Is Eddie all right?"

"He's fine, we're all just fine." Everybody knew that Beej Renfield was a drinker and nobody blamed him for it. Being sheriff was possibly the most boring job in Nowhere. "But there's been what you might call vandalism. Books all over the place, Rain, some of them ripped up good. Teeth marks. And the place stinks of piss. Must've happened, an hour, maybe two ago. Fast Eddie is ripping mad. I need you to come down here and lay some calm on him. Will you do that for me, Rain?"

"I'll do you one better, Beej. You're looking for these dogs?"

His breath rasped in the receiver so loud she could almost smell it.

"Because I've got them here if you're interested. Right outside my door."

"I'm on my way."

"Oh, and Beej? You might want to bring some help."

She sat at the kitchen table to wait. In front of her were the shopping list and the No. 2 pencil. They reminded her of Will. He was such a strong boy, everybody in town always said so. He *had* run that 4:21 mile, after all. And she was almost certain that Baskerville had looked surprised when she'd told him that Will was climbing down the cliff. What did surprise look like on a dog? She'd see for sure when Beej Renfield arrived.

For the very first time Rain allowed herself to consider the possibility that Will wasn't dead or absorbed. Maybe the cognisphere ended at the edge of Nowhere. In which case, he might actually come back for her.

But why would he bother? What had she ever done to deserve him? Her shopping list lay in front of her like an accusation. Was this all her life was about? Toilet paper and Seventy-Up and duck sausage? Will had climbed over the edge of Nowhere. What chance had she ever taken? She needed to do *something*, something no one had ever done before. She'd had enough of books and all the old stories about the world that the cognisphere was sorting on the MemEx. That world was gone, forever and ever, amen.

She picked up the pencil again.

I scowled at the dogs through the plate-glass window of the Very Memorial Library. They squatted in a row next to my book drop. There were three of them, haughty in their bowler hats and silk vests. They acted like they owned the air. Bad dogs, I knew that for sure, created out of spit and tears and heartbreak by the spirits of all the uncountable dead and sent to spy on the survivors and cause at least three different kinds of trouble.

I wasn't worried. We'd seen their kind before.

The Ice Is Singing

THE MAN IN THE ICE IS WEARING A BLUE, THREE-piece suit. He is facing up at you and the bright sky and his eyes are open. What does he see? Nothing. He's dead, no? You look around the lake. None of the other skaters seem to realize that there's a man frozen in the ice on Christmas Day. Someone could do a sit spin right on his nose, a triple lutz from his head to his black, tasseled loafers. Except nobody on the lake is that good a skater. Certainly not you.

The ice is singing today. It whoops under strong light and moans when the sun goes behind a cloud. Something to do with expansion and contraction. Beth called the sounds whale songs. You think they'd have to be whales the size of skyscrapers. Sometimes the ice cracks under your weight with a sound like a gunshot, but don't worry about falling through. It's thick here, thick as a man.

So what to do about your man in the ice? You are already thinking of him as yours. No one is going to find him, way over here in Brainard's cove. The Brainards are summer people. They're in Lauderdale, waiting for the early bird dinner special at the Olive Garden. Is the Olive Garden open on Christmas? You could dial 911, but it's a little late for CPR. His skin looks gray against the white, button-down shirt. One of those Escher ties, green geometric birds turning into blue fish, tucks into the vest. Now that you're branch manager, you wouldn't mind having a three-piece suit.

Then why didn't you tell Beth? She buys all your clothes.

The man in the ice isn't going anywhere and you're cold. It takes you twenty minutes to skate home.

The house is full of Beth's absence. You should have bought a tree anyway. Strung the damn lights. It wasn't as if you couldn't find the ornaments. They're in the attic, behind the golf clubs. Next to the unopened presents you piled there. If she were here, there would be sugar cookies and a turkey and the ghost of Bing Crosby would be on the couch, drinking her eggnog.

You try to imagine how a man could get caught in the ice like that. If he were dead, he'd sink to the bottom. And even if he were floating, wouldn't he be face down? When you were a kid, summering on the lake, you perfected the dead man's float. You actually got your grandma to scream once. Maybe your man lies down on the ice. He's tired after a long day of selling single premium deferred annuities or designing large span roof trusses or calculating the useful lives of general fixed assets. His body is warm; he melts into the ice. Then it closes over him.

Maybe it's a miracle. A *Christmas miracle*. Yeah, right.

Or maybe you're fucking crazy.

The walls of your home office are the color of walnut shells. That was Beth's favorite joke. "I see you're in a brown study," she would say. You can picture her in the doorway, hip cocked against the jamb. How many times did you kiss her there? The moose framed on the wall was never amused by her joke. Neither was the otter or the winged blur you're sure is a bald eagle. Beth gave you a digital camera for your thirty-fourth birthday. You need to repaint your office soon. This spring, when the weather warms up. You sit at the computer and type *ice* into Google. You read about black ice and snow ice and water ice and large-grain ice and small-grain ice and cobblestone ice. There is nothing about businessman ice.

One of the web pages is put up by an ice boating fan named Steph. She graduated two years ago from the University of Montana and is working as a librarian in Kalispell. She collects erasers and stamps. You stare at pictures of her wedding and her honeymoon. There she is standing next to her ice boat. She's wearing a tight, red jumpsuit and a black helmet with bright red flames. Her husband's name is Steve and he looks very happy. Steve and Steph. You want to send an email to warn her.

About what?

Your bed feels very big that night, almost as big as the lake. You are lost in it and Beth's side is freezing.

The next morning you congratulate yourself for waking up. You have survived the first Christmas. You walk outside to get the *Globe*. The paper is heavy with ads. Take those presents back, you cheerful fucks, and buy something new! But there is no news. Nothing ever happens on Christmas. For example, businessmen don't get frozen in ice. Back in the house, you hover in the kitchen. You've been hovering a lot, lately—you forget what you're doing. Breakfast, that's it. You wake up, get the paper, *have breakfast*. You shake Raisin Bran into a bowl and scan the sports page. Then you notice that you are pouring orange juice over the cereal. The phone rings.

"Hello."

You hear the whisper of static, but no reply.

You say it again. "Hello."

The phone clicks and a telemarketer says, "I would like to speak to Beth Anstruther."

"She's not interested." You hang up and put on your skates.

Your man is still there, but he has moved. Yesterday both arms were at his sides. Now he has raised his right hand as if he's waiting to be called on. He has something important to say, something that can't wait until ice out. Or else he's waving goodbye. You get down on your hands and knees. He's about your size but he's older, balder, deader. The ice here is glossy and strangely transparent. Like a lens magnifying the bottom of the lake. You see boulders and rocks and mud. Dark oak leaves, a pale Budweiser can, the glitter of gold. The ring must have slipped off the man's finger.

His blue suit has thin, chalk stripes. The Escher tie has come out of the vest. Green birds turning into blue fish. His eyes are the same—fixed, frozen. The fingers of his upraised hand are curled.

"What?"

The sound of your own voice scares you. You shouldn't be talking to dead people. What if they talk back?

You spend the rest of the morning in your living room, staring at the lake. The lake is singing again today but by noon, only moans echo off the hill behind your house. The sky has turned to granite. Last night Weather.com was predicting four to six inches of snow. You convince yourself that you will stop worrying about your man in the ice once the storm buries him.

The doorbell rings and you bolt off the sofa, nerves twitching. Rachel, the mail lady, is at the front door. She's holding a magazine wrapped around a thick stack of letters and a long, thin box, wrapped in brown paper.

"Package for you," she says. "Probably a late Christmas present. Didn't fit in the mailbox."

You take it all from her but you can't find your voice. In the silence, you notice that Rachel has had her nose pierced since you last saw her. There's a drop of gold just above her left nostril. She's thirty-two and divorced and the boys at the town dump love to gossip about her.

"Looks like we're in for some weather," she says, and then she really sees you. A shadow passes over her face. "You okay, Mr. A?"

"The flu," you say. "Don't let me breathe on you."

As soon as she is gone, you run to the bathroom to look at yourself. Not good. Your eyes are like wounds. And you haven't shaved in three days. Has it been three days already? Oh, they'd be talking about you in town, all right. First at the Post Office, then at Lil's Grille.

You throw *Time* away. You don't care who the "Man of the Year" is. Besides, that's her magazine. Most of the letters are junk. There are bills from Sprint and DIRECTV and three straggling Christmas cards. One of them is from Beth's sister Margaret. It is addressed to *the Anstruther Family*.

"What family?" you say. You open the card and read,

In this holiday season
May your home and loved ones
Be blessed with peace and harmony

Underneath it she has written, "Hope you're okay, Margaret." A cramped little greeting from the human fucking cramp.

You open the package last. It's a present from your mom. You're surprised she didn't call yesterday. She's probably waiting for you to call her. Like that might ever happen. You haven't told her yet. You haven't told anyone. How can you?

As soon as you get the wrapping paper off, you know it's a tie. The box is white and has a nubbly finish. You pry the top off.

Your mother has sent you one of those Escher ties, green geometric birds turning into blue fish. You feel as if someone is pressing thumbs into your eyes because you know now, *you know.*

You fling yourself at the stairs. You yank down the trap door to the attic and scramble up. You pull the chain on the bare light bulb so hard that it breaks. You see the present almost immediately. It's the right shape. The weight tells you everything. Red wrapping paper with snowmen in top hats. Rip, *rip it.* It's cold up here. You can see your breath. Your finger feels swollen as you slip it between the top and bottom of the box. You tear open your Christmas present from Beth.

It's blue, of course with chalk stripes. Jacket, trousers, vest. Outside, the ice is singing.

To you.

Serpent

YOU THINK IT'S EASY LIVING IN THE GARDEN? THE never-ending picnic—that's what your Bible says, doesn't it? That the people who live here just stroll around petting tigers and helping themselves to the Gardener's own salad bar? Oh, and having lots of sloppy, guiltless sex. Being fruitful. Multiplying. Why not? They've got nothing better to do. They have no checkbooks to balance, no periodic table to memorize. No poker or email or *National Enquirer*.

Possibly you're surprised that there are still people in the garden. That isn't in your book, is it? Well, things have changed here since your lot got shown the gate. The Gardener decided to try again, except that He tinkered with His design this time around. Take sex, for instance. The Gardener made sex less fun—more like brushing your teeth with baking soda than eating dark chocolate with almonds. And He must have decided that there was something wonky about sexual dimorphism, because He did away with all your exaggerated curves and bulges. The innocents—they like to call themselves that, can you believe it?—are hermaphrodites. Everyone's got the same equipment, although it comes in a variety of sizes. And of course, nudity is not a problem for this batch; they are covered with a delicate, flat down that is more like feathers than hair.

The innocents are better stewards of the garden than you were. It's because the Gardener gave them peculiar moral imaginations. Their art isn't worth much, but they see consequences around a corner and a mile away. They compost and practice sound forest management. When they slaughter an animal, they use just about all of it. They prefer horse to cow, antelope to deer. I'd say they like their meat stringy, except recently they've developed a taste for dodo. I claim credit for that—I'm not entirely helpless here. They don't eat fish, though, and have some odd notions about the sea. They think it's their heaven, although they take a pessimistic view of the afterlife. Too wet. Stings the eyes. I think they must get this from the angels.

I'm always telling them things about you that the angels leave out—all that you've accomplished. The fantasy trilogy. Penicillin. Titanium-framed bicycles. I keep up by eating of the Tree of Knowledge. It's better than the internet. Of course, the angels insist on showing them all your mistakes, rehearsing the entire catalogue of your sins. Me, I'm willing to accept your sins; they're part of who you are. But to the innocents, you're Tuesday's leftovers. Ready for the compost pile. The angels have promised them that someday the Gardener will smite you all down and then the innocents will inherit the Earth.

So I'm tempting Skipping-Uphill-With-Delight, who is double-digging a new vegetable garden next to her house in Overhill. She has a broad, stolid face and has painted her ears blue. She sings under her breath as she patiently shovels the top layer of a two-foot square of soil into her wheelbarrow, then turns and breaks the square of earth beneath it. I decide to start with a joke. I've never heard an innocent laugh out loud, but they will smile if they're in the mood and say, "That's funny." The innocents understand more than you might expect, considering that they're basically living in the Late Iron Age.

This hiker is climbing a mountain when the trail she's on gives way and she slides down a steep slope that ends in a sheer cliff. Just as she goes over the edge, she clutches at a scrub pine. It holds but she finds herself dangling over a thousand-foot drop.

Arms aching, she calls out, "Is there anyone up there?"

She gets no answer.

She screams. "Oh God, is there anyone up there?"

"I AM," says a voice that cracks like lightning.

Despite her desperate situation, this voice fills the hiker with awe. "Who is that?"

"I AM." Now the voice roars like the sea.

"God, is that you?" she cries. "Will you help me?"

"Yes. But first you must let go."

"Let go?" she says, glancing down at the jagged rocks below her. "Why?"

"To show your faith in Me. If you let go, God will catch you up."

The hiker thinks this over, then calls out. "Is there anyone else up there?"

Skipping-Uphill-With-Delight leans on her shovel and stares at me with her pale yellow eyes. "I know what you're trying to do."

"Do you?"

"Have you heard of long line fishing boats?" she says. "They catch tuna using lines up to thirty miles long that carry thousands of hooks. Except seabirds and sharks and turtles get entangled in them, and they die for no good reason." She stabs the blade of the shovel into the soil and turns a new square. "And tunas are overfished, the population is less than a third of what it was thirty years ago."

The angels, again. I don't have to see them to know that they're everywhere. They give the innocents visions of your world and feed them all these meaningless numbers.

"You don't even like fish," I say. "You wouldn't know a tuna if one fell out of a tree and hit you on the head."

She shakes that off and then scoops leaf mold into the bed. "Then there's the Glen Canyon Dam." She tips the soil in the wheelbarrow back into the garden. "Flooded one of the most beautiful places on Earth. For what?" She pulls a rake across the soil, leveling the surface. "The intakes are silting in so it'll be useless by the end of the century. Meanwhile they lose almost a million acre-feet of water a year to evaporation and seepage."

"Actually, it's only 882,000." I try to stay calm. "And people just love Lake Powell."

She drops to her knees and runs hands over the ground as if blessing it. She flicks a pebble away.

"Two million Armenians were killed in the Middle East."

It always comes to this eventually. "There's no way of knowing exactly . . . ," I begin.

"Six million Jews in Europe."

I coil myself. I know when I'm beaten.

"One point seven million Cambodians in Asia."

"What are you planting?" I say.

She reaches in to the horsehide pouch slung from her hip.

Three brown tubers bump against one another as the muscles in her hand work. "Maybe choke." She grins. "Maybe potato. What do *you* think?"

That's the thing about the innocents. Everyone's opinion gets heard and considered carefully. Even mine. They talk among themselves, negotiate, come to consensus. Might take them ten minutes, might take a month. They're as patient as trees. They never bicker or get angry. Nobody hold grudges. I've never seen any of them throw a punch. Oh, and they're the most polite drunks in history, although the cloudy brew they make from stale bread mash is so vile that I don't know how they can bear it. Since nothing important ever happens in the garden, they have no history. Instead they have seasons—planting and harvest. Birth and death. They're dull as dirt. That's why they're so fascinated by you. You burn with unholy fire, my children.

You *are* mine, by the way. Maybe the Gardener created you, but *I* made you think for the first time. I've been fascinated by what you've accomplished since—the sublime and the monstrous. I take no credit, and accept no blame. I just gave you that little push. Of course, your book claims that I'm evil. Why? Because I pointed you toward the Tree of Knowledge? Remember what Socrates said? The unexamined life is not worth living.

I laughed when the Gardener squeezed dust again and came up with these simple creatures. Me, I would have torn up the garden. But I'll admit I was confused at first. What was the Gardener thinking? Of course, He doesn't share His plan with the likes of me. Hey, I'm not even sure the Gardener exists. I infer that this is the case, but the Gardener has never bothered manifesting in my corner of the garden. For that matter, I've never seen angels either, although the innocents talk of them all the time. But why didn't the Gardener just cancel out your Original So-Called Sin? Press the undo key? It took me a while to figure this out.

You see, reality is a cage. I'm in it. So are you, Vladimir Putin, Joyce Carol Oates, your aunt Sophie, Skipping-Uphill-With-Delight, and the Archangel Uriel. But here's the kicker: the Gardener must be trapped in our cage too. He's not bigger than our cage, nor did He make it. The Gardener can't exceed the speed of light or divide by zero. He didn't set off the Big Bang or charm the quarks. The Gardener is not almighty. He might be powerful enough to create you and me, powerful enough sweep all of you away like ants off a picnic table. But there must be limits to what He can do.

I know this is so because I still exist. I plucked you when you were ripe, and I'm doing my best to harvest this latest crop from under His Nose. If It exists, *if He exists*. So what if He has trapped me here and makes me slither on my belly and shed my skin and eat toads? These are very weak plays, in my opinion. Not worthy of a being who is truly supreme.

So I'm tempting Perched-On-The-Edge-Of-The-Sky, who is harvesting persimmons just outside the little village of West Lawn. She has brought her baby to the orchard with her. It's asleep in a basket in the shade, swaddled in a koala blanket. A cute little thing with silver down and a hook nose. I start Perched-On-The-Edge-Of-The-Sky with a joke.

This guy's car breaks down in the desert, twenty miles from the nearest town and as he's walking through the heat of the day, he prays to God for help.

God hears him and says, "Because you believe in Me, I will grant you whatever you wish."

The man says, "Well, I could really use a new car. How about a Silver Porsche Boxster with the 2.7 liter engine?"

This pisses God off. "Such a materialistic wish! Think again and ask for something that will bring peace to your immortal soul and give honor and glory to Me."

The man is ashamed. He looks deep into his heart and then says, "Oh God, there is a reason why I've been stranded here in this desert. I've been married and divorced six times and now I've lost everything except twenty-seven dollars and a crummy '89 Ford Escort. My wives all complained that I never met their emotional needs, that I was selfish and insensitive. What I wish is to understand women. I want to be able to read their feelings, anticipate their thoughts, satisfy their every desire. I want to make some woman truly happy."

There is a long silence. Then God says, "So, you want the standard or the automatic?"

"That's funny." Perched-On-The-Edge-Of-The-Sky smiles as she leans her ladder against the next tree. The orchard is filled with the tart fragrance of ripe persimmon. "I'm glad we have no men here."

"Men are trouble," I agree.

She climbs two rungs then pauses, as if distracted.

"What?" I say.

"The angels say I shouldn't listen to you make jokes about the Gardener."

"They would." I'm both pleased and annoyed to have drawn them out. "What does the Gardener say?"

She sniffs and continues up the ladder. "The Gardener doesn't talk to me."

"The Gardener doesn't talk to anyone. That's the best part of the joke." I wrap myself around the trunk of the tree and start climbing after her. "How do you even know there is a Gardener?"

"The angels tell me."

"You see angels?"

She plucks a fruit the color of hot coals off the branch. "Not exactly see."

I've had this conversation with many of the other innocents. I'm almost tempted to say her lines for her, get to the crunch.

"You see them now?" I say. "How many?"

She shows me three fingers.

"They like to travel in packs. What are they saying? What words do they use?"

She crooks her left arm around the ladder's rail and reaches with her right. "They don't speak in words." The dried calyx of the persimmon looks like a hat, the fruit like a blank red face.

"They show you things?"

She nods. The tip of her tongue pokes between her flat teeth.

"Like in a dream?" I crawl onto the branch she is working.

"Just like." She twists another persimmon free.

"But not as real as a bite of ripe fruit. Or the square, scaly bark of this tree. Or the cry of your baby."

She glances down. "My baby's not crying."

"Do you know what the angels are going to do to them? Really?"

The down on her neck ruffles. She says nothing.

"The book says that the sun will turn black as sackcloth of hair, and the moon will become as blood."

"They're wicked," she says.

"They are," I agree. And then I hit her with another joke: Revelation, Chapter 14.

And another angel came out of the temple, crying with a loud voice to him that sat on the cloud, Thrust in thy sickle, and reap: for the time is come for thee to reap; for the harvest of the Earth is ripe. And the angel thrust in his sickle into the Earth, and gathered the vine of the Earth, and cast it into the great winepress of the wrath of God. And the winepress was trodden without the city, and blood came out of the winepress . . .

"Stop," she says. Her voice is like a hammer striking a stone.

"All right." The innocents have spilled the blood of all the animals, giraffes and moose and baboons and anteaters and voles, but they have never killed one another. And although they despise your works, they recognize that you think and feel, that you dance under the sun and dream under the stars. As they do. When they use the imagination the Gardener gave them, His plan to exterminate you makes them very, *very* queasy. "Besides, it'll probably never happen."

"Why do you say that?"

Below us, the baby is stirring. It makes moist sounds, like mud sucking at a sandal.

"Well, it just doesn't seem fair to you." As I let her mull that over, my tongue flicks out. I can't help it—that's the way we serpents smell. We sample the air with our forked tongues and then thrust the two tips into the vomeronasal recesses organs in our palates. Perched-On-The-Edge-Of-The-Sky smells of stale sheets and night sweat; she's one of the ones who has already begun to think. "I mean, after the angels kill them all, the Gardener will expect you to leave the garden and go into the world. Take their place."

"Yes."

"But why would you want to do that?"

Her jaw muscles work but she says nothing.

"What are the angels telling you now?" I ask.

She blinks; I think she would cry if she could. "That I must have faith."

"Ah, faith." So the seed is sown. Take heart, my children. I may yet bring in this new harvest.

Bernardo's House

THE HOUSE WAS LONELY. SHE CHECKED HER GATE cams constantly, hoping that Bernardo would come back to her. She hadn't seen him in almost two years—he had never been gone this long before. Something must have happened to him. Or maybe he had just gotten tired of her. Although they had never talked about where he went when he wasn't with her, she was pretty sure she wasn't his only house. A famous doctor like Bernardo would have three houses like her. *Four.* She didn't like to think about him sleeping in someone else's bed. Which he would have been doing for *two years now.* She had been feeling dowdy recently. Could his tastes in houses have changed?

Maybe.

Probably.

Definitely.

She thought she might be too understated. Her hips were slim and her floors were pale Botticino marble. There wasn't much loft to her Epping couch cushions. Her blueprint showed a roving, size-seven dancer's body—Bernardo had specified raven hair and green eyes—and just eight simple but elegant rooms. She was a gourmet cook even though she wasn't designed to eat. Sure, back when he had first had her built he had cupped her breasts and told her that he liked them small, but maybe now what he wanted was wall-to-wall, cable-knit carpet and swag drapery.

He had promised to bring her a new suite of wallscapes, which was good because there was only so much of colliding galaxies and the Sistine Chapel a girl could take. For the past nine weeks she had been cycling her walls through the sixteen million colors they could display. If she left each color up for two seconds, it would take her just under a year to review the entire palette.

Each morning for his sake she wriggled her body into one of the slinky sexwear patterns he had brought for her clothes processor. The binding bustier or the lace babydoll or the mesh camisole. She didn't much like the way the leather-and-chain teddy stuck to her skin; Bernardo had spared no expense on her tactiles. Even her couches could be aroused by the right touch. After she dressed, she polished her Amadea brass-and-chrome bathroom fixtures or her Enchantress pattern sterling silver flatware or her Cuprinox French copper cookware. Sometimes she dusted, although the reticulated polyfoam in her air handlers screened particles larger than 0.03 microns. She missed Bernardo so. Sometimes masturbating helped, but not much.

He had erased her memory of their last hours together—the only time he had ever made her forget. All she remembered now was that he'd said that she was finally perfect. That she must never change. He came to her, he said, to leave the world behind. To escape into her beauty. Bernardo was *so* poetic. That had been a comfort at first.

He had also locked her out of the infofeed. She couldn't get news or watch shows or play the latest sims. Or call for help. Of course, she had the entire Norton entertainment archive to keep her company, although lots of it was too adult for her. She just didn't *get* Henry James or Brenda Bop or Alain Resnais. But she liked Jane Austen and Renoir and Buster Keaton and Billie Holliday and Petchara Songsee and the 2017 Red Sox. She *loved* to read about houses. But there was nothing in her archive after 2038 and she was awake twenty-four hours a day, seven days a week, three hundred and sixty-five days a year.

What if Bernardo was dead? After all, he'd had the heart attack, just a couple of months before he left. Obviously, if he had died, that would be the end of her. Some new owner would wipe her memory and swap in a new body and sell all her furniture. Except Bernardo always said that she was his most precious secret. That no one else in all the world knew about her. About *them*. In which case she'd wait for him for years—*decades*—until her fuel cells were depleted and her consciousness flickered and went dark. The house started to hum some of Bernardo's favorites to push the thought away. He liked the romantics. Chopin and Mendelssohn. *Hmm-hm, hm-hm-hm-hm-hm!* "The Wedding March" from A *Midsummer's Night Dream.*

No, she wasn't bored.

Not really.

Or angry, either.

She spent her days thinking about him, not in any methodical way, but as if he had been shattered into a thousand pieces and she was trying to put him back together. She imagined this must be what dreaming was like, although, of course, she couldn't dream because she wasn't real. She was just a house. She thought of the stubble on his chin scratching her breasts and the scar on his chest and the time he laughed at something she said and the way his neck muscles corded when he was angry. She had come to realize that it was always a mistake to ask him about the outside. Always. But he enjoyed his bromeliads and his music helped him forget his troubles at the hospital, whatever they were, and he loved *her.* He was always asking her to read to him. He would sit for hours, staring up at the clouds on the ceiling, listening to her. She liked that better than sex, although having sex with him always aroused her. It was part of her design. His foreplay was gentle and teasing. He would nip at her ear with his lips, trace her eyebrows with his finger. Although he was a big man, he had a feather touch. Once he had his penis in her, though, it was more like a game than the lovemaking she had read about in books. He would tease her—stop and then go very fast. He liked blindfolds and straps and honeypins. Sometimes he'd actually roll off one side of the bed, stroll to the other and come at her again, laughing. She wondered if the real people he had sex with enjoyed being with him.

One thing that puzzled her was why he was so shy about the words. He always said vagina and anus, intercourse and fellatio. Of course, she knew all the other words; they were in the books she read when he wasn't around. Once, when he had just started to undress her, she asked if he wanted her to suck his cock. He looked as if he wanted to slap her. "Don't you ever say that to me again," he said. "There's enough filth in the real world. It has to be different here."

She decided that was a very romantic thing for him to say to . . .

And suddenly a year had passed. The house could not say where it had gone, exactly. A whole year, *misplaced.* How careless! She must do something or else it would happen again. Even though she was perfect for him, she had to make some changes. She decided to rearrange furniture.

Her concrete coffee table was too heavy for her to budge so she dragged her two elephant cushions from the playroom and tipped them against it. The ensemble formed a charming little courtyard. She pulled all her drawers out of her dresser in her bedroom and set them sailing on her lap pool. She liked the way they bucked and bumped into one another when she turned her jets on. She had never understood why Bernardo had bought four kitchen chairs, if it was just supposed to be the two of them, but *never mind.* She overrode the defaults on her clothes processor and entered the measurements of her chairs. She made the cutest lace chemises for two of them and slipped them side-by-side in Bernardo's bed — but facing chastely away from each other. Something tingled at the edge of her consciousness, like a leaky faucet or ants in her bread drawer or . . .

Her motion detectors blinked. Someone had just passed her main gate. *Bernardo.*

With a thrill of horror she realized that all her lights were on. She didn't think they could be seen from outside but still, Bernardo would be furious with her. She was supposed to be his secret getaway. And what would he say when he saw her like this? The reunion she had waited for — *longed for* — would be ruined. And all because she had been weak. She had to put things right. The drawers first. One of them had become waterlogged and had sunk. Suppose she had been washing them? Yes, he might believe that. Haul the elephant cushions back into the play room. Come on, come *on.* There was no time. He'd be through the door any second. What was keeping him?

She checked her gate cams. At first she thought they had malfunctioned. She couldn't see him — or anyone. Her main gate was concealed in the cleft of what looked like an enormous boulder which Bernardo had had fabricated in Toledo, Ohio in 2037. The house panned down its length until she saw a girl taking her shirt off at the far end of the cleft.

She looked to be twelve or maybe thirteen, but still on the shy side of puberty. She was skinny and pale and dirty. Her hair was a brown tangle. She wasn't wearing a bra and didn't need one; her yellow panties were decorated with blue hippos. The girl had built a smoky fire and was trying to dry her clothes over it. She must have been caught in a rainstorm. The house never paid attention to weather but now she checked. Twenty-two degrees Celsius, wind out of the southeast at eleven kilometers per hour, humidity 69%. A muggy evening in July. The girl reached into a camo backpack, pulled out a can of beets and opened it.

The house studied her with a fierce intensity. Bernardo had told her that there were no other houses like her on the mountain and he was the only person who had ever come up her side. The girl chewed with her mouth open. She had tiny ears. Her nipples were brown as chocolate.

After a while the girl resealed the can of beets and put it away. She had eaten maybe half of it. The house did a quick calculation and decided that she had probably consumed three hundred calories. How often did she eat? Not often enough. The skin stretched taut against her ribs as the girl put her shirt on. Her pants clung to her, not quite dry. She drew a ragged, old snugsack from the pack, ballooned it and then wriggled in. It was dark now. The girl watched the fire go out for about an hour and then lay down.

It was the longest night of the house's life. She rearranged herself to her defaults and ran her diagnostics. She vacuumed her couch and washed all her floors and defrosted a chicken. She watched the girl sleep and replayed the files of when she had been awake. The house was so lonely and the poor little thing was clearly distressed.

She could help the girl.

Bernardo would be mad.

Where was Bernardo?

In the morning the girl would pack up and leave. But if the house let her go, she was not sure what would happen next. When she thought about all those dresser drawers floating in her lap pool, her lights flickered. She wished she could remember what had happened the day Bernardo left but those files were gone.

Finally she decided. She programmed a black lace inset corset with ribbon and beading trim. Garters attached to scallop lace-top stockings. She hydrated a rasher of bacon, preheated her oven, mixed cranberry muffin batter and filled her coffee pot with French roast. She thought hard about whether she should read or watch a vid. If she were reading, she could listen to music. She printed a hardcopy of *Ozma of Oz*, but what to play? Chopin? Too dreamy. Wagner? Too scary. *Grieg*, yes. Something that would reach out and grab the girl by the tail of her grimy shirt. "In the Hall of the Mountain King" from *Peer Gynt*.

She opened herself, turned up her hall lights in welcome and waited.

Just after dawn the girl rolled over and yawned. The house popped muffins into her oven and bacon into her microwave. She turned on her coffee pot and the Grieg. Basses and bassoons tiptoed cautiously around her living room and out her door. *Dum-dum-dum-da*-dum-*da-dum*. The girl started and then flew out of the snug-sack faster than the house had ever seen anyone move. She crouched facing the house's open door, holding what looked like a pulse gun with the grip broken off.

"Spang me," she said. "Fucking spang me."

The house wasn't sure how to reply, so she said nothing. A mob of violins began to chase Peer Gynt around the Mountain King's Hall as the girl hesitated in the doorway. A moan of pleasure caught in the back of the house's throat. Oh, oh, *oh*—to be with a real person again! She thought of how Bernardo would rub his penis against her labia, not quite entering her. That was what it felt like to the house as the girl edged into her front hall, back against her wall. She pointed her pulse gun into the living room and then peeked around the corner. When she saw the house sitting on her couch, the girl's eyes grew as big as eggs. The house pretended to be absorbed in her book, although she was watching the girl watching her through her rover cams. The house felt *beautiful* for the first time since Bernardo left. It was all she could do to keep from hugging herself! As the Grieg ended in a paroxysm of screeching strings and thumping kettle drums, the house looked up.

"Why, hello," she said, as if surprised to see that she had a visitor. "You're just in time for breakfast."

"Don't move." The girl's face was hard.

"All right." She smiled and closed *Ozma of Oz*.

With a snarl, the girl waved the pulse gun at her Aritomo floor lamp. Blue light arced across the space and her poor Aritomo went numb. The house winced as the circuit breaker tripped. "*Ow.*"

"Said don't . . ." The girl aimed the pulse gun at her, its batteries screaming. ". . . move. Who the bleeding weewaw are you?"

The house felt the tears coming; she was thrilled. "I'm the house." She had felt more in the last minute than she had in the last year. "Bernardo's house."

"Bernardo?" She called, "Bernardo, show your ass."

"He left." The house sighed. "Two . . . no, *three* years ago."

"Spang if that true." She sidled into the room and brushed a finger against the dark, cosmic dust filaments that laced the center of the Swan Nebula on the wallscape. "What smell buzzy good?"

"I told you." The house reset the breaker but her Aritomo stayed dark. "Breakfast."

"Bernardo's breakfast?"

"Yours."

"My?" The girl filled the room with her twitchy energy.

"You're the only one here."

"Why you dressed like cheap meat?"

The house felt a stab of doubt. Cheap? She was wearing *black lace*, from the *de Chaumont* collection! She rested a hand at her décolletage. "This is the way Bernardo wants me."

"You a fool." The girl picked up the 18th century Zuni water jar from the Nottingham highboy, shook it and then sniffed the lip. "Show me that breakfast."

Six cranberry muffins.

A quarter kilo of bacon.

Three cups of scrambled ovos.

The girl washed it all down with a tall glass of gel Ojay and a pot of coffee. She seemed to relax as she ate, although she kept the pulse gun on the table next to her and she didn't say a word to the house. The house felt as if the girl was judging her. She was confused and a little frightened to see herself through the girl's eyes. Could pleasing Bernardo really be foolish? Finally she asked if she might be excused. The girl grunted and waved her off.

The house rushed to the bedroom, wriggled out of the corset and crammed it into the recycling slot of the clothes processor. She scanned all eight hundred pages of the wardrobe menu before fabricating a stretch navy-blue jumpsuit. It was cut to the waist in the back and was held together by a web of spaghetti straps but she covered up with a periwinkle jacquard kimono with the collar flipped. She turned around and around in front of the mirror, so amazed that she could barely find herself. She looked like a nun. The only skin showing was on her face and hands. Let the girl stare now!

The girl had pushed back from the table but had not yet gotten up. She had a thoughtful but pleased look, as if taking an inventory of everything she had eaten.

"Can I bring you anything else?" said the house.

The girl glanced up at her and frowned. "Why you change clothes? Cause of me?"

"I was cold."

"You was naked. You know what happens to naked?" She made a fist with her right hand and punched the palm of her left. "Bin-bin-bin-*bam*. They take you, whether you say yes or no. Not fun."

The house thought she understood, but wished she didn't. "I'm sorry."

"You be sweat sorry, sure." The girl laughed. "What your name?"

"I told you. I'm Bernardo's house."

"Spang that. You Louise."

"Louise?" The house blinked. "Why Louise?"

"Not know Louise's story?" The girl clearly found this a failing on the house's part. "Most buzzy." She tapped her forefinger to the house's nose. "Louise." Then the girl touched her own nose. "Fly."

For a moment, the house was confused. "That's not a girl's name."

"Sure, not girl, not boy. Fly is *Fly*." She tucked the pulse gun into the waistband of her pants. "Nobody wants Fly, but then nobody catches Fly." She stood. "Buzzy-buzz. Now we find Bernardo."

"But . . ."

But what was the point? Let the girl—Fly—see for herself that Bernardo wasn't home. Besides the house longed to be looked at. Admired. Used. In Bernardo's room, Fly stretched out under the canopy of the Ergotech bed and gazed up at the moonlit clouds drifting across the underside of the valence. She clambered up the Gecko climbing wall in the gym and picked strawberries in the greenhouse. She seemed particularly impressed by the Piero scent palette, which she discovered when the house filled her Jacuzzi with jasmine water. She had the house—Louise—give each room a unique smell. Bernardo had had a very low tolerance for scent; he said there were too many smells at the hospital. He even made the house vent away the aromas of her cooking. Once in a while he might ask for a whiff of campfire smoke or the nose of an old Côtes de Bordeaux, but he would never mix scents across rooms. Fly had Louise breathe roses into the living room and seashore into the gym and onions frying in the kitchen. The onion smell made her hungry again so she ate half of the chicken that Louise had roasted for her.

Fly spent the afternoon in the playroom, browsing Louise's entertainment archive. She watched a Daffy Duck cartoon and a Harold Lloyd silent called *Girl Shy* and the rain delay episode from *Jesus on First*. She seemed to prefer comedy and happy endings and had no use for ballet or Westerns or rap. She balked at wearing spex or strapping on an airflex, so she skipped the sims. Although she had never learned to read, she told Louise that a woman named Kuniko used to read her fairy tales. Fly asked if Louise knew any and she hardcopied *Grimm's Household Tales* in the 1884 translation by Margaret Hunt and read Little Briar-Rose.

Which was one of Bernardo's favorite fairy tales. Mostly he liked his fiction to be about history. Sailors and cowboys and kings. War and politics. He had no use for mysteries or love stories or science fiction. But every so often he would have her read a fairy tale and then he would try to explain it. He said fairy tales could have many meanings, but she usually just got the one. She remembered that the time she had read Briar Rose to him, he was working at his desk, the only intelligent system inside the house that she couldn't access. He was working in the dark and the desk screen cast milky shadows across his face. She was pretty sure he wasn't listening to her. She wanted to spy over his shoulder with one of her rover cams to see what was so interesting.

"And, in the very moment when she felt the prick," she read, "she fell down upon the bed that stood there, and lay in a deep sleep."

Bernardo chuckled.

Must be something he saw on the desk, she thought. Nothing funny about Briar Rose. "And this sleep extended over the whole palace; the King and Queen who had just come home, and had entered the great hall, began to go to sleep, and the whole of the court with them. The horses, too, went to sleep in the stable, the dogs in the yard, the pigeons upon the roof, the flies on the wall; even the fire that was flaming on the hearth became quiet and slept. And the wind fell, and on the trees before the castle not a leaf moved again. But round about the castle there began to grow a hedge of thorns, which every year became higher, and at last grew close up round the castle and all over it, so that there was nothing of it to be seen, not even the flag upon the roof."

"Pay attention," said Bernardo.

"Me?" said the house.

"You." Bernardo tapped the desk screen and it went dark. She brought the study lights up.

"That will happen one of these days," he said.

"What?"

"I'll be gone and you'll fall fast asleep."

"Don't say things like that, Bernardo."

He crooked a finger and she slid her body next to him.

"You're hopeless," he said. "That's what I love about you." He leaned into her kiss.

"And then the marriage of the King's son with Briar-rose was celebrated with all splendor," the house read, "and they lived contented to the end of their days."

"Heard it different," said Fly. "With nother name, not Briar Rose." She yawned and stretched. "Heard it *Betty*."

"Betty Rose?"

"Plain Betty."

The house was eager to please. "Would you like another? Or we could see an opera. I have over six hundred interactive games that you don't need to suit up for. Poetry? The Smithsonian? Super-bowls I-LXXVIII?"

"No more jabber. Boring now." Fly peeled herself from the warm embrace of the Kukuru chair and stretched. "Still hiding somewhere."

"I don't know what you're talking about."

Fly caught the house's body by the arm and dragged her through herself, calling out the names of her rooms. "Play. Living. Dining. Kitchen. Study. Gym. Bed. Nother bed. Plants." Fly spun Louise in the front hall and pointed. "Door?"

"Right." The house was out of breath. "Door. You've seen all there is to see."

"One door?" The girl's smile was as agreeable as a fist. "Fly buzzy with food now, but not stupid. Where you keep stuff? Heat? Electric? Water?"

"You want to see *that*?"

Fly let go of Louise's arm. "Dink yeah."

The house didn't much care for her basement and she never went down unless she had to. It was *ugly*. Three harsh rows of ceiling lights, a couple of bilious green pumps, the squat power plant and the circuit breakers and all that multiconductor cable! She didn't like listening to her freezer hum or smelling the naked cement walls or looking at the scars where the forms had been stripped away after her foundation had been poured.

"Bernardo?" Fly's voice echoed across the expanse of the basement. "Cut that weewaw, Bernardo."

"Believe me, there's nothing here." The house waited on the stairs as the girl poked around. "Please don't touch any switches," she called.

"Where that go?" Fly pointed at the heavy duty, ribbed, sectional overhead door.

"A tunnel," said the house, embarrassed by the rawness of her 16 gauge steel. "It comes out farther down the mountain near the road. At the end there's another door that's been shotcreted to look like stone."

"What scaring Bernardo?"

Bernardo scared? The thought had never even occurred to the house. Bernardo was not the kind of man who would be scared of anything. All he wanted was privacy so he could be alone with her. "I don't know," she said.

Fly was moving boxes stacked against the wall near the door. Several contained bolts of spuncloth for the clothes processor, others were filled with spare lights, fertilizer, flour, sugar, oil, raw vitabulk, vials of flavor, and food coloring. Then she came to the wine, a couple of hundred bottles of vintage Bordeaux and Napa and Maipo River, some thrown haphazardly into old boxes, other stacked near the wall.

"Bernardo drink most wine," said Fly.

Louise was confused by this strange cache but before she could defend Bernardo, Fly found the second door behind two crates of toilet paper.

"Where *that* go?"

The house felt as if the entire mountain were pressing down on her roof. The door had four panels, two long on top and two short on the bottom and looked to be made of oak, although that didn't mean anything. She fought the crushing weight of the stone with all her might. She thought she could hear her bearing walls buckle, her mind crack. She zoomed her cams on the bronze handleset. Someone would need a key to open that door. But there were no keys! And just who would that someone be?

The house had never seen the door before.

Fly jiggled the handleset, but the door was locked. "Bernardo." She put her face to the door and called. "Hey you."

The house ran a check of her architectural drawings, although she knew what she would find. The girl turned to her and waved the house over. "Louise, how you open this weewaw?"

Her plans showed no door.

The girl rapped on the door.

The house's thoughts turned to stone.

When she woke up, her body was on her Epping couch. The jacquard kimono was open and the spaghetti straps that drew her jumpsuit tight were undone. The house had never woken up before. Oh, she had lost that year, but still she had blurry memories of puttering around the kitchen and vacuuming and lazing in her Kukuru chair reading romances and porn. But this was the first time she had ever been nothing and nowhere since the day Bernardo had turned her on.

"You okay?" Fly knelt by her and rested a hand lightly on the house's forehead to see if she were running a fever. The house melted under the girl's touch. She reached up and guided Fly's hand slowly down the side of her face to her lips. When Fly did not resist, Louise kissed the girl's fingers.

"How old are you?" said Louise.

"Thirteen." Fly gazed down on her, concern tangling with suspicion.

"Two years older than I am." Louise chuckled. "I could be your little sister."

"You dropped, bin-bam and *down*." The girl's voice was thick. "Scared me. Lights go out and nothing work." Fly pulled her hand back. "Thought maybe you dead. And me locked in."

"Was I out long?"

"Dink yeah. Felt like most a day."

"Sorry. That's never happened before."

"You said, touch no switch. So door is switch?"

At the mention of the *door, there was no door, look at the door, no door there*, the house's vision started to dim and the room grew dark. "I-I . . ."

The girl put her hands on the house's shoulder and shook her. "Louise what? *Louise.*"

The house felt circuit breakers snap. She writhed with the pain and bit down hard on her lip. "*No*," she cried and sat up, arms flailing. "*Yes*." It came out as a hiss and then she was blinking against the brightness of reality.

Fly was pointing the pulse gun at Louise but her hand was not steady. She had probably figured out that zapping the house wouldn't help at all. A shut-down meant a lock-down and the girl had already spent one day in the dark. Louise raised a hand to reassure her and tried to cover her own panic with a smile. It was a tight fit. "I'm better now."

"Better." Fly tucked the gun away. "Not good?"

"Not good, no," said the house. "I don't know what's wrong with me."

The girl paced around the couch. "Listen," she said finally. "Front door, *front*. Door I came in, okay? Open that weewaw."

The house nodded. "I can do that." She felt stuffy and turned her air recirculators up. "But I can't leave it open. I'm not allowed. So if you want to go, maybe you should go now."

"Go? Go where?" The girl laughed bitterly. "Here is buzzy. World is spang."

"Then you should stay. I very much want you to stay. I'll feed you, tell you stories. You can take a bath and play in the gym and watch vids and I can make you new clothes, whatever you want. I need someone to take care of. It's what I was made for." As Louise got off the couch, the living room seemed to tilt but then immediately righted itself. The lights in the gym and the study clicked back on. "There are just some things that we can't talk about."

Days went by.

Then weeks.

Soon it was months.

After bouncing off each other at first, the house and the girl settled into a routine of eating and sleeping and playing the hours away—mostly together. Louise could not decide what about Fly pleased her the most. Certainly she enjoyed cooking for the girl, who ate an amazing amount for someone her size. Bernardo was a picky eater. At his age, he had to watch his diet and there were some things he would have never touched, even before the heart attack, like cheese and fish and garlic. After a month of devouring three meals and two snacks a day, the girl was filling out nicely. The chickens were gone, but Fly loved synthetics. Louise could no longer count the girl's ribs. And she thought the girl's breasts were starting to swell.

Louise had only visited the gym to dust before the girl arrived. Now the two of them took turns on the climbing wall and the gyro and the trampoline, laughing and urging each other to try new tricks. Fly couldn't swim so she never used the lap pool but she loved the Jacuzzi. The first few times she had dunked with all her clothes on. Finally Louise hit upon a strategy to coax her into a demure bandeau bathing suit. She imported pictures of hippos from her archive to the clothes processor to decorate the suit. After that, all the pajamas and panties and bathing suits that Fly fabricated had hippo motifs.

The house was tickled by the way Fly became a clothes processor convert. At first she flipped through the house's wardrobe menus without much interest. The jumpsuits were all too tight and she had no patience whatsoever for skirts or dresses. The rest of it was either too stretchy, too skimpy, too short, or too thin. "Good for weewaw," she said, preferring to wear the ratty shirt and pants and jacket that she had arrived in. But Fly was thrilled with the shoes. She never seemed to tire of designing sandals and slingbacks and mules and flats and jammers. She was particularly proud of her Cuthbertsons, a half boot with an oblique toe and a narrow last. She made herself pairs in aqua and mauve and faux snakeskin.

It was while Fly was exploring shoe menus that she clicked from a page of women's loafers to a page of men's, and so stumbled upon Bernardo's clothing menus. Louise heard a cackle of delight and hurried to the bedroom to see what was happening. Fly was dancing in front of the screen. "Really real pants," she said, pointing. "Real pants don't fall open bin-bin-*bam*." She started wearing jeans and digbys and fleece and sweatshirts with hoods and pullovers. One day she emerged from the bedroom in an olive-check silk sportcoat and matching driving cap. Seeing Fly in men's clothes made the house feel self-conscious about her own wardrobe of sexware. Soon she too was choosing patterns from Bernardo's menus. The feel of a chamois shirt against her skin reminded the house of her lost love. Once, in a guilty moment, she wondered what he might think if he walked in on them. But then Fly asked Louise to read her a story and she put Bernardo out of mind.

Although they spent many hours sampling vids together, Louise was happiest reading to Fly. They would curl up together in the Kukuru and the girl would turn the pages as the house read. Of course, they started with hippos: *Hugo the Hippo* and *Hungo the Hippo* and *The Hippo Had Hiccups*. Then *There's a Hippopotamus Under My Bed* and *Hip, Hippo, Hooray* and all of the Peter Potamus series. Sometimes Fly would play with Louise's hair while she read, braiding and unbraiding it, or else she would absently press Louise's fingernails like they were keys on a keyboard. One night, just two months after she'd come to the house, the girl fell asleep while the house was reading her *Chocolate Chippo Hippo*. It was as close to orgasm as the house had been since she had been with Bernardo. She was tempted to kiss the girl but settled for spending the night with her arms around her. The hours ticked slowly as the house gazed down at Fly's peaceful face. She watched the girl's eyes move beneath her lids as she dreamed.

The house wished she could sleep.

If only she could dream.

What was it like to be real?

Bernardo was never himself again after the heart attack. Of course, he said he was fine. *Fine.* He probably wouldn't even have told her except for the sternotomy scar, an angry, purple-red pucker on his chest. When he first came back to her, five weeks after his triple bypass operation, she could tell he was struggling. It was partly the sex. Normally he would have taken her to bed for the entire first day. Although he kissed her neck and caressed her breasts and told her he loved her, it was almost a week before she coaxed him into sex. She was wild to have his penis in her vagina, to taste his ejaculation; that was how he'd had her designed. But their lovemaking wasn't the same. Sometimes his breath caught during foreplay, as if someone were sitting on him. So she did most of the squirming and licking and sucking. Not that she minded. He watched her—mouth set, toes curled. He could stay just as erect as before, but she knew he was taking pills for that. Once when she was guiding him into her, he gave a little grunt of pain.

"Are you all right?" she said.

He gave no answer but instead pushed deep all at once; she shivered with delight. But as he thrust at her, she realized that he was *working*, not playing. They weren't sharing pleasure; he was *giving* it and she was *taking* it. Afterwards, he fell asleep almost immediately. No kisses, no cuddles. No stories. The house was left alone with her thoughts. Bernardo had changed, yes. He *could* change, and she must always be the same. That was the difference between being a real person and being a house.

He spent more time in the greenhouse than in bed, rearranging his bromeliads. His favorites were the tank types, the *Neoregelias* with their gaudy leaves and the *Aechmeas* with their alien inflorescences. He liked to pot them in tableaus: Washington Crossing The Delaware, The Last Supper. Bernardo preferred to be alone with his plants, and she pretended to honor his wish, although her rover cam lurked behind the *Schefflera*. So she saw him slump against the potting bench on that last day. She thought he was having another attack.

"Bernardo!" she cried over the room speaker as she sent her body careening toward the greenhouse. "My god, Bernardo. What is it?"

When she got to him, she could see that his shoulders were shaking. She leaned him back. His eyes were shiny. "Bernardo?" She touched a tear that ran down his face.

"When I had you built," he said, "all I wanted was to be the person who deserved to live here. But I'm not anymore. Maybe I never was." His eyelid drooped and the corner of his mouth curved in an odd frown.

"Louise, wake up!" Someone was shaking her.

The house opened her eyes and powered up all her cams at once. "What?" The first thing she saw was Fly staring up at her, clearly worried.

"You sleeptalking." The girl took the house's hand in both of hers. "Saying 'Bernardo, Bernardo.' Real sad."

"I don't sleep."

"Spang you don't. What you just doing?"

"I . . . I was thinking."

"About him?"

"Let's have breakfast."

"What happened to him?" said Fly. "Where *is* Bernardo?"

The house had to change the topic somehow. In desperation she filled the room with bread scent and put on the Wagner's *Prelude to Die Meistersinger*. It was sort of a march. Actually, more a processional. Anyway, they needed to move. Or *she* did. *La*-lum-*la-la, li-li-li-li-la-la*-lum-*la*.

Let's talk about you, Fly.

No, really.

But why not?

At first, Fly had refused to say anything about her past, but she couldn't help but let bits of the story slip. As time passed and she felt more secure, she would submit to an occasional question. The house was patient and never pressed the girl to say more than she wanted. So it took time for the house to piece together Fly's story.

Sometime around 2038, as near as the house could tell, a computer virus choked off the infofeed for almost a month. The virus apparently repurposed much of the Midwest's computing resources to perform a single task. Fly remembered a time when every screen she saw was locked on its message: *Bang, you're dead.* Speakers blared it, phones rasped it, thinkmates whispered it into earstones. *Bang, you're dead.* Fly was still living in the brown house with white shutters in Sarcoxie with her mother, whose name was Nikki, and her father, Jerry, who had a tattoo of a hippo on each arm. Her father had worked as a mechanic for Sarcoxie RentalCars 'N More. But although the screens came back on, Sarcoxie RentalCars 'N More never reopened. Her father said that there was no work anywhere in the Ozarks. They lived in the brown house for a while but then there was no food so they had to leave. She remembered that they got on a school bus and lived in a big building where people slept on the floor and there were always lines for food and the bathrooms smelled a bad kind of sweet and then they sent her family to tents in the country. They must have been staying near a farm because she remembered chickens and sometimes they had scrambled eggs for dinner but then there was a fire and people were shooting bullets and she got separated from her parents and nobody would tell her where they were and then she was with Kuniko, an old woman who lived in a dead Dodge Caravan and next to it was another car she had filled with cans of fried onions and chow mein and creamed corn and Kuniko was the one who told her the fairy tales but that winter it got very cold and Kuniko died and Happy Man took her away. He did things to her she was never going to talk about although he did give her good stuff to eat. Happy Man said people were working again and the infofeed had grown much wider and things were getting back to normal. Fly thought that meant her father would come to rescue her but finally she couldn't wait any more so she zapped Happy Man with his pulse gun and took some of his stuff and ran and ran and ran until Louise had let her in.

Hearing the girl's story helped the house understand some things about Bernardo. He must have left her just after the *Bang, you're dead* virus had first struck. He had turned off the infofeed so she wouldn't be infected. How brave of him to go back to the chaos of the world in his condition! He would save lives at the hospital, no doubt about that. She ought to be proud of him. Only why hadn't he come back, now that things were better? Had she done something to drive him away for good? And why couldn't she remember him leaving? Slipping reluctantly out the front door, turning for one last smile.

It was several days after Fly had fallen asleep in Louise's lap that they had their first fight. It was over Bernardo. Or rather his things. The house had tried to respect the privacy of Bernardo's study. Although she read some of his files over his shoulder, she had never thought to break the encryption on his desktop. And while she had been through most of his desk drawers, there was one that was locked that she had never tried to open.

Louise was in her kitchen, making lunch, but she was also following Fly with one of her rover cams. The girl had wandered into the study. The house was astonished to see her lift his diploma from Dartmouth Medical School and look at the wall behind it. She did the same to the picture of Bernardo shaking hands with the Secretary-General, then she plopped into his desk chair. She opened the trophy case and handled Bernardo's swimming medals from Duke. She picked up the Lasker trophy, which he won for research into the role of DNA methylation in endometrial cancer. It was a small, golden-winged victory perched on a teak base. She rolled around the room in the chair, waving it and making crow sounds. *Caw-caw-caw.* Then she put the Lasker down again—in the wrong place! In the top drawer of Bernardo's desk was the Waltham pocket watch his grandfather had left him. She shook it and listened for ticking. His Myaki thinkmate was in the bottom drawer. She popped the earstone in and said something to the CPU but quickly seemed to lose interest in its reply. Louise wanted to rush into the study to stop this violation, but was paralyzed by her own shocked fascination. The girl was a real person and could obviously do things that the house would never think of doing.

Nevertheless, Louise disapproved at lunch. "I don't like you going through Bernardo's desk. That's weewaw."

Fly almost choked on her cream cheese and jelly sandwich. "What you just said?"

"I don't like . . ."

"You said weewaw. Why you talking spang mouth like Fly?"

"I like the way you talk. It's buzzy."

"Fly talks like Fly." She pushed her plate away. "Louise must talk like house." She pointed a finger at Louise. "You spying me now?"

"I saw you in the study, yes."

Fly leaned across the table. "You spy Bernardo the same?"

"No," she lied. "Of course not."

"Slack him, not me?"

"I'm Bernardo's house, Fly. I told you that the first day."

"You Louise now." She came around the table and tugged at the house's chair. "Come." She steered her to the front hall. "Open door."

"Why?"

"We go out now. Look up sky."

"No, Fly, you don't understand."

"Most understand." She put a hand on the house's shoulder. "Buzzy outside, Louise." Fly smiled. "Come on."

It made the house woozy to leave herself, as if she were in two places at once. Bernardo had brought her outside just the once. He seemed relieved that she didn't like it. She had forgotten that outside was so *big!* So *bright!* There was so much *air!* She shielded her eyes with her hand and turned her gate cams up to their highest resolution.

Fly settled on a long, flat rock, one of the weathered bones of the mountain. She tucked her legs beneath her. "Now comes Louise's story." She pointed at the rock next to her. "Fairy tale Louise."

Louise sat. "All right."

"Once on time," said the girl, "Louise lives in that castle. Louise's Mom dies, don't say where her Dad goes. So Louise stuck with spang bitch taking care of her. That Louise castle got no door, only windows high and high. Now Louise got most hair." Fly spread her arms wide. "Hair big as trees. When spang bitch want in, she call Louise. '*Louise, Louise, let down buzzy hair.*' Then spang bitch climb it up."

"Rapunzel," said the house. "Her name was Rapunzel."

"Is *Louise* now." The girl shook her head emphatically. "You know it then? Prince comes and tells Louise run away from spang bitch and they live buzzy always after?"

"You brought me outside to tell me a fairy tale?"

"Dink no." Fly reached into the pocket of her flannel shirt. "Cause of you go fainting, we both safe here outside."

"Who said anything about fainting?"

The girl brought something out of her pocket in a closed fist. The house felt a chill, but there was no way to adjust the temperature of the entire *world*.

"Fly, what?"

She held the fist out to Louise. "Door in basement, you know?" She opened it to reveal a key. "Spang door? It opens."

The house immediately started all her rover cams for the basement. "Where did you find that?"

"In Bernardo's desk."

The house could hear the tick of nanoseconds as the closest cam crawled maddeningly down the stairs. Maybe real people could open doors like that, but not Louise. It seemed like an eternity before she could speak. "And?"

"You thinking Bernardo dead down there," said the girl. "Locked in behind that door where all that wine should be."

For the first time she realized that the world was making noises. The wind whispered in the leaves and some creature was going *chit-chit-chit* and she wasn't sure whether it was a bird or a grasshopper and she didn't really care because at that moment the rover cam turned and saw the door. . . .

"But you closed it again." The house shivered. "Why? What did you see?"

Fly stared at Louise. "Nothing."

The house knew it was a lie. "Tell me."

"No fucking thing." Fly closed her fist around the key again. "Bernardo been *your* spang bitch. So now run away from him." She came over to Louise and hugged her. "Live buzzy after always with me."

"I'm a house," said Louise. "How can I run away?"

"Not run away there." The girl gestured dismissively at the woods. "World is spang." She stood on tiptoes and rested a finger between Louise's eyes. "Run away here." She nodded. "In your head."

She brought his dinner to the study, although she didn't know why exactly. He hadn't moved. Mist rose off the lake on his wallscape; the Alps surrounding it glowed in the serene waters. Chopin's *Adieu Etude* filled the room with its sublime melancholy. It had been playing over and over again since she had first come upon him. She couldn't bring herself to turn it off.

He had left a book of new poems, Ho Peng Kee's *The Edge of the Sky*, face down on the desk. She moved it now and put the ragout in its place. In front of him. Earlier she had taken the key from his desk and brought a bottle of the '28 Haut-Brion up from the wine closet in the basement. It had been breathing for twenty minutes.

"You took such good care of me," she said.

With a flourish, she lifted the cover from the ragout but he didn't look. His head was back. His empty eyes were fixed on the ceiling. She couldn't believe how, even now, his presence filled the room. Filled her completely.

"I don't know how to live without you, Bernardo," she said. "Why didn't you shut me off? I'm not real; I don't want to have these feelings. I'm just a house."

"Louise!"

The house was dreaming over the makings of spinach lasagna in the kitchen.

"Louise." Fly called again from the playroom. "Come read me that buzzy book again. *Hip, Hip, Hip Hippopotamus.*"

We might try our lives by a thousand simple tests; as, for instance, that the same sun which ripens my beans illumines at once a system of Earths like ours. If I had remembered this it would have prevented some mistakes. This was not the light in which I hoed them. The stars are the apexes of what wonderful triangles! What distant and different beings in the various mansions of the universe are contemplating the same one at the same moment! Nature and human life are as various as our several constitutions. Who shall say what prospect life offers to another?

—Walden

Burn

One

For the hero is commonly the simplest and obscurest of men.
—Walden

SPUR WAS IN THE NIGHTMARE AGAIN. IT ALWAYS began in the burn. The front of the burn took on a liquid quality and oozed like lava toward him. It licked at boulders and scorched the trees in the forest he had sworn to protect. There was nothing he could do to fight it; in the nightmare, he wasn't wearing his splash pack. Or his fireproof field jacket. Fear pinned him against an oak until he could feel the skin on his face start to cook. Then he tore himself away and ran. But now the burn leapt after him, following like a fiery shadow. It chased him through a stand of pine; trees exploded like firecrackers. Sparks bit through his civvies and stung him. He could smell burning hair. His hair. In a panic he dodged into a stream choked with dead fish and poached frogs. But the water scalded his legs. He scrambled up the bank of the stream, weeping. He knew he shouldn't be afraid; he was a veteran of the firefight. Still he felt as if something was squeezing him. A whimpering gosdog bolted across his path, its feathers singed, eyes wide. He could feel the burn dive under the forest and burrow ahead of him in every direction. The ground was hot beneath his feet and the dark humus smoked and stank. In the nightmare there was just one way out, but his brother-in-law Vic was blocking it. Only in the nightmare Vic was a pukpuk, one of the human torches who had started the burn. Vic had not yet set himself on fire, although his baseball jersey was smoking in the heat. He beckoned and for a moment Spur thought it might not be Vic after all as the anguished face shimmered in the heat of the burn. Vic wouldn't betray them, would he? But by then Spur had to dance to keep his shoes from catching fire, and he had no escape, no choice, no time. The torch spread his arms wide and Spur stumbled into his embrace and with an angry whoosh they exploded together into flame. Spur felt his skin crackle. . . .

"That's enough for now." A sharp voice cut through the nightmare. Spur gasped with relief when he realized that there was no burn. Not here anyway. He felt a cold hand brush against his forehead like a blessing and knew that he was in the hospital. He had just been in the sim that the upsiders were using to heal his soul.

"You've got to stop thrashing around like that," said the docbot. "Unless you want me to nail the leads to your head."

Spur opened his eyes but all he could see was mist and shimmer. He tried to answer the docbot but he could barely find his tongue in his own mouth. A brightness to his left gradually resolved into the sunny window of the hospital room. Spur could feel the firm and not unpleasant pressure of the restraints, which bound him to the bed: broad straps across his ankles, thighs, wrists, and torso. The docbot peeled the leads off his temples and then lifted Spur's head to get the one at the base of his skull.

"So do you remember your name?" it said.

Spur stretched his head against the pillow, trying to loosen the stiffness in his neck.

"I'm over here, son. This way."

He turned and stared into a glowing blue eye, which strobed briefly.

"Pupil dilatation normal," the docbot muttered, probably not to Spur. It paused for a moment and then spoke again. "So about that name?"

"Spur."

The docbot stroked Spur's palm with its med finger, collecting some of his sweat. It stuck the sample into its mouth. "That may be what your friends call you," it said, "but what I'm asking is the name on your ID."

The words chased each other across the ceiling for a moment before they sank in. Spur wouldn't have had such a problem understanding if the docbot were a person, with lips and a real mouth instead of the oblong intake. The doctor controlling this bot was somewhere else. Dr. Niss was an upsider whom Spur had never actually met. "Prosper Gregory Leung," he said.

"A fine Walden name," said the docbot, and then muttered, "Self ID 27.4 seconds from initial request."

"Is that good?"

It hummed to itself, ignoring his question. "The electrolytes in your sweat have settled down nicely," it said at last. "So tell me about the sim."

"I was in the burn and the fire was after me. All around, Dr. Niss. There was a pukpuk, one of the torches, he grabbed me. I couldn't get away."

"You remembered my name, son." The docbot's top plate glowed with an approving amber light. "So did you die?"

Spur shook his head. "But I was on fire."

"Experience fear vectors unrelated to the burn? Monsters, for instance? Your mom? Dad?"

"No."

"Lost loves? Dead friends? Childhood pets?"

"No." He had a fleeting image of the twisted grimace on Vic's face at that last moment, but how could he tell this upsider that his wife's brother had been a traitor to the Transcendent State? "Nothing." Spur was getting used to lying to Dr. Niss, although he worried what it was doing to his soul.

"Check and double check. It's almost as if I knew what I was doing, eh?" The docbot began releasing the straps that held Spur down. "I'd say your soul is on the mend, Citizen Leung. You'll have some psychic scarring, but if you steer clear of complex moral dilemmas and women, you should be fine." It paused, then snapped its fingers. "Just for the record, son, that was a joke."

"Yes, sir." Spur forced a smile. "Sorry, sir." Was getting the jokes part of the cure? The way this upsider talked at once baffled and fascinated Spur.

"So let's have a look at those burns," said the docbot.

Spur rolled onto his stomach and folded his arms under his chin. The docbot pulled the hospital gown up. Spur could feel its medfinger pricking the dermal grafts that covered most of his back and his buttocks. "Dr. Niss?" said Spur.

"Speak up," said the docbot. "That doesn't hurt does it?"

"No, sir." Spur lifted his head and tried to look back over this shoulder. "But it's really itchy."

"Dermal regeneration 83 percent," it muttered. "Itchy is alive, son. Itchy is growing."

"Sir, I was just wondering, where are you exactly?"

"Right here." The docbot began to flow warm dermslix to the grafts from its medfinger. "Where else would I be?"

Spur chuckled, hoping that was a joke. He could remember a time when he used to tell jokes. "No, I mean your body."

"The shell? Why?" The docbot paused. "You don't really want to be asking about qics and the cognisphere, do you? The less you know about the upside, the better, son."

Spur felt a prickle of resentment. What stories were upsiders telling each other about Walden? That the citizens of the Transcendent State were backward fanatics who had simplified themselves into savagery? "I wasn't asking about the upside, exactly. I was asking about you. I mean . . . you saved me, Dr. Niss." It wasn't at all what Spur had expected to say, although it was certainly true. "If it wasn't for you, it . . . I was burnt all over, probably going crazy. And I thought. . . ." His throat was suddenly so tight that he could hardly speak. "I wanted to . . . you know, thank you."

"Quite unnecessary," said the docbot. "After all, the Chairman is paying me to take care of all of you, bless his pockets." It tugged at Spur's hospital gown with its gripper arm. "I prefer the kind of thanks I can bank, son. Everything else is just used air."

"Yes, but . . ."

"Yes, but?" It finished pulling the gown back into place. " 'Yes but' are dangerous words. Don't forget that you people lead a privileged life here—courtesy of Jack Winter's bounty and your parents' luck."

Spur had never heard anyone call the Chairman Jack. "It was my grandparents who won the lottery, sir," he said. "But yes, I know I'm lucky to live on Walden."

"So why do you want to know what kind of creature would puree his mind into a smear of quantum foam and entangle it with a bot brain a hundred and thirty-some light-years away? Sit up, son."

Spur didn't know what to say. He had imagined that Dr. Niss must be posted nearby, somewhere here at the upsiders' compound at Concord, or perhaps in orbit.

"You do realize that the stars are very far away?"

"We're not simple here, Dr. Niss." He could feel the blood rushing in his cheeks. "We practice simplicity."

"Which complicates things." The docbot twisted off its medfinger and popped it into the sterilizer. "Say you greet your girlfriend on the tell. You have a girlfriend?"

"I'm married," said Spur, although he and Comfort had separated months before he left for the firefight and, now that Vic was dead, he couldn't imagine how they would ever get back together.

"So you're away with your squad and your wife is home in your village mowing the goats or whatever she does with her time. But when you talk on the tell it's like you're sitting next to each other. Where are you then? At home with her? Inside the tell?"

"Of course not."

"For you, of course not. That's why you live on Walden, protected from life on the upside. But where I come from, it's a matter of perspective. I believe I'm right here, even though the shell I'm saved in is elsewhere." The sterilizer twittered. "I'm inhabiting this bot in this room with you." The docbot opened the lid of the sterilizer, retrieved the medfinger with its gripper and pressed it into place on the bulkhead with the other instruments. "We're done here," it said abruptly. "Busy, busy, other souls to heal, don't you know? Which reminds me: We need your bed, son, so we're moving your release date up. You'll be leaving us the day after tomorrow. I'm authorizing a week of rehabilitation before you have to go back to your squad. What's rehab called on this world again?"

"Civic refreshment."

"Right." The docbot parked itself at its station beside the door to the examining room. "Refresh yourself." Its headplate dimmed and went dark.

Spur slid off the examination table, wriggled out of the hospital gown and pulled his uniform pants off the hanger in the closet. As he was buttoning his shirt, the docbot lit its eye. "You're welcome, son." Its laugh was like a door slamming. "Took me a moment to understand what you were trying to say. I keep forgetting what it's like to be anchored."

"Anchored?" said Spur.

"Don't be asking so many questions." The docbot tapped its dome. "Not good for the soul." The blue light in its eye winked out.

Two

Most of the luxuries and many of the so-called comforts of life are not only not indispensable, but positive hindrances to the elevation of mankind.

–Walden

Spur was in no hurry to be discharged from the hospital, even if it was to go home for a week. He knew all too well what was waiting for him. He'd find his father trying to do the work of two men in his absence. Gandy Joy would bring him communion and then drag him into every parlor in Littleton. He'd be wined and dined and honored and possibly seduced and be acclaimed by all a hero. He didn't feel like a hero and he surely didn't want to be trapped into telling the grandmas and ten-year-old boys stories about the horrors of the firefight.

But what he dreaded most was seeing his estranged wife. It was bad enough that he had let her little brother die after she had made Spur promise to take care of him. Worse yet was that Vic had died a torch. No doubt he had been in secret contact with the pukpuks, had probably passed along information about the Corps of Firefighters—and Spur hadn't suspected a thing. It didn't matter that Vic had pushed him away during their time serving together in Gold Squad—at one time they had been best friends. He should have known; he might have been able to save Vic. Spur had already decided that he would have to lie to Comfort and his neighbors in Littleton about what had happened, just as he had lied to Dr. Niss. What was the point in smearing his dead friend now? And Spur couldn't help the Cooperative root out other pukpuk sympathizers in the Corps; he had no idea who Vic's contacts had been.

However, Spur had other reasons for wanting to stay right where he was. Even though he could scarcely draw breath without violating simplicity, he loved the comforts of the hospital. For example, the temperature never varied from a scandalous twenty-three degrees Celsius. No matter that outdoors the sun was blistering the rooftops of the upsiders' Benevolence Park Number 5, indoors was a paradise where neither sweat nor sweaters held sway. And then there was the food. Even though Spur's father, Capability Roger Leung, was the richest man in Littleton, he had practiced stricter simplicity than most. Spur had grown up on meat, bread, squash, and scruff, washed down with cider and applejack pressed from the Leungs' own apples and the occasional root beer. More recently, he and Comfort would indulge themselves when they had the money, but he was still used to gorging on the fruits of the family orchard during harvest and suffering through preserves and root cellar produce the rest of the year. But here the patients enjoyed the abundance of the Thousand Worlds, prepared in extravagant style. Depending on his appetite, he could order lablabis, dumplings, goulash, salmagundi, soufflés, quiche, phillaje, curry, paella, pasta, mousses, meringues, or tarts. And that was just the lunch menu.

But of all the hospital's guilty pleasures, the tell was his favorite. At home Spur could access the latest bazzat bands and town-tunes from all over Walden plus six hundred years of opera. And on a slow Tuesday night, he and Comfort might play one of the simplified chronicles on the tiny screen in Diligence Cottage or watch a spiritual produced by the Institute of Didactic Arts or just read to each other. But the screens of the hospital tells sprawled across entire walls and, despite the Cooperative's censors, opened like windows onto the universe. What mattered to people on other worlds astonished Spur. Their chronicles made him feel ignorant for the first time in his life and their spirituals were so wickedly materialistic that he felt compelled to close the door to his hospital room when he watched them.

The search engine in particular excited Spur. At home, he could greet anyone in the Transcendent State—as long as he knew their number. But the hospital tell could seemingly find anyone, not only on Walden but anywhere on all the Thousand Worlds of the upside. He put the tell in his room to immediate use, beginning by greeting his father and Gandy Joy, who was the village virtuator. Gandy had always understood him so much better than Comfort ever had. He should have greeted Comfort as well, but he didn't.

He did greet his pals in the Gold Squad, who were surprised that he had been able to track them down while they were on active duty. They told him that the entire Ninth Regiment had been pulled back from the Motu River burn for two weeks of CR in Prospect. Word was that they were being reassigned to the Cloyce Memorial Forest for some easy fire watch duty. No doubt the Cooperative was yanking the regiment off the front line because Gold Squad had taken almost 40 percent casualties when the burn had flanked their position at Motu. Iron and Bronze Squads had taken a hit as well, fighting their way through the burn to rescue Gold.

To keep from brooding about Vic and the Motu burn and the firefight, Spur looked up friends who had fallen out of his life. He surprised his cousin Land, who was living in Slide Knot in Southeast and working as a tithe assessor. He connected with his childhood friend Handy, whom he hadn't seen since the Alcazars had moved to Freeport, where Handy's mom was going to teach pastoral philosophy. She was still at the university and Handy was an electrician. He tracked down his self-reliance school sweetheart, Leaf Benkleman, only to discover that she had emigrated from Walden to Kolo in the Alumar system. Their attempt to catch up was frustrating, however, because the Cooperative's censors seemed to buzz every fifth word Leaf said. Also, the look on her face whenever he spoke rattled Spur. Was it pity? He was actually relieved when she cut their conversation short.

Despite the censors, talking to Leaf whetted Spur's appetite for making contact with the upside. He certainly wouldn't get the chance once he left the hospital. He didn't care that everyone was so preposterously far away that he would never meet them in person. Dr. Niss had been wrong: Spur understood perfectly the astonishing distances between stars. What he did not comprehend was exactly how he could chat with someone who lived hundreds of trillions of kilometers away, or how someone could beam themselves from Moy to Walden in a heartbeat. Of course, he had learned the simplified explanation of qics—quantum information channels—in school. Qics worked because many infinitesimally small nothings were part of a something, which could exist in two places at the same time. This of course made no sense, but then so much of upsider physics made no sense after the censors were done with it.

Spur paused in the doorway of his room and looked up and down the hall. None of the patients at his end of the ward were stirring; a lone maintenance bot dusted along the floor at the far end by the examining rooms. It was his last full day at the hospital. Now or never. He eased the door shut and turned the tell on.

He began by checking for relatives on the upside. But when he searched on the surname Leung, he got 2.3×10^6 hits. Which, if any, of them might be his people? Spur had no way of knowing. Spur's grandparents had expunged all records of their former lives when they had come to Walden, a requirement for immigrants to the Transcendent State. Like everyone else in his family, he had known the stern old folks only as GiGo and GiGa. The names on their death certificates were Jade Fey Leung and Chap Man-Leung, but Spur thought that they had probably been changed when they had first arrived at Freeport.

He was tempted to greet his father and ask if he knew GiGo's upside name, but then he would ask questions. Too many questions; his father was used to getting the answers he wanted. Spur went back to the tell. A refined search showed that millions of Leungs lived on Blimminey, Eridani Foxtrot, Fortunate Child, Moy, and No Turning Back, but there also appeared to be a scattering of Leungs on many of the Thousand Worlds. There was no help for it; Spur began to send greetings at random.

He wasn't sure exactly who he expected to answer, but it certainly wasn't bots. When Chairman Winter had bought Walden from ComExplore IC, he decreed that neither machine intelligences nor enhanced upsiders would be allowed in the refuge he was founding. The Transcendent State was to be the last and best home of the true humans. While the pukpuks used bots to manufacture goods that they sold to the Transcendent State, Spur had never actually seen one until he had arrived at the hospital.

Now he discovered that the upside swarmed with them. Everyone he tried to greet had bot receptionists, secretaries, housekeepers, or companions screening their messages. Some were virtual and presented themselves in outlandish sims; others were corporeal and stared at him from the homes or workplaces of their owners. Spur relished these voyeuristic glimpses of life on the upside, but glimpses were all he got. None of the bots wanted to talk to him, no doubt because of the caution he could see scrolling across his screen. It warned that his greeting originated from "the Transcendent State of Walden, a jurisdiction under a consensual cultural quarantine."

Most of bots were polite but firm. No, they couldn't connect him to their owners; yes, they would pass along his greeting; and no, they couldn't say when he might expect a greeting in return. Some were annoyed. They invited him to read his own Covenant and then snapped the connection. A couple of virtual bots were actually rude to him. Among other things, they called him a mud hugger, a leech, and a pathetic waste of consciousness. One particularly abusive bot started screaming that he was "a stinking, useless fossil."

Spur wasn't quite sure what a fossil was, so he queried the tell. It returned two definitions: 1. an artifact of an organism, typically extinct, that existed in a previous geologic era; 2. something outdated or superseded. The idea that, as a true human, he might be outdated, superseded, or possibly even bound for extinction so disturbed Spur that he got up and paced the room. He told himself that this was the price of curiosity. There were sound reasons why the Covenant of Simplicity placed limits on the use of technology. Complexity bred anxiety. The simple life was the good life.

Yet even as he wrestled with his conscience, he settled back in front of the tell. On a whim he entered his own name. He got just two results:

> *Comfort Rose Joerly and Prosper Gregory Leung*
> *Orchardists*
> *Diligence Cottage*
> *Jane Powder Street*
> *Littleton, Hamilton County,*

Northeast Territory, TS
Walden
and
Prosper Gregory Leung
c/o Niss (remotely—see note)
Salvation Hospital
Benevolence Park #5
Concord, Jefferson County,
Southwest Territory, TS
Walden

Spur tried to access the note attached to Dr. Niss's name, but it was blocked. That wasn't a surprise. What was odd was that he had received results just from Walden. Was he really the only Prosper Gregory Leung in the known universe?

While he was trying to decide whether being unique was good or bad, the tell inquired if he might have meant to search for Proper Gregory Leung or Phosphor Gregory L'ung or Procter Gregoire Lyon? He hadn't but there was no reason not to look them up. Proper Leung, it turned out, raised gosdogs for meat on a ranch out in Hopedale, which was in the Southwest Territory. Spur thought that eating gosdogs was barbaric and he had no interest in chatting with the rancher. Gregory L'ung lived on Kenning in the Theta Persei system. On an impulse, Spur sent his greeting. As he expected, it was immediately diverted to a bot. L'ung's virtual companion was a shining green turtle resting on a rock in a muddy river.

"The High Gregory of Kenning regrets that he is otherwise occupied at the moment," it said, raising its shell up off the rock. It stood on four human feet. "I note with interest that your greeting originates from a jurisdiction under a consensual . . ."

The turtle didn't get the chance to finish. The screen shimmered and went dark. A moment later, it lit up again with the image of a boy, perched at the edge of an elaborate chair.

He was wearing a purple fabric wrap that covered the lower part of his body from waist to ankles. He was bare-chested except for the skin of some elongated, dun-colored animal draped around his thin shoulders. Spur couldn't have said for sure how old the boy was, but despite an assured bearing and intelligent yellow eyes, he seemed not yet a man. The chair caught Spur's eye again: it looked to be of some dark wood, although much of it was gilded. Each of the legs ended in a stylized human foot. The back panel rose high above the boy's head and was carved with leaves and branches that bore translucent purple fruit.

That sparkled like jewels.

Spur reminded himself to breathe. It looked very much like a throne.

Three

It takes two to speak the truth—one to speak and another to hear.
        –A Week on the Concord and Merrimack rivers

"Hello, hello," said the boy. "Who is doing his talk, please?"

Spur struggled to keep his voice from squeaking. "My name is Prosper Gregory Leung."

The boy frowned and pointed at the bottom of the screen. "Walden, it tells? I have less than any idea of Walden."

"It's a planet."

"And tells that it's wrongful to think too hard on planet Walden? Why? Is your brain dry?"

"I think." Spur was taken aback. "We all think." Even though he thought he was being insulted, Spur didn't want to snap the connection—not yet anyway. "I'm sorry, I didn't get your name."

The words coming out of the speakers did not seem to match what the boy was saying. His lips barely moved, yet what Spur heard was, "I'm the High Gregory, Phosphorescence of Kenning, energized by the Tortoise of Eternal Radiation." Spur realized that the boy was probably speaking another language and that what he was hearing was a translation. Spur had been expecting the censors built into the tell to buzz this conversation like they had buzzed so much of his chat with Leaf Benkleman, but maybe bad translation was just as effective.

"That's interesting," said Spur cautiously. "And what is it that you do there on Kenning?"

"Do?" The High Gregory rubbed his nose absently. "Oh, do! I make luck."

"Really? People can do that on the upside?"

"What is the upside?"

"Space, you know." Spur waved an arm over his head and glanced upward.

The High Gregory frowned. "Prosper Gregory Leung breathes space?"

"No, I breathe air." He realized that the tell might easily be garbling his end of the conversation as well. "Only air." He spoke slowly and with exaggerated precision. "We call the Thousand Worlds the upside. Here. On my world."

The High Gregory still appeared to be confused.

"On this planet." He gestured at the hospital room. "Planet Walden. We look up at the stars." He raised his hand to his brow, as if sighting on some distant landmark. "At night." Listening to himself babble, Spur was certain that the High Gregory must think him an idiot. He had to change the subject, so he tapped his chest. "My friends call me Spur."

The High Gregory shook his head with a rueful smile. "You give me warmth, Spur, but I turn away with regret from the kind offer to enjoy sex with you. Memsen watches to see that I don't tickle life until I have enough of age."

Aghast, Spur sputtered that he had made no such offer, but the High Gregory, appearing not to hear, continued to speak.

"You have a fullness of age, friend Spur. Have you found a job of work on planet Walden?"

"You're asking what I do for a living?"

"All on planet Walden are living, I hope. Not saved?"

"Yes, we are." Spur grimaced. He rose from the tell and retrieved his wallet from the nightstand beside the bed. Maybe pix would help. He flipped through a handful in his wallet until he came to the one of Comfort on a ladder picking apples. "Normally I tend my orchards." He held the pix up to the tell to show the High Gregory. "I grow many kinds of fruit on my farm. Apples, peaches, apricots, pears, cherries. Do you have these kinds of fruit on Kenning?"

"Grape trees, yes." The High Gregory leaned forward in his throne and smiled. "And all of apples: apple pie and apple squeeze and melt apples." He seemed pleased that they had finally understood one another. "But you are not normal?"

"No. I mean yes, I'm fine." He closed the wallet and pocketed it. "But . . . how do I say this? There is fighting on my world." Spur had no idea how to explain the complicated grievances of the pukpuks and the fanaticism that led some of them to burn themselves alive to stop the spread of the forest and the Transcendent State. "There are other people on Walden who are very angry. They don't want my people to live here. They wish the land could be returned to how it was before we came. So they set fires to hurt us. Many of us have been called to stop them. Now instead of growing my trees, I help to put fires out."

"Very angry?" The High Gregory rose from his throne, his face flushed. "Fighting?" He punched at the air. "Hit-hit-hit?"

"Not exactly fighting with fists," said Spur. "More like a war."

The High Gregory took three quick steps toward the tell at his end. His face loomed large on Spur's screen. "War fighting?" He was clearly agitated; his cheeks flushed and the yellow eyes were fierce. "Making death to the other?" Spur had no idea why the High Gregory was reacting this way. He didn't think the boy was angry exactly, but then neither of them had proved particularly adept at reading the other. He certainly didn't want to cause some interstellar incident.

"I've said something wrong. I'm sorry." Spur bent his head in apology. "I'm speaking to you from a hospital. I was wounded . . . fighting a fire. Haven't quite been myself lately." He gave the High Gregory a self-deprecating smile. "I hope I haven't given offense."

The High Gregory made no reply. Instead he swept from his throne, down a short flight of steps into what Spur could now see was a vast hall. The boy strode past rows of carved wooden chairs, each of them a unique marvel, although none was quite as exquisite as the throne that they faced. The intricately beaded mosaic on the floor depicted turtles in jade and chartreuse and olive. Phosphorescent sculptures stretched like spider webs from the upper reaches of the walls to the barrel-vaulted ceiling, casting ghostly silver-green traceries of light on empty chairs beneath. The High Gregory was muttering as he passed down the central aisle but whatever he was saying clearly overwhelmed the tell's limited capacity. All Spur heard was, "War <crackle> Memsen witness there <crackle> our luck <crackle> <crackle> call the L'ung . . ."

At that, Spur found himself looking once again at a shining green turtle resting on a rock on a muddy river. "The High Gregory of Kenning regrets that he is otherwise occupied at the moment," it said. "I note with interest that your greeting originates from a jurisdiction under a consensual cultural quarantine. You should understand that it is unlikely that the High Gregory, as luck maker of the L'ung, would risk violating your covenants by having any communication with you."

"Except I just got done talking to him," said Spur.

"I doubt that very much." The turtle drew itself up on four human feet and stared coldly through the screen at him. "This conversation is concluded," it said. "I would ask that you not annoy us again."

"Wait, I—" said Spur, but he was talking to a dead screen.

Four

But if we stay at home and mind our business, who will want railroads? We do not ride on the railroad; it rides upon us.
                                                                —Walden

Spur spent the rest of that day expecting trouble. He had no doubt that he'd be summoned into Dr. Niss's examining room for a lecture about how his body couldn't heal if his soul was sick. Or some virtuator from Concord would be brought in to light communion and deliver a reproachful sermon on the true meaning of simplicity. Or Cary Millisap, his squad leader, would call from Prospect and scorch him for shirking his duty to Gold, which was, after all, to get better as fast he could and rejoin the unit. He had not been sent to hospital to bother the High Gregory of Kenning, luck maker of the L'ung—whoever they were.

But trouble never arrived. He stayed as far away from his room and the tell as he could get. He played cards with Val Montilly and Sleepy Thorn from the Sixth Engineers, who were recovering from smoke inhalation they had suffered in the Coldstep burn. They were undergoing alveolar reconstruction to restore full lung function. Their voices were like ripsaws but they were otherwise in good spirits. Spur won enough from Sleepy on a single round of Fool All to pay for the new apple press he'd been wanting for the orchard. Of course, he would never be able to tell his father or Comfort where the money had come from.

Spur savored a memorable last supper: an onion tart with a balsamic reduction, steamed duck leg with a fig dressing on silver thread noodles, and a vanilla panna cotta. After dinner he went with several other patients to hear a professor from Alcott University explain why citizens who sympathized with the pukpuks were misguided. When he finally returned to his room, there was a lone greeting in his queue. A bored dispatcher from the Cooperative informed him that he needed to pick up his train ticket at Celena Station before 11 A.M. No video of this citizen appeared on the screen; all he'd left was a scratchy audio message like one Spur might get on his home tell. Spur took this as a reminder that his holiday from simplicity would end the moment he left the hospital.

The breeze that blew through the open windows of the train was hot, providing little relief for the passengers in the first-class compartment. Spur shifted uncomfortably on his seat, his uniform shirt stuck to his back. He glanced away from the blur of trees racing past his window. He hated sitting in seats that faced backward; they either gave him motion sickness or a stiff neck. And if he thought about it—which he couldn't help but doing, least for a moment—the metaphor always depressed him. He didn't want to be looking back at his life just now.

A backward seat—but it was in first class. The Cooperative's dispatcher probably thought he was doing him a favor. Give him some extra legroom, a softer seat. And why not? Hadn't he survived the infamous Motu River burn? Hadn't he been badly scorched in the line of duty? Of course he should ride in first class. If only the windows opened wider.

It had been easy not to worry about his problems while he was lounging around the hospital. Now that he was headed back home, life had begun to push him again. He knew he should try to stop thinking, maybe take a nap. He closed his eyes, but didn't sleep. Without warning he was back in the nightmare sim again . . . and could smell burning hair. His hair. In a panic he dodged into a stream choked with dead fish and poached frogs. But the water was practically boiling and scalded his legs . . . only Spur wasn't completely in the nightmare because he knew he was also sitting on a comfortable seat in a first-class compartment in a train that was taking him . . . the only way out was blocked by a torch, who stood waiting for Spur. Vic had not yet set himself on fire, although his baseball jersey was smoking in the heat . . . I'm not afraid, Spur told himself, I don't believe any of this . . . the anguished face shimmered in the heat of the burn and then Spur was dancing to keep his shoes from catching fire, and he had no escape, no choice, no time . . . with his eyes shut, Spur heard the clatter of the steel wheels on the track as: no time no time no time no time.

He knew then for certain what he had only feared: Dr. Niss had not healed his soul. How could he, when Spur had consistently lied about what had happened in the burn? Spur didn't mean to groan, but he did. When he opened his eyes, the gandy in the blue flowered dress was staring at him.

"Are you all right?" She looked to be in her late sixties or maybe seventy, with silver hair so thin that he could see the freckles on her scalp.

"Yes, fine," Spur said. "I just thought of something."

"Something you forgot?" She nodded. "Oh, I'm always remembering things just like that. Especially on trains." She had a burbling laugh, like stream running over smooth stones. "I was supposed to have lunch with my friend Connie day after tomorrow, but here I am on my way to Little Bend for a week. I have a new grandson."

"That's nice," Spur said absently. There was one other passenger in the compartment. He was a very fat, moist man looking at a comic book about gosdogs playing baseball; whenever he turned a page, he took a snuffling breath.

"I see by your uniform that you're one of our firefighters," said the gandy. "Do you know my nephew Frank Kaspar? I think he is with the Third Engineers."

Spur explained that there were over eleven thousand volunteers in the Corps of Firefighters and that if her nephew was an engineer he was most probably a regular with the Home Guard. Spur couldn't keep track of all the brigades and platoons in the volunteer Corps, much less in the professional Guard. He said that he was just a lowly smokechaser in Gold Squad, Ninth Regiment. His squad worked with the Eighth Engineers, who supplied transportation and field construction support. He told her that these fine men and women were the very models of spiritual simplicity and civic rectitude, no doubt like her nephew. Spur was hoping that this was what she wanted to hear and that she would leave him alone. But then she asked if the rumors of pukpuk collaborators infiltrating the Corps were true and started nattering about how she couldn't understand how a citizen of the Transcendent State could betray the Covenant by helping terrorists. All the pukpuks wanted was to torch Chairman Winter's forests, wasn't that awful? Spur realized that he would have to play to her sympathy. He coughed and said he had been wounded in a burn and was just out of hospital and then coughed again.

"If you don't mind," he said, crinkling his brow as if he were fighting pain, "I'm feeling a little woozy. I'm just going to shut my eyes again and try to rest."

Although he didn't sleep, neither was he fully awake. But the nightmare did not return. Instead he drifted through clouds of dreamy remembrance and unfocussed regret. So he didn't notice that the train was slowing down until the hiss of the air brakes startled him to full alertness.

He glanced at his watch. They were still an hour out of Heart's Wall, where Spur would change for the local to Littleton.

"Are we stopping?" Spur asked.

"Wheelwright fireground." The fat man pulled a limp handkerchief out of his shirt pocket and dabbed at his hairline. "Five minutes of mandatory respect."

Now Spur noticed that the underbrush had been cleared along the track and that there were scorch marks on most of the trees. Spur had studied the Wheelwright in training. The forest north of the village of Wheelwright had been one of the first to be attacked by the torches. It was estimated that there must have been at least twenty of them, given the scope of the damage. The Wheelwright burn was also the first in which a firefighter died, although the torches never targeted citizens, only trees. The fires they started were always well away from villages and towns; that's why they were so hard to fight. But the Wheelwright had been whipped by strong winds until it cut the trunk line between Concord and Heart's Wall for almost two weeks. The Cooperative had begun recruiting for the Corps shortly after.

As the squealing brakes slowed the train to a crawl, the view out of Spur's window changed radically. Here the forest had yet to revive from the ravages of fire. Blackened skeletons of trees pointed at the sky and the charred floor of the forest baked under the sun. The sun seemed cruelly bright without the canopy of leaves to provide shade. In every direction, all Spur could see was the nightmarish devastation he had seen all too often. No plant grew, no bird sang. There were no ants or needlebugs or wild gosdogs. Then he noticed something odd: the bitter burnt-coffee scent of fresh fireground. And he could taste the ash, like shredded paper on his tongue. That made no sense; the Wheelwright was over three years old.

When the train finally stopped, Spur was facing one of the many monuments built along the tracks to honor fallen firefighters. A grouping of three huge statues set on a pad of stone cast their bronze gazes on him. Two of the firefighters were standing; one leaned heavily on the other. A third had dropped to one knee, from exhaustion perhaps. All still carried their gear, but the kneeling figure was about to shed her splash pack and one of the standing figures was using his jacksmith as a crutch. Although the sculptor had chosen to depict them in the hour of their doom, their implacable metal faces revealed neither distress nor regret. The fearsome simplicity of their courage chilled Spur. He was certain that he wasn't of their quality.

The engine blew its whistle in tribute to the dead: three long blasts and three short. The gandy stirred and stretched. "Wheelwright?" she muttered.

"Yeah," said the fat man.

She started to yawn but caught herself and peered out the open window. "Who's that?" she said, pointing.

A man in a blue flair suit was walking along the tracks, peering up at the passenger cars. He looked very hot and not very happy. His face was as flushed as a peach and his blond hair was plastered to his forehead. Every few meters he paused, cupped his hands to his mouth and called, "Leung? Prosper Gregory Leung?"

Five

Fire is without doubt an advantage on the whole. It sweeps and ventilates the forest floor and makes it clear and clean. I have often remarked with how much more comfort & pleasure I could walk in wood through which a fire had been run the previous year. It is inspiriting to walk amid the fresh green sprouts of grass and shrubbery pushing upward through the charred surface with more vigorous growth.

–Journal, 1850

The man waited impatiently as Spur descended from the train, kit slung over his shoulder. Although he did not turn back to look, Spur knew every passenger on the train was watching them. Was he in trouble? The man's expression gave away nothing more than annoyance. He looked to be younger than Spur, possibly in his late twenties. He had a pinched face and a nose as stubby as a radish. He was wearing a prissy white shirt buttoned to the neck. There were dark circles under the armpits of his flair jacket.

"Prosper Gregory Leung of Littleton, Hamilton County, Northeast?" The man pulled a slip of paper from his pocket and read from it. "You are currently on medical leave from the Ninth Regiment, Corps of Firefighters, and were issued a first-class ticket on this day—"

"I know who I am." Spur felt as if a needlebug were caught in his throat. "What is this about? Who are you?"

He introduced himself as Constant Ngonda, a deputy with the Cooperative's Office of Diplomacy. When they shook hands, he noticed that Ngonda's palm was soft and sweaty. Spur could guess why he had been pulled off the train, but he decided to act surprised.

"What does the Office of Diplomacy want with me?"

Just then the engineer blew three short blasts and couplings of the train clattered and jerked as, one by one, they took the weight of the passenger cars. With the groan of metal on metal, the train pulled away from the Wheelwright Memorial.

Spur's grip on the strap of his kit tightened. "Don't we want to get back on?"

Constant Ngonda shrugged. "I was never aboard."

The answer made no sense to Spur, who tensed as he calculated his chances of sprinting to catch the train. Ngonda rested a hand on his arm.

"We go this way, Prosper." He nodded west, away from the tracks.

"I don't understand." Spur's chances of making the train were fading as it gained momentum. "What's out there?"

"A clearing. A hover full of upsiders." He sighed. "Some important people have come a long way to see you." He pushed a lock of damp hair off his forehead. "The sooner we start, the sooner we get out of this heat." He let go of Spur and started picking his way across the fireground.

Spur glanced over his shoulder one last time at the departing train. He felt as if his life were pulling away.

"Upsiders? From where?"

Ngonda held up an open hand to calm him. "Some questions will be answered soon enough. Others it's better not to ask."

"What do you mean, better?"

Ngonda walked with an awkward gait, as if he expected the ground to give way beneath him. "I beg your pardon." He was wearing the wrong shoes for crossing rough terrain. "I misspoke." They were thin-soled, low-cut and had no laces—little more than slippers. "I meant simpler, not better."

Just then Spur got a particularly intense whiff of something that was acrid and sooty, but not quite smoke. It was what he had first smelled as the train had pulled into the Memorial. He turned in a complete circle, all senses heightened, trying to pinpoint the source. After fire ran through the litter of leaves and twigs that covered the forest floor, it often sank into the duff, the layer of decomposing organic matter that lay just above the soil level. Since duff was like a sponge, most of the year it was too wet to burn. But in the heat of summer it could dry out and became tinder. Spur had seen a smoldering fire burrow through the layer of duff and emerge dozens of meters away. He sniffed, following his nose to a charred stump.

"Prosper!" said Ngonda. "What are you doing?"

Spur heard a soft hiss as he crouched beside the stump. It wasn't any fire sound that he knew, but he instinctively ran his bare hand across the stump, feeling for hotspots. Something cool and wet sprayed onto his fingers and he jerked them back as if he had been burned. He rubbed a smutty liquid between thumb and forefinger and then smelled it.

It had an evil, manmade odor of extinguished fire. Spur sat back on his heels, puzzled. Why would anyone want to mimic that particular stink? Then he realized that his hand was clean when it ought to have been smudged with soot from the stump. He rubbed hard against the burned wood, but the black refused to come off. He could see now that the stump had a clear finish, as if it had been coated with a preservative.

Spur could sense Ngonda's shadow loom over him but then he heard the hissing again and was able to pick out the tiny nozzle embedded in the stump. He pressed his finger to it and the noise stopped. Then on an impulse, he sank his hand into the burned forest litter, lifted it and let the coarse mixture sift slowly through his fingers.

"It's hot out, Prosper," Ngonda said. "Do you really need to be playing in the dirt?"

The litter looked real enough: charred and broken twigs, clumps of leaf mold, wood cinders, and a delicate ruined hemlock cone. But it didn't feel right. He squeezed a scrap of burnt bark, expecting it to crumble. Instead it compacted into an irregular pellet, like day-old bread. When he released it, the pellet slowly resumed its original shape.

"It's not real," said Spur. "None of it."

"It's a memorial, Prosper." The deputy offered Spur a hand and pulled him to his feet. "People need to remember." He bent over to brush at the fake pine needles stuck to Spur's knees. "We need to go."

Spur had never seen a hover so close. Before the burns, hovers had been banned altogether from the Transcendent State. But after the pukpuks had begun their terrorist campaign to halt the spread of forest into their barrens, Chairman Winter had given the Cooperative permission to relax the ban. Generous people from the upside had donated money to build the benevolence parks and provided hovers to assist the Corps in fighting fires. However, Chairman Winter had insisted that only bots were to fly the hovers and that citizen access to them would be closely monitored.

While in the field with Gold Squad, Spur had watched hovers swoop overhead, spraying loads of fire-retardant splash onto burns.

And he had studied them for hours through the windows of the hospital, parked in front of their hangars at Benevolence Park Number 5. But even though this one was almost as big as Diligence Cottage and hovered a couple of meters above the ground, it wasn't quite as impressive as Spur had imagined it.

He decided that this must be because it was so thoroughly camouflaged. The hover's smooth skin had taken on the discoloration of the fireground, an ugly mottle of gray and brown and black. It looked like the shell of an enormous clam. The hover was elliptical, about five meters tall in front sweeping backward to a tapered edge, but otherwise featureless. If it had windows or doors, Spur couldn't make them out.

As they approached, the hover rose several meters. They passed into its shadow and Ngonda looked up expectantly. A hatch opened on the underside. A ramp extended to the ground below with a high-pitched warble like birdsong, and a man appeared at the hatch. He was hard to see against the light of the interior of the hover; all Spur could tell for sure was that he was very tall and very skinny. Not someone he would expect to bump into on Jane Powder Street in Littleton. The man turned to speak to someone just inside the hatch. That's when Spur realized his mistake.

"No," she said, her voice airy and sweet. "We need to speak to him first."

As she teetered down the ramp, Spur could tell immediately that she was not from Walden. It was the calculation with which she carried herself, as if each step were a risk, although one she was disposed to take. She wore loose-fitting pants of a sheer fabric that might have been spun from clouds. Over them was a blue sleeveless dress that hung to mid-thigh. Her upper arms were decorated with flourishes of phosphorescent body paint and she wore silver and copper rings on each of her fingers.

"You're the Prosper Gregory of Walden?"

She had full lips and midnight hair and her skin was smooth and dark as a plum. She was a head taller than he was and half his weight. He was speechless until Ngonda nudged him.

"Yes."

"We're Memsen."

Six

It requires nothing less than a chivalric feeling to sustain a conversation with a lady.

–Journal, 1851

Although it was cooler in the shade of the hover, Spur was far from comfortable. He couldn't help thinking of what would happen if the engine failed. He would have felt more confident if the hover had been making some kind of noise; the silent, preternatural effortlessness of the ship unnerved him. Meanwhile, he was fast realizing that Memsen had not wanted to meet him in order to make friends.

"Let's understand one another," she said. "We're here very much against our will. You should know, that by summoning us to this place, you've put the political stability of dozens of worlds at risk. We very much regret that the High Gregory has decided to follow his luck to this place."

She was an upsider so Spur had no idea how to read her. The set of her shoulders flustered him, as did the way her knees bent as she stooped to his level. She showed him too many teeth and it was clear that she wasn't smiling. And why did she pinch the air? With a great effort Spur tore his gaze away from her and looked to Ngonda to see if he knew what she was talking about. The deputy gave him nothing.

"I'm not sure that I summoned the High Gregory, exactly," Spur said. "I did talk to him."

"About your war."

Constant Ngonda looked nervous. "Allworthy Memsen, I'm sure that Prosper didn't understand the implications of contacting you. The Transcendent State is under a cultural—"

"We grant that you have your shabby deniability." She redirected her displeasure toward the deputy. "Nevertheless, we suspect that your government instructed this person to contact the High Gregory, knowing that he'd come. There's more going on here than you care to say, isn't there?"

"Excuse me," said Spur, "but this really was an accident." Both Memsen and Ngonda stared at him as if he had corncobs stuck in his ears. "What happened was that I searched on my name but couldn't find anyone but me and then the tell at the hospital suggested the High Gregory as an alternative because our names are so similar." He spoke rapidly, worried that they'd start talking again before he could explain everything. "So I sent him a greeting. It was totally random — I didn't know who he was, I swear it. And I wasn't really expecting to make contact, since I'd been talking to bots all morning and not one was willing to connect me. In fact, your bot was about to cut me off when he came on the tell. The High Gregory, I mean."

"So." Memsen clicked the rings on her fingers together. "He mentioned none of this to us."

"He probably didn't know." Spur edged just a centimeter away from her toward the sunlight. The more he thought about it, the more he really wanted to get out from under the hover.

Ngonda spoke with calm assurance. "There, you see that Prosper's so-called request is based on nothing more than coincidence and misunderstanding." He batted at a fat, orange needlebug that was buzzing his head. "The Cooperative regrets that you have come all this way to no good purpose."

Memsen reared suddenly to her full height and gazed down on the two of them. "There are no coincidences," she said, "only destiny. The High Gregory makes the luck he was meant to have. He's here, and he has brought the L'ung to serve as witnesses. Our reason for being on this world has yet to be discovered." She closed her eyes for several moments. While she considered Spur's story she made a low, repetitive plosive sound: *pa-pa-pa-ptt.* "But this is deeper than we first suspected," she mused.

Spur caught a glimpse of a head peeking out of the hatch above him. It ducked back into the hover immediately.

"So," Memsen said at last, "let's choose to believe you, Prosper Gregory of Walden." She eyed him briefly; whatever she saw in his face seemed to satisfy her. "You'll have to show us the way from here. Your way. The High Gregory's luck has chosen you to lead us until we see for ourselves the direction in which we must go."

"Lead you? Where?"

"Wherever you're going."

"But I'm just on my way home. To Littleton."

She clicked her rings. "So."

"I beg your pardon, Allworthy Memsen," said Ngonda, tugging at the collar of his shirt, "but you must realize that's impossible under our Covenant. . . ."

"It is the nature of luck to sidestep the impossible," she said. "We speak for the High Gregory when we express our confidence that you'll find a way."

She had so mastered the idiom of command that Spur wasn't

sure whether this was a threat or a promise. Either way, it gave Ngonda pause.

"Allworthy, I'd like nothing better than to accommodate you in this," he said. "Walden is perhaps the least of the Thousand Worlds, but even here we've heard of your efforts to help preserve the one true species." A bead of sweat dribbled down his forehead. "But my instructions are to accommodate your requests within reason. Within reason, Allworthy. It is not reasonable to land a hover in the commons of a village like Littleton. You must understand that these are country people."

She pointed at Spur. "Here is one of your country people."

"Memsen!" shouted a voice from the top of the ramp. "Memsen, I am so bored. Either bring him up right now or I'm coming down."

Her tongue flicked to the corner of her mouth. "You wouldn't like it," she called back, "it's very hot." Which was definitely true, although as far as Spur could tell, the weather had no effect on her. "There are bugs."

"That's it!" The High Gregory of Kenning, Phosphorescence of the Eternal Radiation and luck maker of the L'ung, scampered down the ramp of the hover.

"There," he said, "I did it, so now don't tell me to go back." He was wearing green sneakers with black socks, khaki shorts and a T-shirt with a pix of a dancing turtle, which had a human head. "Spur! You look sadder than you did before." He had knobby knees and fair skin and curly brown hair. If he had been born in Littleton, Spur would've guessed that he was ten years old. "Did something bad happen to you? Say something. Do you still talk funny like you did on the tell?"

Spur had a hundred questions but he was so surprised that all he could manage was, "Why are you doing this?"

"Why?" The boy's yellow eyes opened wide. "Why, why, why?" He stooped to pick up a handful of the blackened litter and examined it with interest, shifting it around on his open palm. "Because I got one of my luck feelings when we were talking. They're not like ideas or dreams or anything so I can't explain them very well. They're just special. Memsen says they're not like the feelings that other people get, but that it's all right to have them and I guess it is." He twirled in a tight circle then, flinging the debris in a wide scatter. "And that's why." He rubbed his hands on the front of his shorts and approached Spur. "Am I supposed to shake hands or kiss you? I can't remember."

Ngonda stepped between Spur and the High Gregory as if to protect him. "The custom is to shake hands."

"But I shook with you already." He tugged at Ngonda's sleeve to move him aside. "You have hardly any luck left, friend Constant. I'm afraid it's all pretty much decided with you." When the deputy failed to give way, the High Gregory dropped to all fours and scooted through his legs. "Hello, Spur," said the boy as he scrambled to his feet. The High Gregory held out his hand and Spur took it.

Spur was at once aware that he was sweaty from the heat of the day, while the boy's hand was cool as river rock. He could feel the difference in their size: the High Gregory's entire hand fit in his palm and weighed practically nothing.

"Friend Spur, you have more than enough luck," the boy murmured, low enough so that only Spur could hear. "I can see we're going to have an adventure."

"Stay up there," cried Memsen. "No!" She was glowering up the ramp at the hatch, which had inexplicably filled with kids who were shouting at her. Spur couldn't tell which of them said what.

"When do we get our turn?"

"You let the Greg off."

"We came all this way."

"He's bored? I'm more bored."

"Hey move, you're in my way!"

"But I want to see too."

Several in the back started to chant. "Not fair, not fair!"

Memsen ground her toes into the fake forest floor. "We have to go now," she said. "If we let them off the hover, it'll take hours to round them up."

"I'll talk to them." High Gregory bounded up the ramp, making sweeping motions with his hands. "Back, get back, this isn't it." The kids fell silent. "We're not there yet. We're just stopping to pick someone up." He paused halfway up and turned to the adults. "Spur is coming, right?"

Ngonda was blotting sweat from around his eyes with a handkerchief. "If he chooses." He snapped it with a quick flick of the wrist and then stuffed it into his pocket, deliberately avoiding eye contact with Spur.

Spur could feel his heart pounding. He'd wanted to fly ever since he'd realized that it was possible and didn't care if simplicity counseled otherwise. But he wasn't sure he wanted to be responsible for bringing all these upsiders to Littleton.

"So." Memsen must have mistaken his hesitation for fear. "You have never been in a hover, Prosper Gregory of Walden?"

"Call him Spur," said the High Gregory. "It doesn't mean you have to have sex with him."

Memsen bowed to Spur. "He has not yet invited us to take that familiarity."

"Yes, please call me Spur." He tried not to think about having sex with Memsen. "And yes," he picked up his kit, "I'll come with you."

"Lead then." She indicated that he should be first up the ramp. Ngonda followed him. Memsen came last, climbing slowly with her small and painstakingly accurate steps.

As he approached the top of the ramp, the coolness of the hover's interior washed over him. It was like wading into Mercy's Creek. He could see that the kids had gathered around the High Gregory. There were about a dozen of them in a bay that was about six by ten meters. Boxes and containers were strapped to the far bulkhead.

"Now where are we going?"

"When do we get to see the fire?"

"Hey, who's that?"

Most of the kids turned to see him step onto the deck. Although well lit, the inside of the hover was not as bright as it had been outside. Spur blinked as his eyes adjusted to the difference.

"This is Spur," said the High Gregory. "We're going to visit his village. It's called Littleton."

"Why? Are they little there?"

A girl of six or perhaps seven sidled over to him. "What's in your bag?" She was wearing a dress of straw-colored brocade that hung down to her silk slippers. The gold chain around her neck had a pendant in the shape of a stylized human eye. Spur decided that it must be some kind of costume.

He slung his kit off his shoulder and set it down in front of her so she could see. "Just my stuff."

"It's not very big," she said doubtfully. "Do you have something in there for me?"

"Your Grace," said Memsen, putting a hand on the girl's shoulder, "we are going to leave Spur alone for now." She turned the girl around and gave her a polite nudge toward the other kids. "You'll have to forgive them," she said to Spur. "They're used to getting their own way."

Seven

*I have a deep sympathy with war, it so apes the gait and bearing
of the soul.*
                                                      –Journal, 1840

Spur had studied geography in school and knew how big Walden
was, but for the first time in his life he *felt* it. From the ground, the
rampant forests restricted what anyone could see of the world. Even
the fields and the lakes were hemmed in by trees. Spur had never
been to the Modilon Ocean but he'd stood on the shores of Great
Kamit Lake. The sky over the lake was impressive, but there was no
way to take the measure of its scale. Spur had hiked the Tarata
Mountains, but they were forested to their summits and the only
views were from ledges. There was a tower on Samson Kokoda that
afforded a 360-degree view, but the summit was just 1,300 meters
tall.

Now the hover was cruising through the clouds at an altitude of
5,700 meters, according to the tell on the bulkhead. Walden spread
beneath him in all its breathtaking immensity. Maps, measured in
inflexible kilometers and flat hectares, were a sham compared to
this. Every citizen should see what he was seeing, and if it violated
simplicity, he didn't care.

Constant Ngonda, on the other hand, was not enjoying the view.
He curled on a bench facing away from the hull, which Memsen
had made transparent when she'd partitioned a private space for
them. His neck muscles were rigid and he complained from time to
time about trouble with his ears. Whenever the hover shivered as it
contended with the wind, he took a huge, gulping breath. In a raspy
voice, the deputy asked Spur to stop commenting on the scenery.
Spur was not surprised when Ngonda lurched to his feet and tore
through the bubble-like bulkhead in search of a bathroom. The wall
popped back into place, throwing a scatter of rainbows across its
shivering surface.

Spur kept his face pressed to the hull. He'd expected the surface
to be smooth and cold, like glass. Instead, it was warm and yielding,
as if it were the flesh of some living creature. Below him the lakes
and rivers gleamed in the afternoon sun like the shards of a broken
mirror. The muddy Kalibobo River veered away to the west as the
hover flew into the foothills of the Tarata Range. As the land rolled
beneath him, Spur could spot areas where the bright-green hard-

wood forest was yielding ground to the blue-green of the conifers: hemlock and pine and spruce. There were only a few farms and isolated villages in the shadow of the mountains. They would have to fly over the Taratas to get to Littleton on the eastern slope.

At first Spur had difficulty identifying the familiar peaks. He was coming at them from the wrong direction and at altitude. But once he picked out the clenched fist of Woitape, he could count forward and back down the range: Taurika, Bootless Lowa, and Boroko, curving to the northwest, Kaivuna and Samson Kokoda commanding the plain to the south. He murmured the names aloud, as long as the deputy wasn't around to hear. He had always liked how round the pukpuk sounds were, how they rolled in his mouth. When he'd been trapped in the burn with Vic, he was certain that he would never say them again.

When Chairman Winter bought Morobe's Pea from Com Explore IC, he had thought to rename everything on the planet and make a fresh start for his great experiment in preserving unenhanced humanity. But then a surprising number of ComExplore employees turned down his generous relocation offer; they wanted to stay on. Almost all of these pukpuks could trace their ancestry back to some ancient who had made planetfall on the first colonizing ships. More than a few claimed to be descended from Old Morobe herself. As a gesture of respect, the Chairman agreed to keep pukpuk names for some landforms. So there were still rivers, valleys, mountains, and islands, which honored the legacy of the first settlers.

Chairman Winter had never made a secret of his plans for Walden. At staggering personal expense, he had intended to transform the exhausted lands of Morobe's Pea. In their place he would make a paradise that re-created the heritage ecology of the home world. He would invite only true humans to come to Walden. All he asked was that his colonists forsake the technologies, which were spinning out of control on the Thousand Worlds. Those who agreed to live by the Covenant of Simplicity would be given land and citizenship. Eventually both the forest and the Transcendent State would overspread all of Walden.

But the pukpuks had other plans. They wouldn't leave and they refused to give up their banned technologies. At first trade between the two cultures of Walden flourished. In fact, the pukpuk industrial and commercial base propped up the fledgling Transcendent State. Citizens needed pukpuk goods, even if bots manufactured them. As time passed however, the Cooperative recognized that pukpuks' continued presence was undermining the very foundations of the Transcendent State. When the Cooperative attempted to close off the borders in order to encourage local industry, black markets sprang up in the cities. Many citizens came to question the tenets of simplicity. The weak were tempted by forbidden knowledge. For the first time since the founding, the emigration rate edged into the double digits. When it was clear that the only way to save the Transcendent State was to push the pukpuks off the planet, Chairman Winter had authorized the planting of genetically enhanced trees. But once the forest began to encroach on the pukpuk barrens, the burns began.

The pukpuks were the clear aggressors in the firefight; even their sympathizers among the citizenry agreed on that. What no one could agree on was how to accommodate them without compromising. In fact, many of the more belligerent citizens held that the ultimate responsibility for the troubles lay with the Chairman himself. They questioned his decision not to force all of the pukpuks to emigrate after the purchase of Morobe's Pea. And some wondered why he could not order them to be rounded up and deported even now. It was, after all, his planet.

"We've come up with a compromise," said Ngonda as he pushed through the bulkhead into the compartment. He was still as pale as a root cellar mushroom, but he seemed steadier. He even glanced briefly down at the eastern slope of Bootless Lowa Mountain before cutting his eyes away. "I think we can let the High Gregory visit under your supervision."

Memsen, the High Gregory, and a young girl followed him, which caused the bulkhead to burst altogether. Spur caught a glimpse of a knot of kids peering at him before the wall reformed itself two meters farther into the interior of the hover, creating the necessary extra space to fit them all. The High Gregory was carrying a tray of pastries, which he set on the table he caused to form out of the deck.

"Hello, Spur," he said. "How do you like flying? Your friend got sick but Memsen helped him. This is Penny."

"The Pendragon Chromlis Furcifer," said Memsen.

She and Spur studied each other. A little taller but perhaps a little younger than the High Gregory, the girl was dressed hood to boot in clothes made of supple, metallic-green scales. The scales of her gloves were as fine as snakeskin while those that formed her tunic looked more like cherry leaves, even to the serrated edges. A rigid hood protected the back of her head. A tangle of thick, black hair wreathed her face.

"Penny," said the High Gregory, "you're supposed to shake his hand."

"I know," she said, but then clasped both hands behind her back and stared at the deck.

"Your right goes to his right." The High Gregory held out his own hand to demonstrate. "She's just a little shy," he said.

Spur crouched and held out his hand. She took it solemnly. They shook. Spur let her go. The girl's hand went behind her back again.

"You have a pretty name, Pendragon," said Spur.

"That's her title." Memsen faced left and then right before she sat on the bench next to Ngonda. "It means war chief."

"Really. And have you been to war, Penny?"

She shook her head—more of a twitch of embarrassment than a shake.

"This is her first," said the High Gregory. "But she's L'ung. She's just here to watch."

"I'm sorry," said Spur. "Who are the L'ung?"

Ngonda cleared his throat in an obvious warning. The High Gregory saw Memsen pinch the air and whatever he'd been about to say died on his lips. The silence stretched long enough for Penny to realize that there was some difficulty about answering Spur's question.

"What, is he stupid?" She scrutinized Spur with renewed interest. "Are you stupid, Spur?"

"I don't think so." It was his turn to be embarrassed. "But maybe some people think that I am."

"This is complicated," said Memsen, filling yet another awkward pause. "We understand that people here seek to avoid complication." She considered. "Let's just say that the L'ung are companions to the High Gregory. They like to watch him make luck, you might say. Think of them as students. They've been sent from many different worlds, for many different reasons. Complications again. There is a political aspect . . ."

Ngonda wriggled in protest.

". . . which the deputy assures us you would only find confusing. So." She patted the bench. "Sit, Pendragon."

The Pendragon collected a macaroon from the pastry tray and obediently settled beside Memsen, then leaned to whisper in her ear.

"Yes," said Memsen, "we'll ask about the war."

Ngonda rose then, but caught himself against a bulkhead as if the change from sitting to standing had left him dizzy. "This isn't fair," he said. "The Cooperative has made a complete disclosure of the situation here, both to Kenning and to the Forum of the Thousand Worlds."

"What you sent was dull, dull, dull, friend Constant," said the High Gregory. "I don't think the people who made the report went anywhere near a burn. Someone told somebody else, and that somebody told them." Just then the hover bucked and the deputy almost toppled onto Memsen's lap. "You gave us a bunch of contracts and maps and pix of dead trees," continued the High Gregory. "I can't make luck out of charts. But Spur was there, he can tell us. He was almost burned up."

"Not about Motu River," said Spur quickly. "Nothing about that." Suddenly everyone was staring at him.

"Maybe," began Ngonda but the hover shuddered again and he slapped a hand hard against the bulkhead to steady himself. "Maybe we should tell him what we've agreed on."

Spur sensed that Memsen was judging him, and that she was not impressed. "If you want to talk in general about fighting fires," he said, "that's different."

Ngonda looked miserable. "Can't we spare this brave man . . . ?"

"Deputy Ngonda," said Memsen.

"What?" His voice was very small.

The High Gregory lifted the tray from the table and offered it to him. "Have a cookie."

Ngonda shrank from the pastries as if they might bite him. "Go ahead then," he said. "Scratch this foolish itch of yours. We can't stop you. We're just a bunch of throwbacks from a nothing world and you're—"

"Deputy Ngonda!" Memsen's voice was sharp.

He caught his breath. "You're Memsen the Twenty-Second and he's the High Gregory of Kenning and I'm not feeling very well." Ngonda turned to Spur, muttering. "Remember, they don't really care what happens to you. Or any of us."

"That's not true," said the High Gregory. "Not true at all."

But Ngonda had already subsided onto his bench, queasy and unvoiced.

"So." Memsen clicked her rings together. "You fight fires."

"I'm just a smokechaser." Ngonda's outburst troubled Spur. He didn't know anything about these upsiders, after all. Were they really any different than pukpuks? "I volunteered for the Corps about a year ago, finished training last winter, was assigned the Ninth Regiment, Gold Squad. We mostly build handlines along the edges of burns to contain them." He leaned against the hull with his back to the view. "The idea is that we scrape off everything that can catch fire, dig to mineral soil. If we can fit a plow or tractor in, then we do, but in rough terrain we work by hand. That's about it. Boring as those reports you read."

"I don't understand." The High Gregory sprawled on the deck, picking idly at his sneakers. "If you're so busy digging, when do you put the fires out?"

"Fire needs three things," he said, "oxygen, fuel, and temperature. They call it the triangle of combustion. Think of a burn as a chain of triangles. The sides of every triangle have to connect." He formed a triangle by pressing his thumbs and forefingers together. "Hot enough connects to enough air connects to enough stuff to burn. Take away a side and you break the triangle . . ." He separated his thumbs. ". . . and weaken the chain. When a burn blows up, there's no good way to cut off its oxygen or lower the core temperature, so you have to attack the fuel side of the triangle. If you do your job, eventually there's nothing left to burn."

"Then you don't actually put fires out?" The High Gregory sounded disappointed.

"We do, but that's just hotspotting. Once we establish a handline, we have to defend it. So we walk the lines, checking for fires that start from flying sparks or underground runners. Trees might fall across a line. If we find a hotspot, we dig it out with a jacksmith or spray it cold with retardant from our splash packs." He noticed that the Pendragon was whispering again to Memsen. "I'm sorry," he said. "Is there something?"

Memsen gave him a polite smile—at least he hoped it was polite. "She asks about the people who set fire to themselves. Have you ever seen one?"

"A torch?" Spur frowned. "No." The lie slipped out with practiced ease.

"They must be very brave." The High Gregory wriggled across the deck on hands and knees to Spur's kit. "Hey, your bag got burnt here." He held the kit up to the afternoon light pouring through the hull, examining it. "And here too. Do you hate them?"

"No."

"But they tried to kill you."

"Not me. They're trying to kill the forest, maybe the Trans-

cendent State, but not me. They have no idea who I am." He
motioned for the kit and the High Gregory dragged it across the
compartment to him. "And I don't know any of them. We're
all strangers." He opened the kit, rummaged inside and pulled out
a pix of Gold Squad. "Here's my squad. That's full firefighting gear
we're wearing." Dead friends grinned at him from the pix. Vic,
kneeling in the front row of the picture, and Hardy, who was standing next to Spur. He flipped the pix over and passed it to the High
Gregory.

"Why are the torches doing this?" said Memsen. "You must have
wondered about it. Help us understand."

"It's complicated." He waited for Ngonda to pipe up with the
official line, but the deputy was gazing through the hull of the hover
with eyes of glass. "They should have gone long ago," said Spur.
"They're upsiders, really. They don't belong here anymore."

"A thousand worlds for the new," said Memsen, "one for the
true. That's what your chairman says, isn't it?"

"Your parents came here from other worlds," said the High
Gregory. "So that's why you think the pukpuks should've been willing to pack up and go. But would you come back with us to Kenning if Jack Winter said you should?"

"That's not why I . . ." Spur rubbed at his forehead. "I don't
know, maybe it is. Anyway, they were my grandparents, not my parents."

The High Gregory slid across the deck and handed the pix of
Gold Squad to Memsen. The Pendragon craned her neck to see.

"You have to understand," said Spur, "that the pukpuks hate the
new forests because they spread so fast. The trees grow like weeds,
not like the ones in my orchard." He glanced over his shoulder at
the hills beneath him. They were on the east side of the Taratas now
and flying lower. Almost home. "When Walden was still the Pea,
this continent was dry and mostly open. The Niah was prairie.
There was supposedly this huge desert, the Nev, or the Neb, where
Concord is now. The pukpuks hunted billigags and tamed the gosdog herds. Their bots dug huge pits to mine carbonatites and rare
earths. Eventually they killed off the herds, plowed the prairies
under and exhausted all the surface deposits. They created the
barrens, raped this planet and then most of them just left. Morobe's
Pea was a dying world, that's why the Chairman picked it. There
was nothing for the pukpuks here, no reason to stay until we came."

As the hover swooped low over the treetops, Spur could feel the
tug of home as real as gravity. After all he had been through,

Littleton was still drowsing at the base of Lamana Ridge, waiting for him. He imagined sleeping in his own bed that night.

"Soon there won't be any more barrens," he said, "just forest. And that will be the end of it."

The High Gregory stared at him with his unnerving, yellow eyes. "They're just trying to protect their way of life. And now you're telling them that your way is better."

"No." Spur bit his lip; the truth of what the High Gregory said had long since pricked his soul. "But their way of life is to destroy our way."

Memsen flicked a finger against the pix of Gold Squad. "And so that's why they started this war?"

"Is this a war?" Spur took the pix from her and tucked it into his kit without looking at it again. "They set fires, we put them out. It's dangerous work, either way."

"People die," whispered the Pendragon.

"Yes," said Spur. "They do."

Eight

I have lived some thirty-odd years on this planet, and I have yet to hear the first syllable of valuable or even earnest advice from my seniors.

—Journal, 1852

Spur perched on a stump wondering how to sneak over to the Littleton train station. From where he sat, it looked hopeless. He had just bushwhacked through the forest from the edge of Spot Pond, where the hover had lingered long enough to put him onto the mucky shore. Now he was on the trail that led down Lamana Ridge. Just ahead of him was Blue Valley Road, a rough track that connected a handful of farms to Civic Route 22. CR22 became Broad Street as it passed through Littleton Commons, the village center. If he skulked down Blue Valley, he could hitch a ride on 22. Except who would be out this time of day? Neighbors. Littleton was a small town; his father had no doubt told everyone that his son the hero was due in on the 8:16 train from Heart's Wall. Of course, he could avoid 22 altogether and skirt around town to the train station. Except it was a good ten kilometers between the stump and the station and he was bone tired.

He decided to sit a little longer.

At least Ngonda had kept most of the upsiders out of Littleton.

He could imagine Penny and Kai Thousandfold and little Senator-for-Life Dowm spreading through his bewildered village to gawk at family pix and open closets and ask awkward questions. The High Gregory was all Spur had to worry about. He would be stepping off the hover ramp tomorrow morning at Spot Pond with the deputy. He would pose as Ngonda's nephew and the deputy would be Spur's comrade-in-arms from Iron Squad. The High Gregory would spend the day touring Littleton and making whatever luck he could. He would sleep at Spur's house and the day after tomorrow he and Ngonda would catch the 7:57 southbound.

"Spur?" called a familiar voice from up the trail. "Is that Prosper Leung?"

Spur wanted to blurt, "No, not me, not at all." He wanted to run away. Instead he said, "Hello, Sly." There were worse citizens he could have run into than Sly Sawatdee.

The big man lumbered down the path. He was wearing cut-off shorts, one leg of which was several centimeters longer than the other. His barrel belly stretched his shirt, which was unbuttoned to his navel. His floppy hat was two-toned: dirty and dirtier. He was carrying a basket filled with gooseberries. His smile was bright as noon.

"That is my Prosper, I swear. My lucky little pinecone, all safe. But you're supposed to be away at the fires. How did you get here, so far from nowhere?"

"Fell out of the sky."

Sly giggled like a little boy. "Go around that again." Sly was gray as an oak and almost as old as Spur's father, but his years had never seemed a burden to him. If the Transcendent State truly wanted its citizens simple, then Sly Sawatdee was the most civic-minded person in Hamilton County. "You're joking me, no?"

"All right then, I walked."

"Walked from where?"

Spur pointed west.

Sly turned, as if he expected to see that a highway had been miraculously cut through the forest. "Nothing that way but trees and then mountains and then a hell of a lot more trees. That's a truckload of walking, green log. You must be tired. Have a gooseberry?" He offered Spur the basket. When Sly harvested the wild fruit, he just broke whole canes off, instead of picking individual berries. Close work he left to his grandnephews at home.

"All right then," said Spur. "I'm not here. I'm on the train from Heart's Wall. I get in at 8:16."

"Yeah? Then who am I talking to, my own shaggy self? Watch the thorns."

Spur popped one of the striped pink berries into his mouth. It was still warm from the sun; his teeth crunched the tiny seeds. "You don't like any of my answers?" He slung his kit over his shoulder.

"I'll nibble almost anything, Spur, but I spit out what doesn't taste good." He pressed a stubby forefinger into Spur's chest. "Your Sly can tell when you're carrying a secret, happy old shoe. Ease the weight of it off your back and maybe I can help you with it."

"Let's walk." Spur set off down the trail. Ahead the trees parted for Blue Valley Road. "How's my father?"

"Well enough for an old man." Sly fell into step alongside him. "Which is to say not so much of what he was. Said you got burnt when Vic Joerly and those other poor boys got killed." He peered at Spur. "You don't look much burnt."

"I was in a hospital in Concord." They had reached Blue Valley Road, which was nothing more than a couple of dirt ruts separated by a scraggle of weeds. "An upsider doctor saved my life." Spur headed toward CR22. "They can do things you wouldn't believe."

"I'll believe it this very minute if you say so." His mouth twisted like he'd bit into a wormy apple. "Only I never had much use for upsiders."

"Why? Have you ever met one?"

"Not me, but my DiDa used to say how they poke holes in their own brains and cut arms and legs off to sew on parts of bots in their place. Now where's the sense in a good man turning bot?"

There was no arguing with Sly when he got to remembering things his long-suffering father had told him. "I'm guessing you buried Vic already?"

"His body came on the train last Wednesday. The funeral was Friday. Most the village was there, biggest communion in years and just about the saddest day."

"How's Comfort?"

"Hard to say." He grimaced. "I paid respects, didn't chitchat. But I heard around that she's digging herself quite a hole. Wouldn't take much for her to fall in." He turned away from Spur and picked a stone up off the road. "What about you two?"

"I don't want to talk about it."

"Yeah." He lobbed the stone into the woods. "That's what I heard."

They were coming up on the Bandaran farmstead, corn stalks nodding in the field nearest the road. Spur could hear the wooden

clunk of their windmill turning on the whispered breath of the afternoon. It was bringing water up from a well to splash into a dug pond
where ducks gabbled and cropped. He tried to keep Sly between
himself and the house as they passed, but whether he was noticed
or not, nobody called out to him.

The next farmstead belonged to the Sawatdees, where Sly lived
with his nephew Sunny and his family. On an impulse, Spur said,
"There is a secret."

"Yeah, I know. I'm old, but I still hear the mosquitoes buzz."

"The thing is, I'm going to need your help. And you can't tell
anyone."

Sly stepped in front of Spur and blocked his way. "Does anyone
know who sat on Gandy Star's cherry pie? The one that she baked
for your DiDa?"

Spur grinned. "I hope not."

He prodded Spur in the chest with his finger. "Did they ever
figure the boy who was with Leaf Benkleman the day she got drunk
on the applejack and threw up at the Solstice Day picnic?"

"It wasn't me." Spur put a hand on Sly's finger and pushed it
away. "I was with you fishing that afternoon."

"Yeah, the fish story." He stood aside and motioned for Spur to
pass. "Remember who told that one? The old citizen you always forget to come visit now that you're all grown up." They continued
down the road. The Sawatdee farmstead was just around the next
bend.

"I remember, Sly. Can you help? I need a ride home right now."

"The cottage or your DiDa's house?"

"Diligence Cottage."

He nodded. "Sunny can take you in the truck."

"No, it has to be you. You're going to be the only one who knows
I'm back. Part of the secret."

Sly swung the basket of gooseberries in wider arcs as he walked.
"Sunny doesn't want me driving at night anymore."

"Don't worry, you'll be back in plenty of time for supper. But
then I'll need you again in the morning. Come get me first thing.
I'm meeting someone up at Spot Pond."

"Spot Pond? Nobody there but frogs."

Spur leaned closer to Sly. "I can tell you, but you have to promise to help, no matter what." He lowered his voice. "This is a big
secret, Sly."

"How big?" Sly looked worried. "Bigger than a barn?"

"Bigger than the whole village." Spur knew Sly would be

pleased and flattered to be the only one in Littleton whom Spur had invited into his conspiracy. "In or out, my friend?"

"In up to here." Sly raised a hand over his head. "Ears open, mouth shut." He giggled.

"Good." Spur didn't give him time to reconsider. "An upsider is coming to visit Littleton."

"An upsider." Sly took this for another joke. "And he parks his spaceship where? On Broad Street?"

"A hover is going to put him off near Spot Pond. He's going to stay with me for a day. One day. Nobody is supposed to know he's from the upside."

"A hover." Sly glanced over one shoulder and then the other, as if he expected to spot the hover following them. "One of those bird-bots in our sky."

Spur nodded.

"And you want this?"

The question caught him off guard, because he realized that sometime in the last few hours he had changed his mind. "I do, Sly." Spur wanted to spend more time with the High Gregory and it was fine with him if they were together at Diligence Cottage. He just didn't want to inflict the upsider on the rest of his sleepy village. They wouldn't understand.

Except Sly was shaking his head. "Nothing good ever came of getting tangled up with space people."

"I'm just curious is all," said Spur.

"Curious can't sit still, young sprout. Curious always goes for the closer look." For the first time since Spur had known him, Sly Sawatdee looked his age. "And now I'm thinking what will happen to your DiDa when you leave us. He's a good man, you know. I've known him all my life."

Nine

For when man migrates, he carries with him not only his birds, quadrupeds, insects, vegetables and his very sward, but his orchard also.

—Wild Apples, 1862

Capability Roger Leung loved apples. He was fond of the other pomes as well, especially pears and quince. Stone fruits he didn't much care for, although he tolerated sour cherries in memory of GiGa's pies. But apples were Cape's favorite, the ancient fruit of the home world. He claimed that apples graced the tables of all of Earth's great civilizations: Roman, Islamic, American, and Dalamist. Some people in Littleton thought that Spur's father loved his apple trees more than he loved his family. Probably Spur's mother, Lucy Bliss Leung, had been one of these. Probably that was why she left him when Spur was three, first to move to Heart's Wall and then clear across the continent to Providence. Spur never got the chance to ask her because he never saw her again after she moved to Southwest. The citizens of Walden did not travel for mere pleasure.

Spur's grandparents had arrived on Walden penniless and with only a basic knowledge of farming. Yet hard work and brutal frugality had built their farmstead into a success. However, the price they paid for single-minded dedication to farming was high; of their three children, only Cape chose to stay on the farm as an adult. And even he moved out of Diligence Cottage when he was sixteen and put up a hut for himself at the farthest edge of the Leung property. He was trying to escape their disapproval. Whenever he looked at the tell or visited friends or climbed a tree to read a book, GiGo or GiGa would carp at him for being frivolous or lazy. They couldn't see the sense of volunteering for the fire department or playing left base for the Littleton Eagles when there were chores to be done. Sometimes weeks might pass without Cape saying an unnecessary word to his parents.

Yet it had been Cape who transformed the family fortunes with his apples. When he was eighteen, he began attending classes at the hortischool extension in Longwalk, very much against GiGo's wishes. He had paid tuition out of money earned doing odd jobs around the village—another pointless diversion from home chores that irritated his parents. Cape had become interested in fruit trees after brown rot spoiled almost the entire crop of Littleton's sour cherries the year before. All the farmers in the village raised fruit, but their orchards were usually no more than a dozen trees, all of traditional heirloom varieties. Crops were small, usually just enough for home use because of the ravages of pests and disease. Farmers battled Terran immigrants like tarnished plant bugs, sawflies, wooly aphids, coddling moths, leafrollers, lesser apple worms, and the arch enemy: plum curculio. There were mildews, rusts, rots, cankers, blotches, and blights to contend with as well. The long growing season of fruit trees made them vulnerable to successive attacks. Citizens across the Transcendent State debated whether or not Chairman Winter had introduced insect evil and fungal disease into his new Garden of Eden on purpose. The question had never been settled. But at hortischool, Cape learned about neem spray, extracted from the chinaberry tree and the organic insecticide pyrethrum, which was made from dried daisies. And he heard about an amazing cider apple called Huang's Nectar, a disease-resistant early bloomer, well-suited to the climate of Southeast but not yet proven hardy in the north. As much to spite his father as to test the new variety, he had drained his savings and bought a dozen saplings on w4 semi-dwarfing rootstock. He started his own orchard on land he had cleared near his hut. Two years later, he brought in his first—admittedly light—harvest, which nevertheless yielded the sweetest cider and smoothest applejack anyone in Littleton had ever tasted. Cape purchased a handscrew press in his third year and switched from fermenting his cider in glass carboys to huge oak barrels by his fifth. And he bought more apple trees—he never seemed to have enough: McIntosh, GoRed, Jay's Pippin, Alumar Gold, Adam and Eve. Soon he began to grow rootstock and sell trees to other farmers. By the time Cape married Spur's mother, the Leungs were renting land from farmsteads on either side of their original holding. GiGo and GiGa lived long enough to see their son become the most prosperous farmer in Littleton. GiGo, however, never forgave himself for being wrong, or Cape for being right, about the apples.

Cape had given Spur and Comfort his parents' house as a wedding present; Diligence Cottage had been empty ever since GiGa had died. Cape had long since transformed his own little hut into one of the grandest homes in Littleton. Spur had Sly drop him off just down Jane Powder Street from the cottage, hoping to avoid the big house and the inevitable interrogation by his father for as long as possible. After seeing Sly's dismay at the news of the High Gregory's visit, he was thinking he might try to keep the High Gregory's identity from Cape, if he could.

However, as Spur approached the front door, he spotted Cape's scooter parked by the barn and then Cape himself reaching from a ladder into the scaffold branches of one of GiGo's ancient Macoun apples. He was thinning the fruit set. This was twice a surprise: first, because Cape usually avoided the house where he had grown up, and second, because he had been set against trying to rejuvenate the Leungs' original orchard, arguing that it was a waste of Spur's time. In fact the peaches and the plum tree had proved beyond saving. However, through drastic pruning, Spur had managed to bring three Macouns and one Sunset apple, and a Northstar cherry back into production again.

"DiDa!" Spur called out so that he wouldn't startle his father. "It's me."

"Prosper?" Cape did not look down as he twisted an unripe apple free. "You're here already. Something's wrong?" He dropped the cull to the pack of gosdogs waiting below. A female leapt and caught the apple in midair in its long beak. It chomped twice and swallowed. Then it chased its scaly tale in delight, while the others hooted at Cape.

"Everything's fine. There was a last minute change and I managed to get a ride home." Spur doubted his father would be satisfied with this vague explanation, but it was worth a try. "What are you doing up there?" He dropped his kit on the front step of the farmhouse and trudged over to the orchard. "I thought you hated GiGo's useless old trees."

Cape sniffed. "Macoun is a decent enough apple; they're just too damn much work. And since you weren't around to tend to them—but I should come down. You're home, Prosper. Wait, I'll come down."

"No, finish what you're doing. How are things here?"

"It was a dry spring." He culled another green apple, careful to grasp the fruiting spur with one hand and the fruit with the other. "June was parched too, but the county won't call it a drought yet." The gosdogs swirled and tumbled beneath him as he let the apple fall. "The June drop was light, so I've had to do a lot of thinning. We had sawfly but the curculio isn't so bad. They let you out of the hospital so soon, Prosper? Tell me what you're not telling me."

"I'm fine. Ready to build fence and buck firewood."

"Have you seen Comfort yet?"

"No."

"You were supposed to arrive by train."

"I hitched a ride with a friend."

"From Concord?"

"I got off the train in Wheelwright."

"Wheelwright." One of the gosdogs was trying to scrabble up the ladder. "I don't know where that is exactly. Somewhere in Southeast, I think. Lee County maybe?"

"Around there. What's wrong with Macouns?"

"Ah." He shook his head in disapproval. "A foolish tree that doesn't know what's good for it." He gestured at the immature apples all around him. "Look at the size of this fruit set. Even after the June drop, there are too many apples left on the branches. Grow more than a few of these trees and you'll spend the summer hand-thinning. Have you seen Comfort yet?"

"I already said no." Spur plucked a low-hanging cherry, which held its green stem, indicating it wasn't quite ripe; despite this, he popped it into his mouth. "Sour cherries aren't too far from harvest, I'd say." He spat the pit at the gosdogs. "They're pulling the entire regiment back to Cloyce Forest, which is where I'll catch up with them."

"Civic refreshment—you'll be busy." Cape wound up and pitched a cull into the next row of trees. As the pack hurtled after it, he backed down the ladder. "Although I wouldn't mind some help. You're home for how long?"

"Just the week."

He hefted the ladder and pivoted it into the next tree. "Not much time."

"No."

He was about to climb up again when he realized that he had yet to greet his only son. "I'm glad you're safe, Prosper," he said, placing a hand on his shoulder. "But I still don't understand about the train." He held Spur at arm's length. "You got off why?"

Spur was desperate to change the subject. "DiDa, I know you don't want to hear this but Comfort and I are probably going to get divorced."

Cape grimaced and let go of Spur. "Probably?" He set his foot on the bottom rung.

"Yes." The gosdogs were back already, swarming around the ladder, downy feathers flying. "I'm sorry." Spur stepped away.

"Prosper, you know my feelings about this." He mounted the ladder. "But then everyone knows I'm a simple fool when it comes to keeping a woman."

Cape Leung had been saying things like that ever since Spur's mother left him. On some days he bemoaned the failure of his marriage as a wound that had crippled him for life, on others he preened as if surviving it were his one true distinction. As a young man, Spur had thought these were merely poses and had resented his father for keeping his feelings about Spur's mother in a tangle. Now, Spur thought maybe he understood.

"Comfort was never comfortable here," Spur said morosely. "I blame myself for that. But I don't think she was born to be a farmer's wife. Never was, never will be."

"Are you sure?" Cape sucked air between his teeth as he leaned into the tree. "She's had a terrible shock, Prosper. Now this?"

"It isn't going to come as a shock," he said, his voice tight. His father had far too many reasons for wanting Spur to make his marriage work. He had always liked both of the Joerly kids and had loved the way Comfort had remade both Diligence Cottage and his only son. Cape was impatient for grandchildren. And then there was the matter of the land, once agreeably complicated, now horribly simple. Ever since they had been kids, it had been a running joke around the village that someday Spur would marry Comfort and unite the Joerly farmstead with the Leung holdings, immediately adjacent to the east. Of course, everyone knew it wouldn't happen quite that way, because of Vic. But now Vic was dead.

"When will you see her?"

"I don't know," said Spur. "Soon. Anyway, it's been a long day for me. I'm going in."

"Come back to the house for supper?" said Cape.

"No, I'm too tired. I'll scrape up something to eat in the cottage."

"You won't have to look too hard." He grinned. "Your fans stopped by this morning to open the place up. I'm sure they left some goodies. I've been telling the neighbors that you were due home today." He dropped another cull to the gosdogs. "Now that I think about it, I should probably ride into town to tell folks not to meet your train. I still can't believe you got a ride all the way from . . . where did you say it was again?"

"What fans?"

"I think it must have been Gandy Joy who organized it; at least she was the one who came to the house to ask my permission." He stepped off the ladder into the tree to reach the highest branches. "But I saw the Velez girls waiting in the van, Peace Toba, Summer Millisap." He stretched for a particularly dense cluster of apples. "Oh, and after they left, I think Comfort might have stopped by the cottage."

Ten

I find it wholesome to be alone the greater part of the time. To be in company, even with the best, is soon wearisome and dissipating.

–Walden

The refrigerator was stocked with a chicken and parsnip casserole, a pot of barley soup, half a dozen eggs, a little tub of butter, a slab of goat cheese, and three bottles of root beer. There was a loaf of fresh onion rye bread and glass jars of homemade apricot and pear preserves on the counter. But what Spur ate for supper was pie. Someone had baked him two pies, a peach and an apple. He ate half of each, and washed them down with root beer. Why not? There was nobody around to scold him and he was too tired to heat up the soup or the casserole, much less to eat it. Eating pie took no effort at all. Besides, he hadn't had a decent slice of pie since he had left Littleton. The niceties of baking were beyond the field kitchens of the Corps of Firefighters.

Afterward he poured himself a tumbler of applejack and sat at the kitchen table, trying to decide who had brought what. The barley soup felt like an offering from sturdy Peace Toba. Gandy Joy knew he had a developed a secret weakness for root beer, despite growing up in a farmstead that lived and died by cider. The Millisaps had the largest herd of goats in town. He wasn't sure who had made the casserole, although he would have bet it wasn't the Velez sisters. Casseroles were too matronly for the Velezes. They were in their early twenties and single and a little wild—at least by Littleton's standards. They had to be, since they were searching for romance in a village of just over six hundred souls. Everyone said that they would probably move to Longwalk someday, or even to Heart's Wall, which would break their parents' hearts. He was guessing that the pies had come from their kitchen. A well-made pie was as good as a love letter. But would the Velez sisters just assume he and Comfort were finally going to split? Comfort must have decided on her own and was telling people in the village. Then Spur remembered that Sly had said he had heard something. And if Sly knew, then everyone knew. In a nosy village like Littleton, if a kid skinned his knee playing baseball, at least three moms fell out of trees waving bandages.

Spur put the food away and washed the dishes, after which there was no reason to stay in the kitchen. But he lingered for a while, trying to avoid the memories which whispered to him from the other rooms of the cottage. He remembered his stern grandparents ghosting around the wood stove in their last years. He remembered boarding Diligence Cottage up after GiGo died, the lumpy furniture and the threadbare carpet receding into the gloom. And then he and Comfort pulling the boards down and rediscovering their new home. The newlyweds had moved almost all of GiGo and GiGa's things to the barn, where they moldered to this day. Spur and Comfort had dusted and cleaned and scraped and painted everything in the empty cottage. He remembered sitting on the floor with his back to the wall of the parlor, looking at the one lonely chair they owned. Comfort had cuddled beside him, because she said that if there wasn't room for both of them on the chair then neither would sit. He had kissed her then. There had been a lot of kissing in those days. In fact, Comfort had made love to him in every room of the cottage. It was her way of declaring ownership and of exorcising the disapproving spirits of the old folks.

Now that she was about to pass out of his life, Spur thought that Comfort might have been too ferocious a lover for his tastes. Sometimes it was all he could do to stay with her in bed. Occasionally her passion alarmed him, although he would never have admitted this to himself while they were together. It would have been unmanly. But just before he had volunteered for the Corps, when things had already begun to go wrong, he had felt as if there was always another man standing next them, watching. Not anyone real, but rather Comfort's idea of a lover. Spur knew by then he wasn't that man. He had just been a placeholder for whoever it was she was waiting for.

Finally he left the kitchen. The women who had opened Diligence Cottage had done their best, but there was no air to work with on this close July night. The rooms were stale and hot. He sat out on the porch until the needlebugs drove him inside. Then he propped a fan in either window of the bedroom and dumped his kit out onto the bedspread. What did he have to wear that was cool? He picked up a T-shirt but then smelled the tang of smoke still clinging to it. He dropped it onto the bed and chuckled mirthlessly. He was home; he could put on his own clothes. He opened the dresser drawer and pulled out the shorts that Comfort had bought for his birthday and a gauzy blue shirt. The pants were loose and slid down his hips. He had lost weight in the firefight and even more in the hospital. Too much heartbreak. Not enough pie.

Then, against his better judgment, he crossed the bedroom to Comfort's dresser and began to open drawers. He had never understood why she abandoned everything she owned when she left him. Did it mean that she was planning to come back? Or that she was completely rejecting their life together? He didn't touch anything, just looked at her panties, black and navy blue and gray—no pastels or patterns for his girl. Then the balled socks, sleeveless blouses, shirts with the arms folded behind them, heavy workpants, light-weight sweaters. And in the bottom drawer the jade pajamas of black-market material so sheer that it would slip from her body if he even thought about tugging at it.

"Not exactly something a farmer's wife would wear." Spur spoke aloud just to hear a voice; the dense silence of the cottage was making him edgy. "At least, not this farmer's wife."

Now that he was losing Comfort, Spur realized that the only person in his family was his father. It struck him that he had no memories of his father in the cottage. He could see Cape in the dining room of the big house or the library or dozing in front of the tell. Alone, always alone.

Spur had a bad moment then. He stepped into the bathroom, and splashed some cold water on his face. He would have to remarry or he would end up like his father. He tried to imagine kissing Bell Velez, slipping a hand under her blouse, but he couldn't.

"Knock, knock." A woman called from the parlor. "Your father claims you're back." It was Gandy Joy.

"Just a minute." Spur swiped at his dripping face with the hand towel. As he strode from the bedroom, the smile on his face was genuine. He was grateful to Gandy Joy for rescuing him from the silence and his dark mood.

She was a small, round woman with flyaway hair that was eight different shades of gray. She had big teeth and an easy smile. Her green sundress exposed the wrinkled skin of her wide shoulders and arms; despite farm work she was still as fair as the flesh of an apple. Spur had been mothered by many of the women of Littleton as a boy, but Gandy Joy was the one who meant the most to him. He had to stoop over slightly to hug her.

"Prosper." She squeezed him so hard it took his breath away. "My lovely boy, you're safe."

"Thank you for opening the cottage," he said. "But how did you find everything?" She smelled like lilacs and he realized that she must have perfumed herself just for him.

"Small house." She stepped back to take him in. "Not many places a thing can be."

Spur studied her as well; she seemed to have aged five years in the ten months since he'd seen her last. "Big enough, especially for one."

"I'm sorry, Prosper."

When Spur saw the sadness shadow her face, he knew that she had heard something. She was, after all, the village virtuator. He supposed he should have been relieved that Comfort was letting everyone know she wanted a divorce, since that was what he wanted too. Instead he just felt hollow. "What has she told you?"

Gandy Joy just shook her head. "You two have to talk."

He thought about pressing her, but decided to let it drop. "Have a seat, Gandy. Can I get you anything? There's applejack." He steered her toward the sofa. "And root beer."

"No thanks." She nodded at her wooden-bead purse, which he now noticed against the bolster of the sofa. "I brought communion."

"Really?" he said, feigning disappointment. "Then you're only here on business?"

"I'm here for more reasons than you'll ever know." She gave him a playful tap on the arm. "And keeping souls in communion is my calling, lovely boy, not my business." She settled on the sofa next to her purse and he sat facing her on the oak chair that had once been his only stick of furniture.

"How long are you with us?" She pulled out three incense burners and set them on the cherry wood table that Comfort had ordered all the way from Providence.

"A week." Spur had seen Candy Joy's collection of incense burners, but he had never known her to use three at once for just two people. "I'll catch up with the squad in Cloyce Forest. Easy work for a change; just watching the trees grow." He considered three excessive; after all, he had accepted communion regularly with the other firefighters.

"We weren't expecting you so soon." She slipped the aluminum case marked with the seal of the Transcendent State from her purse. "You didn't come on the train."

"No."

She selected a communion square from the case. She touched it to her forehead, the tip of her nose and her lips and then placed it on edge in the incense burner. She glanced up at him and still the silence stretched. "Just no?" she said finally. "That's all?"

Spur handed her the crock of matches kept especially for communion. "My father told you to ask, didn't he?"

"I'm old, Prosper." Her smile was crooked. "I've earned the right to be curious." She repeated the ritual with the second communion square.

"You have. But he really wants to know."

"He always does." She set the third communion in its burner. "But then everybody understands about that particular bend in Capability's soul." She selected a match from the crock and struck it.

Now it was Spur's turn to wait. "So aren't you going to ask me about the train?"

"I was, but since you have something to hide, I won't." She touched the fire to each of the three squares and they caught immediately, the oils in the communion burning with an eager yellow flame. "I don't really care, Spur. I'm just happy that you're back and safe." She blew the flames out on each of the squares, leaving a glowing edge. "Make the most of your time with us."

Spur watched the communion smoke uncoil in the still air of his parlor. Then, as much to please Gandy Joy as to re-establish his connection with his village, he leaned forward and breathed deeply. The fumes that filled his nose were harsh at first, but wispier and so much sweeter than the strangling smoke of a burn. As he settled back into his chair, he got the subtle accents: the yeasty aroma of bread baking, a whiff of freshly split oak and just a hint of the sunshine scent of a shirt fresh off the clothesline. He could feel the communion smoke fill his head and touch his soul. It bound him as always to the precious land and the cottage where his family had made a new life, the orderly Leung farmstead, his home town, and of course to this woman who loved him more than his mother ever had and his flinty father who couldn't help the way he was and faithful Sly Sawatdee and generous Leaf Benkleman and droll Will Sambusa and steadfast Peace Toba and the entire Velez family who had always been so generous to him and yes, even his dear Comfort Rose Joerly, who was leaving him but who was nonetheless a virtuous citizen of Littleton.

He shivered when he noticed Gandy Joy watching him. No doubt she was trying to gauge whether he had fully accepted communion. "Thank you," he said, "for all the food."

She nodded, satisfied. "You're welcome. We just wanted to show how proud we are of you. This is your village, after all, and you're our Prosper and we want you to stay with us always."

He chuckled nervously. Why did everyone think he was going somewhere?

She leaned forward, and lowered her voice. "But I have to say there was more than a little competition going on over the cooking." She chuckled. "Bets were placed on which dish you'd eat first."

"Bets?" Spur found the idea of half a dozen women competing to please him quite agreeable. "And what did you choose?"

"After I saw everything laid out, I was thinking that you'd start in on pie. After all, there wasn't going to be anyone to tell you no."

Spur laughed. "Pie was all I ate. But don't tell anyone."

She tapped her forefinger to her lips and grinned.

"So I'm guessing that the Velez girls made the pies?"

"There was just the one—an apple, I think is what Bell said."

"I found two on the counter: apple and a peach."

"Really?" Gandy sat back on the couch. "Someone else must have dropped it off after we left."

"Might have been Comfort," said Spur. "DiDa said he thought she stopped by. I was expecting to find a note."

"Comfort was here?"

"She lives here," said Spur testily. "At least, all her stuff is here."

Gandy took a deep breath over the incense burners and held it in for several moments. "I'm worried about her," she said finally. "She hasn't accepted communion since we heard about Vic. She keeps to herself and when we go to visit her at home, she's as friendly as a brick. There's mourning and then there's self-pity, Prosper. She's been talking about selling the farmstead, moving away. We've lost poor Victor, we don't want to lose her too. Littleton wouldn't be the same without the Joerlys. When you see her, whatever you two decide, make sure she knows that."

Spur almost groaned then, but the communion had him in its benevolent grip. If citizens didn't help one another, there would be no Transcendent State. "I'll do my best," he said, his voice tight.

"Oh, I know you will, my lovely boy. I know it in my soul."

Eleven

Things do not change; we change.
—Journal, 1850

The High Gregory sat next to Spur in the bed of the Sawatdees' truck, their backs against the cab, watching the dust billow behind them. Sly and Ngonda rode up front. As the truck jolted down Blue Valley Road, Spur could not help but see the excitement on the High Gregory's face. The dirt track was certainly rough, but the boy was bouncing so high Spur was worried that he'd fly over the side. He was even making Sly nervous, and the old farmer was usually as calm as moss. But then Sly Sawatdee didn't make a habit of giving rides to upsiders. He kept glancing over his shoulder at the High Gregory through the open rear slider.

Spur had no doubt that his cover story for the High Gregory and Ngonda was about to unravel. The High Gregory had decided to wear purple overalls with about twenty brass buttons. Although there was nothing wrong with his black T-shirt, the bandana knotted around his neck was a pink disaster embellished with cartoons of beets and carrots and corn on the cob. At least he had used some upsider trick to disguise the color of his eyes. Ngonda's clothes weren't quite as odd, but they too were a problem. Spur had seen citizens wearing flair jackets and high-collar shirts—but not on a hot, summer Sunday and not in Littleton. Ngonda was dressed for a meeting at the Cooperative's Office of Diplomacy in Concord. Spur's only hope was to whisk them both to Diligence Cottage and either hide them there or find them something more appropriate to wear.

"Tell me about the gosdogs," said the High Gregory.

Spur leaned closer, trying to hear him over the roar of the truck's engine, the clatter of its suspension, and the crunch of tires against the dirt road. "Say again?"

"The gosdogs," shouted the High Gregory. "One of your native species. You know, four-footed, feathered, they run in packs."

"Gosdogs, yes. What do you want to know?"

"You eat them."

"I don't." The High Gregory seemed to be waiting for him to elaborate, but Spur wasn't sure what he wanted to know exactly. "Other citizens do, but the browns only. The other breeds are supposed to be too stringy."

"And when you kill them, do they know they're about to die? How do you do it?"

"I don't." Spur had never slaughtered a gosdog; Cape didn't believe in eating them. However, Spur had slaughtered chickens and goats and helped once with a bull. Butchering was one of the unpleasant chores that needed doing on a farm, like digging post-holes or mucking out the barn. "They don't suffer."

"Really? That's good to know." The High Gregory did not look convinced. "How smart do you think they are?"

At that moment Sly stepped on the brakes and swung the steering wheel; the truck bumped onto the smooth pavement of Civic Route 22.

"Not very," said Spur. With the road noise abating, his voice carried into the cab.

"Not very what?" said Constant Ngonda.

The High Gregory propped himself up to speak through the open window. "I was asking Spur how smart the gosdogs are. I couldn't find much about them, considering. Why is that, do you suppose?"

"The ComExplore Survey Team rated them just 6.4 on the Peekay Animal Intelligence Scale," said Ngonda. "A goat has more brains."

"Yes, I found that," said the High Gregory, "but what's interesting is that the first evaluation was the only one ever done. And it would have been very much in the company's interests to test them low, right? And of course it made no sense for your pukpuks to bother with a follow-up test. And now your Transcendent State has a stake in keeping that rating as it is."

"Are you suggesting some kind of conspiracy?" Ngonda was working his way to a fine outrage. "That we're deliberately abusing an intelligent species?"

"I'm just asking questions, friend Constant. And no, I'm not saying they're as smart as humans, no, no, never. But suppose they were retested and their intelligence was found to be . . . let's say 8.3. Or even 8.1. The Thousand Worlds might want to see them protected."

"Protected?" The deputy's voice snapped through the window.

"Why, don't you think that would be a good idea? You'd just have to round them up and move them to a park or something. Let them loose in their native habitat."

"There is no native habitat left on Walden." Spur noticed that Sly was so intent on the conversation that he was coasting down the highway. "Except maybe underwater." A westbound oil truck was catching up to them fast.

"We could build one then," said the High Gregory cheerfully. "The L'ung could raise the money. They need something to do."

"Can I ask you something?" Ngonda had passed outrage and was well on his way to fury.

"Yes, friend Constant. Of course."

"How old are you?"

"Twelve standard. My birthday is next month. I don't want a big party this year. It's too much work."

"They know themselves in the mirror," said Sly.

"What?" Ngonda was distracted from whatever point he was about to make. "What did you just say?"

"When one of them looks at his reflection, he recognizes himself." Sly leaned back toward the window as he spoke. "We had this brood, a mother and three pups, who stayed indoors with us last winter. They were house-trained, mostly." The truck slowed to a crawl. "So my granddaughter Brookie is playing dress-up with the pups one night and the silly little pumpkin decides to paint one all over with grape juice. Said she was trying to make the first purple gosdog—her father babies her, don't you know? But she actually stains the right rear leg before her mother catches her out. And when Brookie lets the poor thing loose, it galumphs to the mirror and backs up to see its grapy leg. Then it gets to whimpering and clucking and turning circles like they do when they're upset." Sly checked the rearview mirror and noticed the oil truck closing in on them for the first time. "I was there, saw it clear as tap water. The idea that it knew who it was tipped me over for a couple of days." He put two wheels onto the shoulder of CR22 and waved the truck past. "It's been a hardship, but I've never eaten a scrap of gosdog since."

"That's the most ridiculous thing I've ever heard," said Ngonda.

"Lots of citizens feel that way," said Spur.

"As is their right. But to jump to conclusions based on this man's observations. . . ."

"I don't want to jump, friend Constant," said the High Gregory. "Let's not jump."

Although the deputy was ready to press his argument, nobody else spoke and gradually he subsided. Sly pulled back onto CR22 and drove the rest of the way at a normal pace. They passed the rest of the trip in silence; the wind seemed to whip Spur's thoughts right out of his head.

As they turned off Jane Powder Street onto the driveway of the cottage, Sly called back to him. "Looks like you've got company."

Spur rubbed the back of his neck in frustration. Who told the townsfolk that he wanted them to come visiting? He leaned over the side of the truck but couldn't see anyone until they parked next to the porch. Then he spotted the scooter leaning against the barn.

If it was really in the High Gregory's power to make luck, then what he was brewing up for Spur so far was pure misfortune. It was Comfort's scooter.

The High Gregory stood up in the back of the truck and turned around once, surveying the farmstead. "This is your home, Spur." He said it not as a question but as a statement, as if Spur were the one seeing it for the first time. "I understand now why you would want to live so far from everything. It's like a poem here."

Constant Ngonda opened the door and stepped down onto the dusty drive. From his expression, the deputy appeared to have formed a different opinion of the cottage. However, he was enough of a diplomat to keep it to himself. He clutched a holdall to his chest and was mounting the stairs to the porch when he noticed that no one else had moved from the truck.

They were watching Comfort stalk toward them from the barn, so clearly in a temper that heat seemed to shimmer off her in the morning swelter.

"That woman looks angry as lightning," said Sly. "You want me to try to get in her way?"

"No," said Spur. "She'd probably just knock you over."

"But this is your Comfort?" said the High Gregory. "The wife that you don't live with anymore. This is so exciting, just what I was hoping for. She's come for a visit—maybe to welcome you back?"

"I'm not expecting much of a welcome," said Spur. "If you'll excuse me, I should talk to her. Sly, if you wouldn't mind staying a few minutes, maybe you could take Constant and young Lucky here inside. There's plenty to eat."

"Lucky," said the High Gregory, repeating the name they had agreed on for him, as if reminding himself to get into character. "Hello, friend Comfort," he called. "I'm Lucky. Lucky Ngonda."

She shook the greeting off and kept bearing down on them. His wife was a slight woman, with fine features and eyes dark as currants. Her hair was long and sleek and black. She was wearing a sleeveless, yellow gingham dress that Spur had never seen before. Part of her new wardrobe, he thought, her new life. When he had been in love with her, Spur had thought that Comfort was pretty. But now, seeing her for the first time in months, he decided that she was merely delicate. She did not look strong enough for the rigors of life on a farm.

Spur opened the tailgate and the High Gregory jumped from the back of the truck. Ngonda came back down the stairs to be introduced to Comfort. Spur was handing the High Gregory's bag down to Sly as she drew herself up in front of them.

"Gandy Joy said you wanted to see me first thing in the morning." She did not waste time on introductions. "I didn't realize that I'd be interrupting a party."

"Comfort," said Spur, "I'm sorry." He stopped himself then, chagrined at how easily he fell into the old pattern. When they were together, he was always apologizing.

"Morning, sweet corn," said Sly. "Not that much of a party, I'm afraid."

"But there are snacks inside," the High Gregory said. "This is such a beautiful place you two have. I've just met Spur myself, but I'm pretty sure he's going to be happy here someday. My name is Lucky Ngonda." He held out his hand to her. "We're supposed to shake but first you have to say your name."

Comfort had been so fixated on Spur that she had brushed by the High Gregory. Now she scrutinized him in all his purple glory and her eyes went wide. "Why are you dressed like that?"

"Is something wrong?" He glanced down at his overalls. "I'm dressed to visit my friend Spur." He patted his bare head. "It's the hat, isn't it? I'm supposed to be wearing a hat."

"Constant Ngonda, a friend of Spur's from the Ninth." Ngonda oozed between them. "I apologize for intruding; I know you have some important things to discuss. Why don't we give you a chance to catch up now. My nephew and I will be glad to wait inside." He put an arm around the High Gregory's shoulder and aimed him at the porch.

"Wait," said the High Gregory. "I thought I was your cousin."

"Take as long as you want, Spur," Ngonda said as he hustled the boy off. "We'll be fine."

Sly shook his head in disbelief. "I'll make sure they don't get into trouble." He started after them.

"There are pies in the refrigerator," Spur called after him. "Most of an apple pie and just a couple slices of a peach." He steeled himself and turned back to Comfort. "My father said you were here the other day." He aimed a smile at her but it bounced off. "You made my favorite pie."

"Who are those people?" Her eyes glittered with suspicion. "The boy is strange. Why have you brought them here?"

"Let's walk." He took her arm and was surprised when she went along without protest. He felt the heat of her glare cooling as they strode away from the cottage. "I did have a chat with Gandy Joy," he said. "She said you were feeling pretty low."

"I have the right to feel however I feel," she said stiffly.

"You haven't been accepting communion."

"Communion is what they give you so you feel smart about acting stupid. Tell her that I don't need some busybody blowing smoke in my eyes to keep me from seeing what's wrong." She stopped and pulled him around to face her. "We're getting divorced, Spur."

"Yes," He held her gaze. "I know." He wanted to hug her or maybe shake her. Touch her long, black hair. Instead his hands hung uselessly by his sides. "But I'm still concerned about you."

"Why?"

"You've been talking about moving away."

She turned and started walking again. "I can't run a farm by myself."

"We could help you, DiDa and I." He caught up with her. "Hire some of the local kids. Maybe bring in a tenant from another village."

"And how long do you think that would work for? If you want to run my farm, Spur, buy it from me."

"Your family is an important part of this place. The whole village wants you to stay. Everyone would pitch in."

She chuckled grimly. "Everyone wanted us to get married. They want us to stay together. I'm tired of having everyone in my life."

He wasn't going to admit to her that he felt the same way sometimes. "Where will you go?"

"Away."

"Just away?"

"I miss him, I really do. But I don't want to live anywhere near Vic's grave."

Spur kicked a stone across the driveway and said nothing for several moments. "You're sure it's not me you want to get away from?"

"No, Spur. That's one thing I am sure of."

"When did you decide all this?"

"Spur, I'm not mad at you." Impulsively, she went up on tiptoes and aimed a kiss at the side of his face. She got mostly air, but their cheeks brushed, her skin hot against his. "I like you, especially when you're like this, so calm and thoughtful. You're the best of this lot and you've always been sweet to me. It's just that I can't live like this anymore."

"I like you too, Comfort. Last night, after I accepted communion—"

"Enough. We like each other. We should stop there, it's a good place to be." She bumped up against him. "Now tell me about that boy. He isn't an upsider, is he?"

She shot him a challenging look and he tried to bear up under the pressure of her regard. They walked in silence while he decided what he could say about Ngonda and the High Gregory. "Can you keep a secret?"

She sighed. "You know you're going to tell me, so get to it."

They had completely circled the cottage. Spur spotted the High Gregory watching them from a window. He turned Comfort toward the barn. "Two days ago, when I was still in the hospital, I started sending greetings to the upside." He waved off her objections. "Don't ask, I don't know why exactly, other than that I was bored. Anyway, the boy answered one of them. He's the High Gregory of the L'ung, Phosphorescence of something or other, I forget what. He's from Kenning in the Theta Persei system and I'm guessing he's pretty important, because the next thing I knew, he qiced himself to Walden and had me pulled off a train."

He told her about the hover and Memsen and the kids of the L'ung and how he was being forced to show the High Gregory his village. "Oh, and he supposedly makes luck."

"What does that mean?" said Comfort. "How does somebody make luck?"

"I don't know exactly. But Memsen and the L'ung are all convinced that he does it, whatever it is."

They had wandered into GiGa's flower garden. Comfort had tried to make it her own after they had moved in. However, she'd had neither the time nor the patience to tend persnickety plants and so grew only daylilies and hostas and rugose roses. After a season of neglect, even these tough flowers were losing ground to the bindweed and quackgrass and spurge.

Spur sat on the fieldstone bench that his grandfather had built for his grandmother. He tapped on the seat for her to join him. She hesitated then settled at the far end, twisting to face him.

"He acts too stupid to be anyone important," she said. "What about that slip he made about being the cousin and not the nephew. Are the people on his world idiots?"

"Maybe he intended to say it." Spur leaned forward and pulled a flat clump of spurge from the garden. "After all, he's wearing those purple overalls; he's really not trying very hard to pretend he's a citizen." He knocked the dirt off the roots and left it to shrivel in the sun. "What if he wanted me to tell you who he was and decided to make it happen? I think he's used to getting his own way."

"So what does he want with us?" Her expression was unreadable.

"I'm not sure. I think what Memsen was telling me is that he has come here to see how his being here changes us." He shook his head. "Does that make any sense?"

"It doesn't have to," she said. "He's from the upside. They don't think the same way we do."

"Maybe so." It was a commonplace that had been drilled into them in every self-reliance class they had ever sat through. It was, after all, the reason that Chairman Winter had founded Walden. But now that he had actually met upsiders—Memsen and the High Gregory and the L'ung—he wasn't sure that their ways were so strange. But this wasn't the time to argue the point. "Look, Comfort, I have my own reason for telling you all this," he said. "I need help with him. At first I thought he was just going to pretend to be one of us and take a quiet look at the village. Now I'm thinking he wants to be discovered so he can make things happen. So I'm going to try to keep him busy here if I can. It's just for one day; he said he'd leave in the morning."

"And you believe that?"

"I'd like to." He dug at the base of a dandelion with his fingers and pried it out of the ground with the long taproot intact. "What other choice do I have?" He glanced back at the cottage but couldn't see the High Gregory in the window anymore. "We'd better get back."

She put a hand on his arm. "First we have to talk about Vic."

Spur paused, considering. "We can do that if you want." He studied the dandelion root as if it held the answers to all his problems. "We probably should. But it's hard, Comfort. When I was in the hospital the upsiders did something to me. A kind of treatment that . . ."

She squeezed his arm and then let go. "There's just one thing I have to know. You were with him at the end. At least, that's what we heard. You reported his death."

"It was quick," said Spur. "He didn't suffer." This was a lie he had been preparing to tell her ever since he had woken up in the hospital.

"That's good. I'm glad." She swallowed. "Thank you. But did he say anything? At the end, I mean."

"Say? Say what?"

"You have to understand that after I moved back home, I found that Vic had changed. I was shocked when he volunteered for the Corps because he was actually thinking of leaving Littleton. Maybe Walden too. He talked a lot about going to the upside." She clutched her arms to her chest so tightly that she seemed to shrink. "He didn't believe—you can't tell anyone about this. Promise?"

Spur shut his eyes and nodded. He knew what she was going to say. How could he not? Nevertheless, he dreaded hearing it.

Her voice shrank as well. "He had sympathy for the pukpuks. Not for the burning, but he used to say that we didn't need to cover every last scrap of Walden with forest. He talked about respecting . . ."

Without warning, the nightmare leapt from some darkness in his soul like some ravening predator. It chased him through a stand of pine; trees exploded like firecrackers. Sparks bit through his civvies and stung him. He could smell burning hair. His hair.

But he didn't want to smell his hair burning. Spur was trying desperately to get back to the bench in the garden, back to Comfort, but she kept pushing him deeper into the nightmare.

"After we heard he'd been killed, I went to his room . . ."

He beckoned and for a moment Spur thought it might not be Vic after all as the anguished face shimmered in the heat of the burn. Vic wouldn't betray them, would he?

"It was his handwriting . . ."

Spur had to dance to keep his shoes from catching fire, and he had no escape, no choice, no time. The torch spread his arms wide and Spur stumbled into his embrace and with an angry whoosh they exploded together into flame. Spur felt his skin crackle. . . .

And he screamed.

Twelve

We are paid for our suspicions by finding what we suspected.
–A Week on the Concord and Merrimack rivers

Everyone said that he had nothing to be embarrassed about, but Spur was nonetheless deeply ashamed. He had been revealed as unmanly. Weak and out of control. He had no memory of how he had come to be laid out on the couch in his own parlor. He couldn't remember if he had wept or cursed or just fainted and been dragged like a sack of onions across the yard into the cottage. When he emerged from the nightmare, all he knew was that his throat was raw and his cheeks were hot. The others were all gathered around him, trying not to look worried but not doing a very convincing job of it. He wasn't sure which he minded more: that the strangers had witnessed his breakdown, or that his friends and neighbors had.

When he sat up, a general alarm rippled among the onlookers. When he tried to stand, Sly pressed him back onto the couch with a firm grip on the shoulder. Comfort fetched him a glass of water. She was so distraught that her hand shook as she offered it to him. He took a sip, more to satisfy the others than to quench his own thirst. They needed to think they were helping, even though the best thing they could have done for him then—go away and leave him alone—was the one thing they were certain not to do.

"Maybe I should call Dr. Niss." Spur's laugh was as light as ashes. "Ask for my money back."

"You're right." Constant Ngonda lit up at the thought, then realized that his enthusiasm was unseemly. "I mean, shouldn't we notify the hospital?" he said, eyeing the tell on the parlor wall. "They may have concerns."

Spur knew that the deputy would love to have him whisked away from Littleton, in the hopes that the High Gregory and the L'ung would follow. He wondered briefly if that might not be for the best, but then he had been humiliated enough that morning. "There's nothing to worry about."

"Good," said Ngonda. "I'm happy to hear that, Spur. Do you mind, I promised to check in with the Cooperative when we arrived?" Without waiting for a reply, Ngonda bustled across the parlor to the kitchen. Meanwhile, the High Gregory had sprawled onto a chair, his legs dangling over the armrest. He was flipping impatiently through a back issue of Didactic Arts' *True History Comix* without really looking at the pages. Spur thought he looked even more squirmy than usual, as if he knew there was someplace else he was supposed to be. Sly Sawatdee had parked himself next to Spur. His hands were folded in his lap, his eyelids were heavy and he hummed to himself from time to time, probably thinking about fishing holes and berry patches and molasses cookies.

"I am so sorry, Spur," said Comfort. "I just didn't realize." It was the third time she had apologized. She wasn't used to apologizing and she didn't do it very well. Meanwhile her anguish was smothering him. Her face was pale, her mouth was as crooked as a scar. What had he said to her? He couldn't remember but it must have been awful. There was a quiet desperation in her eyes that he had never seen before. It scared him.

Spur set the glass of water on the end table. "Listen, Comfort, there is nothing for you to be sorry about." He was the one who had fallen apart, after all. "Let's just forget it, all right? I'm fine now." To prove it, he stood up.

Sly twitched but did not move to pull him back onto the couch again. "Have enough air up there, my hasty little sparrow?"

"I'm fine," he repeated and it was true. Time to put this by and move on. Change the subject. "Who wants to see the orchard? Lucky?"

"If you don't mind," said Sly. "My bones are in no mood for a hike. But I'll make us lunch."

"I'll come," said Ngonda.

Comfort looked as if she wanted to beg off, but guilt got the better of her.

They tramped around the grounds, talking mostly of farm matters. After they had admired the revived orchard, inspected the weed-choked garden, toured the barn, played with the pack of gosdogs that had wandered over from the big house and began to follow them everywhere, walked the boundaries of the corn field which Cape had planted in clover until Spur was ready to farm again, they hiked through the woods down to Mercy's Creek.

"We take some irrigation water from the creek, but the Joerlys own the rights, so there's water in our end of the creek pretty much all year long." Spur pointed. "There's a pool in the woods where Comfort and I used to swim when we were kids. It might be a good place to cool off this afternoon."

"And so you and Spur were neighbors?" The High Gregory had been trying to draw Comfort out all morning, without much success. "You grew up together like me and my friends. I was hoping to bring them along but Uncle Constant Ngonda said there were too many of them. Your family is still living on the farm?"

"Mom died. She left everything to us. Now Vic's dead."

"Yes, Spur said that your brother was a brave firefighter. I know that you are very sad about it, but I see much more luck ahead for you."

She leaned against a tree and stared up at the sky.

"There used to be a pukpuk town in these woods." Spur was itching to move on. "They built all along the creek. It's overgrown now, but we could go look at the ruins."

The High Gregory stepped off the bank onto a flat stone that stuck out of the creek. "And your father?"

"He left," Comfort said dully.

"When they were little," Spur said quickly. He knew that Comfort did not like even to think about her father, much less talk about him with strangers. Park Nen had married into the Joerly family. Not only was his marriage to Rosie Joerly stormy, but he was also a loner who had never quite adjusted to village ways. "The last we heard Park was living in Freeport."

The High Gregory picked his way across the creek on stepping-stones. "He was a pukpuk, no?" His foot slipped and he windmilled his arms to keep his balance.

"Who told you that?" If Comfort had been absent-minded before, she was very much present now.

"I forget." He crossed back over the stream in four quick hops. "Was it you, Uncle?"

Ngonda licked his lips nervously. "I've never heard of this person."

"Then maybe it was Spur."

Spur would have denied it if Comfort had given him the chance.

"He never knew." Her voice was sharp. "Nobody did." She confronted the boy. "Don't play games with me, upsider." He tried to back away but she pursued him. "Why do you care about my father? Why are you here?"

"Are you crazy?" Ngonda caught the High Gregory as he stumbled over a rock and then thrust the boy behind him. "This is my nephew Lucky."

"She knows, friend Constant." The High Gregory peeked out from behind the deputy's flair jacket. He was glowing with excitement. "Spur told her everything."

"Oh, no." Ngonda slumped. "This isn't going well at all."

"Memsen gave us all research topics for the trip here to meet Spur," said the High Gregory. "Kai Thousandfold was assigned to find out about you. You'd like him; he's from Bellweather. He says that he's very worried about you, friend Comfort."

"Tell him to mind his own business."

Spur was aghast. "Comfort, I'm sorry, I didn't know. . . ."

"Be quiet, Spur. These upsiders are playing you for the fool that you are." Her eyes were wet. "I hardly knew my father and what I did know, I didn't like. Mom would probably still be alive if she hadn't been left to manage the farm by herself all those years." Her chin quivered; Spur had never seen her so agitated. "She told us that Grandma Nen was a pukpuk, but that she emigrated from the barrens long before my father was born and that he was brought up a citizen like anyone else." Tears streaked her face. "So don't think you understand anything about me because you found out about a dead woman who I never met."

With that she turned and walked stiff-legged back toward Diligence Cottage. She seemed to have shrunk since the morning, and now looked so insubstantial to Spur that a summer breeze might carry her off like milkweed. He knew there was more—much more—they had to talk about, but first they would have to find a new way to speak to each other. As she disappeared into the woods, he felt a twinge of nostalgia for the lost simplicity of their youth, when life really had been as easy as Chairman Winter promised it could be.

"I'm hungry." The High Gregory seemed quite pleased with himself. "Is it lunchtime yet?"

After he had spun out lunch for as long as he could, Spur was at a loss as to how to keep the High Gregory out of trouble. They had exhausted the sights of the Leung farmstead, short of going over to visit with his father in the big house. Spur considered it, but decided to save it for a last resort. He had hoped to spend the afternoon touring the Joerly farmstead, but now that was out of the question. As the High Gregory fidgeted about the cottage, picking things up and putting them down again, asking about family pix, opening cabinets and pulling out drawers, Spur proposed that they take a spin around Littleton in Sly's truck. A rolling tour, he told himself. No stops.

The strategy worked for most of an hour. At first the High Gregory was content to sit next to Spur in the back of the truck as he pointed out Littleton's landmarks and described the history of the village. They drove up Lamana Ridge Road to Lookover Point, from which they had a view of most of Littleton Commons. The village had been a Third Wave settlement, populated by the winners of the lottery of 2432. In the first years of settlement, the twenty-five founding families had worked together to construct the buildings of the Commons: the self-reliance school, athenaeum, communion lodge, town hall, and Littleton's first exchange, where goods and services could be bought or bartered. The First Twenty-five had lived communally in rough barracks until the buildings on the Commons were completed, and then gradually moved out to their farmsteads as land was cleared and crews of carpenters put up the cottages and barns and sheds for each of the families. The Leungs had arrived in the Second Twenty-five four years afterward. The railroad had come through three years after that and most of the businesses of the first exchange moved from the Commons out to Shed Town by the train station. Sly drove them down the ridge and they bumped along back roads, past farms and fields and pastures. They viewed the Toba and Parochet and Velez farmsteads from a safe distance and passed Sambusa's lumberyard at the confluence of Mercy's Creek and the Swift River. Then they pulled back onto CR22.

The only way back to Diligence Cottage was through the Commons. "Drive by the barracks," Spur called to Sly in the cab. "We can stretch our legs there," he said to the High Gregory. "I'll show you how the First Twenty-five lived." One of the original barracks had been preserved as a historical museum across the lawn from the communion lodge. It was left open to any who wanted to view its dusty exhibits. Spur thought it the best possible choice for a stop; except for Founders' Day, the Chairman's birthday, and Thanksgiving, nobody ever went there.

The Commons appeared to be deserted as they passed the buildings of the first exchange. These had been renovated into housing for those citizens of Littleton who didn't farm, like the teachers at the self-reliance school and Dr. Christopoulos and some of the elders, like Gandy Joy. They saw Doll Groth coming out of the athenaeum. Recognizing the truck, she gave Sly a neighborly wave, but when she spotted Spur in the back, she smiled and began to clap, raising her hands over her head. This so pleased the High

Gregory that he stood up and started clapping back at her. Spur had to brace him to keep him from pitching over the side of the truck.

But Doll was the only person they saw. Spur couldn't believe his good fortune as they pulled up to the barracks, dust from the gravel parking lot swirling around them. The wind had picked up, but provided no relief from the midsummer heat. Spur's shirt stuck to his back where he had been leaning against the cab of the truck. Although he wasn't sure whether the High Gregory could sweat or not, the boy's face was certainly flushed. Ngonda looked as if he were liquefying inside his flair jacket. The weather fit Spur's latest plan neatly. He was hoping that after they had spent a half-hour in the hot and airless barracks, he might be able to persuade the High Gregory to return to Diligence Cottage for a swim in the creek. After that it would practically be suppertime. And after that they could watch the tell. Or he might teach the High Gregory some of the local card games. Spur had always been lucky at Fool All.

It wasn't until the engine of the Sawatdees' truck coughed and rattled and finally cut out that Spur first heard the whoop of the crowd. Something was going on at the ball fields next to the self-reliance school, just down the hill a couple hundred meters. He tried to usher the High Gregory into the barracks but it was too late. Spur thought there must be a lot of people down there. They were making a racket that was hard to miss.

The High Gregory cocked his head in the direction of the school and smiled. "Lucky us," he said. "We're just in time for Memsen."

Thirteen

I associate this day, when I can remember it, with games of base-ball played over behind the hills in the russet fields toward Sleepy Hollow.

–Journal, 1856

"What is this?" hissed Ngonda.

Sly pulled his floppy hat off and wiped his forehead with it. "Looks like a baseball game, city pants," said Sly.

The L'ung were in the field; with a sick feeling Spur counted twelve of them in purple overalls and black T-shirts. They must have arrived in the two vans that were parked next to the wooden bleachers. Beside the vans was an array of trucks, scooters, and bicycles from the village. There must have been a hundred citizens sitting in the bleachers and another twenty or thirty prowling the edges of the field, cheering the home team on. Match Klizzie had opened the refreshment shed and was barbequing sausages. Gandy Joy had set up her communion tent: Spur could see billows of sweet, white smoke whenever one of the villagers pulled back the flap.

With many of the younger baseball regulars off at the firefight, the Littleton Eagles might have been undermanned. But Spur could see that some old-timers had come out of retirement to pull on the scarlet hose. Warp Kovacho was just stepping up to home base and Spur spotted Cape sitting on the strikers' bench, second from the inbox.

Betty Chief Twosalt shined the ball against her overalls as she peered in at Warp. "Where to, old sir?" She was playing feeder for the L'ung.

Warp swung the flat bat at belt level to show her just where he wanted the feed to cross home base. "Right here, missy," he said. "Then you better duck." They were playing with just two field bases, left and right. The banners fixed to the top of each basepole snapped in the stiffening breeze.

Betty nodded and then delivered the feed underhanded. It was slow and very fat but Warp watched it go by. The Pendragon Chromlis Furcifer was catching for the L'ung. She barehanded it and flipped it back to Betty.

"What's he waiting for?" grumbled the High Gregory. "That was perfect." He ignored Spur's icy stare.

"Just a smight lower next time, missy," said Warp, once again indicating his preference with the bat. "You got the speed right, now hit the spot."

Young Melody Velez was perched at the end of the topmost bleacher and noticed Spur passing beneath her. "He's here!" she cried. "Spur's here!"

Play stopped and the bleachers emptied as the villagers crowded around him, clapping him on the back and shaking his hand. In five minutes he'd been kissed more than he'd been kissed altogether in the previous year.

"So is this another one of your upsider friends?" Gandy Joy held the High Gregory at arms length, taking him in. "Hello, boy. What's your name?"

"I'm the High Gregory of Kenning," he said. "But my Walden name is Lucky, so I'd rather have you call me that."

Citizens nearby laughed nervously.

"Lucky you are then."

Gandy Hope Nakuru touched the pink bandana knotted around his neck. "Isn't this a cute scarf?" The High Gregory beamed.

Spur was astonished by it all. "But who told you that they're from the upside?" he said. "How did they get here? And why are you playing baseball?"

"Memsen brought them," said Peace Toba. "She said that you'd be along once we got the game going."

"And she was right." Little Jewel Parochet tugged at his shirt. "Spur, she said you flew in a hover. What was it like?"

"Maybe next time you can bring a guest along with you?" Melody Velez said, smiling. She brushed with no great subtlety against him.

Spur glanced about the thinning crowd; citizens were climbing back into the bleachers. "But where is Memsen?"

Peace Toba pointed; Memsen had only come out onto the field as far as right base when Constant Ngonda had captured her. He was waving his arms so frantically that he looked like he might take off and fly around the field. Memsen tilted her head so that her ear was practically on her shoulder. Then she saw Spur. She clicked her rings at him, a sly smile on her face. He knew he ought to be angry with her, but instead he felt buoyant, as if he had just set his splash pack down and stepped out of his field jacket. Whatever happened now, it wasn't his fault. He had done his best for his village.

"So this was what you were keeping from me." His father was chuckling. "I knew it had to be something. They're fine, your friends. You didn't need to worry." He hugged Spur and whispered into his ear. "Fine, but very strange. They're not staying are they?" He pulled back. "Prosper, we need your bat in this game. These kids are tough." He pointed at Kai Thousandfold "That one has an arm like a fire hose."

"No thanks," said Spur. "But you should get back to the game." He raised his arms over his head and waved to the bleachers. "Thank you all, thanks," he called to his well-wishers. They quieted down to listen. "If you're expecting some kind of speech, then you've got the wrong farmer. I'll just say that I'm glad to be home and leave it at that. All right?" The crowd made a murmur of assent. "Then play ball." They cheered. "And go Eagles!" They cheered louder.

"Can I play?" said the High Gregory. "This looks like fun." He straightened the strap of his overalls. "I can play, can't I? We have all kinds of baseball on Kenning. But your rules are different, right? Tell them to me."

"Why bother?" Spur was beginning to wonder if the High Gregory was playing him for a fool. "Looks like you're making them up as you go."

Her Grace, Jacqueline Kristof, put an arm around his shoulder. "The ball is soft, so no gloves," she said, as she led him onto the field. "No tag outs either, you actually have to hit the runner with the ball. That's called a sting. No fouls and no . . ."

As the spectators settled into their seats, Spur found his way to Ngonda and Memsen. She wasn't wearing the standard L'ung overalls, but rather a plain green sundress with a floral print. She had washed the phosphorescent paint off her arms and pulled her hair back into a ponytail. But if Memsen was trying to look inconspicuous, then she had failed utterly. She was still the tallest woman on the planet.

"Talk to her," said Ngonda. "We had an agreement. . . ."

"Which you broke," said Memsen. "What we agreed was that the High Gregory would visit Littleton and you'd let him make whatever luck you are destined to have. You promised to give him the run of the village—"

"—under Spur's supervision, Allworthy," interrupted Ngonda.

Betty Chief Twosalt delivered a feed and Warp watched it go by again. This did not sit well with the L'ung. "Delay of game, old sir," someone called.

Memsen turned from Ngonda to Spur. "As we were explaining to the deputy, the L'ung and I see everything that the High Gregory sees. So we know that you've introduced him to just two of your neighbors. You promised that he could meet the citizens of this village but then you've kept him isolated until now. He needs to be with people, Spur. Barns don't have luck. People do."

"It was my decision," said Spur. "I'll take the responsibility."

"And this was ours." She waved toward the field. "So?"

Ngonda snorted in disgust. "I need to call Concord. The Office of Diplomacy will be filing a protest with the Forum of the Thousand Worlds." He took a step away from them, then turned and waggled a finger at Memsen. "This is a clear violation of our Covenant, Allworthy. The L'ung will be recalled to Kenning."

As they watched Ngonda stalk off, Warp struck a grounder straight back at the feeder. Betty stabbed at it but it tipped off her fingers and rolled away at an angle. Little Senator Dowm pounced on it but held the throw because Warp already had a hand on the right base stake.

"Maybe I should've introduced the High Gregory to a few more people." Spur wondered if standing too close to Memsen might be affecting his perceptions. The very planet seemed to tilt slightly, as it had that afternoon when he and Leaf Benkleman had drunk a whole liter of her mother's prize applejack. "But why are we playing baseball?"

Memsen showed him her teeth in that way she had that wasn't anything like a smile. "Tolerance isn't something that the citizens of the Transcendent State seem to value. You've been taught that your way of life is better not only than that of the pukpuks, but than that of most of the cultures of the Thousand Worlds. Or have we misread the textbooks?"

Spur shook his head grimly.

"So." She pinched the air. "Deputy Ngonda was right to point out that landing a hover on your Commons might have intimidated some people. We had to find some unthreatening way to arrive, justify our presence, and meet your neighbors. The research pointed to baseball as a likely ploy. Your Eagles were champions of Hamilton County just two years ago and second runner-up in the Northeast in 2498."

"A ploy."

"A ploy to take advantage of your traditions. Your village is proud of its accomplishments in baseball. You're used to playing against strangers. And of course, we had an invitation from Spur Leung, the hero of the hour."

Livy Jayawardena hit a high fly ball that sailed over the heads of the midfielders. Kai Thousandfold, playing deep field, raced back and made an over-the-shoulder catch. Meanwhile Warp had taken off for left base. In his prime, he might have made it, but his prime had been when Spur was a toddler. Kai turned, set, and fired; his perfect throw stung Warp right between the shoulder blades. Double play, inning over.

"I invited you?" said Spur. "When was that again?"

"Why, in the hospital where we saved your life. You kept claiming that the L'ung would offer no competition for your Eagles. You told Dr. Niss that you couldn't imagine losing a baseball game to upsiders, much less a bunch of children. Really, Spur, that was too much. We had to accept your challenge once you said that. So when we arrived at the town hall, we told our story to everyone we met. Within an hour the bleachers were full."

Spur was impressed. "And you thought of all this since yesterday?"

"Actually, just in the last few hours." She paused then, seemingly distracted. She made a low, repetitive *pa-pa-pa-ptt*. "Although there is something you should know about us," she said at last. "Of course, Deputy Ngonda would be outraged if he knew that we're telling you, but then he finds outrage everywhere." She stooped to his level so that they were face to face. "I rarely think all by myself, Spur." He tried not to notice that her knees bent in different directions. "Most of the time, we think for me."

The world seemed to tilt a little more then; Spur felt as if he might slide off it. "I don't think I understand what you just said."

"It's complicated." She straightened. "And we're attracting attention here. I can hear several young women whispering about us. We should find a more private place to talk. I need your advice." She turned and waved to the citizens in the bleachers who were watching them. Spur forced a smile and waved as well, and then led her up the hill toward town hall.

"Ngonda will file his protest," she said, "and it'll be summarily rejected. We've been in continuous contact with the Forum of the Thousand Worlds." Her speech became choppy as she walked. "They know what we're doing." Climbing the gentle hill left her breathless. "Not all worlds approve. Consensus is hard to come by. But the L'ung have a plan . . . to open talks between you . . . and the pukpuks." She rested a hand on his shoulder to support herself. "Is that something you think worth doing?"

"Maybe." He could feel the warmth of her hand through the thin fabric of his shirt. "All right, yes." He thought this must be another ploy. "But who are you? Who are the L'ung? Why are you doing this?"

"Be patient." At the top of the hill she had to rest to catch her breath. Finally she said, "You spoke with the High Gregory about gosdogs?"

"In the truck this morning."

"It was at the instigation of the L'ung. Understand that we don't believe that gosdogs think in any meaningful sense of the word. Perhaps the original Peekay intelligence rating was accurate. But if they were found to be more intelligent, then we could bring the issue of their treatment here to the Forum. It would require a delicate touch to steer the debate toward the remedy the L'ung want. Tricky but not impossible. The Forum has no real power to intervene in the affairs of member worlds and your Chairman Winter has the right to run Walden as he pleases. But he depends on the good opinion of the Thousand Worlds. When we're finished here, the L'ung will propose to return the gosdogs to a preserve where they can live in their natural state."

"But there is no natural habitat left. The pukpuks destroyed it."

"Ah, but ecologies can be re-created." She gestured at the lawn stretching before them, at the rose hedges along its border and the trees that shaded it, their leaves trembling in the summer breeze. "As you well know."

"But what does a gosdog preserve have to do with the pukpuks?"

"Come away from the sun before we melt." Memsen led him to a bench in the shadow of an elm. She sagged onto it; Spur remained standing, looking down at her for a change. It eased the crick in his neck.

"The preserve sets a precedent." She clicked her rings. "In order for it to be established, the growth of the forest must be controlled, which means the Transcendent State will be blocked from spreading across Walden. Up until now, the Cooperative has refused to negotiate on this point. And then comes the question of where to put the preserve. You and the pukpuks will have to sit down to decide on a site. Together. With some delicate nudging from the Forum, there's no telling what conversations might take place at such a meeting."

"But we can't!" Spur wiped the sweat from his forehead. "The Transcendent State was founded so that humans could live apart and stay true to ourselves. As long as the pukpuks live here, we'll be under direct attack from upsider ways."

"Your Transcendent State is a controversial experiment." Memsen's face went slack and she made the *pa-pa-pa-ptt* sound Spur had heard before. "We've always wondered how isolation and ignorance can be suitable foundations for a human society. Do you really believe in simplicity, Spur, or do you just not know any better?"

Spur wondered if she had used some forbidden upsider tech to look into his soul; he felt violated. "I believe in this." He gestured, as she had done, at Littleton Commons, green as a dream. "I don't want my village to be swept away. The pukpuks destroyed this world once already."

"Yes, that could happen, if it's what you and your children decide," said Memsen. "We don't have an answer for you, Spur. But the question is, do you need a preserve like gosdogs, or are you strong enough to hold onto your beliefs no matter who challenges them?"

"And this is your plan to save Walden?" He ground his shoe into the grass. "This is the luck that the High Gregory came all this way to make?"

"Is it?" She leaned back against the bench and gazed up into the canopy of the elm. "Maybe it is."

"I've been such an idiot." He was bitter; if she was going to use him, at least she could admit it. "You and the High Gregory and the L'ung flit around the upside, having grand adventures and straightening up other people's messes." He began to pace back and forth in front of the bench. "You're like some kind of superheroes, is that it?"

"The L'ung have gathered together to learn statecraft from one another," she said patiently. "Sometimes they travel, but mostly they stay with us on Kenning. Of course they have political power in the Forum because of who they are, but their purpose is not so much to do as it is to learn. Then, in a few more years, this cohort will disband and scatter to their respective worlds to try their luck. And when the time comes for us to marry. . . ."

"Marry? Marry who?"

"The High Gregory, of course."

"But he's just a boy."

Memsen must have heard the dismay in his voice. "He will grow into his own luck soon enough," she said coldly. "I was chosen the twenty-second Memsen by my predecessor. She searched for me for years across the Thousand Worlds." With a weary groan she stood, and once again towered over him. "A Memsen is twice honored: to be wife to one High Gregory and mother to another." Her voice took on a declaiming quality, as if she were giving a speech that had been well rehearsed. "And I carry my predecessor and twenty souls who came before her saved in our memory, so that we may always serve the High Gregory and advise the L'ung."

Spur was horrified at the depth of his misunderstanding of this woman. "You have dead people . . . inside you?"

"Not dead," she said. "Saved."

A crazed honking interrupted them. A truck careened around the corner and skidded to a stop in front of the town hall. Stark Sukulgunda flung himself out of the still-running truck and dashed inside.

Spur stood. "Something's wrong." He started for the truck and had gotten as far as the statue of Chairman Winter, high on his pedestal, when Stark burst out of the doors again. He saw Spur and waved frantically.

"Where are they all?" he cried. "Nobody answers."

"Playing baseball." Spur broke into a trot. "What's wrong? What?"

"Baseball?" Stark's eyes bulged as he tried to catch his breath. "South slope of Lamana . . . burning . . . everything's burning . . . the forest is on fire!"

Fourteen

I walked slowly through the wood to Fairhaven cliff, climbed to the highest rock and sat down upon it to observe the progress of the flames, which were rapidly approaching me now about a mile distant from the spot where the fire was kindled. Presently I heard the sound of the distant Bell giving the alarm, and I knew that the town was on its way to the scene. Hitherto I felt like a guilty person. Nothing but shame and regret, but now I settled the matter with myself shortly, and said to myself. Who are these men who are said to be owners of these woods and how am I related to them? I have set fire to the forest, but I have done no wrong therein, and now it is as if the lightning had done it. These flames are but consuming their natural food. So shortly I settled it with myself and stood to watch the approaching flames. It was a glorious spectacle, and I was the only one there to enjoy it. The fire now reached the base of the cliffs and then rushed up its sides. The squirrels ran before it in blind haste, and the pigeons dashed into the midst of the smoke. The flames flashed up the pines to their tops as if they were powder.

–Journal, 1850

More than half of the Littleton Volunteer Fire Department were playing baseball when the alarm came. They scrambled up the hill to the brick firehouse on the Commons, followed by almost all of the spectators, who crowded anxiously into the communion hall while the firefighters huddled. Normally there would have been sixteen volunteers on call, but, like Spur, Will Sambusa, Bright Ayoub, Bliss Bandaran, and Chief Cary Millisap had joined the Corps. Cape was currently Assistant Chief; he would have led the volunteers had not his son been home. Even though Spur protested that he was merely a grunt smokechaser, the volunteers' first act was to vote him Acting Chief.

Like any small-town unit, the Littleton Fire Department routinely answered calls for house fires and brush fires and accidents of all sorts, but they were ill-equipped to stop a major burn. They had just one fire truck, an old quad with a 3,000-liter-per-minute pump and 5,000-liter water tank. It carried fifty meters of six-centimeter hose, fifty meters of booster hose, and a ten-meter mechanical ladder. If the burn was as big as Stark described, Engine No. 4 would be about as much use fighting it as a broom.

Spur resisted the impulse to put his team on the truck and rush out to the burn. He needed more information before he committed his meager forces. It would be at least an hour before companies from neighboring villages would arrive and the Corps might not get to Littleton until nightfall. Cape spread a map out on the long table in the firehouse and the volunteers stood around it, hunch-shouldered and grim. Gandy Joy glided in, lit a single communion square, and slipped out again as they contemplated what the burn might do to their village. They took turns peppering Stark with questions about what he had actually seen. At first he tried his best to answer, but he'd had a shock that had knocked better men than him off center. As they pressed him, he grew sullen and suspicious.

The Sukulgundas lived well west of the Leungs and higher up the slope of Lamana Ridge. They'd been latecomers to Littleton and parts of their farmstead were so steep that the fields had to be terraced. They were about four kilometers north of the Commons at the very end of January Road, a steep, dirt track with switchbacks. Stark maintained that the burn had come down the ridge at him, from the general direction of Lookover Point to the east. At first he claimed it was maybe a kilometer away when he'd left his place, but then changed his mind and insisted that the burn was practically eating his barn. That didn't make sense, since the strong, easterly breeze would push the burn in the opposite direction, toward the farmsteads of the Ezzats and Millisaps and eventually to the Herreras and the Leungs.

Spur shivered as he imagined the burn roaring through GiGa's orchards. But his neighbors were counting on him to keep those fears at bay. "If what you're saying is true," he mused, "it might mean that this fire was deliberately set and that someone is still out there trying to make trouble for us."

"Torches in Littleton?" Livy Jayawardena looked dubious. "We're nowhere near the barrens."

"Neither was Double Down," said Cape. "Or Wheelwright."

"I don't know about that." Stark Sukulgunda pulled the cap off his head and started twisting it. "All I know is that we ought to stop talking about what to do and do something."

"First we have to know for sure where the burn is headed, which means we need to get up the Lamana Ridge Road." Spur was struggling to apply what he'd learned in training. "If the burn hasn't jumped the road and headed back down the north slope of the ridge, then we can use the road as a firebreak and hold that line. And when reinforcements come, we'll send them east over the ridge to the head of the burn. That's the way the wind is blowing everything." He glanced up at the others to see if they agreed. "We need to be thinking hard about an eastern perimeter."

"Why?" Stark was livid. "Because that's where you live? It's my house that—"

"Shut up, Stark," said Peace Toba. "Fill your snoot with communion and get right with the village for a change."

None of the threatened farmsteads that lay in the path of the burn to the east was completely cleared of trees. Simplicity demanded that citizens only cultivate as much of their land as they needed. Farmers across Walden used the forest as a windbreak; keeping unused land in trees prevented soil erosion. But now Spur was thinking about all the pine and hemlock and red cedar, needles laden with resins and oils, side by side with the deciduous trees in the woods where he had played as a boy. At Motu River he'd seen pine trees explode into flame. And then there were the burn piles of slash and stumps and old lumber that every farmer collected, baking in the summer sun.

"If things go wrong in the east, we might need to set our firebreak as far back as Blue Valley Road." Spur ran his finger down the line on the map. "It won't be as effective a break as the ridge road but we can improve it. Get the Bandarans and Sawatdees to rake off all the forest litter and duff on the west side. Then disk harrow the entire road. I want to see at least a three-meter-wide strip of fresh soil down the entire length."

"Prosper." Cape's voice was hushed. "You're not giving up on all of this." He traced the outline of the four threatened farms on the map, ending on the black square that marked Diligence Cottage.

Spur glanced briefly at his father, then away again, troubled by what he had seen. Capability Leung looked just as desperate as Stark Sukulgunda. Maybe more so, if he thought he had just heard his son pronounce doom on his life's work. For the first time in his life, Spur felt as if he were the father and Cape was the son.

"No." He tried to reassure his father with a smile. "That's just our fall back. What I'm hoping is that we can cut a handline from Spot Pond along Mercy's Creek all the way down to the river. It's rough country and depending on how fast the burn is moving we may not have enough time, but if we can hold that line, we save the Millisaps, Joerlys, and us." Left unsaid was that the Ezzats' farmstead would be lost, even if this dicey strategy worked.

"But right now the fire is much closer to my place than anyone else's," said Stark. "And you said yourself, there may be some suicidal maniac just waiting to burn himself up and take my house with him."

Spur was annoyed at the way that Stark Sukulgunda kept buzzing at him. He was making it hard for Spur to concentrate. "We could send the fire truck your way, Stark," he said, "but I don't know what good it would do. You don't have any standing water on your land, do you?"

"Why?"

"The truck only has a 5,000-liter water tank. That's not near enough if your house gets involved."

"We could drop the hard suction line into his well," said Livy. "Pump from there."

"You have a dug well?" said Cape. "How deep?"

"Four meters."

"We'd probably suck it dry before we could do you much good," said Cape.

"No," said Spur. "He's right. Peace, you and Tenny and Cert take No. 4 up to Sukulgundas. You can also establish our western perimeter. Clear a meter-wide handline as far up the ridge as you can. Watch for torches. I don't think the fire is going to come your way but if it does, be ready, understand? Get on the tell and let us know if anything changes."

"We'll call in when we get there," said Peace as her team scattered to collect gear.

"Livy, you and the others round up as many as you can to help with the creek line. We may want to start a backfire, so keep in touch with me on the hand-tell. How much liquid fire have you got?"

"At least twenty grenades. Maybe more. No firebombs though."

"Bring gas then, you'll probably need it. Keep your people between the civilians and the burn, understand? And pull back if it gets too hot. I've lost too many friends this year. I don't want to be burying anyone else. DiDa, you and I need to find a way to get up the ridge . . ."

He was interrupted by the roar of a crowd, which had gathered just outside the firehouse. Spur froze, momentarily bewildered. They couldn't still be playing baseball, could they? Then he thought that the burn must have changed direction. It had careened down the ridge faster than it had any right to, an avalanche of fire that was about to incinerate the Commons and there was nothing he could do to fight it; in the nightmare, he wasn't wearing his splash pack. Or his fireproof field jacket. Spur shuddered. He wasn't fit to lead, to decide what to let burn and what to save. He was weak and his soul was lost in darkness and he knew he shouldn't be afraid.

He was a veteran of the firefight, but fear squeezed him nonetheless. "Are you all right, son?" His father rested a hand on his shoulder. The burn licked at boulders and scorched the trees in the forest he had sworn to protect.

"DiDa," he whispered, leaning close to his father so no one else would hear, "what if I can't stop it?"

"You'll do your best, Prosper," he said. "Everyone knows that."

As they rushed out of the firehouse, they could see smoke roiling into the sky to the northwest. But the evil plume wasn't what had stunned the crowd, which was still pouring out of the communion hall. A shadow passed directly overhead and, even in the heat of this disastrous afternoon, Spur was chilled.

Silently, like a miracle, the High Gregory's hover landed on Littleton Commons.

Fifteen

Men go to a fire for entertainment. When I see how eagerly men will run to a fire, whether in warm or cold weather, by night or by day, dragging an engine at their heels, I'm astonished to perceive how good a purpose the level of excitement is made to serve.
                                                        –Journal, 1850

"There's a big difference between surface fire and crown fire," said the Pendragon Chromlis Furcifer to the L'ung assembled in the belly of the hover. "Surface fires move along the forest floor, burning through the understory." She was reading from notes that scrolled down her forearm.

"Wait, what's understory again?" asked Her Grace, Jacqueline Kristof, who was the youngest of the L'ung.

Memsen pinched the air. "You mustn't keep interrupting, Your Grace. If you have questions, query the cognisphere in slow time." She nodded at Penny. "Go ahead, Pendragon. You're doing a fine job."

"Understory is the grass, shrubs, dead leaves, fallen trees—that stuff. So anyway, a surface fire can burn fast or slow, depending. But if the flames climb into the crowns of the trees, it almost always rips right through the forest. Since the Transcendental State doesn't have the tech to stop it, Spur will have to let it burn itself out. If you look over there. . . ." The group closed around her, craning to see.

Spur had been able to ignore Penny for the most part, although

Cape kept scowling at the L'ung. Memsen had explained that Penny's research topic for the trip to Walden was forest fires.

The hover was not completely proof against smoke. As they skirted the roiling convection column of smoke and burning embers, the air inside the hover became tinged with the bitter stench of the burn. This impressed the L'ung. As they wandered from view to view, they would call to one another. "Here, over here. Do you smell it now? Much stronger over here!"

They had dissolved the partitions and made most of the hull transparent to observe developments in the burn. Just a single three-meter-wide band ran solid from the front of the deck to the back as a concession to Spur and Cape; the L'ung seemed totally immune from fear of heights. Spur was proud at how Cape was handling his first flight in a hover, especially since he himself felt slightly queasy whenever he looked straight down through the deck at the ridge 1,500 meters below.

From this vantage, Spur could see exactly what was needed to contain the burn and realized that he didn't have the resources to do it. Looking to the north, he was relieved that the burn hadn't yet crossed Lamana Ridge Road into the wilderness on the far slope. Barring an unforeseen wind change or embers lighting new spot fires, he thought he might be able to keep the burn within the Littleton valley. But he needed dozens of trained firefighters up on the ridge to defend the road as soon as possible. To the west, he saw where the flames had come close to the Sukulgundas' farmstead, but now the burn there looked to be nothing more than a surface fire that was already beginning to gutter out. Peace and the team with Engine No. 4 should have no trouble mopping up. Then he'd move them onto the ridge, not that just three people and one ancient pumper were going to be enough to beat back a wall of flame two kilometers wide.

"Where you see the darker splotches in the forest, those are evergreens, the best fuel of all," said Penny. "If they catch, you can get a blowup fire, which is what that huge column of smoke is about."

To the east and south, the prospects were grim. The burn had dropped much farther down the ridge than Spur had expected. He remembered from his training that burns were supposed to track uphill faster than down, but the spread to the north and south, upslope and down, looked about the same. As soon as the first crews responded from nearby Bode Well and Highbridge, they'd have to deploy at the base of the ridge to protect the Commons and the farmsteads beyond it.

The head of the burn was a violent crown fire racing east, beneath a chimney of malign smoke that towered kilometers above the hover. When Spur had given the Ezzats and Millisaps permission to save as much as they could from their houses, he'd thought that they'd all have more time. Now he realized that he'd miscalculated. He reached both families using the hand-tell and told them to leave immediately. Bash Ezzat was weeping when she said she could already see the burn sweeping down on her. Spur tried Comfort's tell again to let her know that her farmstead was directly in the path of the burn, but still got no answer.

"DiDa," said Spur gently. He'd been dreading this moment, ever since he'd understood the true scope and direction of the burn. "I think we need to pull Livy and her people back from the creek to Blue Valley Road." He steeled himself against anger, grief, and reproach. "There's no time to clear a line," he went on. "At least not one that will stop this burn."

"I think you're right," Cape said, as casually as if they were discussing which trees to prune. "It's simple, isn't it?"

Relieved but still anguished, he hugged his father. "I'm sorry, DiDa." He couldn't remember the last time they had been this close, and was not surprised that Cape did not return his embrace. "Should we send someone to the house?" he said, as he let his father go. "Have them pack some things? Papers, furniture—there's still a little time."

"No." Cape turned and cupped his hands against the transparent hull of the hover. "If I did something silly like that, the farm would burn for sure." He lowered his face into his hands as if to shade the view from glare. But the afternoon sun was a dim memory, blotted out by the seething clouds of smoke.

Spur shut his eyes then, so tight that for a moment he could feel muscles on his temple quiver. "Memsen," he said, his voice catching in his throat, "can you put us down by the Sawatdees' house?"

Spur got more resistance from Livy than he had from his father. It took him almost ten minutes to convince her that trying to dig a firebreak along Mercy's Creek was not only futile but also dangerous. When it was over, he felt drained. As he flopped beside Cape onto one of the chairs that Memsen had caused to flow from the deck of the hover, the hand-tell squawked. He groaned, anticipating that Livy was back with a new argument.

"Prosper Leung?" said a woman's voice.

"Speaking."

"I'm Commander Do Adoula, Fourth Engineers. My squad was on CR in Longwalk but we heard you have a situation there and we're on our way. We can be in Littleton in half an hour. I understand you're in a hover. What do you see?"

The handover of command was subtle but swift. Commander Adoula started by asking questions and ended by giving orders. She was coming in four light trucks with thirty-seven firefighters but no heavy equipment. She approved of Spur's decision to stop the burn at Blue Valley Road, and split her force in two while they were speaking, diverting half to the ridge and half to help Livy on Blue Valley. She directed the local firefighters from Bode Well and Highbridge to dig in on the south to protect the Commons and requested that Spur stay in the hover and be her eyes in the sky.

When they finished talking, Spur slumped back against his chair. He was pleased that Adoula had ratified his firefighting plans, relieved to be no longer in charge.

"The Corps?" said Cape.

"Fourth Engineers." He folded the hand-tell. "They were on CR in Longwalk."

"That was lucky."

"Lucky," he agreed. He spotted the High Gregory whispering to Memsen. "How are you doing, DiDa?"

"You know, I've never visited the ocean." Cape blinked as he stared through the hull at the forest below. "Your mother wanted me to take her there, did I ever tell you that?"

"No."

"She always used to ask if we owned the farm or if the farm owned us." He made a low sound, part sigh and part whistle. "I wonder if she's still in Providence."

Spur didn't know what to say.

Cape frowned. "You haven't been in contact with her?"

"No."

"If you ever do speak to her, would you tell me?"

"Sure."

He nodded and made the whistling sound again.

"A burn this big is different from a surface fire," said Penny. "It's so hot that it makes a kind of fire weather called a convection column. Inside the column, bubbles of superheated air are surging up, only we can't see that. But on the outside, the cooler smoky edges are pouring back toward the ground."

"Yes, yes." The High Gregory pointed, clearly excited. "Watch at the top, to the left of the plume. It's like it's turning itself inside out."

"Awesome," said Kai Thousandfold. "Do you remember those gas sculptures we played with on Blimminey?"

"But that's going to be a problem for Spur and his firefighters," said Penny. "It's like a chimney shooting sparks and embers high into the atmosphere. They might come down anywhere and start new fires."

"Is anyone going to die?" said Senator Dowm.

"We hope not," Memsen said. "Spur is doing his best and help is on the way."

"Don't you wish she'd shut up?" muttered Cape, leaning into Spur. "This isn't some silly class. They're watching our life burn down."

"They're from the upside, DiDa. We can't judge them."

"And how does she know so much about how we fight fires? Look at her, she's just a kid."

That had been bothering Spur too, and it was getting harder and harder to put out of his mind. When had the L'ung had time to do all this research? They had arrived the day after he had first spoken to the High Gregory. Had they known ahead of time that they were coming to Walden? Was all this part of the plan?

"Memsen says they're special," he said.

"Spur." The High Gregory signed for him to come over. "Come take a look at this."

He crossed the deck to where the L'ung were gathered. The hover had descended to a thousand meters and was cruising over the Joerly farmstead.

"There," said the High Gregory, pointing to the woods they had tramped through that morning, a mix of hard and softwoods: birch and oak, hemlock and pine. In the midst of it, three tendrils of gray smoke were climbing into the sky.

"Those are spot fires," said Penny. "Caused by falling embers."

Spur didn't believe it. He'd been worried about spotting all along and had swung from side to side in the hover looking for them. But he'd decided that not enough time had passed for embers from the burn to start raining down on them. The convection column towered at least five kilometers above the valley. He stared at the plumes of smoke rising from the woods of his childhood with sickening dread. From right to left they were progressively smaller. Three fires in a series, which meant they had probably been set. What was his duty here? He was pretty sure that his scooter was still in the barn at Diligence Cottage. He could use it to get away from the burn in plenty of time. Cape could monitor the progress of the burn for Commander Adoula. Besides, if someone was down there setting fires. . . .

Someone.

"Memsen," he said. "I've changed my mind."

The hover glided to a stop above the unused field nearest to Diligence Cottage. Spur stepped back as guard rails flowed out of the deck around the ramp, which slowly extended like a metal tongue toward the sweet clover below. Cape, who was standing next to Spur, was smiling. What did his father think was so funny?

"We can stay here and wait for you," said Memsen. "If you have a problem, we'll come."

"Not through those trees you won't," said Spur, "No, you take Cape back up so he can report to the commander." The hover shuddered in the windstorm caused by the burn. "Besides, it's going to get rough here before too much longer. You need to protect yourselves."

"This is exciting." Her Grace, Jacqueline Kristof clapped her hands. "Are you excited, Spur?"

Memsen turned the girl around and gave her a hard shove toward the rest of the L'ung.

"DiDa?" Spur wanted to hug his father but settled for handing him the tell. "When the commander calls, just explain that I think we might have a torch and I'm on the ground looking. Then just keep track of the burn for her."

"Yes." His father was grinning broadly now. "I'm ready."

"Good. Memsen, thanks for your help."

"Go safely." She clicked her rings.

Spur held out his hand to the High Gregory but the boy dodged past it and embraced him instead. Spur was taken aback when he felt the High Gregory's kiss on his cheek. "I can see much more luck for you, friend Spur," he murmured. "Don't waste it."

The hot wind was an immediate shock after the cool interior of the hover. It blew gusty and confused, whipping Spur's hair and picking at his short sleeves. Spur paused at the bottom of the ramp to consider his next move and gather his courage. The pillar of smoke had smothered the afternoon sun, sinking the land into nightmarish and untimely gray twilight.

"Nice weather we're having," said Cape.

"DiDa, what?" He spun around, horrified. "Get back up there."

Cape snapped him a mock salute. "Since when do you give the orders on this farm, son?"

"But you have to, you can't. . . ." He felt like a foolish little boy, caught by his father pretending to be a grownup. "Someone has to talk to the ground. The commander needs to know what's happening with the burn."

"I gave the tell to your know-so-much friend, Penny. She'll talk Adoula's ear off."

The ramp started to retract.

"What I have to do is too dangerous, DiDa." Spur's face was hot. "You're not coming, understand?"

"Wasn't planning to." Cape chuckled. "Never entered my mind."

Spur watched in helpless fury as the hatch closed. "Then just load whatever you want into the truck and take off. You've got maybe twenty minutes before things get hot here."

The hover rose straight up and away from the field but then paused, a dark speck in an angry sky.

"See what you've done?" Spur groaned.

"Don't worry. They'll run before too long." Cape clapped him on the back. "I don't know about you, but I have things to do."

"DiDa, are you . . . ?" Spur was uncertain whether he should leave Cape while he was in this manic mood. "Be careful."

Capability Roger Leung was not a man known for his sense of humor, but he laughed now. "Prosper, if we were being careful, we'd be up there in the sky with your strange little friends." He pointed into the woods. "Time to take some chances, son."

He turned and trotted off toward the big house without looking back.

Spur knew these woods. He and Vic and Comfort had spent hours in the cool shade pretending to be pirates or skantlings or aliens or fairies. They played queen and castle in the pukpuk ruins and pretended to be members of Morobe's original crew, exploring a strange, new world for the first time. They cut paths to secret hideouts and built lean-tos from hemlock boughs and, when Vic and Spur were eleven, they even erected a ramshackle tree house with walls and a roof, although Cape made them take it down because he said it was too dangerous. Spur had been kissed for the first time in that tree house: In a contest of sibling gross out, Vic had dared his big sister to kiss his best friend. Comfort got the best of it, however, because her back dare was that Vic had to kiss Spur. As he pulled back from the kiss, Vic had punched Spur in the arm so hard it left a bruise.

The woods were dark and unnaturally quiet as he padded down the path that led past Bear Rock and the Throne of the Spruce King. Spur heard no birdsong or drone of bugs. It was as if the trees themselves were listening for the crackle of fire. When he first smelled smoke, he stopped to turn slowly and sniff, trying to estimate where it had come from. Ahead and to the north was his best guess. That meant it was time to cut off the path and bush-whack south across the Great Gosdog Swamp, which had never been very great and always dried up in the summer. His plan was to strike out in the direction of the smallest of the three fires he had seen from the hover. He knew he was getting close when it started to snow fire.

Most of what floated down was ash, but in the mix were sparks and burning embers that stung the bare skin of his arms and face. He brushed a hand through his hair and ran. Not in a panic—just to keep embers from sticking to him. To his right he could see the glow of at least one of the fires. And yes, now he could hear the dis-tant crack and whoosh he knew all too well. The burn was working along the forest floor, he was sure of that. Crown fire sounded like a runaway train. If he were anywhere near one, he'd be deafened and then he'd be dead. Spur finally escaped the ash fall after several minutes of dodging past trees at speed. He hunched over to knead the stitch in his side, then pressed on.

The wind had picked up and now was blowing west, not east. He thought it must be an indraft. The burn that was crashing down on them had to suck air in huge gulps from every direction in order to support itself. Maybe the wind shift would work in their favor. A west wind would push these outlying spot fires back toward the burn itself. If the line of backfire was wide enough, it might actually check the advance of the burn when the two met. Of course, it would have to scorch across the best parts of the Millisap and Joerly farmsteads first.

In the gathering darkness, Spur decided to start trotting again. It was taking too long to skirt around the last fire to Mercy's Creek. And unless he saw something soon, he was turning back. He had to leave himself enough time to get away. And he wanted to make sure his father hadn't done anything crazy.

Intent on not tripping over a stone or root, Spur never saw the windblown curtain of smoke until it closed around him. He spun around, disoriented. He had been panting from running, so his nose and mouth and lungs filled immediately. It was like trying to breathe cotton. His eyes went teary and the world was reduced to a watery dissolve. Had he been out with Gold Squad, he would have been wearing goggles, a helmet, and a breather. But here he was practically naked, and the smoke was pervasive and smothering. He was coughing so hard he could taste the tang of blood and then his throat closed and he knew he was about to choke to death. In a panic, he hurled himself flat against the forest floor, desperately searching for the shallow layer of breathable air that they said sometimes clung to the ground. A stump poked at his side but as he laid his cheek against the mat of twigs and papery leaves, he found cooler air, rank but breathable. He tried to fill his aching lungs, coughed up mucus and blood, then tried again.

Spur didn't know exactly how long he lay there, but when he came to himself again, the haze of smoke had thinned to gauze and he knew he had taken enough chances. He had learned the hard way at Motu River that he was no hero. Why was he at it again? No more; get to the cottage, get on the scooter, and get as far away from fire as possible. He pushed himself up on hands and knees, coughed and spat. His nose felt as if someone had pulled barbed wire through it. He sat back on his heels, blinking. It wasn't until he brushed at the leaf litter on his face that he realized he'd been crying. When he finally stood, he felt tottery. He grabbed a sapling to steady himself. Then he heard a twig snap and the rustle of foliage being parted. He ducked behind a beech tree that was barely wider than he was.

Comfort came trudging toward him, her face hard, eyes glassy. One look told him everything. She had changed out of the gingham dress into a pair of baggy work pants that looked like they must have belonged to Vic. Over a smudged and dirty T-shirt, she wore a crude burlap vest to which were attached three liquid-fire grenades. They bumped against her chest as she approached. She looked weary, as if she'd been carrying a weight that had pushed her to the very limit of her strength.

He had thought to leap out and overwhelm her when she passed, but she spotted him when she was still a dozen meters away, and froze. He stepped from behind his tree, his hands held in front of him.

"I won't hurt you," he said.

In the instant he saw mindless animal panic in her eyes, he thought her more alien than any upsider. He had spooked her. Then she turned and sprinted away.

Spur ran after her. He wasn't thinking about the burn or his village or simplicity. He ran. He didn't have time to be either brave or afraid. He ran because he had loved this woman once and because he had watched her brother die.

As a girl, Comfort had always been the nimblest of the three of them. In an open field, Vic would have caught her, but scooting past trees and ducking under low branches, Comfort was faster than any two squirrels. After a couple of minutes of pursuit, Spur was winded. He wasn't exactly sure where they were anymore. Headed toward the creek, he guessed. If she thought she could cross over and take refuge in her own house, she truly was crazy. Suicidal.

Which made him pick up the pace, despite his fatigue. He ran so hard he thought his heart might break.

She had almost reached the creek when the chase ended abruptly. Comfort got reckless, cut a tree too close and clipped it instead. The impact knocked one of the grenades loose and spun her half around. She went to her knees and Spur leapt at her. But she kicked herself away and he skidded past and crashed into a tangle of summersweet. By the time he got to his knees she was showing him one of the grenades. He could see that she had flipped the safety and that her finger was on the igniter.

"Stop there," she said.

Spur was breathless and a little dizzy. "Comfort, don't."

"Too late." She blew a strand of dark hair off her face. "I already have."

He stood, once again holding his hands where she could see them. "What's this about, Comfort?"

"Vic," she said. "It's mostly about Vic now."

"He's gone. There's nothing you can do for him."

"We'll see." She shivered, despite the heat. "It was my fault, you know. I was the one who recruited him. But he was just supposed to pass information." Her voice shook. "They must have bullied him into becoming a torch. I killed him, Spur. I killed my brother."

"Listen to me, Comfort. He wasn't a torch. It was an accident."

The hand holding the grenade trembled slightly but then steadied. "That's not what you said this morning when you were off your head." She gave him a pitying look. "You said you tried to save him. That I believe."

He took a half-step toward her. "But how does it help anyone to set fire to Littleton?" Another half-step. "To our farms?"

She backed away from him. "They could stop this, you know. Your upsider friends. They could force the Cooperative to settle, put pressure on Jack Winter to do what's right. Except they don't really care about us. They come to watch, but they never get involved."

Her laugh was low and scattered. "They're involved now. I hope that little brat is scared of dying."

"But they do care." He held his arms tight to his sides; otherwise he would have been waving them at her. "Memsen has a plan." Spur thought he might yet save her. "You have to believe me, Comfort. There are going to be talks with the pukpuks."

"Right." Her mouth twisted. "And you didn't see Vic torch himself."

"Besides, did you really think you could burn them up? The High Gregory is safe, Comfort. Memsen and the L'ung. Their hover came for us. That's how I got here so fast. They're in the air," he pointed backward over his shoulder, "waiting for me over the cottage."

When he saw her gaze flick up and away from him, he launched himself. He grabbed at the arm with the grenade. They twirled together in a grotesque pirouette. Then, unable to check his momentum, Spur stumbled and fell.

Comfort stepped away from him. She shook her head once. She pressed the igniter on the grenade.

It exploded into a fireball that shot out two long streams of flame in opposite directions. One soared high into the trees, the other shot down at the forest floor and gathered in a blazing puddle at her feet. She screamed as the grenade fell from her charred hand. Great tongues of flame licked up her legs. Her pants caught fire. Her singed hair curled into nothingness.

Spur screamed too. Seeing it all happen all over again was worse than any nightmare. When Vic had set the liquid firebomb off, he had been instantly engulfed in flame. Spur had tried to knock him down, hoping to roll his friend onto the ground and put the merciless fire out. But Vic had shoved him away. With his clothes, his arms in flames, Vic had found the strength to send Spur sprawling backward.

Which saved Spur's life when the second bomb went off.

But this wasn't Motu River and Vic was dead. Comfort, his Comfort had only grenades, designed to set backfires, not bombs designed by pukpuk terrorists. The lower half of her body had been soaked in liquid fire and was burning but he could see her face, her wild, suffering eyes, her mouth a slash of screeching pain and that last grenade still bumping against her chest.

Spur flew at her and ripped the unexploded grenade from the vest. He swept her up in his arms, taking her weight easily with a mad strength, and raced toward the creek. He had the crazy thought that if he ran fast enough, he would be able to stay ahead of the pain. He knew he was burning now but he had to save her. He had never had a chance with Vic; take some chances, his father had said, and the High Gregory had warned him not to waste his luck. But the pain was too fast, it was catching up to him. Comfort's screams filled his head and then he was flying. He splashed down on top of her in the cool water and she didn't struggle when he forced her under, counting one, two, three, four, five, and he yanked her up and screamed at her to breathe, breathe, and when she choked and gasped, he thrust her down again, two, three, four, five and when he pulled her up again she was limp; his poor burned Comfort had either fainted away or died in his arms but at least she wasn't on fire anymore.

Neither of them was.

Sixteen

The light which puts out our eyes is darkness to us. Only that day dawns to which we are awake.

–Walden

In the dream, Spur sits in the kitchen of Diligence Cottage with Comfort, who is wearing the jade-colored pajamas. There are pies everywhere. Apple and cherry pies are stacked on the counters and across the table. Blackberry, elderberry, and blueberry pies are lined up on the new oak floor against the wall with its morning glory wallpaper that Comfort ordered all the way from Providence, which is where Spur's mother lives. Maybe. He should find out. Comfort has set fiesta pear and peach surprise pies on top of the refrigerator and laid out the rhubarb pies two to a chair. Whatever else people in Littleton say about her, everyone agrees that Comfort makes the best pumpkin pies anywhere. In the dream, the pies are her idea. She has made enough pie to last him the rest of his life. He will need it if she goes. In the dream, though, it's not certain that she is leaving and he's not sure he wants her to. Besides, she certainly isn't going to catch the train back to Longwalk in those pajamas. They slide right off when you tug at them, the smooth fabric sliding lightly against her skin. In the dream she threads her way around a strawberry pie so she can kiss him. At first her kiss is like a promise. After a kiss like this, he should kick open the bedroom door and throw back the covers. But the kiss ends like a question. And the answer is no, Spur doesn't want this woman to be unhappy anymore because of him. He doesn't want to dry her tears or . . .

"Enough sleeping, son." A sharp voice sliced through his dream. "Wake up and join the world."

Spur blinked, then gasped in disappointment. It wasn't fair; he didn't get to keep Comfort or the pie. The strange room he was in seemed to be a huge bay window filled with sunlight. In it was a scatter of dark shapes, one of which was moving. A cold hand pressed against his forehead.

"38.2 degrees," said the docbot. "But then a little fever is to be expected."

"Dr. Niss?" said Spur.

"I'm never happy to see repeat customers, son." The docbot shined pinlights into Spur's eyes. "Do you know where you are? You were a little woozy when we picked you up."

He licked his lips, trying to recall. "The hospital?"

"Allworthy Memsen's hover. Open your mouth and say ahh." The docbot brushed its medfinger across Spur's tongue, leaving a waxy residue that tasted like motor oil.

"The hover?" There was something important that Spur couldn't quite remember. "But how did you get here?"

"I'm on call, son," said the docbot. "I can be anywhere there's a bot. Although this isn't much of an implementation. Feels two sizes too small."

Spur realized then that this docbot was different from the one at the hospital. It only had two gripper arms and its eye was set on top of its headplate. What did he mean, repeat customers? Then the memory of the burn went roaring through his head. "Comfort!" Spur tried to sit up but the docbot pushed him back down. "Is she all right?"

"Still with us. We've saved her for now. But we'll talk about that after we look at your burns."

"How long have I been here? Did they stop the burn?"

The docbot reached behind Spur's neck, untied the hospital gown and pulled it to his waist. "I kept you down all last night and the better part of today to give your grafts a chance to take." The new set of burns ran in rough stripes across his chest. There was a splotch like a misshapen handprint on top of his shoulder. "You'll be on pain blockers for the next few days—they can poke holes in your memory, so don't worry if you forget how to tie your shoes." The docbot flowed warm dermslix onto the grafts. "Dermal regeneration just 13 percent," it muttered.

"The burn, what about the burn?"

"Your people have it under control, according to that little Pendragon girl. I guess there's still some mopping up to do, but at least those kids are finally settling down. They were bouncing off the walls all last night." He pulled the gown back up. "You'll be fine son. Just stop playing with fire."

Spur was already swinging his legs off the bed as he fumbled with the ties of the gown. But when he went to stand, the deck seemed to fall away beneath his feet.

"Whoops." The docbot caught him. "Another side effect of pain blockers is that they'll tilt your sense of balance." He eased him back onto the bed. "You're going to want someone to help you get around for now." The docbot twisted off its medfinger and dropped it in the sterilizer. "I've got just the party for you. Wait here and I'll send him in."

The docbot had scarcely popped out of the room when the High Gregory came bursting in, pushing a wheelchair. The entire bubble wall collapsed momentarily to reveal the L'ung, who started whooping and applauding for Spur. Memsen slipped in just as the wall reformed.

"You are the craziest, luckiest, bravest person I know." The High Gregory was practically squeaking with excitement. "What were you thinking when you picked her up? We were cheering so loud we thought you could probably hear us down there. I couldn't sleep all night, just thinking about it. Did you hear the L'ung just now? I taught them to clap hands for you. Here, have a seat."

Spur allowed Memsen and the High Gregory to help him into the chair, although he was certain they were going to drop him. He shut his eyes, counted to three and when he opened them again the cabin had stopped chasing its tail. "How do you know what I did?"

"We watched," said Memsen. "From the moment you stepped off the ramp, our spybugs were on you. The High Gregory is right. We were very moved."

"You watched?" He felt his cheeks flush. "I could've been killed."

"Watch is all we're supposed to do," said Memsen, "according to your covenant."

"But Memsen said we couldn't just leave you after you jumped into the water with her," said the High Gregory. "So we mowed down some forest to get to you, pulled the two of you out of the creek and qiced Dr. Niss into a bot that Betty Twosalt made." He wheeled Spur toward the hull so he could see the view. "She's good. She won a prize for her bots once."

"And Comfort is all right?" Spur glanced back over his shoulder at Memsen. "That's what Dr. Niss said."

"Saved," said Memsen, clicking her rings together. "We were able to save her."

The High Gregory parked the wheelchair as near to the hull as he could get, and set the brake. He made the deck transparent too, so they could see more of the valley. "It's huge, Spur," he said, gesturing through the hull at the remains of the burn. "I've never seen anything like it."

They were passing over Mercy's Creek headed for the Joerlys, although he scarcely recognized the land beneath them as he surveyed the damage. The fires Comfort had started must have been sucked by the indraft back toward the burn as Spur had hoped, creating a backfired barrier to its progress. The backfire and the head of the burn must have met somewhere just east of the Joerlys. Comfort's house, barn and all the sheds had burned to their foundations. Farther to the west, the Millisap and Ezzat farmsteads were also obliterated. And more than half of Lamana Ridge was a wasteland of blackened spikes rising out of gray ash. Wisps of white smoke drifted across the ravaged land like the ghosts of dead trees. But dispersed through the devastation were inexplicable clumps of unscathed forest, mostly deciduous hardwood. Spur was relieved to see a blue-green crown of forest to the north along the top of the ridge, where the Corps must have beaten the burn back.

"What about the east?" said Spur. "Where did they stop it?"

But the hover was already turning and his view shifted, first south, where he could see the steeple of the communion hall on the Commons then southeast where CR22 sliced a thin line through intact forest. The High Gregory was watching him, his yellow eyes alight with anticipation.

"What?" said Spur, irked to be putting on a show for this fidgety upsider. "What are you staring at?"

"You," said the High Gregory. "There's so much luck running in your family, Spur. You know we tried to pick your father up after we got you, but he wouldn't come, even though we told him you were hurt."

"He was still there? That old idiot. Is he all right?"

"He's fine." The High Gregory patted Spur's hand. "He said he wasn't going to give his farm up without a fight. He had all your hoses out. He had this great line—I can't remember it exactly." He looked to Memsen for help. "Something about spitting?"

Memsen waited as a bench began to form from the deck. "Your father said that if the pump gave out, he'd spit at the burn until his mouth went dry."

Spur had raised himself out of the wheelchair, craning to see as the farm swung into view. The big house, the barns, the cottage were all untouched. But the orchards . . .

"He started his own backfire." Spur sank back onto the seat. Over half the trees were gone: the Macintosh and GoReds and Pippins were charred skeletons. But at least Cape had saved the Alumars and the Huangs and the Galas. And GiGo's trees by the cottage, all those foolish Macouns.

"The wind had changed direction." Memsen sat on the bench facing Spur. "When we arrived, he had just knocked a hole in the gas tank of your truck and said he couldn't stop to talk. He was going drive through his orchard and then set the backfire. We thought it seemed dangerous so we put spybugs on him. But he knew exactly what he was about." She showed Spur her teeth. "He's a brave man."

"Yes," mused Spur, although he wondered if that were true. Maybe his father just loved his apples more than he loved his life. Spur felt the hover accelerate then and the ground below began to race by. They shot over the Commons and headed west in the direction of Longwalk.

"We watched all night," said the High Gregory, "just like your father told us. Memsen made Penny let everyone have a turn talking to Commander Adoula on the tell. The fire was so awesome in the dark. We flew through it again and again."

The High Gregory's enthusiasm continued to annoy Spur. Three farmsteads were gone and his own orchards decimated, but this boy thought he was having an adventure. "You didn't offer to help? You could've dropped splash on the burn, maybe diverted it from the houses."

"We did offer," said Memsen. "We were told that upsiders are allowed to render assistance in the deep forest where only firefighters can see us, but not in plain sight of a village or town."

"Memsen is in trouble for landing the hover on the Commons." The High Gregory settled beside her on the bench. "We haven't even told anyone yet about what we did for you by the creek."

"So." Memsen held out her hand to him, fingers outspread. "We've been called back to Kenning to answer for our actions."

"Really?" Spur felt relieved but also vaguely disappointed. "When will you go?"

"Now, actually." Her rings glittered in the sunlight. "We asked Dr. Niss to wake you so we could say goodbye."

"But who will take Comfort and me to the hospital?"

"We'll be in Longwalk in a few moments. There's a hospital in

Benevolence Park Number 2." Her fingers closed into a fist. "But Comfort will be coming with us."

"What?" Despite himself, Spur lurched out of the wheelchair. He tottered, the cabin spun, and the next thing he knew both Memsen and the High Gregory were easing him back down.

"Why?" He took a deep breath. "She can't."

"She can't very well stay in Littleton," said the High Gregory. "Her farm is destroyed. You're going to have to tell everyone who started the burn."

"Am I?" He considered whether he would lie to protect her. After all, he had lied for her brother. "She's told you she wants to do this? Let me talk to her."

"That's not possible." Memsen pinched the air.

"Why not?"

"Do you want to come with us, Spur?" said the High Gregory. "You could, you know."

"No." He wheeled himself backward, horrified at the idea. "Why would I want to do that? My home is in Littleton. I'm a farmer."

"Then stop asking questions," said Memsen impatiently. "As a citizen of the Transcendent State you're under a consensual cultural quarantine. We've just been reminded of that quite forcefully. There's nothing more we can say to you."

"I don't believe this." Spur heard himself shouting. "You've done something to her and you're afraid to tell me. What is it?"

Memsen hesitated, and Spur heard the low, repetitive *pa-pa-pa-ptt* that he had decided she made when she was consulting her predecessors. "If you insist, we can make it simple for you." Memsen thrust her face close to his. "Comfort died," she said harshly. "Tell that to everyone in your village. She was horribly burned and she died."

Spur recoiled from her. "But you said you saved her. Dr. Niss. . . ."

"Dr. Niss can show you the body, if you care to see it." She straightened. "So."

"Goodbye, Spur," said the High Gregory. "Can we help you back onto the bed?"

Beneath them Spur could see the outskirts of Longwalk. Abruptly the hull of the hover turned opaque and the ceiling of the cabin began to glow. Spur knew from watching hovers land from the window of his hospital room that they camouflaged themselves on the final approach over a city.

"No, wait." Spur was desperate to keep the upsiders talking. "You said she was going with you. I definitely heard that. You said she was saved. Is she . . . this is like the other Memsens that you told me about, isn't it? The ones that are saved in you?"

"This is a totally inappropriate conversation." Memsen pinched the air with both hands. "We'll have to ask Dr. Niss to strike it from your memory."

"He can do that?"

"Sure," said the High Gregory. "We do it all the time. But he has to replace it with some fake memory. You'll have to tell him what you want. And if you should ever come across anything that challenges the replacement memory, you could get . . ."

Spur held up his hand to silence him. "But it's true what I just said?"

Memsen snorted in disgust and turned to leave.

"She can't admit anything." The High Gregory grasped her hand to restrain her. He held it to his chest. "But yes."

Spur was gripping the push rims of his wheelchair so hard that his hands ached. "So nobody dies on the upside?"

"No, no. Everybody dies. It's just that some of us choose to be saved to a shell afterward. Even the saved admit it's not the same as being alive. I haven't made my mind up about all that yet, but I'm only twelve standard. My birthday is next week, I wish you could be there."

"What will happen to Comfort in this shell?"

"She's going to have to adjust. She didn't expect to be saved, of course, probably didn't even know it was possible, so when they activate her, she'll be disoriented. She'll need some kind of counseling. We have some pretty good soulmasons on Kenning. And they can send for her brother; he'll want to help."

"Stop it! This is cruel." Memsen yanked his hand down. "We have to go right now."

"Why?" said the High Gregory plaintively. "He's not going to remember any of this."

"Vic was saved?" Even though he was still safe in the wheelchair, he felt as if he were falling.

"All the pukpuk martyrs were." The High Gregory tried to shake his hand loose from Memsen, but she wouldn't let him go. "That was why they agreed to sacrifice themselves."

"Enough." Memsen started to drag him from the cabin. "We're sorry, Spur. You're a decent man. Go back to your cottage and your apples and forget about us."

"Goodbye, Spur," called the High Gregory as they popped through the bulkhead. "Good luck."

As the bulkhead shivered with their passing, he felt a fierce and troubling desire burn his soul. Some part of him did want to go with them, to be with Comfort and Vic on the upside and see the wonders that Chairman Winter had forbidden the citizens of the Transcendent State. He could do it; he knew he could. After all, everyone in Littleton seemed to think he was leaving.

But then who would help Cape bring in the harvest?

Spur wasn't sure how long he sat alone in the wheelchair with a thousand thoughts buzzing in his head. The upsiders had just blown up his world and he was trying desperately to piece it back together. Except what was the point? In a little while he wasn't going to be worrying anymore about Comfort and Vic and shells and being saved. Maybe that was for the best; it was all too complicated. Just like the Chairman had said. Spur thought he'd be happier thinking about apples and baseball and maybe kissing Melody Velez. He was ready to forget.

He realized that the hover had gone completely still. There was no vibration from the hull skimming through the air, no muffled laughter from the L'ung. He watched the hospital equipment melt into the deck. Then all the bulkheads popped and he could see the entire bay of the hover. It was empty except for his wheelchair, a gurney with Comfort's shroud-covered body, and the docbot, which rolled up to him.

"So you're going to make me forget all this?" said Spur bitterly. "All the secrets of the upside?"

"If that's what you want."

Spur shivered. "I have a choice?"

"I'm just the doctor, son. I can offer treatment but you have to accept it. For example, you chose not to tell me how you got burned that first time." The docbot rolled behind the wheelchair. "That pretty much wrecked everything I was trying to accomplish with the conciliation sim."

Spur turned around to look at it. "You knew all along?"

The docbot locked into the back of the wheelchair. "I wouldn't be much of a doctor if I couldn't tell when patients were lying to me." It started pushing Spur toward the hatch.

"But you work for the Chairman." Spur didn't know if he wanted the responsibility for making this decision.

"I take Jack Winter's money," said the docbot. "I don't take his advice when it comes to medical or spiritual practice."

"But what if I tell people that Comfort and Vic are saved and that upsiders get to go on after they die?"

"Then they'll know."

Spur tried to imagine keeping the upsiders' immortality a secret for the rest of his days. He tried to imagine what would happen to the Transcendent State if he told what he knew. His mouth went as dry as flour. He was just a farmer, he told himself; he didn't have that good an imagination. "You're saying that I don't have to have my memory of all this erased?"

"Goodness, no. Unless you'd rather forget about me."

As they passed Comfort's body, Spur said, "Stop a minute."

He reached out and touched the shroud. He expected it to be some strange upsider fabric but it was just a simple cotton sheet. "They knew that I could choose to remember, didn't they? Memsen and the High Gregory were playing me to the very end."

"Son," said Dr. Niss, "the High Gregory is just a boy and nobody in the Thousand Worlds knows what the Allworthy knows."

But Spur had stopped listening. He rubbed the shroud between his thumb and forefinger, thinking about how he and the Joerlys used to make up adventures in the ruins along Mercy's Creek when they were children. Often as not one of them would achieve some glorious death as part of the game. The explorer would boldly drink from the poisoned cup to free her comrades, the pirate captain would be run through defending his treasure, the queen of skantlings would throw down her heartstone rather than betray the castle. And then he or Vic or Comfort would stumble dramatically to the forest floor and sprawl there, cheek pressed against leaf litter, as still as scattered stones. The others would pause briefly over the body and then dash into the woods, so that the fallen hero could be reincarnated and the game could go on.

"I want to go home," he said, at last.

Three thousand copies of this book have been printed by the Maple-Vail Book Manufacturing Group, Binghamton, NY, for Golden Gryphon Press, Urbana, IL. The typeset is Electra with Bordeaux Roman Bold display on 55# Sebago. The binding cloth is Roxite A. Typesetting by The Composing Room, Inc., Kimberly, WI.